"KATE WILHELM'S
CAUTIONARY MESSAGE
COMES THROUGH
LOUD AND CLEAR."
—*The New York Times*

WHERE LATE THE SWEET BIRDS SANG
has been awarded the coveted Hugo Award
for best science fiction novel of the year at
the 35th annual Sun Con Science Fiction
Convention.

Since its publication, WHERE LATE THE
SWEET BIRDS SANG has won the Locus
Award for best novel of the year, and was
nominated for a Nebula Award as best
novel of the year.

Kate Wilhelm, the second woman ever to
have won the "best novel" Hugo Award,
received a Nebula Award in 1968 for the
year's best short story, "The Planners."

She is the author of *The Clewiston
Test*, *The Infinity Box* and *Margaret
and I*, all published by Pocket Books.

Books by Kate Wilhelm

The Clewiston Test
The Infinity Box
Margaret and I
Where Late the Sweet Birds Sang

Published by POCKET BOOKS

WHERE
LATE
THE
SWEET
BIRDS
SANG

by KATE WILHELM

PUBLISHED BY POCKET BOOKS NEW YORK

Part One of this book first appeared in *Orbit 15*, edited by
Damon Knight; copyright © 1974 by Damon Knight.

**POCKET BOOKS, a Simon & Schuster division of
GULF & WESTERN CORPORATION
1230 Avenue of the Americas, New York, N.Y. 10020**

Published by arrangement with Harper & Row, Publishers, Inc.
Library of Congress Catalog Card Number: 75-6379

ISBN: 0-671-83613-7

First Pocket Books printing January, 1977

10   9   8   7   6   5   4   3

POCKET and colophon are trademarks of Simon & Schuster.

Printed in the U.S.A.

For Valerie,
Kris, and Leslie,
with love

PART ONE

Where Late
the Sweet Birds Sang

Chapter 1

What David always hated most about the Sumner family dinners was the way everyone talked about him as if he were not there.

"Has he been eating enough meat lately? He looks peaked."

"You spoil him, Carrie. If he won't eat his dinner, don't let him go out and play. You were like that, you know."

"When I was his age, I was husky enough to cut down a tree with a hatchet. He couldn't cut his way out of a fog."

David would imagine himself invisible, floating unseen over their heads as they discussed him. Someone would ask if he had a girl friend yet, and they would *tsk-tsk* whether the answer was yes or no. From his vantage point he would aim a ray gun at Uncle Clarence, whom he especially disliked, because he was fat, bald, and very rich. Uncle Clarence dipped his biscuits in his gravy, or in syrup, or more often in a mixture of sorghum and butter that he stirred together on his plate until it looked like baby shit.

"Is he still planning to be a biologist? He should go to med school and join Walt in his practice."

He would point his ray gun at Uncle Clarence and cut a neat plug out of his stomach and carefully ease it out, and Uncle Clarence would ooze from the opening and flow all over them.

"David." He started with alarm, then relaxed again. "David, why don't you go out and see what the other kids are up to?" His father's quiet voice, saying actually, *That's enough of that.* And they would turn their collective mind to one of the other offspring.

As David grew older, he learned the complex relationships that he merely accepted as a child. Uncles, aunts, cousins, second cousins, third cousins. And the honorary members—the brothers and sisters and parents of those who had married into the family. There were the Sumners and Wistons and O'Gradys and Heinemans and the Meyers and Capeks and Rizzos, all part of the same river that flowed through the fertile valley.

He remembered the holidays especially. The old Sumner house was rambling with many bedrooms upstairs and an attic that was wall-to-wall mattresses, pallets for the children, with an enormous fan in the west window. Someone was forever checking to make certain that they hadn't all suffocated in the attic. The older children were supposed to keep an eye on the younger ones, but what they did in fact was to frighten them night after night with ghost stories. Eventually the noise level would rise until adult intervention was demanded. Uncle Ron would clump up the stairs heavily and there would be a scurrying, with suppressed giggles and muffled screams, until everyone found a bed again, so that by the time he turned on the hall light that illuminated the attic dimly, all the children would seem to be sleeping. He would pause briefly in the doorway, then close the door, turn off the light, and tramp back down the stairs, apparently deaf to the renewed merriment behind him.

Whenever Aunt Claudia came up, it was like an apparition. One minute pillows would be flying, someone would be crying, someone else trying to read by flashlight, several of the boys playing cards by another flashlight, some of the girls huddled together whispering what had to be delicious secrets, judging by the way they blushed and looked desperate if an adult came upon them suddenly, and then the door would snap open, the light would fall on the disorder, and she would be standing there. Aunt Claudia was very tall and thin, her nose was too big, and she was tanned to a permanent old-leather color. She would stand there, immobile and terrible, and the children would creep back into bed without a sound. She would not move until everyone was back where he or she belonged, then she would close the door soundlessly. The silence would drag on and on. The ones nearest to the door would hold their breath, trying to hear breathing on the other side. Eventually someone would become brave enough to open the door a crack, and if she were truly gone, the party would resume.

The smells of holidays were fixed in David's memory. All the usual smells: fruit cakes and turkeys, the vinegar that went in the egg dyes, the greenery and the thick, creamy smoke of bayberry candles. But what he remem-

9

bered most vividly was the smell of gunpowder that they all carried at the Fourth of July gathering. The smell that permeated their hair and clothes lasted on their hands for days and days. Their hands would be stained purple-black by berry picking, and the color and smell were one of the indelible images of his childhood. Mixed in with it was the smell of the sulfur that was dusted on them liberally to confound the chiggers.

If it hadn't been for Celia, his childhood would have been perfect. Celia was his cousin, his mother's sister's daughter. She was one year younger than David, and by far the prettiest of all his cousins. When they were very young they promised to marry one day, and when they grew older and it was made abundantly clear that no cousins might ever marry in that family, they became implacable enemies. He didn't know how they had been told. He was certain that no one ever put it in words, but they knew. When they could not avoid each other after that, they fought. She pushed him out of the hayloft and broke his arm when he was fifteen, and when he was sixteen they wrestled from the back door of the Winston farmhouse to the fence, fifty or sixty yards away. They tore the clothes off each other, and he was bleeding from her fingernails down his back, she from scraping her shoulder on a rock. Then somehow in their rolling and squirming frenzy, his cheek came down on her uncovered chest, and he stopped fighting. He suddenly became a melting, sobbing, incoherent idiot and she hit him on the head with a rock and ended the fight.

Up to that point the battle had been in almost total silence, broken only by gasps for breath and whispered language that would have shocked their parents. But when she hit him and he went limp, not unconscious, but dazed, uncaring, inert, she screamed, abandoning herself to terror and anguish. The family tumbled from the house as if they had been shaken out, and their first impression must have been that he had raped her. His father hustled him to the barn, presumably for a thrashing. But in the barn his father, belt in hand, looked at him with an expression that was furious, and strangely sympathetic. He didn't touch David, and only after he had turned and left did David realize that tears were still running down his face.

In the family there were farmers, a few lawyers, two doctors, insurance brokers and bankers and millers, hard-

10

ware merchandisers, other shopkeepers. David's father owned a large department store that catered to the upper-middle-class clientele of the valley. The valley was rich, the farms in it large and lush. David always supposed that the family, except for a few ne'er-do-wells, was rather wealthy. Of all his relatives his favorite was his father's brother Walt. Dr. Walt, they all called him, never uncle. He played with the children and taught them grown-up things, like where to hit if you really meant it, where not to hit in a friendly scrap. He seemed to know when to stop treating them as children long before anyone else in the family did. Dr. Walt was the reason David had decided very early to become a scientist.

David was seventeen when he went to Harvard. His birthday was in September and he didn't go home for it. When he did return at Thanksgiving, and the clan had gathered, Grandfather Sumner poured the ritual before-dinner martinis and handed one to him. And Uncle Warner said to him, "What do you think we should do about Bobbie?"

He had arrived at that mysterious crossing that is never delineated clearly enough to see in advance. He sipped his martini, not liking it particularly, and knew that childhood had ended, and he felt a profound sadness and loneliness.

The Christmas that David was twenty-three seemed out of focus. The scenario was the same, the attic full of children, the food smells, the powdering of snow, none of that had changed, but he was seeing it from a new position and it was not the wonderland it had been. When his parents went home he stayed on at the Wiston farm for a day or two, waiting for Celia's arrival. She had missed the Christmas Day celebration, getting ready for her coming trip to Brazil, but she would be there, her mother had assured Grandmother Wiston, and David was waiting for her, not happily, not with any expectation of reward, but with a fury that grew and caused him to stalk the old house like a boy being punished for another's sin.

When she came home and he saw her standing with her mother and grandmother, his anger melted. It was like seeing Celia in a time distortion, as she was and would be, or had been. Her pale hair would not change much, but her bones would become more prominent and the almost emptiness of her face would have written on it a message of concern, of love, of giving, of being decisively herself, of a strength unsuspected in her frail body. Grandmother Wiston was a beautiful old lady, he thought in wonder, amazed that he never had seen her beauty before. Celia's mother was more beautiful than the girl. And he saw the resemblance to his own mother in the trio. Wordlessly, defeated, he turned and went to the rear of the house and put on one of his grandfather's heavy jackets because he didn't want to see her at all now and his own outdoor clothing was in the front hall closet too near where she was standing.

He walked a long time in the frosty afternoon, seeing very little, and shaking himself from time to time when he realized that the cold was entering his shoes or making his ears numb. He should turn back, he thought often, but he walked on. And he found that he was climbing the slope to the antique forest that his grandfather had taken him to once, a long time ago. He climbed and became warmer, and at dusk he was under the branches of the tiers of trees that had been there since the beginning of time. They or others that were identical to them. Waiting. Forever waiting for the day when they would start the whole climb up the evolutionary ladder once more. Here were the relicts his grandfather had brought him to see. Here was a silverbell, grown to the stature of a large tree, where down the slopes, in the lower reaches, it remained always a shrub. Here the white basswood grew alongside the hemlock and the bitternut hickory, and the beeches and sweet buckeyes locked arms.

"David." He stopped and listened, certain he had imagined it, but the call came again. "David, are you up here?"

He turned then and saw Celia among the massive tree trunks. Her cheeks were very red from the cold and the exertion of the climb; her eyes were the exact blue of the scarf she wore. She stopped six feet from him and opened her mouth to speak again, but didn't. Instead she drew off a glove and touched the smooth trunk of a beech tree. "Grandfather Wiston brought me up here, too, when I was twelve. It was very important to him that we understand this place."

David nodded.

She looked at him then. "Why did you leave like that? They all think we're going to fight again."

"We might," he said.

She smiled. "I don't think so. Never again."

12

"We should start down. It'll be dark in a few minutes." But he didn't move.

"David, try to make Mother see, will you? You understand that I have to go, that I have to do something, don't you? She thinks you're so clever. She'd listen to you."

He laughed. "They think I'm clever like a puppy dog."

Celia shook her head. "You're the one they'd listen to. They treat me like a child and always will."

David shook his head, smiling, but he sobered again very quickly and said, "Why are you going, Celia? What are you trying to prove?"

"Damn it, David. If you don't understand, who will?" She took a deep breath and said, "Look, you do read the newspapers, don't you? People are starving in South America. Most of South America will be in a state of famine before the end of this decade if they aren't helped almost immediately. And no one has done any real research in tropical farming methods. Practically no one. That's all lateritic soil and no one down there understands it. They go in and burn off the trees and underbrush, and in two or three years they have a sunbaked plain as hard as iron. Okay, they send some of their bright young students here to learn about modern farming, but they go to Iowa, or Kansas, or Minnesota, or some other dumb place like that, and they learn farming methods suited to temperate climates, not tropical. Well, we trained in tropical farming and we're going to start classes down there, in the field. It's what I trained for. This project will get me a doctorate."

The Wistons were farmers, had always been farmers. "Custodians of the soil," Grandfather Wiston had said once, "not its owners, just custodians."

Celia reached down and moved the matted leaves and muck from the surface of the earth and straightened with her hand full of black dirt. "The famines are spreading. They need so much. And I have so much to give! Can't you understand that?" she cried. She closed her hand hard, compacting the soil into a ball that crumbled again when she opened her fist and touched the lump with her forefinger. She let the soil fall from her hand and carefully pushed the protective covering of leaves back over the bared spot.

"You followed me to tell me good-bye, didn't you?" David said suddenly, and his voice was harsh. "It's really

13

good-bye this time, isn't it?" He watched her and slowly she nodded. "There's someone in your group?"

"I'm not sure, David. Maybe." She bowed her head and started to pull her glove on again. "I thought I was sure. But when I saw you in the hall, saw the look on your face when I came in . . . I realized that I just don't know."

"Celia, you listen to me! There aren't any hereditary defects that would surface! Damn it, you know that! If there were, we simply wouldn't have children, but there's no reason. You know that, don't you?"

She nodded. "I know."

"For God's sake! Come with me, Celia. We don't have to get married right away, let them get used to the idea first. They will. They always do. We have a resilient family, you and me. Celia, I love you."

She turned her head, and he saw that she was weeping. She wiped her cheeks with her glove, then with her bare hand, leaving dirt streaks. David pulled her to him, held her and kissed her tears, her cheeks, her lips. And he kept saying, "I love you, Celia."

She finally drew away and started back down the slope, with David following. "I can't decide anything right now. It isn't fair. I should have stayed at the house. I shouldn't have followed you up here. David, I'm committed to going in two days. I can't just say I've changed my mind. It's important to me. To the people down there. I can't just decide not to go. You went to Oxford for a year. I have to do something too."

He caught her arm and held her, kept her from moving ahead again. "Just tell me you love me. Say it, just once, say it."

"I love you," she said very slowly.

"How long will you be gone?"

"Three years. I signed a contract."

He stared at her in disbelief. "Change it! Make it one year. I'll be out of grad school then. You can teach here. Let their bright young students come to you."

"We have to get back, or they'll send a search party for us," she said. "I'll try to change it," she whispered then. "If I can."

Two days later she left.

David spent New Year's Eve at the Sumner farm with his parents and a horde of aunts and uncles and cousins. On New Year's Day, Grandfather Sumner made an announcement. "We're building a hospital up at Bear Creek, this side of the mill."

David blinked. That was a mile from the farm, miles from anything else at all. "A hospital?" He looked at his uncle Walt, who nodded.

Clarence was studying his eggnog with a sour expression, and David's father, the third brother, was watching the smoke curl from his pipe. They all knew, David realized. "Why up here?" he asked finally.

"It's going to be a research hospital," Walt said. "Genetic diseases, hereditary defects, that sort of thing. Two hundred beds."

David shook his head in disbelief. "You have any idea how much something like that would cost? Who's financing it?"

His grandfather laughed nastily. "Senator Burke has graciously arranged to get federal funds," he said. His voice became more caustic. "And I cajoled a few members of the family to put a little in the kitty." David glanced at Clarence, who looked pained. "I'm giving the land," Grandfather Sumner went on. "So here and there we got support."

"But why would Burke go for it? You've never voted for him in a single campaign in his life."

"Told him we'd dig out a lot of stuff we've been sitting on, support his opposition. If he was a baboon, we'd support him, and there's a lot of family these days, David. A heap of family."

"Well, hats off," David said, still not fully believing it. "You giving up your practice to go into research?" he asked Walt. His uncle nodded. David drained his cup of eggnog.

"David," Walt said quietly, "we want to hire you."

He looked up quickly. "Why? I'm not into medical research."

"I know what your specialty is," Walt said, still very quietly. "We want you for a consultant, and later on to head a department of research."

"But I haven't even finished my thesis yet," David said, and he felt as if he had stumbled into a pot party.

"You'll do another year of donkey work for Selnick and eventually you'll write the thesis, a bit here, a dab there. You could write it in a month, couldn't you, if you had time?" David nodded reluctantly. "I know," Walt said, smiling faintly. "You think you're being asked to give up a lifetime career for a pipe dream." There was no trace of a smile when he added, "But, David, we believe that lifetime won't be more than two to four years at the very most."

Chapter 2

David looked from his uncle to his father, to the other uncles and cousins in the room, and finally to his grandfather. He shook his head helplessly. "That's crazy. What are you talking about?"

Grandfather Sumner let out his breath explosively. He was a large man with a massive chest and great bulging biceps. His hands were big enough to carry a basketball in each. But it was his head that was his most striking feature. It was the head of a giant, and although he had farmed for many years, and later overseen the others who did it for him, he had found time to read more extensively than anyone else that David knew. There was no book, except the contemporary best sellers, that anyone could mention that he wasn't aware of, or hadn't read. And he remembered what he read. His library was better than most public libraries.

Now he leaned forward and said, "You listen to me, David. You listen hard. I'm telling you what the goddamn government doesn't dare admit yet. We're on the first downslope of a slide that is going to plummet this economy, and that of every other nation on earth, to a depth that they never dreamed of.

"I know the signs, David. The pollution's catching up to us faster than anyone knows. There's more radiation in the atmosphere than there's been since Hiroshima— French tests, China's tests. Leaks. God knows where all of it's coming from. We reached zero population growth a couple of years ago, but, David, we were trying, and other nations are getting there too, and they aren't trying. There's famine in one-fourth of the world right now. Not ten years from now, not six months from now. The fam-

16

ines are here and they've been here for three, four years already, and they're getting worse. There're more diseases than there's ever been since the good Lord sent the plagues to visit the Egyptians. And they're plagues that we don't know anything about.

"There's more drought and more flooding than there's ever been. England's changing into a desert, the bogs and moors are drying up. Entire species of fish are gone, just damn gone, and in only a year or two. The anchovies are gone. The codfish industry is gone. The cod they are catching are diseased, unfit to use. There's no fishing off the west coast of the Americas.

"Every damn protein crop on earth has some sort of blight that gets worse and worse. Corn blight. Wheat rust. Soybean blight. We're restricting our exports of food now, and next year we'll stop them altogether. We're having shortages no one ever dreamed of. Tin, copper, aluminum, paper. Chlorine, by God! And what do you think will happen in the world when we suddenly can't even purify our drinking water?"

His face was darkening as he spoke, and he was getting angrier and angrier, directing his unanswerable questions to David, who stared at him with nothing at all to say.

"And they don't know what to do about any of it," his grandfather went on. "No more than the dinosaurs knew how to stop their own extinction. We've changed the photochemical reactions of our own atmosphere, and we can't adapt to the new radiations fast enough to survive! There have been hints here and there that this is a major concern, but who listens? The damn fools will lay each and every catastrophe at the foot of a local condition and turn their backs on the fact that this is global, until it's too late to do anything."

"But if it's what you think, what could they do?" David asked, looking to Dr. Walt for support and finding none.

"Turn off the factories, ground the airplanes, stop the mining, junk the cars. But they won't, and even if they did, it would still be a catastrophe. It's going to break wide open. Within the next couple of years, David, it's going to break." He drank his eggnog then and put the crystal cup down hard. David jumped at the noise.

"There's going to be the biggest bust since man began scratching marks on rocks, that's what! And we're getting ready for it! I'm getting ready for it! We've got the land

17

and we've got the men to farm it, and we'll get our hospital and we'll do research in ways to keep our animals and our people alive, and when the world goes into a tailspin we'll be alive and when it starves we'll be eating."

Suddenly he stopped and studied David with his eyes narrowed. "I said you'd leave here convinced that we've all gone mad. But you'll be back, David, my boy. You'll be back before the dogwoods bloom, because you'll see the signs."

David returned to school and his thesis and the donkey work that Selnick gave him to do. Celia didn't write, and he had no address for her. In response to his questions his mother admitted that no one had heard from her. In February in retaliation for the food embargo, Japan passed trade restrictions that made further United States trade with her impossible. Japan and China signed a mutual aid treaty. In March, Japan seized the Philippines, with their fields of rice, and China resumed its long-dormant trusteeship over the Indochina peninsula, with the rice paddies of Cambodia and Vietnam.

Cholera struck in Rome, Los Angeles, Galveston, and Savannah. Saudi Arabia, Kuwait, Jordan, and other Arab-bloc nations issued an ultimatum: the United States must guarantee a yearly ration of wheat to the Arab bloc and discontinue all aid to the state of Israel or there would be no oil for the United States or Europe. They refused to believe the United States could not meet their demands. International travel restrictions were imposed immediately, and the government, by presidential decree, formed a new department with cabinet status: the Bureau of Information.

The redbuds were hazy blurs of pink against the clear, May-softened sky when David returned home. He stopped by his house only long enough to change his clothes and get rid of his boxes of college mementos before he drove out to the Sumner farm, where Walt was staying while he oversaw the construction of his hospital.

Walt had an office downstairs. It was a clutter of books, notebooks, blueprints, correspondence. He greeted David as if he hadn't been away at all. "Look," he said. "This research of Semple and Frerrer, what do you know about it? The first generation of cloned mice showed no deviation, no variation in viability or potency, nor did the second or third, but with the fourth the viability descreased

· 18

sharply. And there was a steady, and irreversible, slide to extinction. Why?"

David sat down hard and stared at Walt. "How did you get that?"

"Vlasic," Walt said. "We went to med school together. He went on in one direction, I in another. We've corresponded all these years. I asked him."

"You know his work?"

"Yes. His rhesus monkeys show the same decline during the fourth generation, and on to extinction."

"It isn't just like that," David said. "He had to discontinue his work last year—no funds. So we don't know the life expectancies of the later strains. But the decline starts in the third clone generation, a decline of potency. He was breeding each clone generation sexually, testing the offspring for normalcy. The third clone generation had only twenty-five percent potency. The sexually reproduced offspring started with that same percentage, and, in fact, potency dropped until the fifth generation of sexually reproduced offspring, and then it started to climb back up and presumably would have reached normalcy again."

Walt was watching him closely, nodding now and then. David went on. "That was the clone-three strain. With the clone-four strain there was a drastic change. Some abnormalities were present, and life expectancy was down seventeen percent. The abnormals were all sterile. Potency was generally down to forty-eight percent. It was downhill all the way with each sexually reproduced generation. By the fifth generation no offspring survived longer than an hour or two. So much for clone-four strain. Cloning the fours was worse. Clone-five strain had gross abnormalities, and they were all sterile. Life-expectancy figures were not completed. There was no clone-six strain. None survived."

"A dead end," Walt said. He indicated a stack of magazines and extracts. "I had hoped that they were out of date, that there were newer methods, perhaps, or an error had been found in their figures. It's the third generation that is the turning point then?"

David shrugged. "My information could be out of date. I know Vlasic stopped last year, but Semple and Frerrer are still at it, or were last month. They may have something newer than I know. You're thinking of livestock?"

"Of course. You know the rumors? They're just not

breeding well. No figures are available, but, hell, we have our own livestock. They're down by half."

"I heard something. Denied by the Bureau of Information, I believe."

"It's true," Walt said soberly.

"They must be working on this line," David said. "Someone must be working on it."

"If they are, no one's telling us about it," Walt said. He laughed bitterly and stood up.

"Can you get materials for the hospital?" David asked.

"For now. We're rushing it like there's no tomorrow, naturally. And we're not worrying about money right now. We'll have things that we won't know what to do with, but I thought it would be better to order everything I can think of than to find out next year that what we really need isn't available."

David went to the window and looked at the farm; the green was well established by now, spring would give way to summer without a pause and the corn would be shiny, silky green in the fields. Just like always. "Let me have a look at your lab equipment orders, and the stuff that's been delivered already," he said. "Then let's see if we can wrangle me travel clearance out to the coast. I'll talk to Semple; I've met him a few times. If anyone's doing anything, it's that team."

"What is Selnick working on?"

"Nothing. He lost his grant, his students were sent packing." David grinned at his uncle suddenly. "Look, up on the hill, you can see a dogwood ready to burst open. Some of the blooms are already showing."

Chapter 3

David was bone tired, every muscle seemed to ache at once, and his head was throbbing. For nine days he had been on the go, to the coast, to Harvard, to Washington, and now he wanted nothing more than to sleep, even if the world ground to a stop while he was unaware. He had taken a train from Washington to Richmond, and there, unable to rent a car, or buy gasoline if a car had been available, he had stolen a bicycle and pedaled the rest of the way. He never realized his legs could ache so much.

"You're sure that bunch in Washington won't be able to get a hearing?" Grandfather Sumner asked.

"No one wants to hear the Jeremiahs," David said. Selnick had been one of the group, and he had talked to David briefly. The government had to admit the seriousness of the coming catastrophe, had to take strict measures to avert it, or at least alleviate it, but instead, the government chose to paint glowing pictures of the coming upturn that would be apparent by fall. During the next six months those with sense and money would buy everything they could to see them through, because after that period of grace there would be nothing to buy.

"Selnick says we should offer to buy his equipment. The school will jump at the chance to unload it right now. Cheap." David laughed. "Cheap. A quarter of a million possibly."

"Make the offer," Grandfather Sumner said brusquely. And Walt nodded thoughtfully.

David stood up shakily and shook his head. He waved at them and went off to his bed.

People still went to work. The factories were still producing, not as much, and none of the nonessentials, but they were converting to coal as fast as possible. He thought about the darkened cities, the fleets of trucks rusting, the corn and wheat rotting in the fields. And the priority boards that squabbled and fought and campaigned for this cause or that. It was a long time before his twitching muscles relaxed enough for him to lie quietly, and a longer time before he could relax his mind enough to sleep.

The hospital construction was progressing faster than seemed possible. There were two shifts at work; again a case of damn-the-cost. Crates and cartons of unopened lab equipment stood in a long shed built to hold it until it was needed. David went to work in a makeshift laboratory trying to replicate Frerrer's and Semple's tests. And in early July, Harry Vlasic arrived at the farm. He was short, fat, near-sighted, and short-tempered. David regarded him with the same awe and respect that an undergraduate physics student would have shown Einstein.

"All right," Vlasic said. "The corn crop has failed, as

predicted. Monoculture! Bah! They'll save sixty percent of the wheat, no more than that. This winter, hah, just wait until winter! Now where is the cave?"

They took him to the cave entrance, which was just over a hundred yards from the hospital. Inside the cave they used lanterns. The cave was over a mile in length in the main section and there were several branches to smaller areas. Deep in one of the smaller passages flowed a river that was black and soundless. Spring water, good water. Vlasic nodded again and again. When they finished the cave tour he was still nodding. "It's good," he said. "It'll work. The laboratories go in there, underground passage from the hospital, safe from contamination. Good."

They worked sixteen hours a day that summer and into the fall. In October the first wave of flu swept the country, worse than the outbreak of 1917-1918. In November a new illness appeared, and here and there it was whispered that it was plague, but the government Bureau of Information said it was flu. Grandfather Sumner died in November. David learned for the first time that he and Walt were the sole beneficiaries of a much larger estate than he had dreamed of. And the estate was in cash. Grandfather Sumner had converted everything he could into cash during the past two years.

In December the members of the family began to arrive, leaving the towns and villages and cities scattered throughout the valley to take up residence in the hospital and staff buildings. Rationing, black markets, inflation, and looting had turned the cities into battle mounds. And the government was freezing all assets of every business —nothing could be bought or sold without approval. The army was occupying the buildings, and government employees were overseeing the strict rationing that had been imposed.

The family brought their stocks with them. Jeremy Streit brought his hardware merchandise in four truckloads. Eddie Beauchamp brought his dental equipment. David's father brought all that he could from his department store. The family had diversified, and there were representative supplies from almost every conceivable area of business and professional endeavor.

With the failure of radio and television communication, there was no way for the government to cope with

22

the rising panic. Martial law was declared on December 28. Six months too late.

There was no child left under eight years of age when the spring rains came, and the original 319 people who had come to the upper valley had dwindled to 201. In the cities the toll had been much higher.

David studied the fetal pig he was getting ready to dissect. It was wrinkled and desiccated, its bones too soft, its lymph glands lumpy, hard. Why? Why did the fourth generation decline? Harry Vlasic came to watch briefly, then walked away, his head bowed in thought. Not even he could come up with any answers, David thought, almost with satisfaction.

That night David, Walt, and Vlasic met and went over it all again. They had enough livestock to feed the two hundred people for a long time, through cloning and sexual breeding of the third generation. They could clone up to four hundred animals at a time. Chickens, swine, cattle. But if the livestock all became sterile, as seemed indicated, then the food supply was limited.

Watching the two older men, David knew that they were purposely skirting the other question. If the people also became sterile, how long would they need a continuing supply of food? He said, "We should isolate a strain of sterile mice, clone them, and test for the reemergence of fertility with each new generation of clones."

Vlasic frowned and shook his head. "If we had a dozen undergraduate students, perhaps," he said drily.

"We have to know," David said, feeling hot suddenly. "You're both acting like this is just a five-year emergency plan to tide us over a bad few years. What if it isn't that at all? Whatever is causing the sterility is present in all the animals. We have to know."

Walt looked at David briefly and said, "We don't have the time or the facilities to do any research like that."

"That's a lie," David said flatly. "We can generate all the electricity we can use, more than enough power. We have equipment we haven't even unloaded yet. . . ."

"Because there's no one who can use it yet," Walt said patiently.

"I can. I'll do it in my free time."

"What free time?"

"I'll find it." He stared at Walt until his uncle shrugged permission.

23

In June, David had his preliminary answers. "The A-four strain," he said, "has twenty-five percent potency." Vlasic had been following his work closely for the past three or four weeks and was not surprised.

Walt stared at him in disbelief. "Are you sure?" he whispered after a moment.

"The fourth generation of cloned sterile mice showed the same degeneracy that all clones show by then," David said wearily. "But they also had a twenty-five percent fertility factor. The offspring have shorter lives, but more fertile members. This trend continues to the sixth generation, where fertility is up to ninety-four percent and life expectancy starts to climb again, and then it's on its way to normalcy steadily." He had it all on the charts that Walt now studied. A, A^1, A^2, A^3, A^4, and their offspring by sexual reproduction, a, a^1, a^2 . . . There were no clone strains after A^4; none had survived to maturity.

David leaned back and closed his eyes and thought about bed and a blanket up around his neck and black, black sleep. "Higher organisms must reproduce sexually or die out, and the ability to do so is there. Something remembers and heals itself," he said dreamily.

"You'll be a great man when you publish," Vlasic said, his hand on David's shoulder. He then moved to sit next to Walt, to point out some of the details that Walt might miss. "A marvelous piece of work," he said softly, his eyes glowing as he looked over the pages. "Marvelous." Then he glanced back at David. "Of course, you are aware of the other implications of your work."

David opened his eyes and met Vlasic's gaze. He nodded. Puzzled, Walt looked from one to the other of them. David got up and stretched. "I have to sleep," he said.

But it was a long time before he slept. He had a single room at the hospital, more fortunate than most, who were sleeping doubled up. The hospital had more than two hundred beds, but few single rooms. The implications, he mused. He had been aware of them from the start, although he had not admitted it even to himself, and was not ready to discuss it now. They weren't certain yet. Three of the women were pregnant finally, after a year and a half of barrenness. Margaret was near term, the baby well and kicking at the moment. Five more weeks, he thought. Five more weeks, and perhaps he never would have to discuss the implications of his work.

But Margaret didn't wait five weeks. In two weeks she

24

delivered a stillborn child. Zelda had a miscarriage the following week, and in the next week May lost her child. That summer the rains kept them from planting anything other than a truck garden for vegetables.

Walt began testing the men for fertility, and reported to David and Vlasic that no man in the valley was fertile.

"So," Vlasic said softly, "we now see the significance of David's work."

Chapter 4

Winter came early in sheets of icy rain that went on day after day after day. The work in the laboratories increased, and David found himself blessing his grandfather for his purchase of Selnick's equipment, which had come with detailed instructions for making artificial placentas as well as nearly completed work on computer programs for synthetic amniotic fluids. When David had gone to talk to Selnick about the equipment, Selnick had insisted—madly, David had thought at the time—that he take everything or nothing. "You'll see," he had said wildly. "You'll see." The following week he had hanged himself, and the equipment was on its way to the Virginia valley.

They worked and slept in the lab, leaving only for meals. The winter rains gave way to spring rains, and a new softness was in the air.

David was leaving the cafeteria, his mind on the work in the lab, when he felt a tug on his arm. It was his mother. He hadn't seen her for weeks, and would have brushed past her with a quick hello if she hadn't stopped him. She looked strange, childlike. He turned from her to stare out the window, waiting for her to release his arm.

"Celia's coming home," she said softly. "She's well, she says."

David felt frozen; he continued to stare out the window seeing nothing. "Where is she now?" He listened to the rustle of cheap paper and when it seemed that his mother was not going to answer him, he wheeled about. *"Where is she?"*

"Miami," she said finally, after scanning the two pages. "It's postmarked Miami, I think. It's over two weeks old. Dated May 28. She never got any of our mail." She pressed the letter into David's hand. Tears overflowed her eyes, and heedless of them she walked away.

David didn't read the letter until his mother had left the cafeteria. *I was in Colombia for a while, eight months, I think. And I got a touch of the bug that nobody wants to name.* The writing was spindly and uncertain. She was not well then. He looked for Walt.

"I have to go get her. She can't walk in on that gang at the Wiston place."

"You know you can't leave now."

"It isn't a question of can or can't. I have to."

Walt studied him for a moment, then shrugged. "How will you get there and back? No gas. You know we don't dare use any for anything but the harvest."

"I know," David said impatiently. "I'll take Mike and the cart. I can stay on the back roads with Mike." He knew that Walt was calculating, as he had done, the time involved, and he felt his face tightening, his hands clenching. Walt simply nodded. "I'll leave as soon as it's light in the morning." Again Walt nodded. "Thanks," David said suddenly. He meant for not arguing with him, for not pointing out what both already knew—that there was no way of knowing how long he would have to wait for Celia, that she might never make it to the farm.

Three miles from the Wiston farm, David unhitched the cart and hid it in thick underbrush. He swept over the tracks where he had left the dirt road, and then led Mike into the woods. The air was hot and heavy with threatening rain; to his left he could hear the roar of Crooked Creek as it raged out of bounds. The ground was spongy and he walked carefully, not wanting to sink to his knees in the treacherous mud here in the lowlands. The Wiston farm always had been flood-prone; it enriched the soil, Grandfather Wiston had claimed, not willing to damn nature for its periodic rampages. "God didn't mean for this piece of ground to have to bear year after year after year," he said. "Comes a time when the earth needs a rest, same as you and me. We'll let it be this year, give it some clover when the ground dries out."

David started to climb, still leading Mike, who whinnied softly at him now and again. "Just to the knob, boy," David said quietly. "Then you can rest and eat meadow grass until she gets here."

Grandfather Wiston had taken him to the knob once, when David was twelve. He remembered the day, hot and still like this day, he thought, and Grandfather Wiston had been straight and strong. At the knob his grandfather had paused and touched the massive bole of a white oak tree. "This tree saw the Indians in that valley, David, and the first settlers, and my great-grandfather when he came along. It's our friend, David. It knows all the family secrets."

"Is it still your property up here, Grandfather?"

"Up to and including this tree, son. Other side's national forest land, but this tree, it's on our land. Yours too, David. One day you'll come up here and put your hand on this tree and you'll know it's your friend, just like it's been my friend all my life. God help us all if anyone ever lays an ax to it."

They had gone on that day, down the other side of the knob, then up again, farther and steeper this time until once more his grandfather paused for a few moments, his hand on David's shoulder. "This is how this land looked a million years ago, David." Time had shifted suddenly for the boy; a million years, a hundred million, was all the same distant past, and he imagined the tread of the giant reptiles. He imagined that he smelled the fetid breath of a tyrannosaur. It was cool and misty under the tall trees, and below them the saplings grew, with their branches spread horizontally, as if to catch any stray bit of sunlight that penetrated the high canopy. Where the sun did find a path through, it was golden and soft, the sun of another time. In even deeper shadows grew bushes and shrubs, and at the foot of it all were the mosses and lichens, liverworts and ferns. The arching, heaving roots of the trees were clothed in velvet emerald plants.

David stumbled and, catching his balance, came to rest against the giant oak tree that was, somehow, his friend. He pressed his cheek against the rough bark for a few moments, then he pushed himself away and looked up through the luxuriant branches; he could see no sky through them. When it rained, the tree would protect him from the full force of the storm, but he needed shelter from the fine drops that would make their way through the leaves to fall quietly on the absorbent ground.

27

Before he started to build a lean-to, he examined the farm through his binoculars. Behind the house, there was a garden being tended by five people; impossible to tell if they were male or female. Long-haired, jeans, barefoot, thin. It didn't matter. He noted that the garden was not producing yet, that the plants were sparse and frail. He studied the east field, aware that it was changed but not certain what was different. Then he realized that it was growing corn. Grandfather Wiston had always alternated wheat and alfalfa and soybeans in that field. The lower fields were flooded, and the north field was grown up in grasses and weeds. He swept the glasses slowly over the buildings. He spotted seventeen people altogether. No child younger than eight or nine. No sign of Celia, nor of any recent use of the road, which was also grown up with weeds. No doubt the people down there were just as happy to let the road hide under weeds.

He built a lean-to against the oak, where he could lie down and observe the farm. He used fir branches to roof the shelter, and when the storm came half an hour later he stayed dry. Rivulets ran among the garden rows below, and the farmyard turned silver and sparkly from this distance, although he knew that closer it would simply be muddy water inches deep. The ground was too saturated in the valley to absorb any more water. It would have to run off into Crooked Creek, which was inching higher and higher toward the north field and the vulnerable corn there.

By the third day the water had started to invade the cornfield, and he pitied the people who stood and watched helplessly. The garden was still being tended, but it would be a meager harvest. By now he had counted twenty-two people; he thought that was all of them. During the storm that lashed the valley that afternoon, he heard Mike whinny and he crawled from the lean-to and stood up. Mike, down the slope of the knob, wouldn't mind the rain too much, and he was protected from the wind. Still, he whinnied again, and then again. Cautiously, holding his shotgun in one hand, shielding his eyes from the lashing rain with the other, David edged around the tree. A figure stumbled up the knob haltingly, head bowed, stopping often, then moving on again, not looking up, probably blinded by the rain. Suddenly David threw the shotgun under the lean-to and ran to meet her. "Celia!" he cried. "Celia!"

She stopped and raised her head. The rain ran over her cheeks and plastered her hair to her forehead. She dropped the shoulder bag that had weighed her down and ran toward him, and only when he caught her and held her tight and hard did he realize that he was weeping, as she was.

Under the lean-to he pulled off her wet clothes and rubbed her dry, then wrapped her in one of his shirts. Her lips were blue, her skin seemed almost translucent; it was unearthly white.

"I knew you'd be here," she said. Her eyes were very large, deep blue, bluer than he remembered, or bluer in contrast to her pale skin. Before, she had been always sunburned.

"I knew you'd come here," he said. "When did you eat?"

She shook her head. "I didn't believe it was this bad here. I thought it was propaganda. Everyone thinks it's propaganda."

He nodded and lighted the Sterno. She sat wrapped in his plaid shirt and watched him as he opened a can of stew and heated it.

"Who are those people down there?"

"Squatters. Grandmother and Grandfather Wiston died last year. That gang showed up. They gave Aunt Hilda and Uncle Eddie a choice, join them or get out. They didn't give Wanda any chance at all. They kept her."

She stared down into the valley and nodded slowly. "I didn't know it was this bad. I didn't believe it." Without looking back at him, she asked then, "And Mother, Father?"

"They're dead, Celia. Flu, both of them. Last winter."

"I didn't get any letters," she said. "Almost two years. They made us leave Brazil, you know. But there wasn't any transportation home. We went to Colombia. They promised to let us go home in three months. And then they came one night, late, almost at dawn, and said we had to get out. There were riots, you know."

He nodded, although she was still staring down at the farm and couldn't see. He wanted to tell her to weep for her parents, to cry out, so that he could take her in his arms and try to comfort her. But she continued to sit motionlessly and speak in a dead voice.

"They were coming for us, for the Americans. They

29

blame us, for letting them starve. They really believe that everything is still all right here. I did too. No one believed any of the reports. And the mobs were coming for us. We left on a small boat, a skiff. Nineteen of us. They shot at us when we got too near Cuba."

David touched her arm and she jerked and trembled. "Celia, turn around and eat now. Don't talk any longer. Later. You can tell us about it later."

She looked at him and slowly shook her head. "Never again. I'll never mention any of it again, David. I just wanted you to know there was nothing I could do. I wanted to come home and there wasn't any way."

She didn't look quite so blue-cold now, and he watched with relief as she started to eat. She was hungry. He made coffee, the last of his coffee ration.

"You want me to fill you in on anything here?"

She shook her head. "Not yet. I saw Miami, and the people, all trying to get somewhere else, standing in line for days, standing on the trains. They're evacuating Miami. People are falling dead, and they're just leaving them where they fall." She shivered violently. "Don't tell me anything else yet."

The storm was over, and the night air was cool. They huddled under a blanket and sat without talking, drinking hot black coffee. When the cup began to tilt in Celia's hand, David took it from her and gently lowered her to the bed he had prepared. "I love you, Celia," he said softly. "I've always loved you."

"I love you, too, David. Always." Her eyes were closed and her lashes were very black on her white cheeks. David leaned over and kissed her forehead, pulled the blanket higher about her, and watched her sleep for a long time before he lay down beside her and also slept.

During the night she roused once, moaning, twisting about, and he held her until she quieted. She didn't wake up completely, and what words she said were not intelligible.

The next morning they left the oak tree and started for the Sumner farm. She rode Mike until they got to the cart; by then she was trembling with exhaustion and her lips were blue again, although the day was already hot. There wasn't room for her to lie down in the cart, so he padded the back of the wooden seat with his bedroll and blanket, where she could at least put her head back and rest, when the road wasn't too bumpy and the cart didn't jounce too hard. She smiled faintly when he covered her legs with another shirt, the one he had been wearing.

"It isn't cold, you know," she said matter-of-factly. "That goddamn bug does something to the heart, I think. No one would tell us anything about it. My symptoms all involve the circulatory system."

"How bad was it? When did you get it?"

"Eighteen months ago, I think. Just before they made us leave Brazil. It swept Rio. That's where they took us when we got sick. Not many survived it. Hardly any of the later cases. It became more virulent as time went on."

He nodded. "Same here. Something like sixty percent fatal, increasing up to eighty percent by now, I guess."

There was a long silence then, and he thought that perhaps she had drifted off to sleep. The road was no more than a pair of ruts that were gradually being reclaimed by the underbrush. Already grass covered it almost totally, except where the rains had washed the dirt away and left only rocks. Mike walked deliberately and David didn't hurry him.

"David, how many are up at the northern end of the valley?"

"About one hundred ten now," he said. He thought, two out of three dead, but he didn't say it.

"And the hospital? Was it built?"

"It's there. Walt is running it."

"David, while you're driving, now that you can't watch me for reactions or anything, just tell me about it here. What's been happening, who's alive, who's dead. Everything."

When they stopped for lunch, hours later, she said, "David, will you make love to me now, before the rains start again?"

They lay under a stand of yellow poplars, and the leaves rustled incessantly though no wind could be felt. Under the susurrous trees, their own voices became whispers. She was so thin and so pale, and inside she was so warm and alive; her body rose to meet his and her breasts seemed to lift, to seek his touch, his lips. Her fingers were in his hair, on his back, digging into his flanks, strong now, then relaxed and trembling, then clenched into fists that opened spasmodically; and he felt her nails distantly, aware that his back was being clawed, but distantly, distantly. And finally there were only the susurrant leaves and now and then a long, heaving sigh.

31

"I've loved you for more than twenty years, did you realize that?" he said after a long time.

She laughed. "Remember when I broke your arm?"

Later, in the cart again, her voice came from behind him, softly, sadly. "We're finished, aren't we, David? You, I, all of us?"

He thought, Walt be damned, promises be damned, secrecy be damned. And he told her about the clones developing under the mountain, in the laboratory deep in the cave.

Chapter 5

Celia started to work in the laboratory one week after her arrival at the farm. "It's the only way I'll ever get to see you at all," she said gently when David protested. "I promised Walt that I would work only four hours a day to start. Okay?"

David took her through the lab the following morning. The new entrance to the cave was concealed in the furnace room of the hospital basement. The door was steel, set in the limestone rock that underlay the area. As soon as they stepped through the doorway, the air was cold and David put a coat about Celia's shoulders. "We keep them here at all times," he said, taking a second coat from a wall hanger. "Twice government inspectors have come here, and it might look suspicious if we put them on to go down the cellar. They won't be back."

The passageway was dimly lighted, the floor was smooth. It went four hundred feet to another steel door. This one opened into the first cave chamber, a large, high-domed room. It had been left almost as they had found it, with stalactites and stalagmites on all sides, but now there were many cots, picnic tables and benches, and a row of cooking tables and serving tables. "Our emergency room, for the hot rains," David said, hurrying her through the echoing room. There was another passage, narrower and tougher than the first. At the end of this passage was the animal experiment room.

One wall had been cut through and the computer installed, looking grotesquely out of place against a wall of pale pink travertine. In the center of the room were tanks and vats and pipes, all stainless steel and glass. On either side of these were the tanks that held the animal embryos. Celia stared without moving for several moments, then turned to look at David with startled eyes. "How many tanks do you have?"

"Enough to clone six hundred animals of varying sizes," he said. "We took a lot of them out, put them in the lab on the other side, and we're not using all that we have here. We're afraid our supplies of chemicals will run out, and so far we haven't come up with alternatives that we can extract from anything at our disposal here."

Eddie Beauchamp came from the side of the tanks, jotting figures in a ledger. He grinned at David and Celia. "Slumming?" he asked. He checked his figures against a dial and adjusted it a fraction, and continued down the row checking the other dials, stopping now and again to make a minor adjustment.

Celia's eyes questioned David, and he shook his head. Eddie didn't know what they were doing in the other lab. They walked past the tanks, row after row of them, all sealed, with only needles that moved now and then and the dials on the sides to indicate that there was anything inside. They returned to the corridor. David led her through another doorway, a short passage, then into the second laboratory, this one secured by a lock that he had a key for.

Walt looked up as they entered, nodded, and turned again to the desk where he was working. Vlasic didn't even look up. Sarah smiled and hurried past them and sat down before a computer console and began to type. Another woman in the room didn't seem to be aware that anyone had come in. Hilda. Celia's aunt. David glanced at Celia, but she was staring wide-eyed at the tanks, and in this room the tanks were glass-fronted. Each was filled with a pale liquid, a yellow so faint that the color seemed almost illusory. Within the tanks, floating in the liquid, were sacs, no larger than small fists. Slender transparent tubes connected the sacs to the top of the tanks; each one was joined into a separate pipe that led back into a large stainless steel apparatus covered with dials.

33

Celia walked slowly down the aisle between the tanks, stopped once midway, and didn't move again for a long time. David took her arm. She was trembling slightly.

"Are you all right?"

She nodded. "I . . . it's a shock, seeing them. I . . . maybe I didn't quite believe it." There was a film of perspiration on her face.

"Better take off the coat now," David said. "We have to keep it pretty warm in here. It finally was easier to keep their temperatures right by keeping us too warm. The price we pay," he said, smiling slightly.

"All the lights? The heat? The computer? You can generate that much electricity?"

He nodded. "That'll be our tour tomorrow. Like everything else around here, the generating system has bugs in it. We can store enough power for no longer than six hours, and we just don't let it go out for more than six hours. Period."

"Six hours is a lot. If you stop breathing for six minutes, you're dead." With her hands clasped behind her, she stepped closer to the shiny control system at the end of the room. "This isn't the computer. What is it?"

"It's a computer terminal. The computer controls the input of nutrients and oxygen, and the output of toxins. The animal room is on the other side of that wall. Those tanks are linked to it, too. Separate set of systems, but the same machinery."

They went through the nursery for the animals, and then the nursery for the human babies. There was the dissection room, several small offices where the scientists could withdraw to work, the stockrooms. In every room except the one where the human clones were being grown, people were working. "They never used a Bunsen burner or a test tube before, but they have become scientists and technicians practically overnight," David said. "And thank God for that, or it never would have worked. I don't know what they think we're doing now, but they don't ask questions. They just do their jobs."

Walt assigned Celia to work under Vlasic. Whenever David looked up to see her in the laboratory, he felt a stab of joy. She increased her workday to six hours. When David fell into bed exhausted after fourteen or sixteen hours, she was there to hold him and love him.

In August, Avery Handley reported that his shortwave contact in Richmond warned of a band of marauders who were working their way up the valley. "They're bad," he said gravely. "They took over the Phillotts' place, ransacked it, and then burned it to the ground."

After that they kept guards posted day and night. And that same week Avery announced that there was war in the Middle East. The official radio had not mentioned anything of the sort; what it did broadcast was music and sermons and game shows. Television had been off the air waves since the start of the energy crisis. "They're using the bomb," Avery said. "Don't know who, but someone is. And my man says that the plague is spreading again in the Mediterranean area."

In September they fought off the first attack. In October they learned the band was grouping for a second attack, this time with thirty to forty men. "We can't keep fighting them off," Walt said. "They must know we have food here. They'll come from all directions this time. They know we're watching for them."

"We should blow up the dam," Clarence said. "Wait until they're in the upper valley and flood them out."

The meeting was being held in the cafeteria, with everyone present. Celia's hand tightened in David's, but she didn't protest. No one protested.

"They'll try to take the mill," Clarence went on. "They probably think there's wheat there, or something." A dozen men volunteered to stand guard at the mill. Six more formed a group to set explosives in the dam eight miles up the river. Others formed a scouting party.

David and Celia left the meeting early. He had volunteered for everything, and each time had been turned down. He was not one of the expendable ones. The rains had become "hot" again, and the people were all sleeping in the cave. David and Celia, Walt, Vlasic, the others who worked in the various labs, all slept there on cots. In one of the small offices David held Celia's hand and they whispered before they fell asleep. Their talk was of their childhood.

Long after Celia fell asleep he stared into the blackness, still holding her hand. She had grown even thinner, and earlier that week when he had tried to get her to leave the lab to rest, Walt had said, "Leave her be." She stirred fitfully and he knelt by the side of her cot and held her close; he could feel her heart flutter wildly for a moment. Then she was still again, and slowly he released her and sat on the stone floor with his eyes closed. Later he heard Walt moving about, and the creaking of his cot in the next office. David was getting stiff, and finally he returned to his own bed and fell asleep.

The next day the people worked to get everything up to high ground. They would lose three houses when the dam was blown up, the barn near the road, and the road itself. Nothing could be spared, and board by board they carried a barn up the hillside and stacked the pieces. Two days later the signal was given and the dam was destroyed.

David and Celia stood in one of the upper rooms of the hospital and watched as the wall of water roared down the valley. It was like a jet takeoff; a crowd furious with an umpire's decision; an express train out of control; a roar like nothing he had ever heard, or like everything he had ever heard, recombined to make this noise that shook the building, that vibrated in his bones. A wall of water, fifteen feet high, twenty feet high, raced down the valley, accelerating as it came, smashing, destroying everything in its path.

When the roar was gone and the water stood high on the land, swirling, thick with debris, Celia said in a faint voice, "Is it worth this, David?"

He tightened his arm about her shoulders. "We had to do it," he said.

"I know. But it seems so futile sometimes. We're all dead, fighting right down the line, but dead. As dead as those men must be by now."

"We're making it work, honey. You know that. You've been working right there. Thirty new lives!"

She shook her head. "Thirty more dead people. Do you remember Sunday school, David? They took me every week. Did you go?"

He nodded.

"And Wednesday-night Bible school? I keep thinking of it now. And I wonder if this isn't God's doing after all. I can't help it. I keep wondering. And I had become an atheist." She laughed and suddenly spun around. "Let's go to bed, now. Here in the hospital. Let's pick a fancy room, a suite. . . ."

He reached for her, but suddenly a violent gust of wind drove a hard blast of rain against the window. It came like that, without preliminary, just a sudden deluge. Celia shuddered. "God's will," she said dully. "We have to get back to the cave, don't we?"

They walked through the empty hospital, through the long, dimly lighted passage, through the large chamber where the people were trying to find comfortable positions on the cots and benches, through the smaller passages and finally into the lab office.

"How many people did we kill?" Celia asked, stepping out of her jeans. She turned her back to put her clothes on the foot of her cot. Her buttocks were nearly as flat as an adolescent boy's. When she faced him again, her ribs seemed to be straining against her skin. She looked at him for a moment, and then came to him and held his head tight against her chest as he sat on his cot and she stood naked before him. He could feel her tears as they fell onto his cheek.

There was a hard freeze in November, and with the valley flooded and the road and bridges gone, they knew they were safe from attack, at least until spring. The people had moved out of the cave again, and work in the lab went on at the same numbing pace. The fetuses were developing, growing, moving now with sudden motions of feet and elbows. David was working on substitutes for the chemicals that already were substituting for amniotic fluids. He worked each day until his vision blurred, or his hands refused to obey his directions, or Walt ordered him out of the lab. Celia was working longer hours now, still resting in the middle of the day for several hours, but she returned after that and stayed almost as late as David did.

He passed her chair and kissed the top of her head. She looked up at him and smiled, then returned to her figures. Peter started a centrifuge. Vlasic made a last adjustment on the end tank of nutrients that were to be diluted and fed to the embryos, then called out, "Celia, you ready to count chicks?"

"One second," she said. She made a notation, put her pencil in the open book, and stood up.

David was aware of her, as he always was, even when totally preoccupied with his own work. He was aware that she stood up, that she didn't move for a moment, and when she said, in a tremulous voice that betrayed disbelief, "David . . . David . . ." he was already starting to his feet. He caught her as she crumpled.

Her eyes were open, her look almost quizzical, asking

what he could not answer, expecting no answer. A tremor passed through her and she closed her eyes, and although her lids fluttered, she did not open them again.

Chapter 6

Walt looked David over and shrugged. "You look like hell," he said.

David made no response. He knew he looked like hell. He felt like hell. He watched Walt as if from a great distance.

"David, are you going to pull yourself together? You just giving up?" He didn't wait for a reply. He sat down on the only chair in the tiny room and leaned forward, cupping his chin in his hands, staring at the floor. "We've got to tell them. Sarah thinks there'll be trouble. So do I."

David stood at the window, looking at the bleak landscape, done in grays and blacks and mud colors. It was raining, but the rain had become clean. The river was a gray swirling monster that he could glimpse from up here, a dull reflection of the dull sky.

"They might try to storm the lab," Walt went on. "God knows what they might decide to do."

David made no motion but continued to stare at the sullen sky.

"God damn it! You turn around here and listen to me, you asshole! You think I'm going to let all this work, all this planning, go up in one irrational act! You think I won't kill anyone who tries to stop it now!" Walt had jumped up with his outburst, and he swung David around and yelled into his face. "You think I'm going to let you sit up here and die? Not today, David. Not yet. What you decide to do next week, I don't give a damn, but today I need you, and you, by God, are going to be there!"

"I don't care," David said quietly.

"You're going to care! Because those babies are going to come busting out of those sacs, and those babies are the only hope we have, and you know it. Our genes, yours, mine, Celia's, those genes are the only thing that stand between us and oblivion. And I won't allow it, David! I refuse it!"

David felt only a great weariness. "We're all dead. Today or tomorrow. Why prolong it? The price is too high for adding a year or two."

"No price is too high!"

Slowly Walt's face seemed to come into focus. He was white, his lips were pale, his eyes sunken. There was a tic in his cheek that David never had seen before. "Why now?" he asked. "Why change the plan and tell them now, so far ahead of time?"

"Because it isn't that far ahead of time." Walt rubbed his eyes hard. "Something's going wrong, David. I don't know what it is. Something's not working. I think we're going to have our hands full with prematures."

In spite of himself David made rapid calculations. "It's twenty-six weeks," he said. "We can't handle that many premature babies."

"I know that." Walt sat down once more, and this time put his head back and closed his eyes. "We don't have much choice," he said. "We lost one yesterday. Three today. We have to bring them out and treat them like preemies."

Slowly David nodded. "Which ones?" he asked, but he knew. Walt told him the names, and again he nodded. He had known that they were not his, not Walt's, not Celia's. "What are you planning?" he asked then, and sat down on the side of his bed.

"I have to sleep," Walt said. "Then a meeting, posted for seven. After that we prepare the nursery for a hell of a lot of preemies. As soon as we're ready we begin getting them out. That'll be morning. We need nurses, half a dozen, more if we can get them. Sarah says Margaret would be good. I don't know."

David didn't know either. Margaret's four-year-old son had been one of the first to die of the plague, and she had lost a baby in stillbirth. He trusted Sarah's judgment, however. "Think between them they can get enough others, tell them what to do, see that they do it properly?"

Walt mumbled something, and one of his hands fell off the chair arm. He jerked upright.

"Okay, Walt, you get in my bed," David said, almost resentfully. "I'll go down to the lab, get things rolling there. I'll come up for you at six thirty." Walt didn't protest, but fell onto the bed without bothering to take off his shoes. David pulled them off. Walt's socks were more holes than not, but probably they kept his ankles warm. David left them on, pulled the blanket over him, and went to the lab.

At seven the hospital cafeteria was crowded when Walt stood up to make his announcement. First he had Avery Handley run down his log of diminishing shortwave contacts, with the accompanying grim stories of plague, famine, disease, spontaneous abortions, stillbirths, and sterility. It was the same story worldwide. They listened apathetically; they could not care any longer what was happening to any part of the world that was not their small part. Avery finished and sat down once more.

Walt looked small, David thought in surprise. He had always thought of him as a fairly large man, but he wasn't. He was only five feet nine, and now he was very thin and hard-looking, like a gamecock, trimmed of all excess with only the essentials needed to carry on the fight remaining. Walt studied the assembled people and deliberately said, "There's not a person in this room hungry tonight. We don't have any more plague here. The rain is washing away the radioactivity, and we have food stores that will carry us for years even if we can't plant crops in the spring. We have men capable of doing just about anything we might ever want done." He paused and looked at them again, from left to right, back again, taking his time. He had their absolute attention. "What we don't have," he said, his voice hard and flat now, "is a woman who can conceive a child, or a man who could impregnate her if she was able to bear."

There was a ripple of movement, like a collective sigh, but no one spoke. Walt said, "You know how we are getting our meat. You know the cattle are good, the chickens are good. Tomorrow, ladies and gentlemen, we will have our own babies developed the same way."

There was a moment of utter silence, of stillness, then they broke. Clarence leaped to his feet shouting at Walt. Vernon fought to get to the front of the room, but there were too many people between him and Walt. One of the women pulled on Walt's arm, almost dragging him over, screaming in his face. Walt yanked free and climbed onto a table. "Stop this! I'm going to answer any questions, but I can't hear any one of you this way."

For the next three hours they questioned, argued,

prayed, formed alliances, reformed them as arguments broke out in the smaller groups. At ten Walt took his place on the table again and called out. "We will recess this discussion until tomorrow night at seven. Coffee will be served now, and I understand we have cakes and sandwiches." He jumped from the table and left before any of them could catch up with him, and he and David hurried to the cave entrance, locking the massive door behind them.

"Clarence was ugly," Walt muttered. "Bastard."

David's father, Walt, and Clarence were brothers, David reminded himself, but he couldn't help regarding Clarence as an outsider, a stranger with a fat belly and a lot of money who expected instant obedience from the world.

"They might organize," Walt said after a moment. "They might form a committee to protest this act of the devil. We'll have to be ready for them."

David nodded. They had counted on delaying this meeting until they had live babies, human babies that laughed and gurgled and took milk from the bottle hungrily. Instead they would have a room full of not-quite-finished preemies, certainly not human-looking, with no more human appeal than a calf born too soon.

They worked all night preparing the nursery. Sarah had enlisted Margaret, Hilda, Lucy, and half a dozen other women, who were all gowned and masked professionally. One of them dropped a basin and three others screamed in unison. David cursed, but under his breath. They would be all right when they had the babies, he told himself.

The bloodless births started at five forty-five, and at twelve thirty they had twenty-five infants. Four died in the first hour, another died three hours later, and the rest of them thrived. The only baby left in the tanks was the fetus that would be Celia, nine weeks younger than the others.

The first visitor Walt permitted in the nursery was Clarence, and after that there was no further talk of destroying the inhuman monstrosities.

There was a celebration party, and names were suggested and a drawing was held to select eleven female names and ten male. In the record book the babies were labeled R-1 strain; Repopulation 1. But in David's mind, as in Walt's, the babies were W-1, D-1, and soon, C-1 . . .

41

For the next months there was no shortage of nurses, male or female, no shortage of help doing any of the chores that so few had done before. Everyone wanted to become a doctor or a biologist, Walt grumbled. He was sleeping more now, and the fatigue lines on his face were smoothing out. Often he would nudge David and tow him along, away from the nursery, propel him toward his own room in the hospital, and see to it that he remained there for a night's sleep. One night as they walked side by side back to their rooms, Walt said, "Now you understand what I meant when I said this was all that mattered, don't you?"

David understood. Every time he looked down at the tiny, pink new Celia he understood more fully.

Chapter 7

It had been a mistake, David thought, watching the boys from the window in Walt's office. Living memories, that's what they represented. There was Clarence, already looking too pudgy—he'd be fat in another three or four years. And a young Walt, frowning in concentration over a problem that he wouldn't put on paper until he had a solution to add. Robert, too pretty almost, but determinedly manly, always trying harder than the others to endure, to jump higher, run faster, hit harder. And D-4, himself . . . He turned away and pondered the future of the boys, all of an age; uncles, fathers, grandfathers, all the same age. He was starting a headache again.

"They're inhuman, aren't they?" he said bitterly to Walt. "They come and go and we know nothing about them. What do they think? Why do they hang so close to each other?"

"Remember that old cliché; generation gap? It's here, I reckon." Walt was looking very old. He was tired, and seldom tried to hide it any longer. He looked up at David and said quietly, "Maybe they're afraid of us."

David nodded. He had thought of that. "I know why

Hilda did it," he said. "I didn't at the time, but now I know." Hilda had strangled the small girl who looked more like her every day.

"Me too." Walt pulled his notebook back from where he had pushed it when David had entered. "It's a bit spooky to walk into a crowd that's all you, in various stages of growth. They do cling to their own kind." He started to write then, and David left him.

Spooky, he thought, and veered from the laboratory, where he had been heading originally. Let the damn embryos do their thing without him. He knew he didn't want to enter because D-1 or D-2 would be there working. The D-4 strain would be the one, though, to prove or disprove the experiment. If Four didn't make it, then chances were that Five wouldn't either, and then what? A mistake. Whoops, wrong, sir. Sorry about that.

He climbed the ridge behind the hospital, over the cave, and sat down on an outcrop of limestone that felt cool and smooth. The boys were clearing another field. They worked well together, with little conversation but much laughter that seemed to arise spontaneously. A line of girls came into view, from nearer the river; they were carrying baskets of berries. Blackberries and gunpowder, he thought suddenly, and he remembered the ancient celebrations of the Fourth of July, with blackberry stains and fireworks, and sulfur for the chiggers. And birds. Thrushes, meadowlarks, warblers, purple martins.

Three Celias came into view, swinging easily with the weight of the baskets, a stair-step succession of Celias. He shouldn't do that, he reminded himself harshly. They weren't Celias, none of them had that name. They were Mary and Ann and something else. He couldn't remember for a moment the third one's name, and he knew it didn't matter. They were each and every one Celia. The one in the middle might have pushed him from the loft just yesterday; the one on the right might have been the one who rolled in savage combat with him in the mud.

Once, three years ago, he had had a fantasy in which Celia-3 had come to him shyly and asked that he take her. In the fantasy he had taken her; and in his dreams for weeks to come, he had taken her, over and over and over again. And he had awakened weeping for his own Celia. Unable to endure it any longer, he had sought out C-3 and asked her haltingly if she would come to his room

43

with him, and she had drawn back quickly, involuntarily, with fear written too clearly on her smooth face for her to pretend it was not there.

"David, forgive me. I was startled . . ."

They were promiscuous, indeed it was practically required of them to be free in their loving. No one could anticipate how many of them eventually would be fertile, what the percentage of boys to girls would be. Walt was able to test the males, but since the tests for female fertility required rabbits which they did not have, he said the best test for fertility was pregnancy. The children lived together, and promiscuity was the norm. But only with one another. They all shunned the elders. David had felt his eyes burning as the girl spoke, still moving away from him.

He had turned and left abruptly and had not spoken to her again in the intervening years. Sometimes he thought he saw her watching him warily, and each time he glared at her and hurried away.

C-1 had been like his own child. He had watched her develop, watched her learn to walk, talk, feed herself. His child, his and Celia's. C-2 had been much the same. A twin, somewhat smaller, identical nevertheless. But C-3 had been different. No, he corrected: his perceptions of her had been different. When he looked at her he saw Celia, and he ached.

He had grown chilled on the ridge, and he realized that the sun had set long ago and the lanterns had been lighted below. The scene looked pretty, like a sentimental card titled "Rural Life." The large farmhouse with glowing windows, the blackness of the barn; closer, the hospital and staff building with the cheerful yellow lights in the windows. Stiffly he descended into the valley again. He had missed dinner, but he was not hungry.

"David!" One of the youngest boys, a Five, called to him. David didn't know whom he had been cloned from. There were people he hadn't known when they were that young. He stopped and the boy ran to him, then past him, calling as he went, "Dr. Walt wants you."

Walt was in his room at the hospital. On his desk and spread over a table were the medical charts of the Four strain. "I've finished," Walt said. "You'll have to double-check, of course."

David scanned the final lines quickly, H-4 and D-4. "Have you told the two boys yet?"

"I told them all. They understand." Walt rubbed his eyes. "They have no secrets from each other," he said. "They understand about the girls' ovulation periods, about the necessity of keeping records. If any of those girls can conceive, they'll do it." His voice was almost bitter when he looked up at David. "They're taking it over completely from now on."

"What do you mean?"

"W-one made a copy of my records for his files. He'll follow it through."

David nodded. The elders were being excluded again. The time was coming when the elders wouldn't be needed for anything—extra mouths to feed, nothing else. He sat down and for a long time he and Walt sat in companionable silence.

In class the following day nothing appeared to be different. No pair bonding, David thought cynically. They accepted being mated as casually as the cattle did. If there was any jealousy of the two fertile males, it was well hidden. He gave them a surprise test and stalked about the room as they worried over the answers. They would all pass, he knew; not only pass, but do exceptionally well. They had motivation. They were learning in their teens what he hadn't grasped in his twenties. There were no educational frills, no distractions. Work in the classroom, in the fields, in the kitchens, in the laboratories. They worked interchangeably, incessantly—the first really classless society. He pulled his thoughts back when he realized that they were finishing already. He had allowed an hour, and they were finishing in forty minutes; slightly longer for the Fives, who, after all, were two years younger than the Fours.

The two oldest Ds headed for the laboratory after class, and David followed them. They were talking earnestly until he drew near. He remained in the laboratory for fifteen minutes of silent work, then left. Outside the door he paused and once more could hear the murmur of quiet voices. Angrily he tramped down the hallway.

In Walt's office he raged, "Damn it, they're up to something! I can smell it."

Walt regarded him with a detached thoughtfulness. David felt helpless before him. There was nothing he could point to, nothing he could attach significance to, but there was a feeling, an instinct, that would not be quieted.

"All right," David said, almost in desperation. "Look

45

at how they took the test results. Why aren't the boys jealous? Why aren't the girls making passes at the two available studs?"

Walt shook his head.

"I don't even know what they're doing in the lab anymore," David said. "And Harry has been relegated to caretaker for the livestock." He paced the room in frustration. "They're taking over."

"We knew they would one day," Walt reminded him gently.

"But there are only seventeen Fives. Eighteen Fours. Out of the lot they might get six or seven fertile ones. With a decreased life expectancy. With an increased chance of abnormality. Don't they know that?"

"David, relax. They know all that. They're living it. Believe me, they know." Walt stood up and put his arm about David's shoulders. "We've done it, David. We made it happen. Even if there are only three fertile girls now, they could have up to thirty babies, David. And the next generation will have more who will be fertile. We have done it, David. Let them carry it now if they want to."

By the end of summer two of the Four-strain girls were pregnant. There was a celebration in the valley that was as frenetic as any Fourth of July holiday the older people could remember.

The apples were turning red on the trees when Walt became too ill to leave his room. Two more girls were pregnant; one of them was a Five. Every day David spent hours with Walt, no longer wanting to work at all in the laboratory, feeling an outsider in the classrooms, where the Ones were gradually taking over the teaching duties.

"You might have to deliver those babies come spring," Walt said, grinning. "Might start a class in delivery procedures. Walt-three is ready, I guess."

"We'll manage," David said. "Don't worry about it. I expect you'll be there."

"Maybe. Maybe." Walt closed his eyes for a moment, and without opening them said, "You were right about them, David. They're up to something."

David leaned forward and unconsciously lowered his voice. "What do you know?"

Walt looked at him and shook his head slightly. "About as much as you did when you first came to me in

46

early summer. No more than that. David, find out what they're doing in the lab. And find out what they think about the pregnant girls. Those two things. Soon." Turning away from David, he added, "Harry tells me they have devised a new immersion suspension system that doesn't require the artificial placentas. They're adding them as fast as they can." He sighed. "Harry has cracked, David. Senile or crazy. W-one can't do anything for him."

David stood up, but hesitated. "Walt, I think it's time you told me. What's wrong with you?"

"Get out of here, damn it," Walt said, but the timbre of his voice was gone, the force that should have propelled David from the room was not there. For a moment Walt looked helpless and vulnerable, but deliberately he closed his eyes, and this time his voice was a growl. "Get out. I'm tired. I need rest."

David walked along the river for a long time. He hadn't been in the lab for weeks, months perhaps. No one needed him in the lab any longer. He felt in the way there. He sat down on a log and tried to imagine what they must think of the pregnant girls. They would revere them. The bearers of life, so few among so many. Was Walt afraid a matriarchy of some sort would develop? It could. They had discussed that years ago, and then dismissed it as one of the things they could not control. A new religion might come about, but even if the elders knew it was happening, what could they do about it? What should they do about it? He threw twigs into the smooth water, which moved without a ripple, all of a piece on that calm, cold night, and he knew that he didn't care.

Wearily he got up and started to walk again, very cold suddenly. The winters were getting colder, starting earlier, lasting longer, with more snows than he could remember from childhood. As soon as man stopped adding his megatons of filth to the atmosphere each day, he thought, the atmosphere had reverted to what it must have been long ago, moister weather summer and winter, more stars than he had ever seen before, and more, it seemed, each night than the night before: the sky a clear, endless blue by day, velvet blue-black at night with blazing stars that modern man had never seen.

The hospital wing where W-1 and W-2 were working now was ablaze with lights, and David turned toward it. As he neared the hospital he began to hurry; there were too many lights, and he could see people moving behind the windows, too many people, elders.

Margaret met him in the lobby. She was weeping silently, oblivious of the tears that ran erratically down her cheeks. She wasn't yet fifty, but she looked older than that; she looked like an elder, David thought with a pang. When had they started calling themselves that? Was it because they had to differentiate somehow, and none of them had permitted himself to call the others by what they were? Clones! he said to himself vehemently. Clones! Not quite human. *Clones.*

"What happened, Margaret?" She clutched his arm but couldn't speak, and he looked over her head at Warren, who was pale and shaking. "What happened?"

"Accident down at the mill. Jeremy and Eddie are dead. A couple of the young people were hurt. Don't know how bad. They're in there." He pointed toward the operating-room wing. "They left Clarence. Just walked away and left him. We brought him up, but I don't know." He shook his head. "They just left him there and brought up their own."

David ran down the hall toward the emergency room. Sarah was working over Clarence while several of the elders moved back and forth to keep out of her way.

David breathed a sigh of relief. Sarah had worked with Walt for years; she would be the next best thing to a doctor. He flung his coat off and hurried to her. "What can I do?"

"It's his back," she said tightly. She was very pale, but her hands were steady as she swabbed a long gash on Clarence's side and put a heavy pad over it. "This needs stitches. But I'm afraid it's his back."

"Broken?"

"I think so. Internal injuries."

"Where the hell is W-one or W-two?"

"With their own. They have two injuries, I think." She put his hand over the pad. "Hold it tight a minute." She pressed the stethoscope against Clarence's chest, peered into his eyes, and finally straightened and said, "I can't do a thing for him."

"Stitch him up. I'm going to get W-one." David strode down the hall, not seeing any of the elders who moved out of his way. At the door to the operating room he was stopped by three of the young men. He saw an H-3 and

48

said, "We have a man who's probably dying. Where's W-two?"

"Who?" H-3 asked, almost innocently.

David couldn't think of the name immediately. He stared at the young face and felt his fist tighten. "You know damn well who I mean. We need a doctor, and you have one or two in there. I'm going to bring one of them out."

He became aware of movement behind him and turned to see four more of them approaching, two girls, two boys. Interchangeable, he thought. It didn't matter which ones did what. "Tell him I want him," he said harshly. One of the newcomers was a C1-2, he realized, and still more harshly he said, "It's Clarence. Sarah thinks his back is broken."

C1-2 didn't change his expression. They had moved very close. They encircled him, and behind him H-3 said, "As soon as they're through in there, I'll tell them, David." And David knew there was nothing he could do, nothing at all.

Chapter 8

He stared at their smooth young faces; so familiar, living memories every one of them, like walking through his own past, seeing his aged and aging cousins rejuvenated, but rejuvenated with something missing. Familiar and alien, known and unknowable. Behind H-3 the swinging door opened and W-1 came out, still in surgical gown and mask, now down about his throat.

"I'll come now," he said, and the small group opened for him. He didn't look again at David after dismissing him with one glance.

David followed him to the emergency room and watched his deft hands as he felt Clarence's body, tested for reflexes, probed confidently along the spinal column. "I'll operate," he said, and that same confidence came through with the words. He motioned for S-1 and W-2 to bring Clarence, and left once more.

At the arrival of W-1, Sarah had moved back out of the way, and now she slowly turned and stripped off the gloves that she had put on in preparing to stitch up Clarence's wound. Warren watched the two young people cover Clarence and strap him securely, then wheel him out the door and down the hall. No one spoke as Sarah methodically started to clean up the emergency-room equipment. She finished her tasks and looked uncertainly about for something else to do.

"Will you take Margaret home and put her to bed?" David asked, and she looked at him gratefully and nodded. When she was gone David turned to Warren. "Someone has to see to the bodies, clean them up, prepare them for burial."

"Sure, David," Warren said in a heavy voice. "I'll get Avery and Sam. We'll take care of it. I'll just go get them now and we'll take care of it. I'll . . . David, what have we done?" And his voice that had been too heavy, too dead, became almost shrill. "What are they?"

"What do you mean?"

"When the accident happened, I was down to the mill. Having a bite with Avery. He was just finishing up down there. Section of the floor caved in, you know that old part where we should have put in a new floor last year, or year before. It gave way somehow. And suddenly there they were, the kids, out of nowhere. No one had time to go get them, to yell for them to come running. Nothing, but there they were. They got their own two out of there and up to the hospital like fire was on their tails, David. Out of nowhere."

He looked at David with a fearful expression, and when David simply shrugged, he shook his head and left the emergency room, looking down the hall first, a quick, involuntary glance, as if to make sure that they would permit him to leave.

Several of the elders were still in the waiting room when David went there. Lucy and Vernon were sitting near the window, staring out at the black night. Since Clarence's wife died, he and Lucy had lived together, not as man and wife, but for companionship, because as children they had been as close as brother and sister, and now each needed someone to cling to. Sometimes sister, sometimes mother, sometimes daughter, Lucy had fussed over him, sewed for him, fetched and carried for him, and now, if he died, what would she do? David went to her and took her cold hand. She was very thin, with dark hair that hadn't started to gray, and deep blue eyes that used to twinkle with merriment, a long, long time ago.

"Go on home, Lucy. I'll wait, and as soon as there is anything to tell you, I promise I'll come."

She continued to stare at him. David turned toward Vernon helplessly. Vernon's brother had been killed in the accident, but there was nothing to say to him, no way to help him.

"Let her be," Vernon said. "She has to wait."

David sat down, still holding Lucy's hand. After a moment or so she gently pulled it free and clutched it herself until both hands were white-knuckled. None of the young people came near the waiting room. David wondered where they were waiting to hear about the condition of their own. Or maybe they didn't have to wait anywhere, maybe they would just know. He pushed the thought aside angrily, not believing it, not able to be rid of it. A long time later W-1 entered and said to no one in particular, "He's resting. He'll sleep until tomorrow afternoon. Go on home now."

Lucy stood up. "Let me stay with him. In case he needs something, or there's a change."

"He won't be left alone," W-1 said. He turned toward the door, paused and glanced back, and said to Vernon, "I'm sorry about your brother." Then he left.

Lucy stood undecided until Vernon took her arm. "I'll see you home," he said, and she nodded. David watched them leave together. He turned off the light in the waiting room and walked slowly down the hall, not planning anything, not thinking about going home, or anywhere else. He found himself outside the office that W-1 used, and he knocked softly. W-1 opened the door. He looked tired, David thought, and wasn't sure that his surprise was warranted. Of course, he should be tired. Three operations. He looked like a young, tired Walt, too keyed up to go to sleep immediately, too fatigued to walk off the tension.

"Can I come in?" David asked hesitantly. W-1 nodded and moved aside, and David entered. He never had been inside this office.

"Clarence will not live," W-1 said suddenly, and his voice, behind David, because he had not yet moved from the door, was so like Walt's that David felt a thrill of

51

something that might have been fear or more likely, he told himself, just surprise again. "I did what I could," W-1 said. He walked around his desk and sat down.

W-1 sat quietly, with none of the nervous mannerisms that Walt exhibited, none of the finger tapping that was as much a part of Walt's conversation as his words. No pulling his ears or rubbing his nose. A Walt with something missing, a dead area. Now, with fatigue drawing his face, W-1 sat unmoving, waiting patiently for David to begin, much the same way an adult might wait for a hesitant child to initiate a conversation.

"How did your people know about the accident?" David asked. "No one else knew."

W-1 shrugged. A time-consumer question, he seemed to imply. "We just knew."

"What are you doing in the lab now?" David asked, and heard a strained note in his voice. Somehow he had been made to feel like an interloper; his question sounded like idle chatter.

"Perfecting the methods," W-1 said. "The usual thing."

And something else, David thought, but he didn't press it. "The equipment should be in excellent shape for years," he said. "And the methods, while probably not the best conceivable, are efficient enough. Why tamper now, when the experiment seems to be proving itself?" For a moment he thought he saw a flicker of surprise cross W-1's face, but it was gone too swiftly and once more the smooth mask revealed nothing.

"Remember when one of your women killed one of us a long time ago, David? Hilda murdered the child of her likeness. We all shared that death, and we realized that each of you is alone. We're not like you, David. I think you know it, but now you must accept it." He stood up. "And we won't go back to what you are."

David stood up also, and his legs felt curiously weak. "What exactly do you mean?"

"Sexual reproduction isn't the only answer. Just because the higher organisms evolved to it doesn't mean it's the best. Each time a species has died out, there has been another higher one to replace it."

"Cloning is one of the worst ways for a higher species," David said slowly. "It stifles diversity, you know that." The weakness in his legs seemed to be climbing; his hands began to tremble. He gripped the edge of the desk.

"That's assuming diversity is beneficial. Perhaps it

52

isn't," W-1 said. "You pay a high price for individuality."

"There is still the decline and extinction," David said. "Have you got around that?" He wanted to end this conversation, to hurry from the sterile office and the smooth unreadable face with the sharp eyes that seemed to know what he was feeling.

"Not yet," W-1 said. "But we have the fertile members to fall back on until we do." He moved around the desk and walked toward the door. "I have to check my patients," he said, and held the door open for David.

"Before I leave," David said, "will you tell me what is the matter with Walt?"

"Don't you know?" W-1 shook his head. "I keep forgetting, you don't tell each other things, do you? He has cancer. Inoperable. It metastasized. He's dying, David. I thought you knew that."

David walked blankly for an hour or more, and finally found himself in his room, exhausted, unwilling yet to go to bed. He sat at his window until it was dawn, and then he went to Walt's room. When Walt woke up he reported what W-1 had told him.

"They'll use the fertile ones only to replenish their supply of clones," he said. "The humans among them will be pariahs. They'll destroy what we worked so hard to create."

"Don't let them do it, David. For God's sake, don't let them do it!" Walt's color was bad, and he was too weak to sit up. "Vlasic's mad, so he'll be of no help. You have to stop them somehow." Bitterly he said, "They want to take the easy way out, give up now when we know everything will work."

David didn't know whether he was sorry or glad that he had told Walt. No more secrets, he thought. Never again. "I'll stop them somehow," he said. "I don't know how, or when. But soon."

A Four brought Walt's breakfast, and David returned to his room. He rested and slept fitfully for a few hours, then showered and went to the cave entrance, where he was stopped by a Two.

"I'm sorry, David," he said. "Jonathan says that you need a rest, that you are not to work now."

Wordlessly David turned and left. Jonathan. W-1. If they had decided to bar him from the lab, they could do it. He and Walt had planned it that way: the cave was impregnable. He thought of the elders, forty-four of them now, and two of that number terminally ill. One of the remaining elders insane. Forty-one then, twenty-nine women. Eleven able-bodied men. Ninety-four clones.

He waited for days for Harry Vlasic to appear, but no one had seen him in weeks, and Vernon thought he was living in the lab. He had all his meals there. David gave that up, and found D-1 in the dining room and offered his help in the lab.

"I'm too bored doing nothing," he said. "I'm used to working twelve hours a day or more."

"You should rest now that there are others who can take the load off you," D-1 said pleasantly. "Don't worry about the work, David. It is going quite well." He moved away, and David caught his arm.

"Why won't you let me in? Haven't you learned the value of an objective opinion?"

D-1 pulled away, and still smiling easily, said, "You want to destroy everything, David. In the name of mankind, of course. But still, we can't let you do that."

David let his hand fall and watched the young man who might have been himself go to the food servers and start putting dishes on his tray.

"I'm working on a plan," he lied to Walt, as he would again and again in the weeks that followed. Daily Walt grew feebler, and now he was in great pain.

David's father was with Walt most of the time now. He was gray and aged but in good health physically. He talked of their boyhood, of the coming hunting season, of the recession he feared might reduce his profits, of his wife, who had been dead for fifteen years. He was cheerful and happy, and Walt seemed to want him there.

In March, W-1 sent for David. He was in his office. "It's about Walt," he said. "We should not let him continue to suffer. He has done nothing to deserve this."

"He is trying to last until the girls have their babies," David said. "He wants to know."

"But it doesn't matter any longer," W-1 said patiently. "And meanwhile he suffers."

David stared at him with hatred and knew that he couldn't make that choice.

W-1 continued to watch him for several more moments, then said, "We will decide." The next morning Walt was found to have died in his sleep.

Chapter 9

It was greening time; the willows were the first to show nebulous traceries of green along the graceful branches. Forsythias and flaming bushes were in bloom, brilliant yellows and scarlets against the gray background. The river was high with spring runoffs up north and heavy March rains, but it was an expected high, not dangerous, not threatening this year. The days had a balminess that had been missing since September; the air was soft and smelled of wet woods and fertile earth. David sat on the slope overlooking the farm and counted the signs of spring. There were calves in the field, and they looked the way spring calves always had looked: thin legs, awkward, slightly stupid. No fields had been worked yet, but the garden was green: pale lettuce, blue-green kale, green spears of onions, dark green cabbage. The newest wing of the hospital, not yet painted, crude compared to the finished brick buildings, was being used already, and he could even see some of the young people at the windows studying. They had the best teachers, themselves, and the best students. They learned amazingly well from one another, better than they had in the early days.

They came out of the school in matched sets: four of this, three of that, two of another. He sought and found three Celias. He could no longer tell them apart; they were all grown-up Celias now and indistinguishable. He watched them with no feeling of desire; no hatred moved him; no love. They vanished into the barn and he looked up over the farm, into the hills on the other side of the valley. The ridges were hazy and had no sharp edges anywhere. They looked soft and welcoming. Soon, he thought. Soon. Before the dogwoods bloomed.

The night the first baby was born, there was another celebration. The elders talked among themselves, laughed at their own jokes, drank wine; the clones left them alone and partied at the other end of the room. When Vernon began to play his guitar and dancing started, David slipped away. He wandered on the hospital grounds for a few minutes, as though aimlessly, and then, when he was certain no one had followed him out, he began to trot toward the mill and the generator. Six hours, he thought. Six hours without electricity would destroy everything in the lab.

David approached the mill cautiously, hoping the rushing water of the creek would mask any sound he might make. The building was three stories high, very large, with windows ten feet above the ground, on the level where the offices were. The ground floor was filled with machinery. In the back the hill rose sharply, and David could reach the windows by bracing himself on the steep incline and steadying himself with one hand on the building, leaving the other free to test the windows. He found a window that went up easily when he pushed it, and in a moment he was inside a dark office. He closed the window, and then, moving slowly with his hands outstretched to avoid any obstacle, he crossed the room to the door and opened it a crack. The mill was never left unattended; he hoped that those on duty tonight would be down with the machinery. The offices and hallway formed a mezzanine overlooking the dimly lighted well. Grotesque shadows made the hallway strange, with deep pools of darkness and places where he would be clearly visible should any one happen to look up at the right moment. Suddenly David stiffened. Voices.

He slipped his shoes off and opened the door wider. The voices were louder, below him. Soundlessly he ran toward the control room, keeping close to the wall. He was almost to the door when the lights came on all over the building. There was a shout, and he could hear them running up the stairs. He made a dash for the door, yanked it open, and slammed it behind him. There was no way to lock it. He pushed a file cabinet an inch or so, gave up on it, and picked up a metal stool by its legs. He raised it and swung it hard against the main control panel. At the same moment he felt a crushing pain against his shoulders, and he stumbled and fell forward as the lights went out.

He opened his eyes painfully. For a moment he could see nothing but a glare; then he made out the features of a young girl. She was reading a book, concentrating on it.

56

Dorothy? She was his cousin Dorothy. He tried to rise, and she looked up and smiled at him.

"Dorothy? What are you doing here?" He couldn't get off the bed. On the other side of the room a door opened and Walt came in, also very young, unlined, with his nice brown hair ruffled.

David's head began to hurt and he reached up to find bandages that came down almost to his eyes. Slowly memory came back and he closed his eyes, willing the memory to fade away again, to let them be Dorothy and Walt.

"How do you feel?" W-1 asked. David felt his cool fingers on his wrist. "You'll be all right. A slight concussion. Badly bruised, I'm afraid. You're going to be pretty sore for a while."

Without opening his eyes David asked, "Did I do much damage?"

"Very little," W-1 said.

Two days later David was asked to attend a meeting in the cafeteria. His head was still bandaged, but with little more than a strip of adhesive now. His shoulder ached. He went to the cafeteria slowly, with two of the clones as escorts. D-1 stood up and offered David a chair at the front of the room. David accepted it silently and sat down to wait. D-1 remained standing.

"Do you remember our class discussions about instinct, David?" D-1 asked. "We ended up agreeing that probably there were no instincts, only conditioned responses to certain stimuli. We have changed our minds about that. We agree now that there is still the instinct to preserve one's species. Preservation of the species is a very strong instinct, a drive, if you will." He looked at David and asked, "What are we to do with you?"

"Don't be an ass," David said sharply. "You are not a separate species."

D-1 didn't reply. None of them moved. They were watching him quietly, intelligently, dispassionately.

David stood up and pushed his chair back. "Then let me work. I'll give you my word of honor that I won't try to disrupt anything again."

D-1 shook his head. "We discussed that. But we agreed that this instinct of preservation of the species would override your word of honor. As it would our own."

David felt his hands clench and he straightened his fingers, forced them to relax. "Then you have to kill me."

"We talked about that too," D-1 said gravely. "We

don't want to do that. We owe you too much. In time we will erect statues to you, Walt, Harry. We have very carefully recorded all of your efforts in our behalf. Our gratitude and affection for you won't permit us to kill you."

David looked about the room, picking out familiar faces. Dorothy. Walt. Vernon. Margaret. Celia. They all met his gaze without flinching. Here and there one of them smiled at him faintly.

"You tell me then," he said finally.

"You have to go away," D-1 said. "You will be escorted for three days, downriver. There is a cart loaded with food, seeds, a few tools. The valley is fertile, the seeds will do well. It is a good time of year for starting a garden."

W-2 was one of the three to accompany him. They didn't speak. The boys took turns pulling the cart of supplies. David didn't offer to pull it. At the end of the third day, on the other side of the river from the Sumner farm, they left him. Before he joined the other two boys who left first, W-2 said, "They wanted me to tell you, David. One of the girls you call Celia has conceived. One of the boys you call David impregnated her. They wanted you to know." Then he turned and followed the others. They quickly vanished among the trees.

David slept where they had left him, and in the morning he continued south, leaving the cart behind, taking only enough food for the next few days. He stopped once to look at a maple seedling sheltered among the pines. He touched the soft green leaves gently. On the sixth day he reached the Wiston farm, and alive in his memory was the day he had waited there for Celia. The white oak tree that was his friend was the same, perhaps larger, he couldn't tell. He could not see the sky through its branches covered with new, vivid green leaves. He made a lean-to and slept under the tree that night, and the next morning he solemnly told it good-bye and began to climb the slopes overlooking the farm. The house was still there, but the barn was gone, and the other outbuildings—swept away by the flood they had started so long ago.

He reached the antique forest where he watched a flying insect beat its wings almost lazily and remembered his grandfather telling him that even the insects here were primitive—slower than their more advanced cousins, less adaptable to hot weather or dry spells.

It was misty and very cool under the trees. The insect

had settled on a leaf, and in the golden sunlight it too seemed golden. For a brief moment David thought he heard a bird's trill, a thrush. It was gone too fast to be certain, and he shook his head. Wishful thinking, no more than wishful thinking.

In the antique forest, a cove forest, the trees waited, keeping their genes intact, ready to move down the slopes when the conditions were right for them again. David stretched out on the ground under the great trees and slept, and in the cool, misty milieu of his dream saurians walked and a bird sang.

PART TWO

Shenandoah

Chapter 10

A July haze hung over the valley, dimming outlines; heat shimmered the air above the fields. It was a day without hard edges. The breeze that moved through the valley was soft and warm. The corn was luxuriant, higher than a man's head. The wheat was golden brown, responsive to any change in the wind; the entire field moved at once, as if it were a single organism rippling a muscle, relieving tension perhaps. Beyond the corn the land broke and tumbled down to meet the river, which looked smooth and unmoving. The river was crystal clear, but from the second floor of the hospital, by a trick of the haze-filtered light, the water became rust-colored and solid, metal dulled by neglect.

Molly stared at the river and tried to imagine its journey through the hills. She let her gaze drift back toward the dock and the boat there, but trees concealed it from the upper floor of the hospital. There was a film of sweat on her face and neck. She lifted her hair from the back of her neck where some of it clung, plastered to her skin.

"Nervous?" Miriam slipped her arm about Molly's waist.

Molly rested her head against Miriam's cheek for a second, then straightened again. "I might be."

"I am," Miriam said.

"Me too," Martha said, and she moved to the window also, and put her arm through Molly's. "I wish they hadn't chosen us."

Molly nodded. "But it won't be for so long." Martha's body was hot against her, and she turned from the window. The apartment had been made from three adjoining hospital rooms with the partitions removed; it was long and narrow with six windows, and not one of them was admitting any breeze that late afternoon. Six cots lined the walls; they were narrow, white, austere.

"Let me do your hair now," Melissa called from the far

end of the room. She had been combing and braiding her own hair for the past half hour, and she turned with a flourish. Dressed in a short white tunic with a red sash, corn-straw sandals on her feet, she looked cool and lovely. Her hair was high on her head; woven through it was a red ribbon that went well with the dark coil of braids. The Miriam sisters were inventive and artistic, the style setters, and this was Melissa's newest creation, which would be copied by the other sisters before the end of the week.

Martha laughed delightedly and sat down and watched Melissa's skillful fingers start to arrange her hair. An hour later when they left their room, walking two by two, they moved like a single organism and looked as alike as the stalks of wheat.

Other small groups were starting to converge on the auditorium. The Louisa sisters waved and smiled; a group of Ralph brothers swept past in a run, their long hair held back by braided bands, Indian fashion; the Nora sisters stepped aside and let Miriam's group pass. They looked awed and very respectful. Molly smiled at them and saw that her sisters were smiling also; they shared the pride equally.

As they turned onto the broader path that led to the auditorium steps, they saw several of the breeders peeking at them over the top of a rose hedge. The faces ducked out of sight, and the sisters turned as one, ignoring them, forgetting them instantly. There were the Barry brothers, Molly thought, and tried to pick out Ben. Six little Claras ran toward them, stopped abruptly, and stared at the Miriam sisters until they went up the stairs and into the auditorium.

The party was held in the new auditorium, where the chairs had been replaced by long tables that were being laden with delicacies usually served only at the annual celebration days: The Day of the First Born; Founding Day; The Day of the Flood . . . Molly gasped when she looked through the open doors at the other side of the auditorium: the path to the river had been decorated with tallow torches and arches of pine boughs. Another ceremony would take place at dockside, after the feast. Now music filled the auditorium and sisters and brothers danced at the far end and children scampered among them, playing their own games that appeared governed by random rules. Molly saw her smaller sisters intent on pursuit, and she smiled. Ten years ago that could have been she, and Miri, Melissa; Meg, and Martha. And Miriam would have been somewhere else, having been eluded again, wringing her hands in frustration or stamping her foot in anger that her little sisters were not behaving properly. Two years older than they, she carried her responsibility heavily.

Most of the women wore white tunics with gaudy sashes, and only the Susan sisters had chosen to dress in skirts that swept the floor as they whirled about, now joined hand to hand, now apart, like a flower opening and closing. The men wore tunics, longer and cut more severely than the women's, and had knotted cords from which hung leather pouches, each one decorated with the symbol of the family of brothers to whom the wearer belonged. Here a stag head, there a coiled snake, or a bird in flight, or a tall pine tree . . .

The Jeremy brothers had worked out an intricate dance, more subdued than the flower dance, but requiring ·concentration and endurance. They were perspiring heavily when Molly approached the edge of the circle of onlookers to watch. There were six Jeremy brothers, and Jeremy was only two years older than the rest; there was no discernible difference between any of them. Molly couldn't tell in the confusion of their twisting bodies which one was Jed, who would be one of her fellow travelers down the river of metal.

The music changed, and Molly and her sisters swept out to the floor. Dusk turned to night and the electric lights came on, the bulbs now covered with globes of blue, yellow, red, green. The music grew louder and more and more dancers spun around, while other groups of brothers and sisters lined up at the festive tables. The little Kirby brothers started to cry in unison, and someone took them away to be put to bed. The little Miriam sisters were quiet now, mouselike against a wall, eating cakes with their fingers; all had chosen pink cake with pink icing, which stuck to their fingers, their cheeks, their chins. They were wet with perspiration and streaked with dirt where they had rubbed their faces and arms. One of them was barefoot.

"Look at them!" Miri cried.

"They'll outgrow it," Miriam said, and for a moment Molly felt a stab of something she could not identify. Then the Miriam sisters rushed off in a group to the tables and consulted and disagreed on what to choose and

64

finally ended up with plates filled with identical tidbits: lamb kebobs and sausage-filled pastries, sweet-potato sticks glazed with honey, whole green beans, bright and glistening with a vinegar sauce, tiny steaming biscuits.

Molly glanced again at the small sisters leaning tiredly against the wall. No more pink cakes with pink icing, she thought sadly. One of the little sisters smiled shyly at her and she smiled back, and then went with the others to find a seat, to feast and await the ceremonies.

Roger, the eldest of them all, was the master of ceremonies. He said, "A toast to our brothers and our sister who will venture forth at dawn to find—not new lands to conquer, nor adventures to prove their courage, nor riches of gold or silver, but rather that most priceless discovery of all—information. Information we all need, information that will make it possible for us to erupt into a thousand blooms, a million! Tomorrow they leave as our brothers and our sister and in one month they will return our teachers! Jed! Ben! Harvey! Thomas! Lewis! Molly! Come forward and let us toast you and the most priceless gift you will bring to us, your family!"

Molly felt her cheeks burn with pleasure as she made her way through the crowd, now standing and applauding wildly. At the front of the room she joined the others on stage and waited for the cheering and applause to die, and she saw her little sisters standing on chairs, clapping with abandon, their faces red, smeary—they were going to cry, she thought. They couldn't contain such excitement much longer.

"And now," Roger said, "for each of you we have a gift . . ."

Molly's gift was a waterproof bag to carry her sketch pads and pencils and pens in. It was the first time she had ever owned something not shared by her sisters, something uniquely hers. She felt tears welling, and could not hear the rest of the ceremony, was not aware of the other gifts, and presently they were being led to the dock and the final surprise—a pennant flying from the mast of the small boat that would carry them to Washington. The pennant was the color of the midsummer sky, deep blue so clear that in daylight it would blend into the sky perfectly, and in the middle of it, a diagonal lightning blaze of gleaming silver. A canopy covered the forward section of the boat, and it too was blue and silver.

There was another toast, wine that tingled and made

her head light, and then another, and now Roger was laughing as he said, "The party will continue, but our brave explorers will retire." Jed shook his head, and Roger laughed again. "You have no choice, my brother. Your last toast was doctored, and within an hour you will be sound asleep, so you will start your trip fresh and rested. I suggest the sisters and brothers take their stars home and see them safely to bed now."

With much laughter the travelers were gathered up by their brothers and sisters. Molly protested feebly as her sisters half led, half carried her back to their room.

"I'll repack your things," Miriam said, examining the gift bag. "How beautiful this is! Look, it is all carved . . ."

They undressed her and brushed her hair, and Miri caressed her back and rubbed her shoulders, and Melissa brushed fairy kisses on her neck as she unwound the ribbon from her hair.

Molly felt a pleasant inertia envelop her and she could only smile and sigh as her sisters prepared her for bed, and then two of them unrolled the floor mat and waited there as the others guided her to it, all of them laughing at her unsteady walk, the way she almost buckled at the knees, and her attempts to keep her eyes open. On the mat they caressed and delighted her until she floated away from them entirely, and then they carried her to her own cot and pulled the thin summer blanket over her, and Miri bent over and kissed her eyelids tenderly.

Chapter 11

By the end of the first hour, life in the boat had become routine. The shouts had been lost in the distance and there was only the quiet river and the silent woods and fields and the regular splash of oars.

For weeks they had been in training, and now all six were hardened and worked well together. Lewis, who had designed the boat, stood forward on guard against unexpected hazards. Three of the brothers and Molly rowed in the first hitch, and Ben sat forward, behind Lewis.

There was a covered section forward, with the canopy down now, and a permanently closed-in rear section with four bunks. The forward section could be closed as snugly as the rear. Every available inch of space had been used, mostly for food, extra clothes, medical supplies, and waterproof pouches folded neatly, to be filled with documents, maps, whatever they found of value.

Molly rowed and watched the shoreline. They had left the familiar section of the valley, with its cultivated fields; the land was changing. The valley narrowed, then widened, then narrowed again, with steeply rising cliffs to the left, wooded slopes on the right. In the silent morning the trees were unmoving; there was no sound except the splashing of oars.

Her sisters would be in the food-processing kitchens this week, Molly thought, as she watched the oar dip into the clear water. Laughing together, moving together. Perhaps they missed her already . . . She pulled steadily, lifted the oar, watched it dip again.

"Rock! Ten o'clock, twenty yards!" Lewis called.

They shifted course easily to give it a wide berth.

"Nine o'clock, twenty yards!"

Thomas, in front of Molly, was wide-shouldered, his hair the color of straw, and as straight as straw. A slight breeze lifted it and let it fall over and over. His muscles moved fluidly, and perspiration glazed him. Molly thought he would make a fine drawing, a study in musculature. He turned and said something to Harvey, across the boat from him, and they both laughed.

Now the sun was higher and the heat was in their faces, along with the breeze they created moving through the water, slowly, but steadily, smoothly. Molly could feel sweat on her upper lip. Soon they would have to stop to put the canopy in place. It would offer some wind resistance, but they had decided the pluses were greater than the minuses; the trip was planned to provide the maximum of safety and comfort, and neither was to be sacrificed to speed.

Others had gone down the river as far as the juncture with the Shenandoah. There were rocks ahead, then a smooth, long slide into the broader, and unknown, river. And that afternoon Molly would relinquish her place at the oars and start her real mission, a pictorial diary of the trip, including whatever changes in the maps were necessary.

They tried to use the sail, but the wind in the valley was capricious, and they decided to wait until later, perhaps on the Potomac, and try it there. They stopped and set up the canopy and rested, then returned to the oars, and now Molly sat alone, her sketch pad and the river maps on the seat beside her. Her hands felt stiff and she was content to sit quietly. Finally she started to sketch.

They came to the first rapids later that afternoon, and navigated them without difficulty. They joined the Shenandoah and turned north, and when they rested, they were all subdued and even Jed had nothing to laugh about, no jokes to make.

They slept in the boat, riding gently on the water. Molly thought of her sisters, now in their narrow white beds, the mat rolled up and put away. She fought down tears of loneliness. A high breeze stirred the treetops and she imagined they were whispering. She longed to reach out and touch one of the brothers; it mattered little which one of them. She sighed, and heard someone whisper her name. It was Jed. He slipped into her narrow bunk, and with their arms wrapped tightly about each other, they fell asleep.

On the second night they all paired off and comforted one another before they were able to sleep.

The next day they were forced to a stop by rapids and a waterfall. "It isn't on the map at all," Molly said, standing on the bank with Lewis. The river had been wide and easy, the valley heavily overgrown with bushes and low trees where once corn and wheat had grown. Then the cliffs moved toward the water, which narrowed and deepened and ran swifter, and sometime since the maps had been printed one of the cliffs had shuddered and dropped massive boulders and debris that now choked the river as far ahead as they could see. The water had spread, filled the valley from side to side. They could hear the thunder of a waterfall ahead.

"We should be nearly at the juncture of the north and south branches of the Shenandoah," Molly said. She turned to look at the cliffs. "Probably a couple of miles at the most, over there." She pointed up the cliff that overshadowed them.

Lewis nodded. "We'll have to go back until we find a place to get the boat out of the water, go overland."

Molly consulted her map. "Look, this road. It comes nearly to the river back there, then goes over a couple of hills, about three miles, then back down to the river. That should clear the falls. There's nothing but cliffs on this side between us and the north branch. No road, no trail, nothing."

Lewis ordered lunch, and after they had eaten and rested they turned the boat and began to row against the current, keeping close to shore, watching for a sign of the road. The current was fast here, and they realized for the first time how hard it would be on the return trip, fighting the current all the way home.

Molly sighted the break in the hills where the old road was. They pulled in closer and found a spot where the boat could be hauled out of the water, and prepared for an overland trek. They had brought wheels and axles and axes to cut trees to make a wagon, and four of the brothers began to unpack what they needed.

Folded neatly away were heavy long pants and boots and long-sleeved shirts, protection more against scratches from bushes than cold, which was not expected while they were gone. Molly and Lewis changed clothes hurriedly and left to look for the best way to get through the scrub growth to the road.

They would have to sleep in the woods that night, Molly thought suddenly, and a shudder passed through her. Her sisters would look up from their work uneasily, exchange glances, and return to their chores reluctantly, somehow touched by the same dread she felt. If she were within reach, the others would have come to her, unable to explain why, but irresistibly drawn together.

They had to turn back several times before they found a way the boat could be taken to the road. When they returned to the river, the others had the flat wagon prepared and the boat lashed in place. There was a small fire, on which water was heating for tea. They were all dressed in long pants and boots now.

"We can't stop," Lewis said impatiently, glancing at the fire. "We have about four hours until dark, and we should get to the road and make camp before then."

Ben said quietly, "We can start while Molly has tea and cheese. She is tired and should rest." Ben was the doctor. Lewis shrugged.

Molly watched as they strapped on the harnesses. She held a mug of tea and a piece of cheese the color of old ivory, and at her feet the fire burned lower. She moved away from it, too warm in the heavy pants and shirt. They were starting to move the boat, four of them pulling together, Thomas pushing from behind. He glanced back at her and grinned, and the boat heaved over a rock, settled, and moved steadily to the left and upward.

Molly took her tea and cheese to the edge of the river, pulled off her boots, and sat with her feet in the tepid water. Each of them had a reason for being on this trip, she knew, and felt not at all superfluous. The Miriam sisters were the only ones who could remember and reproduce exactly what they saw. From earliest childhood they had been trained to develop this gift. It was regrettable that the Miriam sisters were slightly built; she been chosen for this one skill alone, not for strength and other abilities, as the brothers had been, but that she was as necessary as any of the others was not doubted by anyone.

The water felt cooler to her feet now, and she began to strip off her clothing. She waded out and swam, letting the water flow through her hair, cleanse her skin, soothe her. When she finished, the fire was almost out and, using her mug, she doused it thoroughly, dressed again, and then began to follow the trail left by the brothers and the heavy boat.

Suddenly and without any warning she felt she was being watched. She stopped, listening, trying to see into the woods, but there was no sound in the forest except the high, soft rustling of leaves. She whirled about. Nothing. She drew in her breath sharply and started to walk again. It was not fear, she told herself firmly, and hurried. There wasn't anything to be afraid of. No animals, nothing. Only burrowing insects had survived: ants, termites . . . She tried to keep her mind on ants—they were the pollinators now—and she found herself looking upward again and again at the swaying trees.

The heat was oppressive, and it seemed the trees were closing in, always closing in, yet never getting any closer. It was being alone for the first time in her life, she told herself. Really alone, out of reach, out of touch. It was loneliness that made her hurry through the undergrowth, now crushed down, hacked out of the way. And she thought, this was why men went mad in the centuries gone by: they went mad from loneliness, from never knowing the comfort of brothers and sisters who were as one, with the same thoughts, the same longings, desires, joys.

She was running, her breath coming in gasps, and she forced herself to stop and breathe deeply a few minutes. She stood leaning against a tree and waited until her pulse was quieter, then she began to walk again, briskly, not letting herself run. But not until she saw the brothers ahead did the fear subside.

That night they made camp in the middle of the rotten roadway deep in the forest. The trees closed over them, blotting out the sky, and their small fire seemed feeble and pale in the immensity of the darkness that pressed in from all sides and above. Molly lay rigidly still, listening for something, anything, for a sound that said they were not alone in the world, that she wasn't alone in the world. But there was no sound.

The next afternoon Molly sketched the brothers. She was sitting alone, enjoying the sun and the water, which had become smooth and deep. She thought of the brothers, how different they were one from another, and her fingers began to draw them in a way she never had drawn before, never had seen before.

She liked the way Thomas looked. His muscles were long and smooth, his cheekbones high and prominent, neatly dividing his face. She drew his face, using only straight lines that suggested the planes of his cheeks, the narrow sharp nose, the pointed chin. He looked young, younger than the Miriam sisters, although they were nineteen and he was twenty-one.

She closed her eyes and visualized Lewis. Very big, over six feet. Very broad. She drew a rocklike form, a long head and a face that seemed to flow, rounded, fleshy with no bony framework, except for his large nose. The nose didn't satisfy her. She closed her eyes and after a moment rubbed out the nose she had drawn and put one back that was slightly off center, a bit crooked. Everything was too exaggerated, she knew, but somehow, in overdoing it, she had caught him.

Harvey was tall and rather thin. And great long feet, she thought, smiling at the figure emerging on her pad. Big hands, round eyes, like rings. You just knew, she thought, he would be awkward, stumble over things, knock things down.

Jed was easy. Rotund, every line a curve. Small, almost delicate hands, small bones. Small features centered in his face, all too close together.

Ben was the hardest. Well proportioned, except for his

head, which was larger than the others', he was not so beautifully muscled as Thomas. And his face was merely a face, nothing outstanding about it. She drew his eyebrows heavier than they should have been, and made him squint, the way he did when he listened closely. She narrowed her eyes studying it. It wasn't right. Too hard. Too firm, too much character, she thought. In ten years he might look more like the sketch than he did now.

"Rocks! Twelve o'clock, thirty yards!" Lewis called.

Guiltily Molly flipped the sketch pad to a clean page and began to draw the river and its hazards.

Chapter 12

Ben was bringing his medical notes up to date. Lewis was finishing his daily log. Thomas sat in the rear of the boat and stared back the way they had come. Ben had been watching him closely for the past three days, uncertain what to expect, not liking the change in attitude that Thomas wasn't even trying to hide any longer.

He wrote: "Separation from our brothers and sisters has been harder on all of us than we expected. Suggest future parties send pairs of likes whenever possible."

If Thomas became ill, he thought, then what? Even back in the hospital they had no provisions for caring for the mentally ill. Insanity was a community threat, a threat to the brothers and sisters who suffered as much as the affected one. Early on, the family had decided that no community threat could be allowed to survive. If any brother or sister became mentally ill, his or her presence was not to be tolerated. And that, Ben told himself sharply, was the law. Their small group could not afford to lose a pair of hands, though, and that was the reality. And when reality and law clashed, then what?

After a glance at Molly, Ben added another note: "Suggest parties be made up equally of males and females." She had been more lonely than any of them, he knew. He had watched her fill page after page of her sketchbook, and wondered if that had substituted in some way for the absence of her sisters. Perhaps when Thomas was confronted with his real work he would no longer stare for long periods and start when anyone touched him or called his name.

"We'll have to change our food-rationing schedule," Lewis said. "We counted on five days only for this leg of the trip, and it's been eight. You want to do the food count, Ben?"

Ben nodded. "Tomorrow when we tie up I'll make an inventory. We might have to cut down." They shouldn't, he knew. He made another note. "Suggest double caloric needs."

Molly's hand slipped out from under her cheek and dangled over the side of her bunk. Ben had intended to lie with her that night, but it didn't matter. They were all too tired even for the comfort of sex. Ben sighed and put his notebook down. The last light was fading from the sky. There was only the soft slap of wavelets against the side of the boat and the sound of deep breathing from the rear section. There was a touch of chill in the air. Ben waited until Thomas was asleep, then he lay down.

Molly dreamed of turning over in the boat, of being unable to get out from under it, of searching for a place to surface where the boat would not cut her off from the air above. The water was pale gold, it was turning her skin golden, and she knew that if she let herself remain still for even one moment she would become a golden statue on the bottom of the river forever. She swam harder, desperate to breathe, aching, flailing, yielding to terror. Then hands reached for her, her own hands, as white as snow, and she tried to grasp them. The hands, dozens of them now, closed on nothing, opened, closed. They missed her again and again, and finally she screamed, "Here I am!" And the water rushed to fill her. She started to sink, frozen, only her mind churning with fear, forming over and over the scream of protest her lips were unable to utter.

"Molly, hush. It's all right." A quiet voice in her ear penetrated finally, and she jerked awake from the dream. "It's all right, Molly. You're all right."

It was very dark. "Ben?" Molly whispered.

"Yes. You were dreaming."

She shuddered and moved over so he could lie beside her. She was shivering; the night air had become very cool since they had turned in to the Potomac. Ben was warm, his arm tight about her, and his other hand warm and gentle as he caressed her cold body.

They made no sound to awaken the others as their bodies united in the sexual embrace, and afterward Molly slept again, hard and tight against him.

All the next day the signs of great devastation grew: houses had burned, others had been toppled by storms. The suburbs were being overgrown with shrubs and trees. Debris made the trip harder; sunken boats and collapsed bridges turned the river into a maze where their progress was measured in feet and inches. Again they had found it impossible to use the sail.

Lewis and Molly were together in the prow of the boat, alert for submerged dangers, sometimes calling out in unison, sometimes singly, warning against hazards, neither of them silent for more than a minute or two at a time.

Suddenly Molly pointed and cried, "Fish! There are fish!"

They stared at the school of fish in wonder, and the boat drifted until Lewis shouted, "Obstacle! Eleven o'clock, ten yards!" They pulled the oars hard and the school of fish vanished, but the gloom had lifted. While they rowed, they talked of ways of netting fish for dinner, of drying fish for the return trip, of the excitement in the valley when they learned that fish had survived after all.

None of the ruins they had seen from the river prepared them for the scene of desolation they came upon on the outskirts of Washington. Molly had seen photographs in books of bombed-out cities—Dresden, Hiroshima—and the destruction here seemed every bit as total. The streets were buried under rubble, here and there vines covered the heaps of concrete, and trees had taken root high above the ground, binding the piles of bricks and blocks and marble together. They stayed on the river until it became impassable, and this time the rapids were created by man-made obstacles: old rusting automobiles, a demolished bridge, a graveyard of buses . . .

"It was worthless," Thomas muttered. "All of this. Worthless."

"Maybe not," Lewis said. "There have to be vaults, basements, fireproof storage rooms . . . Maybe not."

"Worthless," Thomas said again.

"Let's tie up and try to figure out just where we are," Ben said. It was nearly dusk; they couldn't do anything until morning. "I'll start dinner. Molly, can you make out anything from the maps?"

She shook her head, her eyes fixed, staring at the nightmare scene before them. Who had done this? Why? It was as if the people had converged here to destroy this place that had failed them in the end so completely.

"Molly!" Ben's voice sharpened. "There are still a few landmarks, aren't there?"

She stirred and abruptly turned away from the city. Ben looked at Thomas, and from him to Harvey, who was studying the river ahead.

"They did it on purpose," Harvey said. "In the end they must have all been mad, obsessed with the idea of destruction."

Lewis said, "If we can locate ourselves, we'll find the vaults. All this"—he waved his hand—"was done by savages. It's all surface damage. The vaults will be intact."

Molly was turning slowly, examining the landscape in a panoramic survey. She said, "There should be two more bridges, and that will put us at the foot of Capitol Hill, I think. Another two or three miles."

"Good," Ben said quietly. "Good. Maybe it isn't this bad in the center. Thomas, give me a hand, will you?"

Throughout the night the boat moved this way and that as different people, tired but unable to sleep, crept about restlessly, seeking solace from one another.

Before dawn they were all up. They ate quickly and by the first light were on their way over the rubble toward the center of Washington. It appeared that the destruction of the inner city was in fact less than on the fringes. Then they realized that here the buildings had been spaced farther apart; open land gave the illusion of less complete ruin. Also, it was obvious that someone had tried to clear away some of the debris.

"Let's split into pairs here," Lewis said, taking command once more. "Meet back here at noon. Molly and Jed, over there. Ben and Thomas, that way. Harvey and I will start over there." He pointed as he spoke, and the others nodded. Molly had identified the locations for them: the Senate Office Building was up there; the Post Office Building; the General Services Building . . .

"We were naïve," Thomas said suddenly as he and Ben approached the ruined Post Office Building. "We thought there would be a few buildings standing with open doors. All we had to do was walk in, pull out a drawer or two, and get everything we wanted. Be heroes when we got home. Stupid, wasn't it?"

"We've already found out a lot," Ben said quietly.

"What we've learned is that this isn't the way," Thomas said sharply. "We aren't going to accomplish anything."

They circled the building. The front of it was blocked; around the side, one wall was down almost completely; the insides were charred and gutted.

The fourth building they tried to enter had burned also, but only parts of it had been destroyed. Here they found offices, desks, files. "Small business records!" Thomas said suddenly, whirling away from the files to look at Ben excitedly.

Ben shook his head. "So?"

"We came through a room with telephone directories! Where was it?" Again Ben looked mystified, and Thomas laughed. "Telephone directories! They'll list warehouses! Factories! Storage depots!"

They found the room where several directories lay in a pile on the floor, and Thomas began to examine one intently. Ben picked up another of the books and started to open it.

"Careful!" Thomas said sharply. "That paper's brittle. Let's get out of here."

"Will that help?" Ben asked, pointing to the directory Thomas carried.

"Yes, but we need the central office of the telephone company. Maybe Molly can find it."

That afternoon, the next day, and the next the search for useful information continued. Molly updated her Washington map, locating the buildings that contained anything of use, noting the dangerous buildings, the flooded sections—many of the basements were filled with evil-smelling water. She drew many of the skeletons they kept stumbling over. She sketched them as dispassionately as she did the buildings and streets.

On the fourth day they found the central telephone offices, and Thomas stationed himself in one of the rooms and began to go through the directories of the eastern cities, carefully lifting out pages they could use. Ben stopped worrying about him.

On the fifth and sixth days it rained, a steady gray rain that flooded the low-lying areas and brought water above the basement level in some of the buildings. If the rain kept up very long, the whole city would flood, as it evidently had done over and over in the past. Then the skies cleared and the wind shifted and drove in from the north, and they shivered and continued the search.

As she drew, Molly thought: millions of people, hundreds of millions of people, all gone. She drew the ruined Washington Monument, the broken statue of Lincoln and the words of the inscription that remained on the pedestal: *One nation indi* . . . She drew the skeletal frame of the Supreme Court Building . . .

They didn't move camp to the city, but slept aboard the boat every night. They were amassing too much material to take back with them; every evening when they left the city they took back loads of records, books, maps, charts, and after the evening meal each of them went over his own stack of material and tried to sort it. They made extensive notes about the condition of the buildings they explored, the contents, the usefulness of the material in them. The next expedition would be able to go straight to work.

There were the skeletons, some of them on top of the rubble, some half buried, others in the buildings. How easily they could ignore them, Ben mused. Another species, extinct now, a pity. Pass on.

On the ninth evening they made the final choices of what to pack in the boat. They found an intact room in a partially destroyed building and stored the surplus material there for the next group.

On the tenth day they started for home, this time rowing against the current, with a fresh breeze blowing from the northeast, puffing the large single sail they had not been able to use until now. Lewis attached the tiller, and the wind drove them up the river.

Fly, fly! Molly silently urged the boat. She stood in the prow and sang out the hazards, some of them almost before they came into sight. There was a tree stump there, she remembered; and again, a train engine; a sand bar . . . In the afternoon the wind shifted and blew in from due north, and they had to take down the sail or risk being driven onto shore. Gradually the excitement they had all felt earlier gave way to dogged determination, and finally to mindless patience, and when they stopped for the night they all knew they had traveled little more than half the distance they had traveled on this leg of their journey toward the city.

77

That night Molly dreamed of dancing figures. Joyously she ran toward them, arms outstretched, her feet not touching the ground at all as she raced to join them. Then the air thickened and shimmered and the figures were distorted, and when one of them looked at her, the outline of her face was all wrong, her features wrong, one eye too high, her mouth bent out of shape. Molly stopped, staring at the grotesque face. She was drawn toward it relentlessly through the thick air that changed everything. She struggled and tried to hang back, but her feet moved, her body followed, and she could feel the resisting air close about her suffocatingly. The caricature of her own face grimaced, and the figure raised snake-like arms toward her. Molly came wide awake suddenly, and for several moments didn't know where she was. Someone was shouting.

It was Thomas, she realized, and Ben and Lewis were struggling with him, getting him out of his bunk, toward the bow of the boat, the canopied section. Harvey moved to the rear and gradually quiet returned, but it was a long time before Molly could go back to sleep.

By the third day the return trip had turned into a nightmare. The wind became gusty, more dangerous than helpful, and they no longer tried to use the sail. The current was swifter, the water muddy. It must have rained much more inland than it had in Washington. Also, the air had a chill that persisted until midday, when the sun became too hot for the warm clothing they had put on earlier. By sundown it was too cool for the lighter garments they had changed into at the lunch break. They were always too hot or too cold.

Ben and Lewis withdrew from the others and watched the sunset from a rise over the river. "They're hungry, that's part of the trouble," Ben said. Lewis nodded. "Also, Molly has started her menstrual period and she won't let anyone near her. She nearly bit poor Harvey's head off last night."

"I'm not worried about Harvey," Lewis said.

"I know. I don't know if Thomas is going to make it or not. I tranquilized him at dinner. I don't know from one day to the next what to expect from him."

"We can't carry a dead weight home with us," Lewis said grimly. "Even with strict rationing, food's going to be

78

a problem. If he's tranquilized, he'll still need to eat, someone else will have to row for him . . ."

"We'll take him back with us," Ben said, and suddenly he was in command. "We'll need to study him, even if he goes home in restraints."

For a moment they were both silent. "It's the separation, isn't it?" Lewis looked south, toward home. "No one predicted anything like this. We're not like them! We have to scrap the past, the history books, everything. No one predicted this," he said again quietly. "If we get back, we have to make them understand what happens to us away from our own kind."

"We'll get back," Ben said. "And that's why I need Thomas. Who could have foreseen this? Now that we're aware of how different we are from them, we'll be looking harder. I wonder where else differences will show up when we're not expecting them to."

Lewis stood up. "Coming back?"

"In a minute."

He watched Lewis slip down the embankment and board the boat; then he looked at the sky once more. Men had gone out there, he thought in wonder, and he couldn't think why. Singly and in small groups they had gone into strange lands, across wide seas, had climbed mountains where no human foot had ever trod. And he couldn't think why they had done those things. What impulse had driven them from their own kind to perish alone, or among strangers? All those ruined houses they had seen, like the old Sumner house in the valley, designed for one, two, three people, lived in by so few people, deliberately isolating themselves from others of their own kind. Why?

The family used isolation for punishment. A disobedient child left alone in a small room for ten minutes emerged contrite, all traces of rebellion eradicated. They had used isolation to punish David. The doctors knew the full story of the last months that David had lived among them. When he became a threat, they had isolated him permanently, punishment enough. And yet those other men of the distant past had sought isolation, and Ben couldn't think why.

Chapter 13

For two days it had been raining; the wind was gusting at thirty knots and increasing. "We have to get the boat out of the water," Lewis said.

They had covered the entire boat with oiled canvas, but water seeped in through cracks and now and then a wave lapped over the side and spilled down into the boat. More and more frequently something heavy rubbed against the boat or crashed into it.

Molly pumped and visualized the river behind them. There had been a bank hours back, but since then there had been no place they could land safely.

"An hour," Lewis said, as if answering her thoughts. "Shouldn't take more than an hour to get to that low bank."

"We can't go back!" Thomas shouted.

"We can't stay here!" Harvey snapped at him. "Don't be an idiot! We're going to get rammed!"

"I won't go back!"

"What do you think, Ben?" Lewis asked.

They were huddled together in the prow; Molly was in the midsection manning the pump doggedly, trying to pretend her aching muscles away. The boat shuddered under a new impact, and Ben nodded.

"Can't stay here. Not going to be a picnic getting back downriver."

"Let's get at it," Lewis said, and stood up.

They were all wet and cold, and afraid. They were within sight of the swirling waters of the Shenandoah where it joined the Potomac, and the eddies that had nearly swamped them on the first leg of their trip now threatened to break the boat apart. They could get no closer to the Shenandoah until the flood subsided.

"Thomas, relieve Molly at the pump. And, Thomas, remember, you don't think of anything but that pump!

And you keep it going!"

Molly got up, continuing to pump until Thomas was in place, ready to take over without interruption. As she started for the rear oar, Lewis said, "You take the prow." They put the oars back in the locks. The rain pounded them, and Thomas pumped harder. The water was sloshing about their feet, and when the lines to shore were untied the boat swung sharply into the river. The water inside the boat surged back and forth.

"Log! Coming fast! Eight o'clock!" Molly yelled.

They turned the boat, and it shot forward and they were flashing down the river, keeping abreast of the log that was off to their left.

"Stump! Twelve o'clock! Twenty yards!" Molly hardly had time to get the words out. They jerked the boat to the left and flew past the stump. The flood had changed everything. The stump had been ashore when they passed it before. The current became swifter, and they fought to get closer in. "Tree! One o'clock! Twenty yards!" They veered out again and now the log that was pacing them tumbled and came dangerously close. "Log! Nine o'clock! Three yards!"

And on they went in the blinding rain, flying past a newly created shoreline, staying even with the massive log that turned and tumbled alongside them. Suddenly Molly saw the low spot and cried, "Land! Two o'clock, twenty yards!" They drove in sharply to shore. The boat dragged on something hidden in the muddy water and the front half swung out toward the river. It rocked violently and water sloshed in over the side. Lewis and Ben quickly jumped out and, with the brown water swirling about their chests, waded toward shore, dragging the boat in after them. The boat grated over mud and stones, and now the others jumped into the water and dragged the boat higher until it was beached, tilted, but for the moment safe. Molly lay in the mud panting until Lewis said, "We've got to get it higher. The river's rising fast."

It rained throughout the night and they had to move the boat a second time; then the rain stopped and the sun shone, and that night there was a frost.

Ben cut the rations again. The storm had cost them five more days, and the river was swifter when they returned to it, their progress slower than ever.

Thomas was in the worst shape, Ben thought. He was withdrawn, sunken in depression from which no one could rouse him. Jed was next hardest hit. In time, no doubt, his symptoms would match Thomas's. Harvey was irritable; he had turned sullen and suspicious of everyone. He suspected that Ben and Lewis were stealing his food, and he watched them intently at mealtime. Molly was haggard, and she looked haunted; her eyes kept turning toward the south and home, and she seemed to be listening, always listening. Lewis was intent on maintaining the boat, but when he stopped working, that same look was on his big face: listening, watching, waiting. Ben couldn't assess the changes in himself. He knew they were there. Often he would look up suddenly, certain someone had spoken his name softly, only to find no one nearby, no one paying any attention to him. Sometimes he had the feeling that there was a danger he couldn't see, something hanging over him that made him look to the sky, search the trees. But there was never anything to see. . . .

He wondered suddenly when all sexual activity had stopped. In Washington, or immediately after they left. He had decided it wasn't working for him. It was too hard to pretend the other men were his brothers; finally, it had been too unsatisfactory, too frustrating. Somehow it had been better with Molly if only because no pretense had been necessary, but even that had failed. Two people trying to become one, neither quite knowing what the other needed or wanted. Or maybe it was hunger that killed the sexual appetite. He wrote in his notebooks.

Molly, watching him, felt as if a thick clear wall separated her from every living thing on earth. Nothing could get through the wall, nothing could touch her in any way, and where the feeling had aroused terror, never fully dormant any longer, now it simply bemused her to think of it. Every day they got closer to home, and curiously it seemed less from their own efforts than from an irresistible pull. They were powerless not to return home. The pull was steady, dragging them back just as they had dragged the boat up the bank to save it from the flood. Their every act was instinctive. And the terror? She didn't know its source, only that waves of terror coursed through her unexpectedly, and when they did, she felt weak and cold. She could feel her facial muscles tighten during those times, and she was aware of the way her heart leaped, then paused, then raced.

And often when she had been at the oars for a long time, something else happened, and she felt a release. At those times strange visions came to her, strange thoughts that seemed untranslatable into words. She looked about in wonder and the world she saw was unfamiliar, the words she would have used to describe it useless, and only color would do, color and line and light. The terror was stilled, and a gentle peace filled her. Gradually the peace would give way to fatigue and hunger and fear, and then she could mock herself and the visions, and even while mocking, yearn for it all to happen again.

Sometimes when she was forward, watching for hazards, it was almost as if she were alone with the river that seemed to have a voice, and infinite wisdom. The voice murmured too softly to make out the words, but the rhythms were unmistakable: it was speech. One day she wept because she could not understand what it was saying to her. Ben's hand on her shoulder roused her, and she stared at him blankly.

"Did you hear it too?" she asked, keeping her voice as soft as the river's.

"What?" He sounded too brusque, too harsh, and she pulled away. "What do you mean?"

"Nothing. Nothing. I'm just tired."

"Molly, I heard nothing! And you heard nothing! We're pulling in to rest, stretch our legs. You get some tea."

"All right," she said, and started around him. But then she paused. "What was it we heard, Ben? It isn't the river, is it?"

"I told you I heard nothing!" He turned away from her and stood stiffly in the prow of the boat to guide the men at the oars in to shore.

When they turned the last curve in the river and came upon the familiar fields, they had been away from their brothers and sisters for forty-nine days. Thomas and Jed were both drugged into insensibility. The others rowed numbly, starved, dull-eyed, obeying a command stronger than the body's command to stop. When small boats approached and hands took the lines and towed them to the dock, they continued to stare ahead, not believing yet, still in a recurring dream where this had happened repeatedly.

Molly was pulled to her feet and led ashore. She stared at her sisters, who were strangers to her. And this too was

83

a recurring dream, a nightmare. She swayed, and was grateful for the blackness that descended on her.

The sunshine was soft in the room when Molly opened her eyes; it was very early morning and the air was cool and fresh. There were flowers everywhere. Asters and chrysanthemums, purples, yellows, creamy whites. There were dahlias the size of dinner plates, shocking pink, scarlet. The bed was absolutely still, no water lapping about it, no rocking motions. No odors of sweat and moldy clothing. She felt clean and warm and dry.

"I thought I heard you," someone said.

Molly looked at the other side of the bed. Miri, or Meg, or . . . She couldn't tell which one.

"Martha has gone for your breakfast," the girl said.

Miriam joined them and sat on the edge of Molly's bed. "How are you now?"

"I'm all right. I'll get up."

"No, of course you won't get up. Breakfast first, then a rubdown and a manicure, and anything else we can think of that will make you more comfortable, and then if you don't fall asleep again, and if you still want to get up, then you may." Miriam laughed gently at her as Molly started to rise and sank back down again.

"You've been sleeping for two days," said Miri, or Meg, or whoever it was. "Barry's been here four times to check on you. He said you need to sleep all you can, and eat all you can."

There were dim memories of rousing, of drinking broth, of being bathed, but the memories refused to come into sharp focus.

"Are the others all right?" she asked.

"They're all fine," Miriam said soothingly.

"Thomas?"

"He's in the hospital, but he'll be fine too."

For many days they babied her; her blistered hands healed and her back stopped aching, and she regained some of the weight she had lost.

But she had changed, she thought, studying herself in the large mirror at the end of the room. Of course, she was still thin and gaunt. She looked at Miri's smooth face, and knew the difference lay deeper than that. Miri looked empty. When the animation faded, when she was no longer laughing or talking, there was nothing there. Her face became a mask that hid nothing.

"We'll never let you out of sight again!" Martha

whispered, coming up behind her. The others echoed it vehemently.

"I thought of you every day, almost every minute," Miri said.

"And we all thought of you together each evening after dinner. We just sat here in a circle on the mat and thought of you," Melissa said.

"Especially when it got so long," Miri said in a whisper. "We were so afraid. We kept calling you and calling you, silently, but all of us together. Calling you home over and over."

"I heard you," Molly said. Her voice sounded almost harsh. She saw Miriam shake her head at the sisters, and they fell silent. "We all heard you calling. You brought us home," Molly said, softening her voice with an effort.

They hadn't asked her anything about the trip, about Washington, about her sketchbooks, which they had unpacked and must have looked at. Several times she had started to speak of the river, the ruins, and each time she had failed. There was no way she could make them understand. Presently she would have to get to work on the sketches, using them as guides and drawing in detail what she had seen, what it had been like from start to finish. But she didn't want to speak of it. Instead they talked of the valley and what had happened in the seven weeks of Molly's absence. Nothing, she thought. Nothing at all. Everything was exactly as it always had been.

The sisters had been excused from work in order to speed Molly's recovery. They chatted and gossiped and caught up on mending and took walks and read together, and as Molly's strength returned, they played together on the mat in the middle of the room. Molly took no part in their play. Toward the end of the week, when they dragged the mat out and opened it, Miriam poured small glasses of amber wine and they toasted Molly and drew her to the mat with them. Her head was spinning pleasantly and she looked at Miriam, who smiled at her.

How beautiful the sisters are, she thought, how silky their hair, and smooth their skin; each body was unmarred, flawless.

"You've been away so long," Miriam whispered.

"Something's still down there on the river," Molly said foolishly, wanting to weep.

"Bring it home, darling. Reach out and bring back all the parts of you."

85

And slowly she reached out for the other part of herself, the part that had watched and listened and had brought her peace. That was the part that had built the clear hard wall, she thought distantly. The wall had been built to protect her, and now she was tearing it down again.

She felt she was speeding down the river, flying over the water, now swirling brown and muddy and dangerous, now smooth and deep blue-green and inviting, now white foam as it shattered over rocks . . . She sped down the river and tried to find that other self, to submerge it and become whole again with her sisters . . . Over her the trees murmured and beneath her the water whispered back, and she was between them, not touching either, and she knew that when she found that other self she would have to kill it, to destroy it totally, or the whispers would never go away. And she thought of the peace she had found, and the visions she had seen.

Not yet! she cried silently, and stopped her race down the river, and was once more in the room with her sisters. Not yet, she thought again, quietly. She opened her eyes and smiled at Miriam, who was watching her anxiously.

"Is it all right now?" Miriam asked.

"Everything is fine," Molly said, and somewhere she thought she could hear that other voice murmur softly before it faded away. She reached out and put her arms about Miriam's body and drew her down to the mat and stroked her back, her hip, her thigh. "Everything is fine," she whispered again.

Later, when the others slept, she stood shivering by the window and looked out at the valley. Autumn was very early. Each year it came a little earlier than the previous year. But it was warm in the large room; her chill was not caused by the season or the night air. She thought of the mat play and tears stood in her eyes. The sisters hadn't changed. The valley was unchanged. And yet everything was different. She knew something had died. Something else had come alive, and it frightened her and isolated her in a way that distance and the river had not been able to do.

She looked at the dim forms on the beds and wondered if Miriam suspected. Molly's body had responded; she had laughed and wept with the others, and if there had been one part of her not involved, one part alive and watchful, it had not interfered.

She could have done it, she thought. She could have destroyed that other part with Miriam's help, and the help of the sisters. She should have, she thought, and shivered again. Her thoughts were chaotic; there was something that had come to live within her, something that was vaguely threatening, and yet could give her peace as nothing else could. The beginnings of insanity, she thought wildly. She would become incoherent, scream at nothing, try to do violence to others or to herself. Or maybe she was going to die. Eternal peace. But what she had felt was not simply the absence of pain and fear, but the peace that comes after a great accomplishment, a fulfillment.

And she knew it was important that she let the visions come, that she find time to be alone in order to allow them to fill her. She thought of the sisters despairingly: they would never permit her to be alone again. Together they made a whole; the absence of one of them left the others incomplete. They would call and call her.

Chapter 14

Now the harvest had been gathered; apples hung red and heavy on the trees, and the maples blazed like torches against endless blue skies. Sycamores and birches burned gold, and the sumac's red deepened until it looked almost black. Every morning each blade of grass was edged in frost; it gleamed and glistened until it was melted by the rising sun. The passion of the autumn colors never had been so intense, Molly thought. How the light under the maples changed! And the pale glow that surrounded the sycamores!

"Molly?" Miriam's voice roused her from the window, and she turned reluctantly. "Molly, what are you doing?"

"Nothing. Thinking of the work for today."

Miriam paused. "Will it take you much longer? We miss you."

"I don't think so," Molly said, and started for the door.

Miriam moved slightly; her movement was enough to make Molly stop again. "Another two or three weeks," Molly said quickly, not wanting Miriam's hand on her arm.

Miriam nodded, and the moment passed when she could have touched Molly, could have held her. She felt baffled. Again and again when she would have embraced Molly, the moment passed, just as it now had, and they stood apart, not touching.

Molly left her in the large room, and presently Miriam walked to the hospital. "Are you too busy?" she asked, standing in the doorway to Ben's office. "I would like to talk with you."

"Miriam?" The inflection was automatic, as was her slight nod. Only Miriam would come alone; a younger sister would have been accompanied by her. "Come in. It's about Molly, isn't it?"

"Yes." She closed the door and sat down opposite his desk. His desk was covered with papers, notes, his medical notebook that he had carried on the trip with him. She looked from the papers to the man, and thought he was diifferent too. Like Molly. Like all of them who had gone away.

"You told me to come back if it didn't get better," she said. "She's worse than before. She's bringing unhappiness to all the sisters. Can't you do something for her?"

Ben sighed and leaned back in his chair and looked at the ceiling. "It's going to take time."

Miriam shook her head. "You said that before. How is Thomas, and Jed? How are you?"

"We're all coming around," Ben said, smiling slightly. "She will too, Miriam. Believe me, she will."

Miriam leaned toward him. "I don't believe you. I don't think she wants to come back to us. She's resisting us. I wish she hadn't come back at all if this is how she's going to be from now on. It's too hard on the other sisters." She had become very pale, and her voice shook; she turned away from him.

"I'll speak to her," Ben said.

Miriam drew a piece of paper from her pocket. She unfolded it and put it on his desk. "Look at that. What does it mean?"

They were the caricatures Molly had sketched of the brothers early in the trip. Ben studied them, the one of himself in particular. Was he really that grim-looking?

That determined? And surely his eyebrows were not that heavy and menacing?

"She's mocking us! Mocking all of you. She has no right to make fun of our brothers like that," Miriam said. "She's watching all the time, watching her sisters as they work and play. She won't participate unless I give her wine, and even then I can feel a difference. Always watching us. Everyone."

Ben smoothed the sketch paper and asked, "What do you propose we do, Miriam?"

"I don't know. Make her stop working on the drawings of the trip. That's keeping her mind on it, on what happened. Make her join her sisters in their daily work, as she used to. Stop letting her isolate herself for hours in that small room."

"She has to be alone to do the drawings," Ben said. "Just as I have to be alone to write my report, and Lewis has to be alone to assess the capabilities of the boat and the changes needed in it."

"But you and Lewis, the others, are all doing it because you must, and she is doing it because she wants to. She wants to be alone! She looks for excuses to be alone, and she's working on other things, not just the trip drawings. Make her let you in that room, let you see what else she's been doing!"

Ben nodded slowly. "I'll see her today," he said.

After Miriam had gone, Ben studied the sketches again, and he smiled slightly. She certainly had captured them, he thought. Cruelly, coldly, and accurately. He folded the paper and put it in his leather pouch, and thought about Molly and the others.

He had lied about Thomas. He wasn't back to normal, and might never be normal again. He had become almost totally dependent on his brothers. He refused to be separated from them even momentarily, and he slept with one or another of them every night. Jed was somewhat better, but he too showed a need for constant reassurance.

Lewis seemed virtually untouched by the voyage. He had stepped out of this life and back into it almost casually. Harvey was nervous, but less so than he had been a week ago, much less than when he first rejoined his brothers. Eventually he would be well.

And he, Ben. What about Ben? he asked himself mockingly. He was recovered, he decided.

He went to talk to Molly. She had a room in the hospital administration wing. He tapped lightly at the door, then opened it before she answered. They so seldom closed doors, rarely in the day, but it seemed natural for her to have closed her door, just as he felt it natural to close his when he was working. He stood for a moment looking at her. Had she slid something under the paper that lay on her drawing board? He couldn't be certain. She sat with her back to the window, the board tilted before her.

"Hello, Ben."

"Can you spare a few minutes?"

"Yes. Miriam sent you, didn't she? I thought she would."

"Your sisters are very concerned about you."

She looked down at the table and touched a paper.

She was different, Ben thought. No one would ever mistake her for Miriam, or another of the sisters. He came around the table and looked at the drawing. Her sketch pad was open to a page filled with small, hastily done line drawings of buildings, ruined streets, hills of rubble. She was doing a full page of one section of Washington. For a moment he had a curious feeling of being there, seeing the devastation, the tragedy of a lost era; Molly had the power to put images from his mind onto paper. He turned and looked out the window at the hills, which were splashes of color now with the sun full on them.

Watching him, Molly thought: neither Thomas nor Jed would talk with her at all. Thomas shied away as if she carried plague, and Jed remembered other things, urgent things he had to do. Harvey talked too much, and said nothing. And Lewis was too busy.

But she could talk with Ben, she thought. They could relive the trip with each other, they could try to understand what had happened, for whatever had happened to her had happened to him. She could see it in his face, in the way he had turned so abruptly from her drawing. Something lay within him, ready to awaken, ready to whisper to him, if he would let it, just as it lay within her and changed the world she saw. It spoke to her, not in words, but in colors, in symbols that she didn't understand, in dreams, in visions that passed fleetingly through her mind. She watched him where he stood, with the sun shining on him. Light fell on his arm in a way that made each hair gleam golden, a forest of golden trees on a brown plain. He shifted and the twilight on the plain turned the trees black.

"Little sister," he began, and she smiled and shook her head.

"Don't call me that," she said. "Call me . . . whatever you want, but not that." She had disturbed him; a frown came and went, leaving his face unreadable. "Molly," she said. "Just call me Molly."

But now he couldn't think what it was he had started to say to her. The difference was in her expression, he thought suddenly. Physically she was identical to Miriam, to the other sisters, only the expression was changed. She looked more mature, harder? That wasn't it, but he thought it was close to what he meant. Determined. Deeper.

"I want to see you on a regular basis for a while," Ben said abruptly. He hadn't started to say that at all, hadn't even thought of it until he said it.

Molly nodded slowly.

Still he hesitated, puzzled about what else he might say.

"You should set the time," Molly said gently.

"Monday, Wednesday, Saturday, immediately after lunch," he said brusquely. He made a note in his book.

"Starting today? Or should I wait until Monday?"

She was mocking him, he thought angrily, and snapped his book shut. He wheeled about and strode to the door. "Today," he said.

Her voice held him at the door. "Do you think I'm losing my mind, Ben? Miriam does."

He stood with his hand on the knob, not looking at her. The question jolted him. He should reassure her, he knew, say something soothing, something about Miriam's great concern, something. "Immediately after lunch," he said harshly, and let himself out.

Molly retrieved the paper she had slid under the Washington drawing and studied it for a time with her eyes narrowed. It was the valley, distorted somewhat so that she could get in the old mill, the hospital, and the Sumner house, all lined up in a way that suggested relatedness. It wasn't right, however, and she couldn't decide what was wrong. There were faint marks where the people were to go in the drawing, a cluster of them at the mill, more at the entrance to the hospital, a group in the field behind the old house. She erased the marks and sketched in, very lightly, a single figure, a man, who stood in the field. She drew another figure, a woman, walking between the hospital and the house. It was the size of everything, she thought. The buildings, especially the mill, were so large, the figures so small, dwarfed by the things they had made. She thought of the skeletons she had seen in Washington; a body reduced to bones was smaller still. She would make her figures emaciated, almost skeletal, stark . . .

Suddenly she snatched up the paper, crumpled it into a ball, and threw it into the wastecan. She buried her face in her arms.

They would have a "Ceremony for the Lost" for her, she thought distantly. The sisters would be comforted by the others, and the party would last until dawn as they all demonstrated their solidarity in the face of grievous loss. In the light of the rising sun the remaining sisters would join hands, forming a circle, and after that she would cease to exist for them. No longer would she torment them with her new strangeness, her apartness. No one had the right to bring unhappiness to the brothers or sisters, she thought. No one had the right to exist if such existence was a threat to the family. That was the law.

She joined her sisters for lunch in the cafeteria, and tried to share their gaiety as they talked of the coming-of-age party for the Julie sisters that night.

"Remember," Meg said, laughing mischievously, "no matter how many offers we get, we refuse all bracelets. And whoever sees the Clark brothers first slips on a bracelet before he can stop her." She laughed deep in her throat. Twice they had tried to get to the Clark brothers and twice other sisters had beaten them. Tonight they were separating, to take up posts along the path to the auditorium to lie in wait for the young Clark brothers, whose cheeks were still downy, who had crossed the threshold into adulthood only that autumn.

"They'll all cry 'Unfair!'" Miriam said, protesting feebly.

"I know," Meg said, laughing again.

Melissa laughed with her and Martha smiled, looking at Molly. "I'm to be at the first hedge," she said. "You wait by the path to the mill." Her eyes sparkled. "I've got the bracelets all ready. They're red, with six little silver bells tied in place. How he'll jingle, whoever gets the bracelet!" The six bells meant all the sisters were inviting all the brothers.

92

All over the cafeteria groups were huddled just like this, Molly thought, glancing about. Small groups of people, all conspiring, planning their conquests with glee, setting traps . . . Look-alikes, she thought, like dolls.

The Julie sisters had blond hair, hanging loose and held back with tiaras made of deep red flowers. They had chosen long tunics that dipped down low in the back, high in the front in drapes that emphasized their breasts charmingly. They were shy, smiling, saying little, eating nothing. They were fourteen.

Molly looked away from them suddenly and her eyes burned. Six years ago she had stood there, just like that, blushing, afraid and proud, wearing the bracelet of the Henry brothers. The Henry brothers, she thought suddenly. Her first man had been Henry, and she had forgotten that. She looked at the bracelet on her left wrist, and looked away again. One of the sisters had gotten to Clark first, and later Molly and her sisters would play with the Clark brothers on the mat. So smooth still, their faces were as smooth as the Julie faces.

People were trying to match up the bracelets now, and there was much laughter as everyone milled about the long tables and made excuses to examine each other's bracelets.

"Why didn't you come to my office this afternoon?"

Molly whirled about to find Ben at her elbow. "I forgot," she said.

"You didn't forget."

She looked down and saw that he still wore his own bracelet. It was plain, grass braided without adornment, without the brothers' symbol. Slowly, without looking at him, she began to pluck the silver bells from her own bracelet and when there was only one left on it, she slipped the bracelet off her wrist and reached out to put it on his. For a moment he resisted, then he held out his hand and the bracelet slid over his knuckles, over the jutting wrist bone. Only then did Molly look into his face. It was a mask—hard, unfamiliar, forbidding. If she could peel off the mask, she thought, there would be something different.

Abruptly Ben nodded, and turned and left her. She watched him go. Miriam and the others would be angry, she thought. Now there would be an extra Clark brother.

It didn't matter, but Miriam had counted on all of them to participate, and now it would be uneven.

The Julie sisters were dancing with the Lawrence brothers, two by two, and Molly felt a pang of sadness suddenly. Lewis was fertile, perhaps others of his group were also. If one of the Julie sisters conceived and was sent to the breeders' compound, the next party for them would be the Ceremony for the Lost. She watched them and couldn't tell which man was Lewis, which Lawrence, Lester . . .

She danced with Barry, then with Meg and Justin, then with Miriam and Clark, and again with Meg and Melissa and two of the Jeremy brothers; not with Jed, though, who stood against the wall and watched his brothers anxiously. He still wore his own bracelet. The other brothers had an assortment of bracelets on their wrists. Poor Jed, Molly thought, and almost wished she had given hers to him.

She sat with Martha and Curtis and ate a minced-beef sandwich and drank more of the amber wine that made her head swim delightfully. Then she danced with one of the Julie sisters, who was looking solemn now as the hour grew late. Presently the Lawrence brothers would claim them for the rest of the night.

The music changed. One of the Lawrence brothers claimed the girl Molly had danced with; the girl looked at him with a timid smile that appeared, vanished, appeared again. He danced her away.

Molly felt a tap on her arm, and turned to face Ben. He was unsmiling. He held out his arm for her and they danced, not speaking, neither of them smiling. He danced her to the table, where they stopped and he handed her a small glass of wine. Silently they drank, and then walked together from the auditorium. Molly caught a glimpse of Miriam's face as they left. Defiantly she held her back stiffer, her head higher, and went out into the cold night with Ben.

Chapter 15

"I would like to sit down by the river for a little while," she said. "Are you cold?" Ben asked, and when she said yes, he got cloaks for them both.

Molly watched the pale water, changing, always changing, and always the same, and she could feel him near, not touching, not speaking. Thin clouds chased across the face of the swelling moon. Soon it would be full, the harvest moon, the end of Indian summer. The man was so cleanly outlined, so unambiguous, she thought. A misshapen bowl, like an artifact made by inexpert hands that would improve with practice.

The moon in the river moved, separated into long shiny ropes that coiled, slid apart, came together, formed a wide band of luminous water that looked solid, then broke up again. Against the shore the voice of the river was gentle, secretive.

"Are you cold?" Ben asked again. His face was pale in the moonlight, his eyebrows darker than in daylight, straight, heavy. He could have been scowling at her; it was hard to tell. She shook her head, and he turned toward the river again.

The river was alive, she thought, and just when you thought you knew it, it changed and showed another face, another mood. Tonight it was beguiling, full of promise, and even knowing the promises to be false, she could hear the voice whispering to her persuasively, could sense the pull of the river.

And Ben thought of the river, swollen in floodtide, flashing bright over gravel, over rocks, breaking up into foam against boulders. He saw again the small fire on the bank, the figure of the girl standing there silhouetted against the gleaming water while the brothers pulled the boat up the hill.

"I'm sorry I didn't come today," she said suddenly in a

small voice. "I got almost to your door, and then didn't come the rest of the way. I don't know why."

There was a shout of laughter from the auditorium, and he wished he and Molly had walked farther up the river before stopping. A cloud covered the face of the moon and the river turned black, and only its voice was there, and the peculiar smell of the fresh water.

"Are you cold?" he asked again, as if the moonlight had held warmth that now was gone.

She moved closer to him. "Coming home," she said softly, dreamily, "I kept hearing the river talk to me, and the trees, and the clouds. I suppose it was fatigue and hunger, but I really heard them, only I couldn't understand the words most of the time. Did you hear them, Ben?"

He shook his head, and although she couldn't see him now with the cloud over the face of the moon, she knew he was denying the voices. She sighed.

"What would happen if you had an idea, something you wanted to work out alone?" she asked after a moment.

Ben shifted uneasily. "It happens," he said carefully. "We discuss it and usually, unless there's a good reason, a shortage of equipment, or supplies, something like that, whoever has the idea goes ahead with it."

Now the cloud had freed the moon; the light seemed brighter after the brief darkness. "What if the others didn't see the value of the idea?" Molly asked.

"Then it would have no value, and no one would want to waste time on it."

"But what if it was something you couldn't explain exactly, something you couldn't put into words?"

"What is the real question, Molly?" Ben asked, turning to face her. Her face was as pale as the moon, with deep shadows for eyes, her mouth black, not smiling. She looked up at him, and the moon was reflected in her eyes, and she seemed somehow luminous, as if the light came from within her, and he realized that Molly was beautiful. He never had seen it before and now it shocked him that the thought formed, forced itself on him.

Molly stood up suddenly. "I'll show you," she said. "In my room."

They walked back to the hospital side by side, not touching, and Ben thought: of course, the Miriam sisters were all beautiful, most of the sisters were. Just as most of

96

the brothers were handsome. It was a given. And it was meaningless.

She pulled a blind down on the window in her little room and threw her cloak on the chair behind her worktable. Then she pulled out drawings, sorting through them. Finally she handed one to him.

It was a woman, no one he knew, but vaguely familiar. Sara, he realized; changed, but Sara. Beside her, mirrors reached into infinity, and in each mirror was another woman, each Sara, but none exactly like her. Here a scowl tightened the mouth, there a wide smile, another was laughing, another had graying hair, wrinkles . . . He looked at Molly in bewilderment.

She handed him another drawing. There was a tree, nothing more. A tree rising out of a solid rock. An impossible thing and he felt unsettled by it.

Another drawing. She thrust it at him. A tiny boat on a vast sea that filled the paper from margin to margin. There was a solitary figure in the boat, so small it was insignificant, impossible to identify.

He felt upset by the drawings. He looked at Molly on the other side of the drawing table; she was staring at him intently. She looked feverish, her cheeks flushed, her eyes too bright.

"I need help, Ben," she said, her voice low and compelling. "You have to help me."

"What?"

"Ben, I have to do those things in paints. I don't know why, but I have to. And others. It won't work with pencil, or pen and ink. I need color and light! Please!"

She was weeping. Ben stared at her in surprise. This was her secret then? She wanted to paint? He suppressed an urge to smile at her, as if she were a child pleading for what was already hers.

She read his expression and sat down and put her head back against the cloak. She closed her eyes. "Miriam understands, and so do my sisters," she said tiredly, and now the high color in her cheeks faded and she looked very young and weary. "They won't let me do it."

"Why not? What's wrong with painting?"

"I . . . they don't like the way the pictures make them feel. They think it's dangerous. Miriam thinks so. The others will too."

Ben looked at the tiny boat in the endless ocean. "But

you don't have to paint this one, do you? Can't you do something else?"

She shook her head. Her eyes were still closed. "If someone had a bad heart, would you treat his ear because it was easier?" Now she looked at him, and there was no mockery at all in her face.

"Have you talked to Miriam?"

"She took some drawings I did of the brothers on the trip. She didn't like them. She kept them. I don't have to talk to her, or the others. I know what they will say. I bring them only pain anymore." She thought of them with the Clark brothers on the mat, laughing, sipping the amber wine, caressing the smooth boy/man bodies. It wasn't group sex, she thought suddenly. It was male and female broken up into parts, just as the moon broke on the smooth river. The sisters made one organism, female; the Clark brothers made up one organism, male, and when they embraced, the female organism would not be completely satisfied because it was not whole that night. One part of its body was missing, had been missing for a long time. And the missing part, like an amputated limb, caused phantom pain.

"Molly." Ben's voice was gentle. He touched her arm and she started. "Come to my room with me. It is very late. Soon it will be dawn."

"You don't have to," she said. "I thought I wouldn't tell you, that's why I turned around before I got to your office today. Then tonight, I thought I had to tell you because I needed help. You don't have to."

Almost reluctantly Ben said, "Come with me, Molly. To my room. I want you to."

Chapter 16

Snow fell lazily, silently; no wind blew, and the sky seemed low enough to touch. The snow built up on level surfaces, on tree branches, on the needles of the pines and spruces. It sifted down through a crack between a gutter and the roof of the hospital and built a short wall of snow that soon would topple of its own weight. Snow covered the land, unsullied, pure, layer on layer so that in protected spots where no intermittent sun melted it and no wind disturbed it, the snow depth had grown to six, seven, even eight feet. Against the whiteness, shadowed into grays and blues, the river gleamed black. The clouds were so thick the light that lay over the land seemed to come upward from the snow. The light was very dim, and in the distance the snow and sky and air merged and there were no boundaries.

No boundaries, Molly thought. It was all one. She stood at her window. Behind her an easel waited with a painting on it, but she couldn't think of it now. The snow, the strange light that came from below, the wholeness of the scene outside held her.

"Molly!"

She turned sharply. Miriam stood in the doorway, still wearing her outdoor clothing, snow clinging to her shoulders, her hood.

"I said, Meg's been hurt! Didn't you hear me?"

"Hurt? How? What happened?"

Miriam stared at her for a moment, then shook her head. "You didn't know, did you?"

Molly felt disoriented, as if she were a stranger who had wandered in and understood nothing. The painting looked garish, ugly, meaningless to her. Now she could sense Meg's pain and fear, and the sisters' presence easing it. They needed her, she thought clearly, and didn't understand why, and Meg faded from her thoughts. "Where is she?" she asked. "What happened? I'll come with you."

Miriam looked at her and shook her head. "Don't come," she said. "Stay here." She went away.

When Molly learned where Meg was and went to the hospital room to be with her sisters, they would not let her in.

Ben looked at his brothers and shrugged at the question: What were they to do about Molly? Exile her, as they had exiled David? Isolate her in a hospital room? Quarter her with the breeders—the mothers? Ignore the problem? They had discussed every alternative and were satisfied with none.

"There's nothing to indicate she is making progress,"

Barry said. "Nothing to indicate she even wants to resume a normal life."

"Since there's no precedent for anything like this, whatever we decide will have to be the right thing," Bruce said soberly. His thick eyebrows drew together, separated. "Ben, she's your patient. You haven't said a thing. You were certain that allowing her to paint would be therapeutic, but it wasn't. Have you any other suggestions?"

"When I asked permission to withdraw from my work in the lab and study psychology instead, it was refused. The rest of us who went to Washington have made a complete recovery, a functional recovery," he added drily. "Except Molly. We don't know enough to know why, how to treat her, if she'll ever recover. I say, give it time. She isn't needed in the classrooms, let her paint. Give her a room of her own and leave her alone."

Barry was shaking his head. "Psychology is a dead end for us," he said. "It revives the cult of the individual. When a unit is functioning, the members are self-curing. As for letting her remain in the hospital . . . She is a constant source of pain and confusion to her sisters. Meg will be all right, but Molly didn't even know her sister had fallen, had a broken arm. The sisters needed her and she didn't answer. We all know and agree it is our duty to safeguard the well-being of the unit, not the various individuals within it. If there is a conflict between those two choices, we must abandon the individual. That is a given. The only question is how."

Ben stood up and went to the window. He could see the breeders' quarters across the hedge. Not there, he thought vehemently. They would never accept her. They might even kill her if she were put among them. Only a month ago they had had the Ceremony for the Lost for Janet, who was now counted among the breeders, who was undergoing drug and hypnotic conditioning to force her to accept her new status as a fertile female who would bring forth a child as often as the doctors decided it was necessary. And the new children would be transferred to the nursery at birth, and the breeders would then have time to regain good health, to grow strong enough to do it again, and again, and again . . .

"No point in putting her in there," Bob said, going to stand by Ben at the window. "Better if we simply admit there's no solution and resort to euthanasia. It would be less cruel."

Ben felt a weight in his chest and turned toward his brothers. They were right, he thought distantly. "If it happens again," he said, speaking slowly, uncertain where his own thoughts were taking him, "we will have this same agonizing meeting again, the same useless alternatives to discuss and discard."

Barry nodded. "I know. That's what's giving me bad dreams. With more and more people needed to forage, to repair the roads, to make expeditions to the cities, there might be more cases like Molly's."

"Let me have her," Ben said abruptly. "I'll put her in the old Sumner house. We'll have the Ceremony for the Lost and declare her gone. The Miriam sisters will close the gap and feel no more pain, and I'll be able to study this reaction."

"It is very cold in the house," Ben said, "but the stove will warm it. Do you like these rooms?"

They had gone over the entire house, and Molly had chosen the second-floor wing facing the river. There were wide windows without curtains, and the cold afternoon light filled the room, but in the summer it would be warm and bright with sunshine, and always there was the river to gaze at. The adjoining room had been a nursery or a dressing room, she thought. It was smaller with high double windows that reached almost to the ceiling. She would paint in that room. There was a tiny balcony outside the windows.

Already the sounds of music were drifting across the valley as the ceremony began. There would be dancing, a feast, and much wine.

"The electricity is off," Ben said harshly. "The wires are bad. We'll get them fixed as soon as the snow melts."

"I don't care about that. I like the lamps and the fireplace. I can burn wood in the stove."

"The Andrew brothers will keep you supplied with wood. They'll bring anything you need. They will leave everything on the porch."

She moved to the window. The sun, covered with thin clouds, hung on the edge of the hill. It would start its slide down the other side, and darkness would follow swiftly. For the first time in her life she would be alone at night. She stood with her back to Ben, gazing at the river and thinking about the old house, so far away from the other buildings in the valley, hidden by trees and bushes that had grown as high as trees.

If she had a bad dream and stirred in her sleep or cried out, no one would hear her, no one would be at her side to soothe her, comfort her.

"Molly." Ben's voice was still too harsh, as if he were terribly angry with her, and she didn't know why he should be angry. "I can stay with you tonight if you're afraid . . ."

She turned to look at him then, her face shadowed, the cold light and snow and gray sky behind her, and Ben knew she was not afraid. He felt as he had that night by the river: she was beautiful, and the light in the room came from her, from her eyes. "You're happy, aren't you?" he said wonderingly.

She nodded. "I'll make a fire in my fireplace. And then I'll drag that chair up close to it and sit and watch the flames and listen to the music, and after a while, I'll go to bed, and maybe read for a little bit, by lamplight, until I get sleepy . . ." She smiled at him. "It's all right, Ben. I feel . . . I don't know how I feel. Like something's gone that was heavy and hard to live with. It's gone, and I feel light and free and yes, even happy. So maybe I am crazy. Maybe that's what going crazy means." She turned to the window again. "Do the breeders feel happy?" she asked after a moment.

"No."

"What is it like for them?"

"I'll make your fire. The chimney's open. I checked."

"What happens to them, Ben?"

"They are given a course in learning how to be mothers. Eventually they like that life, I think."

"Do they feel free?"

He had started to put logs in the grate, and now he dropped a large one with a crash and stood up. He went to her and swung her away from the window. "They never stop suffering from the separation," he said. "They cry themselves to sleep night after night, and they are on drugs all the time, and they have sessions of conditioning to make them accept it, but every night they cry themselves to sleep. Is that what you wanted to hear? You wanted to think they were as free as you are now, free to be alone, to do what they want with no thought of their responsibilities to the others. It's not like that! We need them, and we use them the only way we can, to do the

102

least harm to the sisters who are not breeders. When they're through breeding, if they are fit, they work in the nursery. If they're not fit, we put them to sleep. Is that what you wanted to hear?"

"Why are you saying this?" she whispered, her face ashen.

"So you won't have any illusions about your little nest here! We can use you, do you understand? As long as you are useful to the community, you'll be allowed to live here like a princess. Just as long as you're useful."

"Useful, how? No one wants to look at my paintings. I've finished the maps and drawings of the trip."

"I'm going to dissect your every thought, your every wish, every dream. I'm going to find out what happened to you, what made you separate yourself from your sisters, what made you decide to become an individual, and when I find out we'll know how never to allow it to happen again."

She stared at him, and now her eyes were not luminous but deeply shadowed, hidden. Gently she pulled loose from his hands on her shoulders. "Examine yourself, Ben. Catch yourself listening to voices no one else can hear. Observe yourself. Who else is angry at the way we treat the breeders? Why did you fight to save my life when the good of the community demanded I be put to sleep, like a used-up breeder? Who else even looks at my paintings? Who else would rather be here in this cold dark room with a madwoman than at the celebration? Our coupling is not joyous, Ben. When we embrace it is a hard, bitter, cruel thing we do, and we are filled with sadness and neither of us knows why. Examine yourself, Ben, and then me, and see if there is a cause you can root out and destroy without destroying the carriers."

Savagely he pulled her to him and pressed her face hard against his chest so she could not speak. She did not struggle against him. "Lies, lies, lies," he muttered. "You are mad." He put his cheek against her hair, and her arms shifted and moved up his back to hold him. He pulled away roughly and stood apart from her. Now the darkness had settled heavily in the room and she was only a shadow against shadows.

"I'm leaving now," he said brusquely. "You shouldn't have any trouble getting a fire started. I lighted the stove downstairs and the heat should be up here soon. You won't be cold."

She didn't speak, and he turned and hurried from the room. Outside, he started to run through the deep snow, and he ran until he could run no longer and his breath was coming in painful gasps. He turned to look at the house; it was no longer visible through the black trees.

Chapter 17

Now the rain was light and steady, and the wind had died down. The tops of the hills were hidden by clouds and the river hidden by mist. There was a steady sound of hammers, muted by the rain, but reassuring. Under the roof of the boat shed people were working, getting the third boat constructed. Last year they had been farmers, teachers, technicians, scientists; this year they were boat builders.

Ben watched the rain. The brief lull ended and the wind screamed through the valley, driving rain before it in waves. The scene dissolved, and there was only the rain beating on the window.

Molly would wonder if he was coming, he thought. The window shook under the increasing force of the rain. Break! he thought. No, she wouldn't wonder. She wouldn't even notice his absence. As suddenly as it had started, the outburst of violence stopped and the sky thinned so that there was almost enough sun to cast shadows. It was all the same to her, he thought, whether he was there or not. While she talked to him, answered his questions, she painted, or sketched, or cleaned brushes; sometimes, restless, she made him walk with her, always up the hills, into the woods, away from the inhabited valley where she was forbidden. And those were the things she would have done alone.

Soon his brothers would join him for the formal meeting they had requested, and he would have to agree to a time for the completion of the report he hadn't even begun. He looked at his notebook on the long table and turned from it to the window once more. The notebook was filled; he had nothing more to ask her, nothing more to extract from her, and he knew as little today as he had known in the fall.

In his pocket was a small package of sassafras, the first of the season, his gift to her. They would brew tea and sit before the fire, sipping the fragrant, hot drink. They would lie together and he would talk of the valley, of the expansion of the lab facilities, the progress on the boats, the plans for cloning foragers and workers who could repair roads or build bridges or do whatever was required to open a route to Washington, to Philadelphia, to New York. She would ask about her sisters, who were working on textbooks, carefully copying illustrations, charts, graphs, and she would nod gravely when he answered and her gaze would flicker over her own paintings that no one in the valley could or would understand. She would talk about anything, answer any question he asked, except about her paintings.

She understood what she did as little as he, and that was in his notes. She was compelled to paint, to draw, to make tangible those visions that were blurred and ambiguous and even hurtful. The compulsion was stronger than her will to live, he thought bitterly. And now his brothers would join him and make a decision about her.

Would they offer her a bag of seeds and an escort down the river?

Heavy clouds rolled down from the mountains and turned off the feeble light, and again the wind blasted the window and pelted it with hard rain. Ben was standing there watching it when his brothers came into the room and seated themselves.

"We'll get right to it," Barry said, just as Ben would have done in his place. "She isn't better, is she?"

Ben sat down to complete the circle and shook his head.

"In fact, if anything, she's worse than she was when she came home," Barry continued. "Isolation has permitted her illness to spread, to intensify, and joining her in isolation, even temporarily, has permitted the disease to infect you."

Ben looked at his brothers in surprise and confusion. Had there been clues, hints that they were thinking along those lines? He realized that by asking the question he had answered another. He should have known. In a perfectly functioning unit there are no secrets. Slowly he shook his head, and he spoke very carefully. "For a time, I believed I was ill also, but I continued to function according to our schedule, our needs, and I dismissed the thoughts that had troubled me. In what way have I given offense?"

Barry shook his head impatiently.

For a moment Ben could sense their unhappiness. "I have a theory about Molly that perhaps applies also to me." They waited. "Always before us, in infancy there was a period when ego development naturally occurred, and if all went well during that period, the individual was formed, separate from his parents. With us such a development is not necessary, or even possible, because our brothers or sisters obviate the need for separate existence, and instead a unit consciousness is formed. There are very old studies of identical twins that recognized this unit or group consciousness, but the researchers were not prepared to understand the mechanism. Very little attention was paid to it, and little further study." He stood up and moved again to the window. The rain was steady and hard now. "I suggest that we all still have the capability for individual ego development latent within us. It becomes dormant when the physiological time passes for its spontaneous emergence, but with Molly, and perhaps with others, if there is enough stimulus, under the proper conditions, this development is activated."

"The proper conditions being separation from the brothers or sisters under stressful circumstances?" Barry asked thoughtfully.

"I think so. But the important thing now," Ben said urgently, "is to let it develop and see what happens. I can't predict her future behavior. I don't know what to expect from one day to the next."

Barry and Bruce exchanged glances, and then looked at the other brothers. Ben tried to interpret the looks and failed. He felt chilled and turned to watch the rain instead.

"We will decide tomorrow," Barry said finally. "But whatever our decision about Molly is, there is another decision that we made that is unaltered. You must not continue to see her, Ben. For your own welfare, and ours, we must forbid your visits to her."

Ben nodded in agreement. "I'll have to tell her," he said.

At the tone in his voice Barry again looked at the other brothers, and reluctantly they agreed.

"Why are you so surprised?" Molly asked. "This had to happen."

"I brought you some tea," Ben said brusquely.

Molly took his package and looked down at it for a long time. "I have a present for you," she said softly. "I was going to give it to you another time, but . . . I'll go get it."

She left and returned quickly with a small packet, no more than five inches square. It was a folded paper and, when opened, it had several faces, all of them variations of Ben's. In the center was a man's massive head, with fierce eyebrows and penetrating eyes, surrounded by four others, all resembling one another enough to show relationship.

"Who are they?"

"In the middle is the old man who owned this house. I found photographs in the attic. That is his son, David's father, and that one is David. That's you."

"Or Barry, or Bruce, or any of the others before us," Ben said curtly. He didn't like the composite picture. He didn't like looking at the faces of men who had lived such different, inexplicable lives, and who looked so much like him.

"I don't think so," Molly said, squinting her eyes at the picture, then studying him. "There's something about the eyes they just don't have. Theirs only see outward, I think, and yours, and those of the other men in the picture, they can look both ways."

Suddenly she laughed and drew him to the fire. "But put it away and let's have our tea, and a cookie. I've been getting more than I can eat and I saved a lot. We'll have a party!"

"I don't want any tea," Ben said. Not looking at her, watching the flames in the grate, he asked, "Don't you even care?"

"Care?"

Ben heard the pain there, sharp, undeniable. He closed his eyes hard.

"Should I weep and howl and tear my clothes, and bang my head on the wall? Should I beg you not to leave me, to stay with me always? Should I throw myself from the topmost window of this house? Should I grow thin and pale and wither away like a flower in the autumn, killed by the cold it never understands? How should I show I care, Ben? Tell me what I should do."

He felt her hand on his cheek and opened his eyes and found they were burning.

"Come with me, Ben," she said gently. "And afterwards perhaps we shall weep together when we say goodbye."

"We promise never to harm her," Barry said quietly. "If she has need of one of us, someone will go care for her. She will be permitted to live out her life in the Sumner house. We shall never display or permit others to display her paintings, but we shall preserve them carefully so that our descendants may study them and understand the steps we have taken today." He paused and then said, "Furthermore, Ben, our brother, will accompany the contingent who will go down the river to set up a base camp for future groups to use." Now he looked up from the paper before him.

Ben nodded gravely. The decisions were just and compassionate. He shared his brothers' anguish, and knew the suffering would not end until the boats returned and they could hold the Ceremony for the Lost for him. Only then would they all be freed again.

Molly watched the boats glide down the river, Ben standing in the prow of the lead boat, the wind streaming his hair. He didn't turn to look at the Sumner house until the boat started around the first curve that would take it out of sight, and then briefly she saw his pale face, and he was gone, the boat was gone.

Molly continued to stand at the wide windows for a long time after the boats had disappeared. She remembered the voice of the river, the answering voices from the high treetops, the way the wind moved the upper levels without stirring a blade of grass. She remembered the silence and darkness that had pressed in on them at night, touching them, testing them, tasting them, the intruders. And her hand moved to her stomach and pressed against the flesh there, against the new life that was growing within her.

The summer heat gave way to early September frosts and the boats returned, and this time another stood in the prow. The trees burned red and gold and snows fell and in January Molly gave birth to her son, alone, un-aided, and lay looking at the infant in the crook of her arm and smiled at him. "I love you," she whispered tenderly. "And your name shall be Mark."

All through the latter stages of her pregnancy Molly had told herself almost daily that tomorrow she would send a message to Barry, that she would submit to his authority and allow herself to be placed in the breeders' quarters. Now, looking at the red infant with his eyes screwed so tightly closed he seemed without eyes, she knew she would never give him up.

Each morning the Andrew brothers brought firewood, her basket of supplies, whatever she asked for, deposited it all on her porch, and left again, and she saw no one, except at a distance. As soon as Mark could understand her words, she began to impress upon him the need for silence while the Andrew brothers were near the house. When he grew older and started to ask "why" about everything, she had to tell him the Andrew brothers would take him away from her and put him in a school and they would never see each other again. It was the first and only time she saw him react with terror, and after that he was as quiet as she when the young doctors were there.

He learned to walk and talk early; he began to read when he was four, and for long periods he would curl up near the fireplace with one of the brittle books from the downstairs library. Some of them were children's books, others were not; he didn't seem to mind. They played hide-and-seek throughout the house and, when the weather was pleasant, up and down the hillside behind the house, out of sight of the others in the valley, who would never under any circumstances enter the woods unless ordered to do so. Molly sang to him and told him stories from the books, and made up other stories when they exhausted the books. One day Mark told her a story, and she laughed delightedly, and after that sometimes she was the storyteller and sometimes he was. While she paainted he drew pictures, or painted also, and more and more often played with the river clay she brought him, and made shapes that they dried in the sun on the balcony.

They wandered farther up the hillside as he became sturdier. One day in the summer when he was five, they remained in the woods for several hours, Molly pointing out the ferns and liverworts to him, drawing his attention to the way the sunlight changed the colors of the delicate green leaves, deepened the rich greens to nearly black.

"Time," she said finally.

He shook his head. "Let's climb to the top and look at the whole world."

"Next time," she said. "We'll bring our lunch and climb all the way up. Next time."

"Promise?"

"Promise."

They walked back down slowly, stopping often to examine a rock, a new plant, the bark of an ancient tree, whatever caught his interest. At the edge of the woods they paused and looked about carefully before leaving the shelter of the trees. Then they ran to the kitchen door hand in hand and, laughing, tried to get through together.

"You're getting too big," Molly cried, and allowed him to enter first.

Mark stopped abruptly, yanked on her hand, and turned to run. One of the Barry brothers stepped from the dining room into the kitchen, and another closed the door to the outside and stood behind them. The other three entered the kitchen silently and stared in disbelief at the boy.

Finally one of them spoke. "Ben's?"

Molly nodded. Her hand clutched Mark's in a grip that must have hurt him. He stood close to her and looked at the brothers fearfully.

"When?" the brother asked.

"Five years ago, in January."

The spokesman sighed heavily. "You'll have to come with us, Molly. The boy too."

She shook her head and felt weak with terror. "No! Leave us alone. We're not hurting anyone! Leave us alone!"

"It's the law," the brother said harshly. "You know it as well as we do."

"You promised!"

"The agreement we made didn't cover this." He took a step closer to her. Mark tore his hand free from her grasp and flew at the doctor.

"Leave my mother alone! Go away! Don't you hurt my mother!"

Someone caught Molly's arms and held her, and another of them caught Mark and lifted him as he kicked and lashed out furiously, screaming all the while.

110

"Don't hurt him!" Molly cried, and struggled to free herself. She hardly felt the pinprick of the injection. Dimly she heard one last scream of anguish from Mark, and then there was nothing.

Chapter 18

Molly blinked and shut her eyes against the glare of a silver frost that covered everything. She stood still and tried to remember where she was, who she was, anything. When she opened her eyes again, the blinding glare still dazzled her. She felt as if she had awakened after a long, nightmare-haunted dream that was becoming more and more dim as she tried to recapture it. Someone nudged her.

"You'll freeze out here," someone said close by. Molly turned to look at the woman, a stranger. "Come on, get inside," the woman said louder. Then she leaned forward and looked at Molly closely. "Oh, you're back, aren't you?"

She took Molly by the arm and guided her inside a warm building. Other women looked up idly and then bent down over their sewing again. Some of them were obviously pregnant. Some of them were dull-eyed, vacant-looking, doing nothing.

The woman helping Molly took her to a chair and stood by her side long enough to say, "Just sit still for a while. You'll start remembering in a little bit." Then she left and took her place at one of the machines and began stitching.

Molly looked at the floor and waited for memories to return, and for a long time there was nothing but the terror of nightmare remembered in emotions, not in details.

They had strapped her to a table, many times, she thought, and they had done things to her that she could not recall. There had been another time when some of the women had held her down and done things to her. She shuddered violently and closed her eyes. The memory receded. Mark, she thought suddenly, very clearly. Mark!

111

She jumped up and looked about wildly. The woman who had befriended her hurried over and caught her arm.

"Look, Molly, they'll put you under again if you make trouble. Understand? Just sit still until our break, and I'll talk to you then."

"Where is Mark?" Molly whispered.

The woman glanced about and said in an undertone, "He's all right. Now sit down! Here comes a nurse."

Molly sat down again and stared at the floor until the nurse glanced about the room and left once more. Mark was all right. There was ice on the ground. Winter. He was six, then. She remembered nothing of the late summer, the fall. What had they done to her?

The hours until the break passed painfully slowly. Occasionally one or another of the women would look at her and there was awareness, not the incurious glances that had been given her before. The word was spreading that she was back, and they were watching her, perhaps to see what she would do now, perhaps to welcome her, perhaps for some reason she couldn't guess. She looked at the floor. Her hands were clenched, her nails digging into her palms. She relaxed them. They had taken her to a hospital room, but not the usual hospital, one in the breeders' quarters. They had examined her thoroughly. She remembered injections, answering questions, pills . . . It was too blurred. Her hands had clenched again.

"Molly, come on. We'll have tea and I'll tell you what I can."

"Who are you?"

"Sondra. Come on."

She should have known, Molly thought, following Sondra. She remembered suddenly the ceremony given for Sondra, who was only three or four years older than she. She had been nine or ten, she thought.

The tea was a pale yellow drink she couldn't identify. After one sip she put it down and looked across the lounge toward the uncovered window. "What month is this?"

"January." Sondra finished her tea and leaned forward and said in a low voice, "Listen, Molly, they've taken you off the drugs and they'll be watching you for the next few weeks to see how you behave. If you cause trouble, they'll put you on something again. You've been conditioned. Just don't fight it, and you'll be all right."

Molly felt she could understand only half of what Sondra was saying to her. Again she looked about the lounge;

112

in here the chairs were comfortable and there were tables at convenient intervals. Women were in clusters of threes and fours, chatting, now and then glancing at her. Some of them smiled, one winked. There were thirty women in the room, she thought in disbelief. Thirty breeders!

"Am I pregnant?" she asked suddenly, and pressed her hands against her stomach.

"I don't think so. If you are, it's still awfully early, but I doubt it. They tried every month since you've been here and it didn't take before. I doubt it took the last time either."

Molly sagged against her chair and closed her eyes hard. That's what they had done to her on the table. She felt tears form and roll down her cheeks and was not able to stop them. Then Sondra's arm was about her shoulders, and she held her tightly.

"It hits all of us like that, Molly. It's the separation, the being alone for the first time. You don't get used to it, but you learn to live with it and it doesn't hurt so much after a while."

Molly shook her head, unable as yet to speak. No, she thought distinctly, it was not the separation, it was the humiliation of being treated like an object, of being drugged and then used, forced to cooperate in that procedure unquestioningly.

"We have to go back now," Sondra said. "You won't have to do anything for another day or two, long enough to collect your thoughts, get used to everything all over again."

"Sondra, wait. You said Mark is all right? Where is he?"

"He's in school with the others. They won't hurt him or anything. They're very good to all the children. You remember that, don't you?"

Molly nodded. "Did they clone him?"

Sondra shrugged. "I don't know. I don't think so." She grimaced then and pressed her hand to her stomach. She looked very old and tired, and except for her bulging stomach, too thin.

"How many times have you been pregnant?" Molly asked. "How long have you been here?"

"Seven, counting now," Sondra said without hesitation. "I was brought here twenty years ago."

Molly stared at her then and shook her head. But she had been nine or ten when they mourned Sondra. "How long have I been here?" she whispered finally.

"Molly, not too fast. Try to relax this first day."

"How long?"

"A year and a half. Now come on."

All afternoon she sat quietly, and the memories became slightly less blurred, but she could not account for a year and a half. It was gone from her life as if a fold had been made and the two ends now touching excluded whatever had happened in the section that made up the loop, a year and a half.

He was seven, then. Seven, no longer an infant. She shook her head. In the afternoon one of the doctors strolled through the room, stopping to speak to several of the women. He approached Molly and she said, "Good afternoon, Doctor," just as the others had done.

"How are you feeling, Molly?"

"Well, thank you."

He moved on.

Molly looked at the floor again. She felt as if she had watched the small interlude from a great distance, unable to alter a nuance of it. Conditioning, she thought. That was what Sondra had meant. How else had they conditioned her? To spread her legs obligingly when they approached with their instruments, with the carefully hoarded sperm? She forced her fingers open again and flexed them. They were sore from gripping so hard.

Suddenly she looked up, but the doctor had gone. Who was he? For a moment she felt dizzy, then the room steadied again. She had called him Doctor, hadn't even questioned the lack of a name. Had it been Barry? Bruce? Another part of her conditioning, she thought bitterly. The breeders were the lost, they no longer had the right to know one of the clones from another. The Doctor. The Nurse. She bowed her head once more.

The routine was easy after a few days. They were given soporifics at bedtime and stimulants at breakfast, all disguised in the thin yellow tea that Molly wouldn't drink. Some of the women wept at night, others succumbed rapidly to the drugged tea and slept heavily. There was a lot of sexual activity; they had their mats, just as everyone else. Through the day they worked in the various departments of the clothing section. They had free time in the late afternoon, books to read, games in the lounge, guitars and violins available to them.

"It really isn't bad," Sondra said a few days after Molly's awakening. "They take good care of us, the very best. If you prick your finger, they come running and watch over you like a baby. It's not bad."

Molly didn't respond. Sondra was tall and heavy, in her sixth month; her eyes varied from brightly alert to dull and unseeing. *They* watched Sondra, Molly thought, and at the least sign of depression or emotional upset they changed the dosage and kept her operating on an even level.

"They don't keep most of the new ones under as long as they did you," Sondra said another time. "I guess that's because most of us were only fourteen or fifteen when we came here, and you were older."

Molly nodded. They had been children, easy to condition into breeding machines who thought it really wasn't that bad a life. Except at night, when many of them wept for their sisters.

"Why do they want so many babies?" Molly asked. "We thought they were reducing the human babies, not increasing the number."

"For workers and road builders, dam builders. They're hurting for materials from the cities, chemicals mostly, I think. They're making more clones of the babies too, we hear. They'll have an army to send out to build their roads and keep the rivers open."

"How do you know so much about what's going on? We always thought you were kept more isolated than that."

"No secrets in this whole valley," Sondra said complacently. "Some of the girls work in the nursery, some in the kitchens, and they hear things."

"And what about Mark? Do you ever hear anything about him?"

Sondra shrugged. "I don't know anything about him," she said. "He's a boy, like the other boys, I guess. Only he doesn't have any brothers. They say he wanders off alone a lot."

She would watch for him, she thought. Sooner or later she would see him over the rose hedge. Before that time arrived, she was summoned to the Doctor's office.

She followed the Nurse docilely and entered the office. The Doctor was behind his desk.

"Good afternoon, Molly."

"Good afternoon, Doctor," she said, and wondered, was he Barry, or Bruce, or Bob . . . ?

"Are the other women treating you all right?"

"Yes, Doctor."

A series of such questions, followed by Yes, Doctor, or No, Doctor. Where was it supposed to go, she wondered, and became more wary.

"Is there anything you want or need?"

"May I have a sketch pad?"

Something changed, and she knew this was the reason for her visit. She had made a mistake; perhaps they had conditioned her not to think of sketching again, never to think again of painting . . . she tried to remember what they had said to her, had done to her. Nothing came. She should not have asked for it, she thought again. A mistake.

The Doctor opened his desk drawer and took out her sketch pad and charcoal pencil. He pushed them across the desk toward her.

Desperately Molly tried to remember. What was he watching for? What was she supposed to do? Slowly she reached for the pad and pencil, and for a moment she felt a tremor in her hand and her stomach churned as a wave of nausea rose. The sensations passed, but she had stopped the forward movement of her hand, and she stared at it. Now she knew. She moistened her lips and started to move her hand again. The sensations returned for a scant moment, long enough to register, then they faded away. She didn't look up at the Doctor, who was watching her closely. Again she moistened her lips. She was almost touching the pad now. Abruptly she jerked her hand back and jumped up from her chair and looked wildly about the room, one hand clutching her stomach, the other pressed against her mouth.

She started to run to the door, but his voice held her. "Come, sit down, Molly. You'll be all right now."

When she looked again at his desk the pad and pencil were gone. Reluctantly she sat down, afraid of what new tricks he might have prepared for her, afraid of the inevitable mistake she was certain to make—and then another year and a half in limbo? A whole lifetime in limbo? She didn't look at the Doctor.

There were a few more inane questions, and she was dismissed. As she walked back to her room she understood why the breeders didn't try to leave the area, why they never spoke to a clone, although they were separated only by a hedge.

All of March was wind-blown and water-soaked, with icy rains that did not let up for days at a time. April's rains were softer, but the river continued to rise through most of the month as the snow water cascaded down from the hills. May started cold and wet, but by midmonth the sun was warm and the farm workers were busy in the fields.

Soon, Molly thought, standing at the rear of the breeders' area, looking up the hillside. The dogwoods were blooming, and over them the redbud trees glowed. The trees were all clothed in new greenery and the ground was fast losing its feel of a wet sponge. Soon, she repeated, and went inside to her sewing table.

Three times she had traversed the inhabited area of the valley. The first time, she had vomited violently; the next time, warned, she had struggled against nausea and terror, and when she passed the clone hospital she had almost fainted. The third time her reaction had been less powerful, and the same feelings had passed through her quickly, as if a memory had been stimulated momentarily.

She might have other, even more drastic reactions to the Sumner house, she thought, but now she knew she did not have to yield to the conditioned responses. Soon, she thought again, bending over her sewing.

Four times they had put her in the breeders' hospital ward and installed a constant temperature gauge, and when the temperature was right, Nurse had come in with her tray and said cheerfully, "Let's try again, shall we, Molly?" And obediently Molly had opened her legs and lain still while the sperm were inserted with the shiny, cold instrument. "Now, remember, don't move for a while," Nurse then said, still cheerful, brisk, and had left her lying, unmoving, on the narrow cot. And two hours later she was allowed to dress and leave again. Four times, she thought bitterly. A thing, an object, press this button and this is what comes out, all predictable, on cue.

She left the breeders' compound on a dark, moonless night. She carried a large laundry bag that she had been filling slowly, secretly, for almost three months. There was no one awake; there was nothing of danger in the valley, perhaps in the entire world, but she hurried, avoiding the path, keeping to the sound-muffling grass. The thick growth surrounding the Sumner house created a darkness that was like a hole in space, a blackness that would swallow up anything that chanced too close. She hesitated, then felt her way between the trees and bushes until she came to the house.

She still had two hours before dawn, another hour or so before her absence was discovered. She left her bundle on the porch and made her way around the house to the back door, which opened at a touch. Nothing happened to her as she entered, and she breathed a sigh of relief. But then no one had expected her to get this far ever again. She felt her way up the stairs to her old room; it was as she had left it, she thought at first, but something was wrong, something had been changed. It was too dark to see anything at all, but the feeling of difference persisted and she found the bed and sat down to wait for dawn so she could see the room, see her paintings.

When she could see, she gasped. Someone had spread her paintings out, had stood them all up around the walls, on chairs, on the old desk she never had used. She went into the other room, where she had painted, and there on the bench that Mark had used for his clay, instead of the half-dozen crude figures he had shaped, there were dozens of clay objects: pots, heads, animals, fish, a foot, two hands . . . Weakly Molly leaned against the doorframe and wept.

The room was bright when she pushed away from the door. She had delayed too long; she had to hurry now. She ran down the stairs and out of the house, picked up her bag, and started climbing the hill. Two hundred feet up she stopped and began to search for the spot she and Mark had found once: a sheltered spot behind blackberry bushes, protected by an overhanging ledge of limestone. From there she could see the house but could not be seen from below. The bushes had grown, the spot was even more hidden than she remembered. When she finally found it she sank down to the ground in relief. The sun was high, they would know by now that she was gone. Presently a few of them would come to look over the Sumner house, not really expecting to find her, but because they were thorough.

They came before noon, spent an hour looking around the house and yard, then left. Probably it would be safe now to return to the house, she thought, but she did not stir from her hole in the hill. They returned shortly before dark, and spent more time going over the same ground they had covered before. Now she knew it was safe to go

118

to the house. They never went out after dark, except in groups; they would not expect her to wander about in the dark alone. She stood up, easing the stiffness out of her legs and back. The ground was damp, and this spot was cool, sheltered from the sun.

She lay on the bed. She knew she would hear him when he entered the house, but she couldn't sleep, except in a fitful, dream-filled doze: Ben lying with her; Ben sitting before the fire sipping pink, fragrant tea; Ben looking at her painting and becoming pale . . . Mark scrambling up the stairs, his legs going this way and that, a frown of determination on his face. Mark squatting over a single leaf of a fern, still rolled tightly at the end, and studying it intently, as if willing it to uncoil as he watched. Mark, his hands pudgy and grimy, gleaming wet, pushing the clay this way, smoothing it, pushing it that way, frowning at it, oblivious of her . . .

She sat up suddenly, wide awake. He had come into the house. She could hear the stairs creak slightly under his feet. He stopped, listening. He must sense her there, she thought, and her heart quickened. She went to the door of the workroom and waited for him.

He had a candle. For a moment he didn't see her. He put the candle down on the table and only then looked around cautiously.

"Mark!" she said softly. "Mark!"

His face was lighted. Ben's face, she thought, and something of hers. Then his face twisted and when she took a step toward him, he took a step backward.

"Mark?" she said again, but now she could feel a hard, cold hand squeezing her heart, making it painful for her to breathe. What had they done to him? She took another step.

"Why did you come here?" he yelled suddenly. "This is *my* room! Why did you come back? I hate you!" he screamed.

Chapter 19

The cold hand squeezed harder. Molly felt for the door-frame behind her and held it tightly. "Why do you come here?" she whispered. "Why?"

"It's all your fault! You spoiled everything. They laugh at me and lock me up . . ."

"And you still come here. Why?"

Suddenly he darted to the workbench and swept it clean. The elephant, the heads, the foot, hands, everything crashed to the floor and he jumped up and down on the pieces, sobbing incoherently, screaming sounds that were not words. Molly didn't move. The rampage stopped as abruptly as it began. Mark looked down at the gray dust, the fragments that remained.

"I'll tell you why you come back," Molly said quietly. She still held the doorframe hard. "They punish you by locking you up in a small room, don't they? And it doesn't frighten you. In the small room you can hear yourself, can't you? In your mind's eye you see the clay, the stone you will shape. You see the form emerging, and it is almost as if you are simply freeing it, allowing it to come into being. That other self that speaks to you, it knows what the shape is in the clay. It tells you through your hands, in dreams, in images that no one but you can see. And they tell you this is sick, or bad, or disobedient. Don't they?"

He was watching her now. "Don't they?" she repeated. He nodded.

"Mark, they'll never understand. They can't hear that other self whispering, always whispering. They can't see the pictures. They'll never hear or get a glimpse of that other self. The brothers and sisters overwhelm it. The whisper becomes fainter, the images dimmer, until finally they are gone, the other self gives up. Perhaps it dies." She paused and looked at him, then said softly, "You come here because you can find that self here, just as I could find my other self here. And that's more important than anything they can give you, or take away from you."

He looked down at the floor, at the shambles of the pieces he had made, and wiped his face with his arm. "Mother," he said, and stopped.

Now Molly moved. Somehow she reached him before he could speak again and she held him tightly and he held her, and they both wept.

"I'm sorry I busted everything."

"You'll make more."

"I wanted to show you."

"I looked at them all. They were very good. The hands especially."

"They were hard. The fingers were funny, but I couldn't make them not funny."

"Hands are the hardest of all."

He finally pushed away from her slightly, and she let him go. He wiped his face again. "Are you going to hide here?"

"No. They'll be back looking for me."

"Why did you come here?"

"To keep a promise," she said softly. "Do you remember our last walk up the hill, you wanted to climb to the top, and I said next time? Remember?"

"I've got some food we can take," he said excitedly. "I hide it here so when I get hungry I'll have something."

"Good. We'll use it. We'll start as soon as it gets light enough to see."

It was a beautiful day, with high thin clouds in the north, the rest of the sky unmarred, breathtakingly clear. Each hill, each mountain in the distance, was sharply outlined; no haze had formed yet, the breeze was gentle and warm. The silence was so complete that the woman and boy were both reluctant to break it with speech, and they walked quietly. When they paused to rest, she smiled at him and he grinned back and then lay with his hands under his head and stared at the sky.

"What's in your big pack?" he asked as they climbed later. She had made a small pack for him to carry, and she still carried the laundry bag, now strapped to her back.

"You'll see," she said. "A surprise."

And later he said, "It's farther than it looked, isn't it? Will we get there before dark?"

"Long before dark," she said. "But it is far. Do you want to rest again?"

He nodded and they sat under a spruce tree. The spruces were coming down the mountains, she thought, recalling in detail old forestry maps of the region.

"Do you still read much?" she asked.

Mark shifted uneasily and looked at the sky, then at the trees, and finally grunted noncommittally.

"So did I," she said. "The old house is full of books, isn't it? They're so brittle, though, you have to be careful with them. After you went to sleep every night I sat up and read everything in the house."

"Did you read the one about Indians?" he asked, and rolled over on his stomach and propped his head up in his cupped hands. "They knew how to do everything, make fires, make canoes, tents, everything."

"And there's one about how boys, a club or something, used to go camping and relearn all the Indian methods. It can still be done," she said dreamily.

"And what you can eat in the woods, and stuff like that? I read that one."

They walked, rested, talked about the books in the old house, talked about the things Mark planned to make, climbed some more, and late in the afternoon they came to the summit of the mountain and looked down over the entire valley, all the way to the Shenandoah River in the distance.

Molly found a spot that was level and sheltered, and Mark finally got to see the surprise she had prepared for him: blankets, some preserved food, fruits, meat, six pieces of cornbread, and corn to pop over the open fire. After they ate, they pushed spruce needles into mounds and Mark rolled up in his blanket and yawned.

"What's that noise?" he asked after a moment.

"The trees," Molly said softly. "The wind moves up there even when we can't feel it down here, and the trees and wind tell each other secrets."

Mark laughed and yawned again. "They're talking about us," he said. Molly smiled in the dark. "I can almost hear the words," he said.

"We're the first human beings they've seen in a long time," she said. "They're probably surprised that there are any more of us around."

"I won't go back either!" Mark shouted at her. They

122

had eaten the last of the cornbread and dried apples, and the fire was out, the ground smoothed around it.

"Mark, listen to me. They will put me back in the breeders' compound. Do you understand? I won't be allowed out again. They will give me medicines that will keep me very quiet and I won't know anything or anyone. That will be my life back there. But you? You have so much to learn. Read all the books in the old house, learn everything you can from them. And one day you might decide to leave, but not until you're a man, Mark."

"I'm staying with you."

She shook her head. "Remember the voices of the trees? When you're lonely, go into the woods and let the trees talk to you. Maybe you'll hear my voice there too. I'll never be far away, if you listen."

"Where are you going?"

"Down the river, to the Shenandoah, to look for your father. They won't bother me there."

Tears stood in his eyes, but he didn't shed them. He lifted his pack and put his arms through the harness. They started down the mountain again. Midway down they stopped. "You can see the valley from here," Molly said. "I won't go any farther with you."

He didn't look at her.

"Good-bye, Mark."

"Will the trees talk to me if you're not there?"

"Always. If you listen. The others are looking to the cities to save them, and the cities are dead and ruined. But the trees are alive, and when you need them, they'll talk to you. I promise you that, Mark."

Now he came to her and hugged her hard. "I love you," he said. Then he turned and started down the hill, and she stood watching him until her tears blinded her and she could no longer see him.

She waited until he emerged from the woods and started across the cleared valley. Then she turned and walked south, toward the Shenandoah. All that night the trees whispered to her. When she awakened, she knew the trees had accepted her; they didn't stop their murmuring as they had always done in the past when she stirred about. Over and under and through their voices she could hear the voice of the river, still far off, and beyond it, she was certain she could hear Ben's voice, growing stronger as she hurried toward him. She could smell the fresh water now; and the voices of the river and the trees and Ben's voice blended as they called to her to hurry. She ran toward him joyously. He caught her and together they floated down, down into the cool, sweet water.

PART THREE

At the
Still Point

Chapter 20

The new dormitory was dark except for the pale lights spaced regularly in the halls. Mark darted down the hallway and went inside one of the rooms. There was too little light to make out details; only the shapes of sleeping boys on the white beds could be seen at first. The windows were dark shadows.

Mark stood by the door silently and waited for his eyes to adjust; the shapes emerged from darkness and became dark and light areas—arms, faces, hair. His bare feet made no sound as he approached the first cot, and again he stopped; this time his wait was shorter. The boy on the cot didn't stir. Slowly Mark opened a small bottle of ink, made from blackberries and walnuts, and dipped a fine brush into it. He had been holding the ink next to his chest; it was warm. Moving very carefully, he leaned over the sleeping boy and quickly painted the numeral 1 on the boy's cheek. The boy didn't move.

Mark backed away from the first bed, went to another, and again paused to make certain the boy was sleeping deeply. This time he painted a 2.

Presently he left the room and hurried to the next one. He repeated the procedure there. If the boy was sleeping on his stomach, his face buried in the covers, Mark painted a number on his hand or arm.

Shortly before dawn Mark put the top back on his bottle of ink and crept to his own room, a cubicle large enough to contain only his cot and some shelves above it. He put the ink on a shelf, making no attempt to hide it. Then he sat cross-legged on his bed and waited.

He was a slightly built boy, with dark, abundant hair that made his head seem overlarge, not conspicuously so, but noticeable if one examined him closely. The only startling feature was his eyes, a blue of such intensity and depth that they were unforgettable. He sat patiently, a slight smile playing on his lips, deepening, leaving, forming again. The light outside his window brightened; it was spring and the air had a luminosity that was missing in other seasons.

Now he could hear voices, and his smile deepened, widened his mouth. The voices were loud and angry. He began to laugh, and was weak from laughter when his door opened and five boys entered. There was so little room they had to line up with their legs tight against his cot.

"Good morning, One, Two, Three, Four, Five," Mark said, choking on the words with new laughter. They flushed angrily and he doubled over, unable to contain himself.

"Where is he?" Miriam asked. She had entered the conference room and was still standing at the door.

Barry was at the head of the table. "Sit down, Miriam," he said. "You know what he did?"

She sat at the other end of the long table and nodded. "Who doesn't? It's all over, that's all anyone's talking about." She glanced at the others. The doctors were there, Lawrence, Thomas, Sara . . . A full council meeting.

"Has he said anything?" she asked.

Thomas shrugged. "He didn't deny it."

"Did he say why he did it?"

"So he could tell them apart," Barry said.

For a brief moment Miriam thought she heard a trace of amusement in his voice, but nothing of it showed on his face. She felt tight with fury, as if somehow she might be held responsible for the boy, for his aberrant behavior. She wouldn't have it, she thought angrily. She leaned forward, her hands pressed on the tabletop, and demanded, "What are you going to do about him? Why don't you control him?"

"This meeting has been called to discuss that," Barry said. "Have you any suggestions?"

She shook her head, still furious, unappeased. She shouldn't even be there, she thought. The boy was nothing to her; she had avoided contact with him from the beginning. By inviting her to the meeting, they had made a link that in reality didn't exist. Again she shook her head and now she leaned back in her chair, as if to divorce herself from the proceedings.

"We'll have to punish him," Lawrence said after a moment of silence. "The only question is how."

127

How? Barry wondered. Not isolation; he thrived on it, sought it out at every turn. Not extra work; he was still working off his last escapade. Only three months ago he had gotten inside the girls' rooms and mixed up their ribbons and sashes so that no group had anything matching. It had taken hours for them to get everything back in place. And now this, and this time it would take weeks for the ink to wear off.

Lawrence spoke again, his voice thoughtful, a slight frown on his face. "We should admit we made a mistake," he said. "There is no place for him among us. The boys his age reject him; he has no friends. He is capricious and willful, brilliant and moronic by turns. We made a mistake with him. Now his pranks are only that, childish pranks, but in five years? Ten years? What can we expect from him in the future?" He directed his questions at Barry.

"In five years he will be downriver, as you know. It is during the next few years that we have to find a way to manage him better."

Sara moved slightly in her chair, and Barry turned to her. "We have found that he is not made repentant by being isolated," Sara said. "It is his nature to be an isolate, therefore by not allowing him the privacy he craves we will have found the correct punishment for him."

Barry shook his head. "We discussed that before," he said. "It would not be fair to the others to force them to accept him, an outsider. He is disruptive among his peers; they should not be punished along with him."

"Not his peers," Sara said emphatically. "You and your brothers voted to keep him here in order to study him for clues in how to train others to endure separate existences. It is your responsibility to accept him among yourselves, to let his punishment be to have to live with you under your watchful eyes. Or else admit Lawrence is right, that we made a mistake, and that it is better to correct the mistake now than to let it continue to compound."

"You would punish us for the misdeeds of the boy?" Bruce asked.

"That boy wouldn't be here if it were not for you and your brothers," Sara said distinctly. "If you'll recall, at our first meeting concerning him, the rest of us voted to rid ourselves of him. We foresaw trouble from the beginning, and it was your arguments about his possible usefulness that finally swayed us. If you want to keep him, then you keep him with you, under your observation, away from the other children, who are constantly being hurt by him and his pranks. He is an isolate, an aberration, a troublemaker. These meetings have become more frequent, his pranks more destructive. How many more hours must we spend discussing his behavior?"

"You know that isn't practical," Barry said impatiently. "We're in the lab half the time, in the breeders' quarters, in the hospital. Those aren't places for a child of ten."

"Then get rid of him," Sara said. She sat back now and crossed her arms over her chest.

Barry looked at Miriam, whose lips were tightly compressed. She met his gaze coldly. He turned to Lawrence.

"Can you think of any other way?" Lawrence asked. "We've tried everything we can think of, and nothing has worked. Those boys were angry enough to kill him this morning. Next time there might be violence. Have you thought what violence would do to this community?"

They were a people without violence in their history. Physical punishment had never been considered, because it was impossible to hurt one without hurting others equally. That didn't apply to Mark, Barry thought suddenly, but he didn't say it. The thought of hurting him, of causing him physical pain, was repugnant. He glanced at his brothers and saw the same confusion on their faces that he was feeling. They couldn't abandon the boy. He did hold clues about how man lived alone; they needed him. His mind refused to probe more deeply than that: they needed to study him. There were so many things about human beings that were incomprehensible to them; Mark might be the link that would enable them to understand.

The fact that the boy was Ben's child, that Ben and his brothers had been as one, had nothing to do with it. He felt no particular bond to the boy. None at all. If anyone could feel such a bond, it should be Miriam, he thought, and looked at her for a sign that she felt something. Her face was stony, her eyes avoided him. Too rigid, he realized, too cold.

And if that were so, he thought coolly, as if thinking about an experiment with insensate material, then it truly was a mistake to keep the boy with them. If that one child had the power to hurt the Miriam sisters as well as the Barry brothers, he was a mistake. It was unthinkable that an outsider could somehow reach in and twist the old hurts so much that they became new hurts, with even more destructive aftermaths.

"We could do it," Bob said suddenly. "There are risks, of course, but we could manage him. In four years," he continued, looking now at Sara, "he'll be sent out with the road crew, and from then on, he won't be a threat to any of us. But we will need him when we begin to reach out to try to understand the cities. He can scout out the paths, survive alone in the woods without danger of mental breakdown through separation. We'll need him."

Sara nodded. "And if we have to have another meeting such as this one, can we agree today that it will be our final meeting?"

The Barry brothers exchanged glances, then reluctantly nodded and Barry said, "Agreed. We manage him or get rid of him."

The doctors returned to Barry's office, where Mark was waiting for them. He was standing at the window, a small dark figure against the glare of sunlight. He turned to face them, and his own face seemed featureless. The sun touched his hair and made it gleam with red-gold highlights.

"What will you do with me?" he asked. His voice was steady.

"Come over here and sit down," Barry said, taking his place behind the desk. The boy crossed the room and sat on a straight chair, perching on the extreme front of it, as if ready to leap up and run.

"Relax," Bob said, and sat on the edge of the desk, swinging his leg as he regarded the boy. When the five brothers were in the room it seemed very crowded suddenly. The boy looked from one to another of them and finally turned his attention to Barry. He didn't ask again.

Barry told him about the meeting, and watching him, he thought, there was a little of Ben, and a little of Molly, and for the rest, he had gone into the distant past, dipped into the gene pool, had come up with strangers' genes, and he was unlike anyone else in the valley. Mark listened intently, the way he listened in class when he was interested. His grasp was immediate and thorough.

"Why do they think what I did was so awful?" he asked when Barry became silent.

Barry looked at his brothers helplessly. This was how it

was going to be, he wanted to say to them. No common grounds for understanding. He was an alien in every way.

Suddenly Mark asked, "How can I tell you apart?"

"There's no need for you to tell us apart," Barry said firmly.

Mark stood up then. "Should I go get my stuff, bring it to your place?"

"Yes. Now, while the others are in school. And come right back."

Mark nodded. At the door he paused, glanced at each in turn once more, and said, "Maybe just a tiny, tiny touch of paint, on the tips of the ears, or something . . . ?" He opened the door and ran out, and they could hear him laughing as he raced down the hall.

Chapter 21

Barry glanced about the lecture room and spotted Mark in the rear, looking sleepy and bored. He shrugged; let him be bored. Three of the brothers were working in the labs, and the fourth was busy in the breeders' quarters; that left the lecture, and Mark had to sit through it if it killed him.

"The problem we raised yesterday, if you'll recall," Barry said then, referring briefly to his notes, "is that we have yet to discover the cause of the decline of the clone strains after the fourth generation. The only way we have got around this to date is through constant replenishment of our stocks by the use of sexually reproduced babies who are cloned before the third month *in utero*. In this way we have been able to maintain our families of brothers and sisters, but admittedly this is not the ideal solution. Can any of you tell me what some of the obvious drawbacks to this system are?" He paused and glanced about. "Karen?"

"There is a slight difference between the babies cloned in the laboratory and those born of human mothers. There is the prenatal influence and also the birth trauma that might alter the sexually reproduced person."

"Very good," Barry said. "Comments, anyone?"

"In the beginning they waited two years before they cloned the babies," Stuart said. "Now we don't, and that makes the family almost as close as if they were all clones."

Barry nodded, then pointed to Carl. "If the human baby has a birth defect, caused by a birth trauma, he can be aborted, and still the cloned babies will be all right."

"That's hardly in the nature of a drawback," Barry said, smiling. There was an answering ripple of amusement throughout the class.

He waited a moment, then said, "The genetic pool is unpredictable, its past is unknown, its constituents so varied that when the process is not regulated and controlled, there is always the danger of producing unwanted characteristics. And the even more dangerous threat of losing talents that are important to our community." He allowed time for this to be grasped, then continued. "The only way to ensure our future, to ensure continuity, is through perfecting the process of cloning, and for this reason we need to expand our facilities, increase our researchers, locate a source of materials to replace what is wearing out and equip the new laboratories, and we need to complete a safe link to that source or sources."

A hand was raised. Barry nodded. "What if we can't find enough equipment in good condition soon enough?"

"Then we will have to go to human implantation of the cloned fetus. We have done this in a number of cases, and we have the methods, but it is wasteful of our few human resources, and it would necessitate changing our timetable drastically to use the breeders this way." He looked over the class, then continued. "Our goal is to remove the need for sexual reproduction. Then we will be able to plan our future. If we need road builders, we can clone fifty or a hundred for this purpose, train them from infancy, and send them out to fulfill their destiny. We can clone boat builders, sailors, send them out to the sea to locate the course of the fish our first explorers discovered in the Potomac. A hundred farmers, to relieve those who would prefer to be working over test tubes than hoeing rows of carrots."

Another ripple of laughter passed over the students.

Barry smiled also; without exception they all worked their hours in the fields.

"For the first time since mankind walked the face of the earth," he said, "there will be no misfits."

"And no geniuses," a voice said lazily, and he looked to the rear of the class to see Mark, still slouched down in his chair, his blue eyes bright, grinning slightly. Deliberately he winked at Barry, then closed both eyes again, and apparently returned to sleep.

"I'll tell you a story if you want," Mark said. He stood in the aisle between two rows of three beds each. The Carver brothers had all had appendicitis simultaneously. They looked at him from both sides, and one of them nodded. They were thirteen.

"Once there was a woji," he said, moving to the window, where he sat cross-legged on a chair with the light behind him.

'What's a woji?"

"If you ask questions, I won't tell it," Mark said. "You'll see as I go along. This woji lived deep in the woods, and every year when winter came he nearly froze to death. That was because the icy rains soaked him and the snow covered him over, and he had nothing at all to eat because the leaves all fell and he ate leaves. One year he got an idea, and he went to a big spruce tree and told it his idea. At first the spruce tree wouldn't even consider his suggestion. The woji didn't go away, though. He kept telling the spruce tree his idea over and over, and finally the spruce tree thought, What did he have to lose? Why not try it? So the spruce tree told the woji to go ahead. For days and days the woji worked on the leaves, rolling them up and making them over into needles. He used some of the needles to sew them all tightly to the tree branches. Then he climbed to the very top of the spruce tree and yelled at the ice wind, and laughed at it and said it couldn't hurt him now, because he had a home and food to eat all winter.

"The other trees heard him and laughed, and they began to tell each other about the crazy little woji who yelled at the ice wind, and finally the last tree, at the place where the trees end and the snow begins, heard the story. It was a maple tree, and it laughed until its leaves shook. The ice wind heard it laughing and came blowing up, storming and throwing ice, and demanded to know what

133

was so funny. The maple tree told the ice wind about the crazy little woji who had challenged his powers to take the leaves off the trees, and the ice wind became madder and madder. It blew harder and harder. The maple leaves turned red and gold with fear and then fell to the ground, and the tree stood naked before the wind. The ice wind blew south and the other trees shivered and turned color and dropped their leaves.

"Finally the ice wind came to the spruce tree and screamed for the woji to come out. He wouldn't. He was hidden deep in the spruce needles where the ice wind couldn't see him or touch him. The wind blew harder and the spruce tree shivered, but its needles held tight and they didn't turn color at all. The ice wind now called up the ice rain to help, and the spruce tree was covered with icicles, but the needles held on and the woji stayed dry and warm. Then the ice wind got madder than ever and called the snow to help, and it snowed deeper and deeper until the spruce tree looked like a mountain of snow, but deep inside, the woji was warm and content, close to the trunk of the tree, and soon the tree shrugged and the snow fell away from it and it knew the ice wind could no longer hurt it.

"The ice wind howled about the tree all winter, but the needles held tight and the woji stayed snug and warm, and if he nibbled on a needle now and then the tree forgave him, because he had taught it not to cringe and turn colors and stand naked all winter shivering before the ice wind just because that's what the other trees did. When spring came the other trees begged the woji to turn their leaves into needles too, and the woji finally agreed. But only for those trees that hadn't laughed at him. And that's why the evergreen trees are evergreen."

"Is that all?" demanded one of the Carver brothers.

Mark nodded.

"What's a woji? You said we'd know when the story was over."

"That's the thing that lives in spruce trees," Mark said, grinning. "He's invisible, but sometimes you can hear him. He's usually laughing." He jumped down from the chair. "I've gotta go." He trotted to the door.

"There's no such thing!" one of the brothers yelled.

Mark opened the door and looked out cautiously. He wasn't supposed to be there. Then he looked over his shoulder and asked the brothers, "How do you know?

Have you ever gone out there to try to hear him laughing?" He left them quickly before a doctor or nurse showed up.

Before dawn one morning near the end of May the families began to gather at the dock once more to see off the six boats and crews of brothers and sisters. There was no gaiety now, there had been no party the night before. Barry stood near Lewis and watched the preparations. They were both silent.

There was no way to draw back now, Barry knew. They had to have the supplies that were in the big cities, or die. That was the alternative they had. The toll had been too high, and he knew no way to reduce it. Special training had helped a little, but not enough. Sending groups of brothers and sisters had helped, but not enough. So far in the four trips downriver, they had lost twenty-two people, and another twenty-four had been affected by the ordeal, perhaps permanently affected, and through them their families. Thirty-six of them this time. They were to stay out until frost, or until the river started its usual fall rise, whichever was first.

Some of them were to build a bypass around the falls; some would dig a canal to link the Shenandoah to the Potomac to avoid the danger of the rough water they now had to face with each trip. Two groups were to go back and forth between the falls and Washington and bring out the supplies that had been found the previous year. One group was on river patrol, to clear the rapids that the capricious rivers renewed each winter.

How many would return this time? Barry wondered. They would stay out longer than any of the others had; their work was more dangerous. How many?

"Having a building at the falls will help," Lewis said suddenly. "It was the feeling of being exposed that made it particularly bad."

Barry nodded. It was what they all reported—they felt exposed, watched. They felt the world was pressing in on them, that the trees moved closer as soon as the sun set. He glanced at Lewis, forgot what he had started to say, and instead watched a tic that had appeared at the corner of his mouth. Lewis was clenching his fists; he stared at the dwindling boats, and the tic jerked and vanished, jerked again.

"Are you all right?" Barry asked. Lewis shook himself

135

and looked away from the river. "Lewis? Is anything wrong?"

"No. I'll see you later." He strode away swiftly.

"There's something about being in the woods in the dark especially that has a traumatic effect," Barry said later to his brothers. They were in the dormitory room they shared; at the far end, apart from them, sat Mark, cross-legged on a cot, watching them. Barry ignored him. They were so used to his presence now that they seldom noticed him at all, unless he got in the way. They usually noticed if he vanished, as he frequently did.

The brothers waited. That was well known, the fear of the silent woods.

"In training the children to prepare for their future roles, we should incorporate experience in living in the woods for prolonged periods. They could start with an afternoon, then go to an overnight camping expedition, and so on, until they are out for several weeks at a time."

Bruce shook his head. "What if they were adversely affected to the point where they could not go out on the expeditions at all? We could lose ten years of hard work that way."

"We could try it with a sample," Barry said. "Two groups, one male, one female. If they show distress after the first exposure, we can slow it down, or even postpone it until they are a year or two older. Eventually they'll have to go out there; we might be able to make it easier on them."

They no longer were holding the number of like clones to six, but had increased them to ten of each group. "We have eighty children almost eleven years old," Bruce said. "In four years they will be ready. If the statistics hold up, we'll lose two-fifths of them within the first four months they are away, either to accidents or psychological stress. I think it's worth a try to condition them to the woods and living apart beforehand."

"They have to have supervision," Bob said. "One of us."

"We're too old," Bruce said with a grimace. "Besides, we know we're susceptible to the psychological stress. Remember Ben."

"Exactly," Bob said. "We're too old to make any difference here. Our young brothers are taking over our functions more and more, and their little brothers are ready to step into their places when needed. We are expendable," he concluded.

"He's right," Barry said reluctantly. "It's our experiment, our obligation to see it through. Draw lots?"

"Take turns," Bruce said. "Each of us to have a crack at it before it's over."

"Can I go too?" Mark asked suddenly, and they all turned to look at him.

"No," Barry said brusquely. "We know you're not hurt by the woods. We don't want anything to go wrong with this, no pranks, no tricks, no bravado."

"You'll get lost then," Mark shouted. He jumped down from his cot and ran to the door and paused there to yell back, "You'll be out in the woods with a bunch of crying babies and you'll all go crazy and the woji will die laughing at you!"

A week later Bob led the first group of boys up into the woods behind the valley. Each carried a small pack with his lunch in it. They wore long pants and shirts and boots. Watching them leave, Barry could not banish the thought that he should have been the first to try it with them. His idea, his risk. He shook his head angrily. What risk? They were going for a hike in the woods. They would have lunch, turn around, and come back down. He caught Mark's glance and for a moment they stared at each other, the man and boy, curiously alike, yet so distant from each other that no similarity was possible.

Mark broke the stare and looked again at the boys, who were climbing steadily and coming to the thicker growths. Soon they were invisible among the trees.

"They'll get lost," he said.

Bruce shrugged. "Not in one hour or two," he said. "At noon they'll eat, turn around, and come back."

The sky was deep blue with puffs of white clouds and a very high band of cirrus clouds with no apparent beginning or end. It would be noon in less than two hours.

Stubbornly Mark shook his head, but he said nothing more. He returned to class, and then went to the dining room for lunch. After lunch he was due to work in the garden for two hours, and he was there when Barry sent for him.

"They aren't back yet," Barry said when Mark entered the office. "Why were you so certain they would be lost?"

"Because they don't understand about the woods," Mark said. "They don't see things."

"What things?"

Mark shrugged helplessly. "Things," he said again. He looked from one brother to another and again shrugged.

"Could you find them?" Bruce asked. His voice sounded harsh, and deep frown lines cut into his forehead.

"Yes."

"Let's go," Barry said.

"The two of us?" Mark asked.

"Yes."

Mark looked doubtful. "I could do it faster alone," he said.

Barry felt a shuldder start, and drew himself away from his desk with a brusque motion. He was holding himself rigidly under control now. "Not you alone," he said. "I want you to show me those things you see, how you can find your way where there's no path. Let's go before it gets any later." He glanced at the boy in his short tunic, barefooted. "Go get changed," he said.

"This is all right for up there," Mark said. "There's nothing under the trees up there."

Barry thought about his words as they headed for the woods. He watched the boy, now ahead of him, now at his side, sniffing the air happily, at home in the silent, dim woods.

They moved quickly and very soon they were deep in the forest where the trees had reached mature growth and made a canopy overhead that excluded the sun completely. No shadows, no way to discover directions, Barry thought, breathing hard as he worked to keep up with the nimble boy. Mark never hesitated, never paused, but moved rapidly with certainty, and Barry didn't know what clues he found, how he knew to go this way and not that. He wanted to ask, but he needed his breath for climbing. He was sweating, and his feet felt like lead as he followed the boy.

"Let's rest a minute," he said. He sat on the ground, his back against a mammoth tree trunk. Mark had been ahead of him, and now he trotted back and squatted a few feet away.

"Tell me what you look for," Barry said after a moment. "Show me a sign of their passage there."

Mark looked surprised at the demand. "Everything shows they came this way," he said. He pointed to the tree that supported Barry's back. "That's a bitternut hickory

138

tree—see, nuts." He brushed the dirt aside and uncovered several nuts. They were half rotted. "The boys found some and threw them. And there," he said, pointing, "see that sprout. Someone bent it to the ground, it still isn't straight again. And the marks of their feet, scuffing the dirt and leaves on the forest floor. It's like a sign saying, this way, this way."

Barry could see the difference when Mark showed him, but when he looked in another direction, he thought he could see scuff marks there also.

"Water," Mark said. "That's a runoff trail from melting snow. It's different."

"How did you learn about the woods? Molly?"

Mark nodded. "She couldn't get lost ever. She couldn't forget how things looked, and if she saw them again, she knew. She taught me. Or else I was born with it, and she showed me how to use it. I can't get lost either."

"Can you teach others?"

"I guess so. Now that I showed you, you could lead, couldn't you?" He had turned his back, scanning the woods, and now faced Barry again. "You know which way to start, don't you?"

Barry looked carefully about them. The scuff marks were on the path they had just made, where Mark had pointed them out. He saw the water trail, and looked harder for the trail they should follow. There was nothing. He looked again at Mark, who was grinning. "No," he said. "I don't know which way to go now."

Mark laughed. "Because it's rocky," he said. "Come on." He started again, this time keeping to the edge of a rocky trail.

"How did you know?" Barry asked. "There's no sign of them among the rocks."

"Because there was no sign anywhere else. It was all that was left. There!" He pointed, and there was another bent tree, this one stronger, older, more firmly rooted. "Someone pulled that spruce down and let it spring back up. Probably more than one did, because it's still not quite straight, and you can see now that the rocks have been kicked around."

The rocky trail deepened and became a creek bed. Mark watched the edges carefully and soon turned again, pointing to scuff marks as he went. The woods were deeper, the gloom more intense here. Thick evergreen trees covered the slope they began to descend, and sometimes they had to wind their way among the branches that touched one another in the spruce forest. The floor was brown, springy with generations of needles.

Barry found himself holding his breath in order not to disturb the silence of the great forest, and he understood why the others talked of a presence, something that watched as they moved among the trees. The silence was so intense, it was like a dream world where mouths open and close and no noise is heard, where musicians' instruments are strangely muted, where one screams and screams silently. Behind him he could sense the trees moving in closer, closer.

Then, suddenly, as if it had been growing a long time and he only now had become aware of it, he found that he was listening to something over and beyond the silence, something that was like a voice, or voices mingling in whispers too distant to make out the words. Like Molly, he thought, and a shiver of fear raced through him. The voices faded. Mark had stopped and was looking about again.

"They doubled back here," he said. "They must have had lunch up there and started back, but here they lost their way. See, they went over too far, and kept going farther and farther from the way they had come."

Barry could see nothing to indicate they had done that, but he knew he was helpless in that dark forest and he could only follow the boy wherever he led.

They climbed again and the spruces thinned out and now there were aspens and cottonwoods bordering a stream.

"You'd think they'd know they hadn't seen this before," Mark said with disgust. He was moving faster now. He stopped again and a grin came and went, leaving him looking worried. "Some of them began to run here," he said. "Wait. I'll see if they regrouped ahead, or if we have to find any of them." He vanished before he finished speaking, and Barry sank to the ground to wait for him. The voices came back almost instantly. He looked at the trees that seemed unmoving, and knew that the branches high above were stirring in the wind, that they made the voicelike whispering, but still he strained to hear the words over and over. He put his head down on his knees and tried to will the voices into silence.

His legs were throbbing, and he was very hot. He could feel trickles of sweat running down his back, and he hunched over more so his shirt was snug across his shoulders, absorbing the sweat. They couldn't send their people out to live in the forests, he knew. This was a hostile environment, with a spirit of malevolency that would stifle them, craze them, kill them. He could feel the presence now, pressing in on him, drawing closer, feeling him . . . Abruptly he stood up and started to follow Mark.

Chapter 22

Barry heard voices again, this time real voices, childish voices, and he waited.

"Bob, are you all right?" he called when his brother came into view. Bob looked bedraggled and there was dirt on his face; he nodded and waved, breathing heavily.

"They were climbing toward the knob," Mark said, suddenly at Barry's side. He had come upon him from a different direction, invisible until he spoke.

Now the boys were straggling into the same area, and they looked worse than Bob. Some of them had been crying. Just as Mark had predicted, Barry thought.

"We thought we might be able to see where we were if we climbed higher," Bob said, glancing at Mark, as if for approval.

Mark shook his head. "Always go down, follow a stream, if you don't know where you are," he said. "It'll go to a bigger stream, then finally to the river, and you can follow it back to where you have to go."

The boys were watching Mark with open admiration. "Do you know the way down?" one of them asked.

Mark nodded.

"Rest a few minutes first," Barry said. The voices were gone now, the woods merely dark woods, uninhabited by anything at all.

Mark led them down quickly, not the way they had gone up, not the way he had followed them, but in a more direct line that had them looking over the valley within half an hour.

"It was a mistake to risk them like that!" Lawrence said angrily. It was the first council meeting since the adventure in the forest.

"It's necessary to teach them to live in the woods," Barry said.

"They won't have to live out there. The best thing we can do with the woods is clear them as quickly as possible. We'll have a shelter for them down below the falls where they'll live, just as they live here, in a clearing."

"As soon as you're away from this clearing, the woods make themselves felt," Barry said. "Everyone has reported the same terror, the feeling of being closed in by the trees, of being threatened by them. They have to learn how to live with that."

"They'll never live in the woods," Lawrence said with finality. "They'll live in a dormitory building on the bank of the river, and when they travel, they'll go by boat, and when they stop, they'll stop in another clearing where there is decent shelter, where the woods have been beaten back and will be kept back." He emphasized his words by hitting his fist on the tabletop as he spoke.

Barry regarded Lawrence bitterly. "We can run the laboratories five more years, Lawrence! Five years! We have almost nine hundred people in this valley right now. Most of them are children, being trained to forage for us, to find those things we need to survive. And they won't find them on the banks of your tamed rivers! They're going to have to make expeditions to New York, to Philadelphia, to New Jersey. And who's going to go before them and clear back the woods for them? We train those children now to cope with the woods, or we'll die, all of us!"

"It was a mistake to rush into this," Lawrence said. "We should have waited until we knew how much we could find and get back to the valley before we got into this so deeply."

Barry nodded. "You can't have it both ways," he said. "We made the decision. Every year we wait, the less there is for us to forage in the cities. And we have to salvage what we can. Without it we die anyway, more slowly perhaps than with the timetable we now have, but in the end it would be the same. We can't exist without the tools, the hardware, the information that's in the cities. And now we're committed to this path, and we have to do our best to see that these children are equipped as well as possible to survive when we send them out."

Five years, he thought, that's all they needed. Five years to find a source of laboratory equipment—tubing, stainless steel tanks, centrifuges . . . Computer components, wiring, wafers . . . They knew the things they needed had been stored carefully, they had the papers to prove that. They would find the right warehouses, weathertight, dry, with acres of well-stacked shelves. It was a gamble, producing so many children in so short a time, but a gamble they had taken knowingly, aware of the consequences if anything went wrong along the way. They might be hungry before the five years were over; whether or not the valley could adequately feed over a thousand people had been endlessly debated. For the kind of restocking they required, they needed a lot of people, and in five years they would know if they had gambled foolishly.

Four hundred fifty children between five and eleven years, that was what was in the kitty, Barry thought. That was the extent of the gamble. And in four years the first eighty of them would leave the valley, possibly forever, but if they returned, if even a few of them returned with materials, with information about Philadelphia or New York, with anything of value, the gamble would have paid off.

It was agreed that the training program as outlined by Barry should be continued on a trial basis, risking no more than three groups—thirty children. And further, if the children were psychologically damaged by the equipment, they were not to be salvaged, and the experiment would be discontinued immediately. Barry left the meeting satisfied.

"What will I get out of it?" Mark demanded.

"What do you mean?"

"I mean, you get a teacher, and the brothers and sisters get training. What do I get?"

"What do you want? You'll have companionship. More than you have now."

"They won't play with me," Mark said. "They'll listen and do what I say because they're afraid and they know I'm not, but they won't play with me. I want my own room again."

Barry glanced at his brothers and knew they would all agree to that instantly. It had been a nuisance having the boy in their communal bedroom. By mutual consent they had not dragged the mat out in his presence, and their talk had been censored—when they remembered he was there. Barry nodded. "Not back in the dormitory, here in this building."

"That's all right."

"Then here's what we'll do. Once a week each group will go out, one hour at a time to start with, and not more than a few minutes from a place where they can see the valley. After several exposures of this limited duration and distance, you'll take them farther, keep them longer. Are there games you could play with them in the woods to help them become accustomed to being there?" There was no longer any question of not including Mark in this phase of the training.

Mark sat on a branch hidden by thick foliage from below and watched the boys stumbling about the edges of the clearing, looking for the path he had left them to follow. It was as if they were blind, he thought wonderingly. All they really cared about was staying close together, not becoming separated even momentarily. This was the third time this week Mark had tried this game with the clones; the other two groups had failed also.

At first he had enjoyed leading them out into the woods; their frank admiration of him had been pleasant, unexpected, and for once he had felt the differences that separated them might be lessened when they learned some of the things he knew, when they could all play together among the whispering trees. He knew now such hopes had been wrong. The differences were more pronounced than ever, and the early admiration was turning into something else, something he could not really understand. They seemed to dislike him more, to be almost afraid of him, certainly resentful of him.

He whistled and watched the reaction pass over them all simultaneously, like grass being blown by a gust of wind. Even knowing the direction, they were not able to find his trail. Disgustedly he left the tree, sliding part way, dropping agilely from branch to branch where it was too rough to slide. He joined the boys and glanced at Barry, who also looked disgusted.

"Are we going back now?" one of the boys asked.

"No," Barry said. "Mark, I want you to take two of the boys a short distance away, try to hide with them. Let's see if the others can find you."

Mark nodded. He glanced at the ten boys and knew it

made no difference which two went with him. He pointed to the two nearest him and turned and went into the woods, the boys at his heels.

Again he left a trail that anyone with eyes could follow, and as soon as they were out of sight of the larger group he began to circle around to get behind the boys in the clearing, not trying for distance at all, since they couldn't follow a trail even three feet. Finally he stopped. He put his fingers to his lips and the other two nodded, and they sat down to wait. They looked desperately afraid, sat touching at the arms, their legs touching. Mark could hear their brothers now, not following the trail, but coming straight for them. Too fast, he thought suddenly. The way they were rushing was dangerous.

The brothers he was with jumped up excitedly, and in a moment the others rushed into sight. Their reunion was jubilant and triumphant, and even Barry looked pleased. Mark drew back and watched, his warning about rushing in strange woods stilled.

"That's enough for today," Barry said. "Very good, boys. Very good indeed. Who knows the way back?"

They were all flushed with their first success in the woods, and they began to point one way after another, laughing, elbowing each other. Barry laughed with them. "I'd better lead you out of here," he said.

He looked about for Mark, but he was not there. For a moment Barry felt a thrill of fear. It passed almost too quickly to be identified, and he turned and started to walk toward the massive oak tree that was the last tree before the long slope down to the valley. At least he had learned that much, he thought, and he knew the boys also should have learned that much by now. The grin of triumph at their earlier success faded, and he felt the weight of doubts and disappointment settle over him again.

Twice more he looked back for Mark and failed to spot him in the dense woods. Mark saw him looking and made no sign. He watched the boys tripping, laughing, touching, and he felt his eyes burn and a strange emptiness almost like nausea gripped him. When they were out of sight down in the valley, he stretched out on the ground and looked up through the thick branches that veiled the sky, breaking it up into fragments of light, black against white, or white through black. By squinting his eyes he could make the black merge and the light pieces take precedence, then recede once more.

"They hate me," he whispered, and the trees whispered back, but he could not make out the words. Just leaves in the wind, he thought suddenly, not voices at all. He sat up and threw a handful of rotted leaves at the nearest tree trunk, and somewhere he thought someone laughed. The woji. "You're not real, either," he said softly. "I made you up. You can't laugh at me."

The sound persisted, grew louder, and suddenly he stood up and looked back over his shoulder at a black cloud bank that had been forming all afternoon. Now the trees were crying out warnings to him, and he began to scramble down the slope, not following the boys and Barry, but heading for the old farmhouse.

The house was completely hidden by a thicket of bushes and trees. Like Sleeping Beauty's castle, he thought, trotting toward it. The wind howled, hurling bits of dirt, twigs, leaves stripped from the trees. He crawled through the bushes and in the shelter the wind seemed very distant. The entire sky was darkening fast, and the wind was dangerous, he knew. Tornado weather, that's what they called it. There had been a rash of tornados two years ago; they all feared them now.

At the house, he didn't pause. He opened the coal chute, concealed by a tangle of ivy, and slid down and landed lightly in the black basement. He felt about for his candle and sulfur matches, and then went upstairs, where he watched the weather through a chink in the boarded-up window in the top bedroom. The house was completely boarded up now, doors, windows, the chimney sealed. They had decided it was not good for him to spend time alone in the old building, but they hadn't known about the coal chute and what they had done actually was to provide him with a sanctuary where no one could follow.

The storm roared through the valley and left as abruptly as it had started. The heavy rain became a spatter, then a drizzle; it stopped and presently the sun was shining again. Mark left the window. There was an oil lantern in the bedroom. He lighted the lamp and looked at his mother's paintings, as he had done many times in the years since she had taken him camping. She knew, he thought. Always that one person, in the fields, at the doorway, on the river or ocean. Always just one. She knew what it was like. Without warning he started to

146

sob, and threw himself down on the floor and wept until he was weak. Then he slept.

He dreamed the trees took him by the hand and led him to his mother and she held him close and sang and told him stories and they laughed together.

"Is it working?" Bob asked. "Can they be trained to live in the wilderness?"

Mark was in the corner of the room, sitting cross-legged on the floor, forgotten by the doctors. He looked up from the book he was reading and waited for the answer.

"I don't know," Barry said. "Not for a lifetime, I don't think. For short periods, yes. But they'll never be woodsmen, if that's what you mean."

"Should we go ahead with the others next summer? Are they getting enough out of it to make a large-scale attempt?"

Bruce shrugged. "It's been a training program for us too," he said. "I know I don't want to keep going back into those dismal woods. I dread my days more and more."

"Me too," Bob said. "That's why I brought this up now. Is there any real point to it?"

"You're thinking about the camp-out next week, aren't you?" Barry asked.

"Yes. I don't want to go. I know the boys are dreading it. You must be anxious about it."

Barry nodded. "You and I are too aware of what happened to Ben and Molly. But what's going to happen to those children when they leave here and have to spend night after night in the woods? If preparation like this can ease it for them, we have to do it."

Mark returned to his book, but he was not seeing it now. What happened to them? he wondered. Why were they all so afraid? There wasn't anything in the woods. No animals, nothing to hurt anyone. Maybe they heard the voices and that made them afraid, he thought. But then, if they heard the voices too, the voices had to be real. He felt his pulse racing suddenly. For several years he had believed the voices were only the leaves, that he was only pretending they were really voices. But if the brothers heard them too, that made them real. The brothers and sisters never made up anything. They didn't know how. He wanted to laugh with joy, but he didn't make a sound to attract attention. They would want to

147

know what was funny, and he knew he could never tell them.

The camp was a large clearing several miles from the valley. Twenty boys, ten girls, two doctors, and Mark sat about the campfire eating, and Mark remembered that other time he had sat eating popcorn at a campfire. He blinked rapidly and the feeling that came with the memory faded slowly. The clones were uneasy, but not really frightened. Their large number was reassuring, and the babble of their voices drowned out the noises of the woods.

They sang, and one of them asked Mark to tell the woji story, but he shook his head. Barry asked lazily what a woji was, and the clones nudged each other and changed the subject. Barry let it drop. One of those things that all children know and adults never do, he thought. Mark told another story and they sang some more, and then it was time to unroll the blankets and sleep.

Much later Mark sat up, listening. One of the boys was going to the latrine, he decided, and lay down again and was asleep almost instantly.

The boy stumbled and clutched a tree to steady himself. The fire was dim now, no more than embers through the tree trunks. He took several more steps and abruptly the embers vanished. For a moment he hesitated, but his bladder urged him on, and he didn't yield to the temptation to relieve himself against a tree. Barry had made it clear they had to use the latrine in the interest of health. He knew the ditch was only twenty yards from the camp, only another few steps, but the distance seemed to grow rather than decrease and he had a sudden fear that he was lost.

"If you get lost," Mark had said, "the first thing to do is sit down and think. Don't run. Calm down and think."

But he couldn't sit down here. He could hear the voices all around him, and the woji laughing at him, and something coming closer and closer. He ran blindly, his hands over his ears trying to blot out the ever louder voices.

Something clutched at him and he felt it ripping his side, felt the blood flowing, and he screamed a high wild shriek that he couldn't stop.

In the camp his brothers sat up and looked about in terror. *Danny!*

148

"What was that?" Barry demanded.

Mark was standing up listening, but now the brothers were calling out, "Danny! Danny!"

"Tell them to shut up," Mark said. He strained to hear. "Make them stay here," he ordered, and trotted into the woods toward the latrine. He could hear the boy now, faintly, dashing madly into trees, bushes, stumbling, screaming. Abruptly the sounds stopped.

Mark paused again to listen, but the woods were silent. There was pandemonium behind him in camp and ahead of him nothing.

He didn't move for several minutes, listening. Danny might have fallen, winded himself. He might be unconscious. There was no way in the dark for Mark to follow him without sounds to lead him. Slowly he turned back to camp. They were all up now, standing in three groups, the two doctors also close to each other.

"I can't find him in the dark," Mark said. "We'll have to wait for morning." No one moved. "Build up the fire," he said. "Maybe he'll see the glow and follow it back."

One group of brothers started to throw wood on the embers, smothering it. Bob took charge, and presently they had a roaring fire again. Danny's brothers sat huddled together, all looking pinched and cold and very afraid. They could find him, Mark thought, but they were afraid to go after him in the black woods. One of them began to cry, and almost as if that had been the signal, they were all weeping. Mark turned from them and went again to the edge of the woods to listen.

With the first faint light of dawn Mark started to follow the trail of the missing boy. He had dashed back and forth, zig-zagging, rebounding from tree to tree. Here he had run forward for a hundred yards, only to crash into a boulder. There was blood. He had been scraped by a spruce branch. Here he had run again, faster this time. Up a rise . . . Mark paused looking at the rise, and he knew what he was going to find. He had been trotting easily, and now he slowed to a walk and followed the trail, not stepping on any of Danny's prints, but keeping to one side, reading what had happened.

At the top of the rise there was a narrow ridge of limestone. There were many such outcroppings in the woods, and almost always when there was a rise such as this, the other side was steep also, sometimes steeper, rockier. He stood on the ridge looking down the thirty feet of sparse growth and rocks, and twisted among them he could see the boy, his eyes open as if he were studying the pale, colorless sky. Mark didn't go down. He squatted several moments looking at the figure below, then turned and went back to camp, not rushing now.

"He bled to death," Barry said after they brought the body back to camp.

"They could have saved him," Mark said. He didn't look at Danny's brothers, who were all gray, waxy-looking, in shock. "They could have gone straight to him." He stood up. "Are we going down now?"

Barry nodded. He and Bob carried the body on a litter made from thin tree branches tied together. Mark led them to the edge of the woods and turned. "I'll go make sure the fire's all the way out," he said. He didn't wait for permission, but vanished among the trees almost instantly.

Barry put the surviving nine brothers in the hospital to be treated for shock. They never emerged, and no one, ever asked about them.

The following morning Barry arrived in the lecture room before the class had assembled. Mark was already in his place at the rear of the room. Barry nodded to him, opened his notes, straightened his desk, and looked up again to find Mark still regarding him. His eyes were as bright as twin blue lakes covered with a layer of ice, Barry thought.

"Well?" he asked finally when it seemed the locked stare would be maintained indefinitely.

Mark didn't look away. "There is no individual, there is only the community," he said clearly. "What is right for the community is right even unto death for the individual. There is no one, there is only the whole."

"Where did you hear that?" Barry demanded.

"I read it."

"Where did you get that book?"

"From your office. It's on one of the shelves."

"You're forbidden to enter my office!"

"It doesn't matter. I've already read everything in it." Mark stood up and his eyes glinted as the light changed in them. "That book is a lie," he said clearly. "They're all lies! I'm one. I'm an individual! *I am one!*" He started for the door.

"Mark, wait a minute," Barry said. "Have you ever

seen what happens to a strange ant when it falls into another ant colony?"

At the door Mark nodded. "But I'm not an ant," he said.

Chapter 23

Late in September the boats reappeared on the river, and the people gathered at the dock to watch. It was a cold, rainy day; already frosts had turned the landscape bleak, and fog over the river obscured everything until the boats were very close. A meeting party set out to help bring in the exhausted people, and when they were all docked and the tally taken, the realization that nine people had been lost wreathed the homecoming in gloom.

The following night they held the Ceremony for the Lost, and the suvivors told their story haltingly. They had brought back five boats, one under tow most of the way. One boat had been swept away at the mouth of the Shenandoah; they had found it smashed and broken up, with no survivors, its load of surgical equipment lost to the river. The second damaged boat had been run aground by a sudden storm that overturned it and ruined its load of maps, directories, warehouse lists—bales and bales of papers that would have proven useful.

The shelter at the falls had been started; the canal had proven disastrous, impossible to dig as proposed. The river flooded in from below and washed it out repeatedly, and all they had succeeded in doing was to make a swampy area that flooded in high water and was a muddy bog when the river fell. And the worst part, they agreed, had been the cold. As soon as they had reached the Potomac the cold had plagued them. There had been frosts; leaves had fallen prematurely, and the river was numbing. Much of the vegetation was dead; only the hardiest plants were surviving. The cold had persisted in Washington, had made the canal digging a hellish task.

The snow came to the valley early that year, on the first

of October. It remained on the ground for a week before the wind shifted and warm southerly breezes melted it. On the infrequent clear days when the sun shone brightly and no mist hid the tops of the surrounding hills and mountains, the snow could still be seen on the high ridges.

Later Barry would be able to look back on that winter and know it had been crucial, but at the time it seemed just one more in the endless string of seasons.

One day Bob called to him to come outside and look at something. No new snow had fallen for several days, and the sun was bright and gave the illusion of warmth. Barry pulled on a heavy cape and followed Bob out. There was a snow sculpture standing in the center of the court-yard between the new dorms. It was a male figure, eight feet tall, nude, its legs fused into a base that was also a pedestal. In one hand the figure carried a club, or perhaps a torch, and the other hand swung at its side. The feeling of motion, of life, had been captured. It was a man on his way to somewhere else, striding along, not to be stopped.

"Mark?" Barry asked.

"Who else?"

Barry approached it slowly; there were others looking at it also, mostly children. A few adults were there, and others came out until there was a crowd about the statue. A small girl stared, then turned and began to roll a snow-ball. She threw it at the figure. Barry caught her arm before she could throw again.

"Don't do that," he said.

She looked at him blankly, looking at the figure even more blankly, and started to inch away He released her, and she darted back through the people. Her sisters ran to her. They touched each other as if to reassure them-selves that all was well.

"What is it?" one of them asked, unable to see over the heads of the people between her and the statue.

"Just snow," the little girl answered. "It's just snow."

Barry stared at her. She was about seven, he thought. He caught her again, and this time lifted her so she could see. "Tell me what that is," he said.

She wriggled to get loose. "Snow," she said. "It's snow."

"It's a man," he said sharply.

She looked at him in bewilderment and glanced at the figure again. Then she shook her head. One by one he

152

held other small children up to see. All they saw was snow.

Barry and his brothers talked to their younger brothers about it later that day, and the younger doctors were impatient at what was clearly, to them, a trifle.

"So the younger children can't see that it's supposed to be the figure of a man. What does it matter?" Andrew asked.

"I don't know," Barry said slowly. And he didn't know why it was important, only that it was.

During the afternoon the sun melted the snow a bit, and overnight it froze solid once more. By morning when the sun hit the statue, it was blinding. Barry went out to look at it several times that day. That night someone, or a group, went out and toppled it and stamped it into the ground.

Two days later four groups of boys reported the disappearance of their mats. They searched Mark's room, other places where he might have hidden them, and came up with nothing. Mark started a new sculpture, this time a woman, presumably a companion piece to the man, and this time the statue remained until spring, long after it was no longer identifiable, but was simply a mound of snow that had melted, frozen, melted repeatedly.

The next incident happened soon after the New Year celebration. Barry was awakened from a deep sleep by an insistent hand on his shoulder.

He sat up feeling groggy and disoriented, as if he had been pulled a long way to find himself in his bed, cold, stupid, blinking without recognition at the younger man standing over him.

"Barry, snap out of it! Wake up!" Anthony's voice registered first, then his face. The other brothers were waking up now.

"What's wrong?" Suddenly Barry was thoroughly awake.

"A breakdown in the computer section. We need you."

Stephen and Stuart were already tearing down the computer when Barry and his brothers got to the laboratory. Several younger brothers were busy disconnecting tubes from the terminal in order to regulate the flow manually. Other young doctors were making a tank-by-tank check of the dials. The scene was of orderly chaos, Barry thought, if there could be such a thing. A dozen people were moving about quickly, each intent on his own job, but each out of place there. The aisles became cluttered when more than two people tried to move among the tanks, and now there were a dozen, and more coming every minute.

Andrew had taken charge, Barry noted with satisfaction. All the newcomers were assigned sections immediately, and he found himself monitoring a row of embryos seven weeks old. There were ninety babies in the tanks at various stages of development. Two groups could be removed and finished in the premature ward, but their chances of survival would be drastically reduced. His group seemed all right, but he could hear Bruce muttering at the other end of the same aisle and he knew there was trouble there. The potassium salts had been increased. The embryos had been poisoned.

The scientists were spoiled, he thought. So used to the computer analysis of the amniotic fluids, they had let their own skills deteriorate. Now trial and error was too slow to save the embryos. The survivor of that group was turned off. No more solitaires. Members of another group had suffered, but this time only four were overdosed. The six survivors were allowed to continue.

Throughout the night they monitored the fluids, added salts as they were needed, diluted the fluids if salt started to build, kept a temperature check and oxygen count, and by dawn Barry felt as if he were swimming through an ocean of congealed amniotic fluids himself. The computer was not yet functioning. The checks would have to be continued around the clock.

The crisis lasted four days, and during that time they lost thirty-four babies, and forty-nine animals. When Barry finally fell into bed exhausted, he knew the loss of the animals was the more grievous. They had depended on those animals for the glandular secretions, for the chemicals they extracted from their bone marrow and blood. Later, he thought, sinking down into the fog of sleep, later he would worry about the implications of the loss.

"No maybes! We have to have the computer parts as soon as the snow melts. If this happens again, I don't know if we can repair it." Everett was a thin, tall computer expert, no more than twenty, possibly not that yet. His older brothers deferred to him, and that was a good sign that he knew what he was talking about.

154

"The new paddle-wheel boats will be ready by summer," Lawrence said. "If a road crew can get out early enough to make certain the bypass is open . . ."

Barry stopped listening. It was snowing again. Large lazy flakes of snow drifted, in no hurry to get to earth, wafted this way and that. He could not see past the first dormitory, only twenty yards from the window he looked through. The children were in school, absorbing everything being presented to them. The laboratory conditions had been stabilized again. It would work out, he told himself. Four years wasn't too long to hold out, and if they could have four years they would be over the line from experimental to proven.

The snow drifted, and he mused at the individuality of each snowflake. Like millions of others before him, he thought, awed by the complexities of nature. He wondered suddenly if Andrew, the self he had been at thirty, had ever felt bemused by the complexities of nature. He wondered if any of the younger children knew each snowflake was different. If they were told that it was so, were ordered to examine the snowflakes as a project, would they see the difference? Would they think it marvelous? Or would they accept it as another of the endless lessons they were expected to learn, and so learn it obediently and derive no pleasure or satisfaction from the new knowledge?

He felt chilled, and turned his attention back to the meeting. But the thoughts would not stop there. They learned everything they were taught, he realized, everything. They could duplicate what had gone before, but they originated nothing. And they couldn't even see the magnificent snow sculpture Mark had created.

After the meeting he walked with Lawrence to inspect the new paddle-wheel boats. "Everything's top priority," he said. "Without exception."

"Trouble is," Lawrence said, "they're right. Everything really is top priority. It's a fragile structure we have here, Barry. Very fragile indeed."

Barry nodded. Without the computers they would have to close down all but a couple dozen of the tanks. Without the parts for the generator, they would have to cut down on electricity, start burning wood for warmth, to cook with, read by tallow candles. Without the boats they could not travel to the cities, where their supplies were rotting away more each season. Without the new supply of workers and explorers they could not maintain the by-pass road around the falls, maintain the rivers so that the paddle boats could navigate them . . .

"You ever read that poem about the want of a nail?" he asked.

"No," Lawrence said, and looked at him questioningly. Barry shook his head.

They watched the crew working on the boat for a few minutes, and then Barry said, "Lawrence, how good are the younger brothers at boat building?"

"The best," Lawrence said promptly.

"I don't mean just following orders. I mean, has one of the younger brothers come up with an idea you could use?"

Lawrence turned to study him again. "What's bothering you, Barry?"

"Have they?"

Lawrence frowned and was silent for what seemed a long time. Finally he shrugged. "I don't think so. I can't remember. But then, Lewis has such clear ideas of what it has to be, I doubt if anyone would even think of contradicting him, or adding to anything he has planned."

Barry nodded. "I thought so," he said, and walked away on the snow-cleared path, edged on either side by a white fence as high as his head. "And it never used to snow this much, either," he said to himself. There. He had said it aloud. He thought he probably was the first one of the inhabitants to say that. It never used to snow this much.

Later that day he sent for Mark, and when the boy stood before him, he asked, "What are the woods like in the winter, when there's snow like now?"

Mark looked guilty for a moment. He shrugged.

"I know you've managed to learn to walk with snow-shoes," Barry said. "And you ski. I've seen your trail leading up into the woods. What is it like?"

Now Mark's eyes seemed to glow with blue fires, and a smile formed, then left. He ducked his head. "Not like summer," he said. "Stiller. And it's pretty." Suddenly he blushed and became silent.

"More dangerous?" Barry asked.

"I guess so. You can't see dips, they fill up with snow, and sometimes snow hangs on ridges so you can't be real sure where the land ends. You could go over an edge that way, I guess, if you didn't know about it."

"I want to train our children in getting around on snowshoes and skis. They might have to be in the woods in winter. They have to have some training. Can they find enough material to make fires?"

Mark nodded.

"We'll start them on making snowshoes tomorrow," Barry said decisively. He stood up. "I'll need your help. I've never seen a pair of snowshoes. I don't know how to begin." He opened the door and before Mark left he asked, "How did you learn to make them?"

"I saw them in a book."

"What book?"

"Just a book," Mark said. "It's gone now."

In the old house, Barry understood. What other books were in the old house? He knew he had to find out. That night when he met with his brothers they talked long and soberly about the conclusions he had drawn.

"We'll have to teach them everything they might ever need," Barry said, and felt a new weariness settle over him.

"The hardest thing we'll have to do," Bruce said thoughtfully after a moment, "will be to convince others that this is so. We'll have to test it, make certain we are right, then prove it. This will put a terrible burden on the teachers, on the older brothers and sisters."

They didn't question his conclusions. Each of them, given his direct observations, would have come up with the same conclusions.

"I think we can devise a few simple tests," Barry said. "I made some sketches this afternoon." He showed them: a stick figure of a man running, climbing stairs, sitting down; a sun symbol, a circle with rays extending from it; a tree symbol, a cone with a stick in the base; a house made of four lines, two parallel, an angle for the roof; a disc moon; a bowl with steam rising from it in wavy lines . . .

"We could have them finish a story," Bruce said. "Keep it as simple as the drawings. A three- or four-line story without an ending, which they must supply."

Barry nodded. They knew what he was after. If the children lacked the imagination to abstract, to fantasize, to generalize, they had to know it now and try to compensate. Within a week their fears were realized. The children under nine or ten could not identify the line drawings,

157

could not complete a simple story, could not generalize a particular situation to a new situation.

"So we teach them everything they'll need to know to survive," Barry said harshly. "And be grateful they seem able to learn whatever we teach."

They would need different lesson material, he knew. Material from the old books in the farmhouse, lessons in survival, in how to build simple lean-tos, how to make fires, how to substitute what was at hand for what was missing . . .

Barry and his brothers went to the old farmhouse with crowbars and hammers, ripped off the boarding at the front entrance, and went inside. While the others examined the yellowed, crumbly books in the library, Barry climbed the stairs to Molly's old rooms. Inside, he stopped and took a deep breath.

There were the paintings, as he remembered them, and more, there were small objects made out of clay. There were wood carvings, a head that had to be Molly, done in walnut, done cleanly, expertly, like but unlike the Miriam sisters. Barry couldn't explain how it differed, but knew it was not like them, and was like Molly. There were works done in sandstone, in limestone, some of them complete, most of them rough, as if he had started them and lost interest. Barry touched the carved likeness of Molly and for no reason he could name, he felt tears forming. He turned abruptly and left the room, closing the door carefully behind him.

He didn't tell his brothers, and he didn't understand the reason for not telling them any more than he had understood the tears he had shed over a piece of wood hacked out by a child. Later that night when images of the head kept intruding when he tried to sleep, he thought he knew why he hadn't told. They would be forced to find and seal off the secret entrance Mark used to enter the house. And Barry knew he couldn't do that.

Chapter 24

The paddle-wheel boat was bedecked with bright ribbons and flowers; it dazzled under the early morning sun. Even the wood pile was decorated. The steam engine gleamed. The troops of young people filed aboard with much laughter and gaiety. Ten of these, eight of those, sixty-five in all. The boat crew stood apart from the young explorer-foragers, watching them warily, as if afraid the carnival spirit of the morning might damage the boat somehow.

And indeed the infectious exuberance of the young people was dangerous in its spontaneity, drawing into itself the onlookers ashore. The gloom of the past expeditions was forgotten as the boat made ready to churn its way downriver. This was different, the mood cried, these young people had been specially bred and trained for this mission. It was their life fulfillment they sought. Who had a better right to rejoice at seeing life's goal within reach?

Tied securely to the side of the paddle boat was a fourteen-foot canoe made of birch bark, and standing protectively by it was Mark. He had boarded before the others, or had slept there, perhaps; no one had seen him arrive, but he was there with his canoe that could outrun anything else on the river, even the big paddle wheel. Mark watched the scene impassively. He was slender, not tall, but his slim body was well muscled and his chest was deep. If he was impatient to be under way, he showed no sign of it. He might have stood there for an hour, a day, a week . . .

The elder members of the expedition now came aboard, and the cheering and singing ashore grew in volume. Nominally the leaders of the expedition, the Gary brothers nodded to Mark and took their places in the stern.

Standing on the dock, Barry watched smoke puff up from the stack as the boat started to foam the water, and he thought about Ben and Molly, and those who had not come back, or had come back only to go into the hospital and never emerge. The children were almost hysterically happy, he thought. They might be going to a circus, or a tournament, or to enlist in the king's service, or to slay dragons . . . His gaze sought Mark's. The bright blue eyes didn't waver, and Barry knew that he at least understood what they were doing, what the dangers were, the prizes. He understood this mission meant the end of the experiment, or a new beginning for them all. He knew, and he, like Barry, was not smiling.

"The terrible heroics of children," Barry muttered.

At his side Lawrence said, "What?" and Barry shrugged and said it was nothing. Nothing.

The boat pulled away steadily now, leaving a wide wake that spread from shore to shore and made waves that broke against the dock. They watched until the boat was out of sight.

The river was swift and muddy, high with runoff from the mountains. Crews had been out for over a month clearing the rapids, marking safe channels among the boulders, repairing the winter damage to the dock at the head of the falls, working on the overland detour. The paddle wheel made good time, and they arrived at the falls shortly after lunch. All afternoon they worked at unloading the boat to transport the supplies to the shelter.

The building at the foot of the falls was a duplicate of the dormitories in the valley, and inside it the large group of travelers found it easy to forget this building was isolated, that it was separate from the others. Each evening the road crew assembled in the building, and the boatmen gathered there, and no one was left outside in the black woods. Here at the shelter the woods had been pushed back to the edge of the hills that rose precipitously behind the clearing. Soybeans and corn would be planted later, when the weather warmed enough. Fertile land was not to be wasted, and those people stationed in the shelter were not to be idle during the weeks between the arrivals and departures of the paddle wheels.

The following day the new expeditionary force loaded the big boat at the foot of the falls, and that night they slept in the shelter. At dawn they would embark on the second phase of the trip to Washington.

Mark allowed no one to handle his pack, or his canoe, which he secured to the second boat. This was the fourth canoe he had made, the largest, and he felt no one else understood the mixture of fragility and strength that combined to make this canoe the only safe way to travel the rivers. He had tried to interest some of the others in canoes, but failed; they didn't want to think about traveling the wild rivers alone.

The Potomac was rougher than the Shenandoah, and there were ice floes in it. No one had mentioned ice floes, Mark thought, and wondered about the source this late in the year. It was mid-April. The forests screened the hills here, and he could only guess there was still snow and ice in the high country. The paddle wheel moved slowly down the river, its crew busy and alert to the dangers of the wide, swift stream. By dark they were well into the Washington area, and tied up that night to a bridge foundation that jutted from the water, a sentinel left behind when the rest of the bridge yielded to the intolerable pressures of water, wind, and age.

Early the next morning they began to unload, and it was here that Mark was to leave the others. It was hoped he would return within two weeks, with good news about the accessibility of a route to Philadelphia and/or New York.

Mark unloaded his own belongings, unslung the canoe and carefully lifted it off the paddle wheel, and then shrugged his backpack into place. He was ready. A long knife was sheathed at his thigh, a rope hung from his braided steerhide belt; he was dressed in hide trousers, moccasins, and a soft leather shirt. The ruined city was oppressive to him; he was eager to be back on the river. Already the transfer was being made; supplies were unloaded, and stacks of materials that had been found and put in storage near the river were being taken aboard. For a few moments Mark watched, then silently he lifted his canoe, swung it over his head, and began to walk.

Throughout the day he walked amid the ruins, always keeping to a northeast direction that eventually would see him clear of the city, into the forest again. He found a small stream and floated his canoe, following the meandering waterway for several hours before it turned south, where he shouldered the canoe and took to the forest. Now the forest was thick and silent, familiar for all its strangeness. Before dark he found a place to camp, and made a fire and cooked his dinner. His supply of dried food was sufficient for two to three weeks, if he didn't find other food to supplement it, but he knew he would find wild food. No forest failed to yield fern tips, or asparagus shoots, or a variety of other edible greens. Here nearer the coast, there was less frost damage than inland.

As the light faded he dug a shallow trench and filled it with soft pine needles, spread his poncho over them, pulled the canoe into position to make a cover, and stretched out on the bed he had made. His worse enemy would be the spring rains, he knew. They could be heavy, and unexpected. He made a few sketches and notes, then rolled on his side and watched the dying fire until it was a glow in the blackness, and soon he was asleep.

The next day he entered Baltimore. It had burned, and there was evidence of a great flood. He didn't explore the ruins. He launched his canoe in Chesapeake Bay and started north. The forest came to the water's edge here, and from the water there were no traces of any of man's works. There was a strong current, the effects of an outgoing tide combined with the flow from the Susquehanna River. Mark fought it for several minutes, then headed for shore to wait for low tide. He should cross the bay, he thought, and hug the shoreline there. As he drew nearer the delta of the Susquehanna the water would be rougher and it might be impossible to get the small boat through at all. There were ice floes here, not large, and mostly flat, as if they had broken away from a river that had frozen over and was only now thawing.

He stretched out on the ground and waited for the tide to turn. Occasionally he checked the water level, and when it stopped falling he sat on the shore and watched until sticks he threw into the water started to float northward, and then he set out once again. This time he started to paddle northeast, heading for open water and the other shore.

The turbulence was minor near the shore, but as he drew nearer the center of the bay he could feel the force of the tide meeeting the rush of the river and, although little of the fierce battle showed on the surface of the water, it was transmitted through the boat; he could feel it in the oar, in the way the small boat pulled to one side, then the other. His arms strained at the paddle, he could feel the tautness of his back and legs as he fought the current and the tide, and he felt only exhilaration at being in the battle.

Abruptly he was through it, and now the tide carried him strongly northward, and he had only to steer and search the shoreline for the best place to make a landing. It was sandy, with sparse growth; the danger there would be hidden rocks that could pierce the bottom of the canoe. The sun was very low when he felt the first gentle scraping of boat on sandy beach, and he sprang out into the cold water and pulled the canoe ashore.

With his canoe safe on high ground, he stood on the beach and looked back the way he had come. Forests, black, solid-looking, the green-blue water streaked with the muddy water of the river, deep blue sky, the sun low in the west, and nowhere another person, nowhere a sign of human life, no buildings, no roads, nothing. Suddenly he threw his head back and laughed, a joyous, almost childish laugh of triumph. It was his. All of it. No one else wanted it. No one was there to contest his ownership, and he claimed it all.

He whistled as he made a fire of driftwood. It burned with incredible colors: greens, blues, copper flames, scarlet. He cooked his dried corn and beef in sea water and marveled at the taste, and when he fell asleep before the last light had faded, he was smiling.

By dawn the next morning he was ready to follow the shoreline north, searching for the old intercoastal waterway that joined Chesapeake Bay with Delaware Bay. When he found it, little remained of the canal; now there was a wide marsh with cattails and marsh grasses hiding the land and water alike. Immediately on entering the marsh the grasses closed in about him and he was cut off from the world. At times the water deepened and no grasses grew in those places, and he was able to move ahead faster, but most of the day he pushed his canoe through the tough stems, using them, clumps of roots, whatever he could find, to propel himself eastward. The sun rose higher and he took off his shirt. No wind moved among the grasses. The sun lowered and the air became cold and he put his shirt back on. He paddled when he could, pushed against the grasses when he could not use the paddle any other way, and slowly he made his way through the marsh. He didn't stop to eat or rest all day; he knew he didn't want to be among the high grasses when the sun went down, when darkness came.

The shadows were very long when he finally felt the difference in the water beneath the boat. He began to move faster now; each dip of his paddle made the boat glide forward in a more natural response, not impeded by the rough, grasping stems that had held him back all day. The grasses parted, thinned out, then disappeared, and there was turbulent, freely moving water before him. He knew he was too tired to fight yet another current, and he let it take him downstream, to land on the shore of Delaware Bay.

The next morning he saw fish. Moving carefully, he opened his pack and found the net he had made the previous winter, to the amusement of the other children. The net was five feet square, and although he had practiced throwing it in the river in the valley, he knew he was inexpert with it, that his first throw would probably be the only chance he would have. He knelt in the canoe, which had begun to drift as soon as he stopped paddling, and waited until the fish swam closer. Closer, he whispered at them, closer. Then he threw, and for a moment the canoe rocked dangerously. He felt the heaviness of the weighted net increase, and jerked and tugged hard and began to pull it in. He gasped when he saw his catch: three large, silvery fish.

He sat back on his heels and studied the fish flopping about, and for a time his mind was a blank about what to do with them. Slowly he began to remember what he had read about cleaning them, how to sun-dry them, or roast them over an open fire . . .

On shore he cleaned the three fish and spread them in the sun on flat rocks to dry. He sat looking at the water and wondered if there were shellfish here also. He took the canoe out again, this time keeping very close to shore. He came to a half-submerged rock where he found a bed of oysters, and on the bottom of the sandy bay there were clams, which disappeared when he disturbed the water. By late afternoon he had gathered many of the oysters and dug pounds and pounds of clams. His fish were not dry, and he knew they would spoil if he didn't do something else. He pondered, staring at the bay, and he realized the ice floes were the answer.

Once more he went out into the water, and this time he maneuvered close enough to one of the larger slabs of ice to get his rope around it and tow it back to shore. He wove a shallow basket of pine branches, put the clams on the bottom, then the oysters, and on top of them the fish. He put the basket on the flat ice, hacked off pieces of the ice with his knife, and put them over everything. Then he relaxed. He had used up almost the whole day in gathering the food, making sure it would not spoil before he could eat it. But he didn't care. Later when he ate roasted fish and wild asparagus, he knew he had never eaten any food half as good.

From where he camped, the Delaware was a black hole in the dark forest. Now and then the blackness was broken by a pale shadow that moved without a sound, as if floating in air. Ice. The river was very high; on the banks some trees were standing in water; there might be others invisible until too late, or rocks, or other perils. Mark considered the hazards of that black river and felt only contentment, and the next morning he entered it and headed for Philadelphia.

It was the cities that depressed him, he thought, staring at the gray ruins on either side of the Schuylkill River. As far as he could see in any direction there was the same vista of gray ruins. The city had burned, but not to the ground as Baltimore had. Some buildings seemed almost intact here, but everywhere the same grayness persisted, the same ugliness of destruction. Trees had started to grow here, but even they were ugly, stunted, sickly-looking.

Mark felt here the same fear that others spoke of feeling in the forest. There was a presence here, and it was malign. He found himself looking back over his shoulder again and again, and determinedly paddled ahead. Soon he would stop and make some sketches of the buildings he could see from the river. Probably he should make some token explorations on foot, he thought reluctantly. He paddled more slowly and examined a grove of trees. They were so badly formed it was hard to determine what kind of trees they were. Aspens, he decided. He tried to imagine their roots searching in the concrete and metal beneath the streets for sustenance, finding only more concrete and metal.

But there had been trees in Washington, he thought, paddling harder to avoid a large, ragged chunk of ice. Those trees had been normal-looking, but these . . . They were less than half full size, misshapen, their branches few and grotesquely twisted. Abruptly Mark pulled up. Radiation, he thought with a chill. This is what radiation poisoning did. Before his mind's eye appeared descriptions and photographs of various kinds of animal and vegetable life deformed by radioactivity.

He turned the canoe and raced back downriver to the juncture with the Delaware. He still had several hours before darkness forced him to stop. For a moment he hesitated, then turned northward once more, this time keeping a wary eye open for deformed plant growth, as well as for chunks of ice, which had become more numerous.

He passed one more place with badly deformed plant life. He kept to the far side of the river and continued to paddle.

Philadelphia went on and on, the ruins more or less uniform. Occasionally there were blocks of buildings that seemed virtually untouched, but now he suspected that was because those areas had been blocked off when they became radioactive. He didn't investigate any of them. Most of the immense buildings were skeletons, but there were still many standing, enough to make a full-scale expedition worthwhile, if the buildings were not contaminated. He knew that problem would have to be solved by Barry or his younger brothers. He continued on. The forests were taking over again, and the trees were well developed here, thick, luxuriant; in some places where the river narrowed, the canopies met overhead, and it was like passing through a tunnel where only his paddle in the water made a sound and the rest of the world held its breath in the twilight stillness.

There was another puzzle here, he thought, studying the banks of the river. The flow was very swift, but the water was low and the banks in places rose several feet to the land above. The river could have been partially dammed; he knew he would have to find out before he returned to Washington.

Daily the weather had become colder, and that night there was frost. The next day he went through Trenton, and as in Philadelphia, the ruins were ubiquitous, the growth stunted and malformed.

Although it took him several miles out of his way, he went through the city in his canoe, and didn't leave it until the woods looked normal again. Then he carried the boat to high ground and secured it and headed north on foot. The Delaware turned west here, and he was bound for New York. That afternoon the rains started.

Mark blazed a trail now; he didn't want to have to make a search for the canoe when he returned. He traveled steadily through the heavy rain, protected by his great poncho, which covered him from crown to feet.

He could find no dry wood for a fire that night, and he chewed his cold beef and wished he had another of the succulent fish instead.

The rain was undiminished the next day, and now he knew that to continue was foolish, that he might lose his direction completely in a world whose boundaries had been erased, with no sky, no sun to plot his course. He searched for a spruce grove and crept under the largest of the trees and huddled in his poncho, dozing, waking, dozing again throughout the day and night. The sighing of the trees wakened him and he knew the rain was over; the trees were shaking off the water, murmuring together about the terrible weather, wondering about the boy who slept among them. He had to find a sunny place, dry out his pack, the poncho, his clothes, dry and oil his moccasins . . . . He crawled out from under the spruce, whispered a thank you, and began to search for a good place to dry out everything, make a fire, have a good meal.

When he came upon the deformed underbrush late that afternoon, he backed up a hundred feet, squatted, and studied the woods before him.

He was at least another day's distance from New York, he suspected, twenty miles, maybe even more. The woods here were too thick to be able to see if the deformities were localized. He retreated half a mile, made camp, and thought about the days ahead. He would not enter any place that he thought had been irradiated. How many days was he willing to detour? He didn't know. Time had stopped for him, and he couldn't be certain now how long he had been in the woods, how long since the paddle wheel had entered Washington. He wondered if the others were all right, if they had found the warehouses, had brought out the stuff they were to collect. He thought how they might blindly stumble through the poisoned areas in Philadelphia, through the poison here. He shuddered.

He followed the edge of the poisoned area for three days, sometimes going north, then west, then north again. He got no nearer the city. A ring of death surrounded it.

He came to a vast swamp where dead trees lay rotting

167

and nothing grew; he could go no farther. The swampy land extended westward as far as he could see; it smelled of salt and decay, like mud flats when the tide went out. He touched the water to his tongue and then turned back. Sea water. That night the temperature plummeted, and the next day the trees and bushes stood blackened. Now he ate his corn and beef hungrily, and wondered if he would find any wild food again. His supply was running low, his raisins were gone, his dried apples nearly gone. He knew he wouldn't starve, but it would be pleasant to have fresh vegetables and fruit, more of the hot flaky fish, or oysters, or a clam broth thick with chewy bits of white meat . . . Resolutely he turned his thoughts away from food and walked a little faster.

He traveled quickly, his own trail easily followed, the blaze marks on the trees like roadmarks—turn here, this way, straight ahead. When he got back to his canoe he went west on the Delaware to satisfy his curiosity about the diminished flow and the ice, which was thicker than before. The rain must have broken more of it loose, he thought. It was difficult going against the swift current, and the floating chunks of ice made the river more hazardous. The land here was flat. When the change came, he knew it instantly. The river became faster, and now there was the white water of rapids, and there was a definite rise in the land on either side of the river. It had cut a channel here, another deeper one farther on. When the rapids became too dangerous for the small boat to navigate, he took the canoe from the water and stored it safely, then continued on foot.

A hill rose before him, barely covered with scrub growth and loose rocks. Carefully he picked his way up it. It was very cold. The trees here looked as they would in early March, or even late February. There were bud swellings, but no leaves, no green, only the black-green of the spruces, still in their winter needles. At the top of the hill he drew in his breath sharply. Before him was a vast sheet of snow and ice, blinding in the sunlight.

In some places the snowfield came to the banks of the river, in others it started a good distance back, and up there, about a mile away, the river was almost jammed with ice. It was a narrow black ribbon winding its way through the glare.

Southward the trees blocked his view, but he could see for miles to the north and west, and there was only snow and ice. White mountains climbed to the clear blue sky, and the valleys had been rounded at the bottoms as the snow accumulated there. The wind shifted and blew into Mark's face, and the cold was numbing, bringing tears to his eyes. The sun seemed to have no warmth here. He was sweating under his leather shirt, but the sight of all that snow, and the chill of the wind when it swept across it, created the illusion that the sun had failed. The illusion made him shiver violently. He turned and hurried down the steep hillside, sliding the last twenty feet or more, aware even as he started the slide that it was dangerous, that he would cause rocks to follow him, that he might be hit by them, injured too badly to move out of the way. He rolled at the bottom and jumped to his feet and ran. He ran a long time, and could hear the rocks crashing behind him.

In his mind the sound was that of the glacier advancing, rolling toward him inexorably, grinding everything to powder.

Chapter 25

Mark was flying. It was glorious to swoop and dive high over the trees and rivers. He soared higher and higher until his body tingled with excitement. He swerved to avoid flying through a billowing white cloud. When he straightened out, there was another white cloud before him; again he swerved, and then again and again. The clouds were everywhere, and now they had joined to form a wall, and the great white wall was advancing on him from every direction. There was no place he could go to avoid being overtaken. He dived, and the dive became a fall, faster and faster. There was nothing he could do to stop it. He fell through the whiteness . . .

Mark came wide awake, shivering hard, his body covered with sweat. His fire was a feeble glow in the blackness. He fed it carefully, blew on his chilled hands while he waited for the scrapings of punk to burn, and then

169

added twigs, and finally branches. Although it would be dawn soon and he would have to extinguish the fire, he fed it until it blazed hot and bright. Then he sat huddled before it. He had stopped shivering, but the nightmare vision persisted and he wanted light and warmth. And he wanted not to be alone.

He traveled very swiftly the next four days, and on the afternoon of the fifth he approached the landing area in Washington where the paddle wheel had docked and the brothers and sisters had set out for the warehouses.

The Peter brothers ran to meet him, helped with the canoe, took his pack, talking all the while.

"Gary said you should go to the warehouse the minute you got in," one of them said.

"We had six accidents so far," another one said excitedly. "Broken arms, legs, stuff like that. Nothing like the other groups had in the past. We're making it!"

"Gary said we'll start for Baltimore or Philadelphia by the end of this week."

"We have a map to show you which warehouse they're doing now."

"We have at least four boatloads of stuff already . . ."

"We've been taking turns. Four days down here getting stuff ready for the boat, cooking, all that, then four days in the warehouses finding stuff . . ."

"It's not bad here, not like we thought it would be. I don't know why the others had so much trouble."

Mark followed them wearily. "I'm hungry," he said.

"There's soup cooking now for dinner," one of them said. "But Gary said . . ."

Mark moved past them to the building they were using for their quarters. Now he could smell the soup. He helped himself, and before he finished eating he began to feel too sleepy to keep his eyes open. The boys kept talking about their successes. "Where are the beds?" Mark asked, interrupting one of them again.

"Aren't you going to the warehouse like Gary said?"

"No. Where are the beds?"

"We'll start for Philadelphia in the morning," Gary said with satisfaction. "You did a good job, Mark. How long will it take us to get to Philadelphia?"

Mark shrugged. "I didn't walk, so I don't know. I've shown you where it's all marshy, maybe impassable by foot. If you can get through, probably eight to ten days.

But you need something to measure the radioactivity."

"You were wrong about that, Mark. There can't be any radioactivity. We weren't at war, you know. No bombs were used here. Our elders would have warned us."

Again Mark shrugged.

"We trust you to get us through," Gary said, smiling now. He was twenty-one.

"I'm not going," Mark said.

Gary and his brothers exchanged glances. Gary said, "What do you mean? That's your job."

Mark shook his head. "My job was to find out if the cities are there, if anything's left in them. I know I reached them by water. I don't know if they can be reached on foot. I know there's been radioactivity, and I'm going back to the valley to report that."

Gary stood up and began to roll the map they had been using to mark the swamps, the changed coastline, the marsh that had been the intercoastal waterway. Not looking directly at Mark, he said, "Everyone in this expedition is under my command, you know. Everyone."

Mark didn't move.

"I order you to go with us," Gary said, and now he looked at Mark.

Mark shook his head. "You won't make it there and back before the weather changes," he said. "You and your brothers don't know anything about the forests. You'll have the same trouble the early expeditions had in coming to Washington. And the boys can't do anything without someone to tell them what to do. What if all the stuff in Philadelphia is radioactive? If you bring it back, you'll kill everyone with it. I'm going back to the valley."

"You're going to take orders just like everyone else!" Gary shouted. "Keep him here!" He motioned to two of his brothers, and they hurried from the room. The other three remained with Mark, who was still sitting cross-legged on the floor where he had been from the beginning of the meeting.

In a few minutes Gary returned; he carried several long strips of birch bark. Now Mark stood up and reached for the bark. It was from his canoe.

Gary thrust the scraps at him. "Now you understand, I hope. We leave in the morning. You'd better get some rest."

Wordlessly Mark left them. He went to the river and examined the ruined boat. Afterward he built a small fire, and when it was burning brightly he put one end of the boat in the flames, and as it burned he pushed it forward until it was totally consumed.

The next morning when the boys assembled to start the trek to Philadelphia, Mark was not among them. His pack was gone, he could not be found. Gary and his brothers consulted angrily and decided to start without him. They had good maps that Mark himself had corrected. The boys were all well trained. There was no reason to feel dependent on a fourteen-year-old. They started off, but there was a pall over them now.

Mark watched from a distance, and throughout the day he kept them in sight. When they camped that night, their first night in the open forest, he was in a tree nearby.

The boys were all right, he thought with satisfaction. As long as their groups were not separated, they would be all right. But the Gary brothers were clearly nervous. They started at noises.

He waited until the camp was still, and then, high in a tree where he could look down on them without being seen, he began to moan. At first no one paid any attention to the noises he made, but presently Gary and his brothers began to peer anxiously at the woods, at one another. Mark moaned louder. The boys were stirring now. Most of them had been asleep when he started. Now there was a restless movement among them.

"Woji!" Mark moaned, louder and louder. "Woji! Woji!" He doubted anyone was still asleep. "Woji says go back! Woji says go back!" He kept his voice hollow, muffled by his hand over his mouth. He repeated the words many times, and ended each message with a thin, rising moan. After a time he added one more word. "Danger. Danger. Danger."

He stopped abruptly in the middle of the fourth "Danger." Even he was aware of the listening forest now. The Gary brothers took torches into the forest around the camp, looking for something, anything. They stayed close to one another as they made the search. Most of the boys were sitting up, as close to the fires as they could get. It was a long time before they all lay down to try to sleep again. Mark dozed in the tree, and when he jerked awake, he repeated the warning, again stopping

172

in the middle of a word, though he wasn't certain why that was so much worse than just stopping. Again the futile search was made, the fires were replenished, the boys sat upright in fear. Toward dawn when the forest was its blackest Mark began to laugh a shrill, inhuman laugh that seemed to echo from everywhere at once.

The next day was cold and drizzly with thick fog that lifted only slightly as the day wore on. Mark circled the straggling group, now whispering from behind them, now from the left, the right, from in front of them, sometimes from over their heads. By midafternoon they were barely moving and the boys were talking openly of disobeying Gary and returning to Washington. Mark noted with satisfaction that two of the Gary brothers were siding with the rebellious boys now.

"Ow! Woji!" he wailed, and suddenly two groups of the boys turned and started to run. "Woji! Danger!"

Others turned now and joined the flight, and Gary shouted at them vainly, and then he and his brothers were hurrying back the way they had come.

Laughing to himself, Mark trotted away. He headed west, toward the valley.

Bruce stood over the bed where the boy lay sleeping. "Is he going to be all right?"

Bob nodded. "He's been half awake several times, babbling about snow and ice most of the time. He recognized me when I examined him this morning."

Bruce nodded. Mark had been sleeping for almost thirty hours. Physically he was out of danger, and probably hadn't been in real danger at all. Nothing rest and food couldn't cure anyway, but his babblings about the white wall had sounded insane. Barry had ordered everyone to leave the boy alone until he awakened naturally. Barry had been with him most of the time, and would return within the hour. There was nothing anyone could do until Mark woke up.

Later that afternoon Barry sent for Andrew, who had asked to be present when Mark began to talk. They sat on either side of the bed and watched the boy stir, rousing from the deep sleep that had quieted him so thoroughly that he had appeared dead.

Mark opened his eyes and saw Barry. "Don't put me in the hospital," he said faintly, and closed his eyes again. Presently he opened his eyes and looked about the room, then back to Barry. "I'm in the hospital, aren't I? Is anything wrong with me?"

"Not a thing," Barry said. "You passed out from exhaustion and hunger, that's all."

"I would like to go to my own room then," Mark said, and tried to rise.

Barry gently restrained him. "Mark, don't be afraid of me, please. I promise you I won't hurt you now or ever. I promise that." For a moment the boy resisted the pressure of his hands, then he relaxed. "Thank you, Mark," Barry said. "Do you feel like talking yet?"

Mark nodded. "I'm thirsty," he said. He drank deeply. He began to describe his trip north. He told it completely, even how he had frightened Gary and his brothers and routed the expedition to Philadelphia. He was aware that Andrew tightened his lips at that part of the story, but he kept his eyes on Barry and told them everything.

"And then you came back," Barry said. "How?"

"Through the woods. I made a raft to cross the river."

Barry nodded. He wanted to weep, and didn't know why. He patted Mark's arm. "Rest now," he said. "We'll get word to them to stay in Washington until we dig up some radiation detectors."

"Impossible!" Andrew said angrily outside the door. "Gary was exactly right in pressing on to Philadelphia. That boy destroyed a year's training in one night."

"I'm going too," Barry had said, and he was with Mark now in Washington. Two of the younger doctors were also with them. The young expedition members were frightened and disorganized; the work had come to a stop, and they had been waiting in the main building for someone to come give them new instructions.

"When did they start out again?" Barry demanded.

"The day after they got back here," one of the young boys said.

"Forty boys!" Barry muttered. "And six fools." He turned to Mark. "Would we accomplish anything by starting after them this afternoon?"

Mark shrugged. "I could alone. Do you want me to go after them?"

"No, not by yourself. Anthony and I will go, and Alistair will stay here and see that things get moving again."

Mark looked at the two doctors doubtfully. Anthony was pale, and Barry looked uncomfortable.

"They've had about ten days," Mark said. "They should be in the city by now, if they didn't get lost. I don't think it would make much difference if we leave now or wait until morning."

"Morning, then," Barry said shortly. "You could use another night's sleep."

They traveled fast, and now and again Mark pointed out where the others had camped, where they had gone astray, where they had realized their error and headed in the right direction again. On the second day his lips tightened and he looked angry, but said nothing until late in the afternoon. "They're too far west, getting farther off all the time," he said. "They might miss Philadelphia altogether if they don't head east again. They must have been trying to bypass the swamps."

Barry was too tired to care, and Anthony merely grunted. At least, Barry thought, stretching out by the fire, they were too tired at night to listen for strange noises, and that was good. He fell asleep even as he was thinking this.

On the fourth day Mark stopped and pointed ahead. At first Barry could see no difference, but then he realized they were looking at the kind of stunted growth Mark had talked about. Anthony unpacked the Geiger counter and it began to register immediately. It became more insistent as they moved ahead, and Mark led them to the left, keeping well back from the radioactive area.

"They went in, didn't they?" Barry said.

Mark nodded. They were keeping their distance from the contaminated ground, and when the counter sounded its warning, they moved south again until it became quieter. That night they decided to keep moving west until they were able to get around the radioactive area, and enter Philadelphia from that direction, if possible.

"We'll run into the snowfields that way," Mark said.

"Not afraid of snow, are you?" Barry said.

"I'm not afraid."

"Right. Then we go west tomorrow, and if we can't turn north by night, we come back and try going east, see if we pick up a trail or anything that way."

They traveled all day through an intermittent rain, and hourly the temperature fell until it was near freezing when they made camp that night.

175

"How much farther?" Barry asked.

"Tomorrow," Mark said. "You can smell it from here."

Barry could smell only the fire, the wet woods, the food cooking. He studied Mark, then shook his head.

"I don't want to go any farther," Anthony said suddenly. He was standing by the fire, too rigid, a listening look on his face.

"It's a river," Mark said. "It must be pretty close. There's ice on all the rivers, and it hits the banks now and then. That's what you hear."

Anthony sat down, but the intent look didn't leave his face. The next morning they headed west again. By noon they were among hills, and now they knew that as soon as they got high enough to see over the trees they would be able to see the snow, if there was any snow to see.

They stood on the hill and stared, and Barry understood Mark's nightmares. The trees at the edge of the snow were stark, like trees in the middle of winter. Beyond them other trees had snow halfway up their trunks, and their naked branches stood unmoving, some of them at odd angles, where the pressure had already knocked them over and the snow had prevented their falling. Up higher there were no trees visible at all, only snow.

"Is it still growing?" Barry asked in a hushed voice.

No one answered. After a few more minutes, they turned and hurried back the way they had come. As they circled Philadelphia heading east, the Geiger counter kept warning them to stay back, and they could get no closer to the city from this direction than they had been able to from the west. Then they found the first bodies.

Six boys had come out together. Two had fallen near each other; the others had left them, continued another half-mile and collapsed. The bodies were all radioactive.

"Don't get near them," Barry said as Anthony started to kneel by the first bodies. "We don't dare touch them," he said.

"I should have stayed," Mark whispered. He was staring at the sprawled bodies. There was mud on their faces. "I shouldn't have left. I should have kept after them, to make sure they didn't go on. I should have stayed."

Barry shook his arm, and Mark kept staring, repeating over and over, "I should have stayed with them. I should . . ." Barry slapped him hard, then again, and Mark bowed his head and stumbled away, reeling into trees and bushes as he rushed away from the bodies, away from Barry and Anthony. Barry ran after him and caught his arm.

"Mark! Stop this! Stop it, do you hear me!" He shook him hard again. "Let's get back to Washington."

Mark's cheeks were glistening with tears. He pulled away from Barry and started to walk again, and he didn't look back at the bodies.

Barry and Bruce waited for Anthony and Andrew, who had requested, demanded, time to talk to them. "It's about him again, isn't it?" Bruce said.

"I suppose."

"Something's got to be done," Bruce said. "You and I both know we can't let him go on this way. They'll demand a council meeting next, and that'll be the end of it."

Barry knew. Andrew and his brother entered and sat down. They both looked grim and angry.

"I don't deny he had a bad time during the summer," Andrew said abruptly. "That isn't the point now. But whatever happened to him has affected his mind, and that is the point. He's behaving in a childish, irresponsible way that simply cannot be tolerated."

Again and again since summer these sessions had been held. Mark had drawn a line of honey from an ant hill up the wall into the Andrew brothers' quarters, and the ants had followed. Mark had soaked every match he could get his hands on in a salt solution, dried them carefully, and restacked them in the boxes, and not one of them had lighted, and he had sat with a straight face and watched one after another of the older brothers try to get a fire. Mark had removed every nameplate from every door in the domitories. He had tied the Patrick brothers' feet together as they slept and then yelled to them to come quickly.

"He's gone too far this time," Andrew said. "He stole the yellow Report to Hospital tags, and he's been sending dozens of women to the hospital to be tested for pregnancy. They're in a panic, our staff is overworked as it is, and no one has time to sort out this kind of insanity."

"We'll talk to him," Barry said.

"That's not good enough any longer! You've talked and talked. He promises not to do that particular thing again, and then does something worse. We can't live with this constant disruption!"

"Andrew, he had a series of terrible shocks last summer. And he's had too much responsibility for a boy his age. He feels a dreadful guilt over the deaths of all those children. It isn't unnatural for him to revert to childish behavior now. Give him time, he'll get over it."

"No!" Andrew said, standing up with a swift, furious motion. "No! No more time! What will it be next?" He glanced at his brother, who nodded. "We feel that we are his targets. Not you, not the others; we are. Why he feels this hostility toward me and my brothers I don't know, but it's here, and we don't want to have to worry about him constantly, wondering what he'll do next."

Barry stood up. "And I say I'll handle it."

For a moment Andrew faced him defiantly, then said, "Very well. But, Barry, it can't go on. It has to stop now."

"It will stop."

The younger brothers left, and Bruce sat down. "How?"

"I don't know how. It's his isolation. He can't talk this out with anyone, doesn't play with anyone . . . We have to force him to participate in those areas where the others would accept him."

Bruce agreed. "Like the Winona sisters' coming-of-age party next week."

Later that day Barry told Mark he was to attend the party. Mark had never been formally accepted into the adult community, and would not be honored by a party just for him.

He shook his head. "No, thank you, I'd rather not."

"I didn't invite you," Barry said grimly. "I'm ordering you to attend and to participate. Do you understand?"

Mark glanced at him quickly. "I understand, but I don't want to go."

"If you don't go, I'm hauling you out of this cozy little room, away from your books and your solitude, and putting you back in our room, back in the lecture rooms when you're not in school or at work. Now do you understand?"

Mark nodded, but didn't look at Barry again. "All right," he said sullenly.

Chapter 26

The party had started already when Mark entered the auditorium. They were dancing at the far end, and between him and the dancers a group of girls stood whispering. They turned to look at him, and one of them left the group. There was giggling behind her, and she motioned her sisters to stop, but the giggling continued.

"Hello, Mark," she said. "I'm Susan."

Before he realized what she was doing she had slipped off her bracelet and was trying to put it over his hand. There were six little bows on the bracelet.

"No," Mark said hurriedly, and jerked away. "I . . . No. I'm sorry." He backed up a step, turned and ran, and the giggling started again, louder than before.

He ran to the dock and stood looking at the black water. He shouldn't have run. Susan and her sisters were seventeen, maybe even a little older. In one night they would have taught him everything, he thought bitterly, and he had turned and run. The music grew louder; soon they would eat and then leave in couples, in groups, everyone but Mark, and the children too young for the mat play. He thought of Susan and her sisters and he was first hot, then cold, then flushing hot again.

"Mark?"

He stiffened. They wouldn't have followed him, he thought in panic. He whirled around.

"It's Rose," she said. "I won't give you my bracelet unless you want it."

She came closer, and he turned his back and pretended to be looking at something in the river, afraid she would be able to see him in the dark, see the redness he could feel pounding in his neck and cheeks, sense his wet palms. Rose, he thought, his age, one of the girls he had trained in the woods. For him to blush and become bashful before her was more intolerable than running from Susan had been.

179

"I'm busy," he said.

"I know. I saw you before. It's all right. They shouldn't have done that, not all of them together. We all told them not to."

He didn't reply, and she moved to his side. "There's nothing to see, is there?"

"No. You'll get cold out here."

"You will too."

"What do you want?"

"Nothing. Next summer I'll be old enough to go to Washington or Philadelphia."

He turned angrily. "I'm going to my room."

"Why did I make you mad? Don't you want me to go to Washington? Don't you like me?"

"Yes. I'm going now."

She put her hand on his arm and he stopped; he felt he couldn't move. "May I go to your room with you?" she asked, and now she sounded like the girl who had asked in the woods if the mushrooms were all dangerous, if the things in the trees had told him how to find his way, if he really could become invisible if he wanted to.

"You'll go back to your sisters and laugh at me like Susan did," he said.

"No!" she whispered. "Never! Susan wasn't laughing at you. They were scared, that's why they were all so nervous. Susan was most scared of all because she was picked to put the bracelet on you. They weren't laughing at you."

As she spoke she released his arm and took a step back from him, then another. Now he could see the pale blur of her face. She was shaking her head as she talked.

"Scared? What do you mean?"

"You can do things no one else can do," she said, still speaking very softly, almost in a whisper. "You can make things no one ever saw, and you can tell stories no one ever heard, and you can disappear and travel through the woods like the wind. You're not like the other boys. Not like our elders. Not like anyone else. And we know you don't like any of us because you never choose anyone to lie with."

"Why did you come after me if you're so afraid of me?"

"I don't know. I saw you run and . . . I don't know."

He felt the hot flush race through him again, and he began to walk. "If you want to go with me, I don't care," he said roughly, not looking back. "I'm going to my room now." He could not hear her footsteps for the pounding in his ears. He walked swiftly, making a wide berth of the auditorium, and he knew she was running to keep up. He led her around the hospital, not wanting to walk down the brightly lighted corridor with her at his heels. At the far end he opened the door and glanced inside before he entered. He let the door go and almost ran to his room, and he heard her quick footsteps as she came after him.

"What are you doing?" she asked at the doorway.

"I'm putting the cover over the window," he said, and his voice sounded angry even to him. "So no one can look at us. I put it there a lot."

"But why?"

He tried not to look at her when he climbed down from the chair, but again and again he found himself watching. She was unwinding a long sash that had gone around her neck, criss-crossed at her breasts, and circled her waist several times. The sash was violet, almost the color of her eyes. Her hair was a pale brown. He remembered that during the summer it had been blond. There were freckles across her nose, on her arms.

She finished with the sash and now lifted her tunic, and with one motion took it off. Suddenly Mark's fingers seemed to come to life and without his willing it they began to pull off his tunic.

Later she said she had to go, and he said not yet, and they dozed with his arms tight about her. When she again said she had to go, he woke up completely. "Not yet," he said. When he woke the second time it was daylight and she was pulling on her tunic.

"You have to come back," Mark said. "Tonight, after dinner. Will you?"

"All right."

"Promise. You won't forget?"

"I won't forget. I promise."

He watched her wind the sash, and when she was gone he reached out and yanked the cover from the window and looked for her. He didn't see her; she must have gone through the building, out the other end. He rolled over and fell asleep again.

And now, Mark thought, he was happy. The nightmares were gone, the sudden flashes of terror that he couldn't explain stopped sweeping over him. The mysteries had been answered, and he knew what the books meant when the authors spoke of finding happiness, as if it

181

were a thing that perseverance would lead one to. He examined the world with new eyes, and everything he saw was beautiful and good.

During the day while studying, he would stop, think with terrible fear that she was gone, lost, had fallen into the river, something. He would drop what he was doing and race from building to building searching for her, not to speak to her, just to see her, to know she was all right. He might find her in the cafeteria with her sisters at such times, and from a distance he would count them and then search for the one with the special something that separated her from all others.

Every night she came to him, and she taught him what she had been taught by her sisters, by the other men, and his joy intensified until he wondered how the others had stood it before him, how he could stand it.

In the afternoons he ran to the old house, where he was making her a pendant. It was the sun, two inches in diameter, made of clay. It had three coats of yellow paint, and he added a fourth. In the old house he read again the chapters on physiology, sexual responses, femininity, everything he could find that touched on his happiness in any way

She would say no one night soon, and he would give her the pendant to show he understood, and he would read to her. Poetry. Sonnets from Shakespeare or Wordsworth, something soft and romantic. And afterward he would teach her to play chess, and they would spend platonic evenings together learning all about each other.

Seventeen nights, he thought, waiting for her. Seventeen nights so far. The cover was over the window, his room was clean, ready. When his door opened and Andrew stood there, Mark jumped up in a panic.

"What's wrong? Has something happened to Rose? What happened?"

"Come with me," Andrew said sternly. Behind him one of his brothers watched.

"Tell me what's wrong!" Mark yelled, and tried to run past them.

The doctors caught his arms and held him. "We'll take you to her," Andrew said.

Mark stopped trying to yank away, and a new coldness seemed to enter him. Wordlessly they walked through the building, out the far end, and along the pathways cleared in the snow to one of the dormitories. Now he struggled again, but briefly, and he permitted them to lead him to one of the rooms. At the door they all stopped, and then Andrew gave Mark a slight push and he entered alone.

"No!" he cried. "No!"

There was a tangle of naked bodies, doing all the things to one another she had told him about. At his scream of anguish she raised her head, as they all did, but he knew it was Rose his eyes had picked out of all the rest. She was on her knees, one of the brothers behind her; she had been nuzzling one of her sisters.

He could see their mouths moving, knew they were talking, yelling. He turned and ran. Andrew got in front of him, his mouth opening, closing, opening. Mark doubled his fist and hit blindly, first Andrew, then the other doctor.

"Where is he?" Barry demanded. "Where did he go this time of night?"

"I don't know," Andrew said sulkily. His mouth was swollen and it hurt.

"You shouldn't have done that to him! Of course he went wild with his first taste of sex. What did you think would happen to him? He's never had it with anyone at all! Why did that foolish girl come to you?"

"She didn't know what to do. She was afraid to tell him no. She tried to explain everything to him, but he wouldn't listen. He ordered her back night after night."

"Why didn't you come to us about it?" Barry asked bitterly. "What made you think shock treatment like that would take care of the problem?"

"I knew you'd say leave him alone. You say that about everything he does. Leave him alone, it'll take care of itself. I didn't think it would."

Barry went to the window and looked out at the black, cold night. The snow was several feet deep, and the temperature dropped to near zero almost every night.

"He'll come back when he gets cold enough," Andrew said. "He'll come back furious with all of us, and with me in particular. But he will come back. We're all he has." He left abruptly.

"He's right," Bruce said. He sounded tired. Barry looked quickly at his brother, then at the others, who had remained silent while Andrew reported. They were as worried about the boy as he was, and as tired as he was

183

of the apparently endless stream of troubles caused by him.

"He can't go to the old house," Bruce said after a moment. "He knows he'd freeze there. The chimney's plugged, he can't have a fire. That leaves the woods. Even he can't survive in the woods at night in this weather."

Andrew had sent a dozen of the younger brothers to search all the buildings, even the breeders' quarters, and another group had gone to the old house to look. There was no sign of Mark. Toward dawn the snow started again.

Mark had found the cave by accident. Picking berries on the cliff over the farmhouse one day, he had felt a cold draft of air on his bare legs and had found the source. A hole in the hill, a place where two limestone rocks came together unevenly. There were caves throughout the hills. He had found several others before this one, and there was the cave where the laboratories were.

He had dug carefully behind one of the limestone slabs, and gradually had opened the mouth of the cave enough to get through it. There was a narrow passage, then a room, another passage, another larger room. Over the years since finding it he had taken in wood to burn, clothes, blankets, food.

That night he huddled in the second room and stared dry-eyed into the fire he had made, certain no one would ever find him. He hated them all, Andrew and his brothers most of all. As soon as the snow melted, he would run away, forever. He would go south. He would make a longer canoe, a seventeen-foot one this time, and steal enough supplies to last him and he would keep going until he reached the Gulf of Mexico. Let them train the boys and girls themselves, let them find the warehouses, find the dangerous radioactive places if they could. First he would burn down everything in the valley. And then he would go.

He stared at the flames until his eyes felt afire. There were no voices in the cave, only the fire crackling and popping. The firelight flickered over the stalagmites and stalactites, making them appear red and gold. The smoke was carried away from his face and the air was good; it even felt warm after the cold night air. He thought about the time he and Molly had hidden on the hillside near the cave entrance while Barry and his brothers searched for them. At the thought of Barry, his mouth tightened. Barry, Andrew, Warren, Michael, Ethan . . . All doctors, all the same. How he hated them!

He rolled in his blanket and when he closed his eyes, he saw Molly again, smiling gently at him, playing checkers, digging mud for him to model. And suddenly the tears came.

He never had explored the cave past the second room, but in the days that followed, he began a systematic exploration. There were several small openings off the room, and one by one he investigated them, until he was brought up by a sealed passage, or a drop-off, or a ceiling so high he couldn't get to any of the holes there might be up there. He used torches, and his steps were sometimes reckless, but he didn't care if he fell or not, if he got trapped or not. He lost track of how many days he had been in the cave; when he was hungry he ate, when he was thirsty he went to the entrance, scooped up snow, and took it back with him to melt. When he was sleepy he slept.

On one of his last exploratory trips he heard water running, and he stopped abruptly. He had traveled far, he knew. Over a mile. Maybe two miles. He tried to remember how long his torch had been when he started. Almost full length, and now it was less than a third of that. Another torch hung on his belt, just in case he needed it, but he never had gone so far that he had needed a second torch to get back.

He had lighted the second torch before he came upon the cave river. Now he felt a new excitement as he realized this had to be the same water that ran through the laboratory cave. It was one system, then, and even if no opening existed other than the one cut by the river, the two sections were linked.

He followed the river until it vanished into a hole in the cave wall; he would have to swim to go any further. He squatted and stared at the hole. The river appeared in the laboratory cave from just such a hole.

Another time he would come back with his rope and more torches. He turned to go back to his large room with the fire and food, and now he paid attention to his torch so he could estimate how far he traveled, how far that wall was from his familiar section of the cave. But he knew where he was. He knew on the other side of that wall there was the laboratory, and beyond it the hospital and the dormitories.

He slept one more time in the cavern, and the next day he left it to return to the community. He had eaten very little for the past few days; he felt half starved and was very tired.

The snow was inches deeper than it had been, and it was snowing when he arrived in the valley once more. It was nearly dark by the time he got to the hospital building and entered. He saw several people but spoke to no one and went straight to his room, where he pulled off his outer clothes and fell into bed. He was nearly asleep when Barry appeared in the doorway.

"Are you all right?" Barry asked.

Mark nodded silently. Barry hesitated a moment, then entered. He stood over the bed. Mark looked up at him without speaking, and Barry reached down and touched his cheek, then his hair

"You're cold," he said. "Are you hungry?"

Mark nodded.

"I'll bring you something," Barry said. But before he opened the door he turned once more. "I'm sorry," he said. "Mark, I'm truly sorry." He left quickly.

After he was gone Mark realized they had thought he was dead, and the look he had seen on Barry's face was the same look he could remember seeing on Molly's face a long time ago.

He didn't care, he thought. They couldn't do anything now to make up for what they had done to him. They hated him and thought he was weak, thought they could control him the way they controlled the clones. And they were wrong. It wasn't enough for Barry to say he was sorry; they would all be sorry before he was done.

When he heard Barry returning with food, he closed his eyes and pretended to be asleep, not willing to see again that soft, vulnerable look.

Barry left the tray, and when he was gone, Mark ate ravenously. He pulled the cover over him and before he fell asleep he thought again of Molly. She had known he'd come to feel like this and she had said to wait, wait until he was a man, to learn everything he could first. Her face and Barry's face seemed to blend together, and he fell asleep.

Chapter 27

Andrew had called the meeting, was in charge from start to finish. No one disputed his authority now to take control of the council meetings. Barry watched him from a side chair and tried to feel some of the excitement the younger brother showed.

"Those of you who want to look over the charts and records, please do so. I have given you the barest summary, not our methods. We can reproduce indefinitely through cloning. We have finally solved the problem that has plagued us from the beginning, the problem of the fifth-generation decline. The fifth, sixth, tenth, one-hundredth, they'll all be perfect now."

"But only those clones from our youngest people survive," Miriam said drily.

"We'll work that out too," Andrew said impatiently. "In manipulating the enzymes there are some organisms that react with what appears to be almost an allergic collapse. We'll find out why and take care of it."

Miriam was looking very old, Barry realized suddenly. He hadn't noticed it before, but her hair was white and her face was thin, with fine lines around her eyes, and she looked tired unto death.

She looked at Andrew with a disarming smile. "I expect you to be able to solve the problem you have created, Andrew," she said, "but will the younger doctors be able to?"

"We shall continue to use the breeders," Andrew said with a touch of impatience. "We'll use them to clone those children who are particularly intelligent. We'll go to implantations of clones using the breeders as hosts to ensure a continuing population of capable adults to carry on affairs . . ."

Barry found his attention wandering. The doctors had gone over it all before the council meeting; nothing new would come out here. Two castes, he thought. The leaders, and the workers, who were always expendable. Was that what they had foreseen in the beginning? He knew it was not possible to find any answers to his question. The clones wrote the books, and each generation had felt free to change the books to conform to their own beliefs. He had made a few such changes himself, in fact. And now Andrew would change them again. And this would be the final change; none of the new people would ever think of altering anything.

". . . even more costly in terms of manpower than we expected," Andrew was saying. "The glaciers are moving into Philadelphia at an accelerating rate. We may have only two or three more years to bring out what is salvageable, and it is costing us dearly. We will need hundreds of foragers to go south and east to the coastal cities. We now have some excellent models—the Edward brothers proved especially adept at foraging, as did your own little sisters, the Ella sisters. We'll use them."

"My little Ella sisters couldn't transcribe a landscape to a map if you strung them by the heels and threatened to slice them inch by inch until they did," Miriam said sharply. "That's exactly what I'm talking about. They can do only those things they have been taught, exactly as they've been taught."

"They can't draw maps, but they can return to where they've been," Andrew said, no longer trying to conceal his displeasure at the turn the meeting had taken. "That's all we require of them. The implanted clones will do the thinking for them."

"Then it's true," Miriam said. "If you change the formula, you can produce only those clones you are talking about."

"Right. We can't handle two different chemical processes, two formulae, two kinds of clones. We've decided this is the best way to proceed at this time, and meanwhile we'll be working on the process, I can assure you. We shall wait until the tanks are empty, in seven months, then make the changes. And we are working out a timetable to plan for the best time to clone the council members and those others who are needed in leadership capacities. We are not rushing into a new procedure without considering every aspect, I promise you, Miriam. At each step we will inform this group of our progress . . ."

In a tightly thatched lean-to near the mill Mark rested

on his elbow and looked at the girl at his side. She was his age, nineteen. "You're cold," he said.

She nodded. "We won't be able to do this much longer."

"You could meet me in the old farmhouse," he said.

"You know I can't."

"What happens if you try to cross the line? A dragon comes out and breathes fire on you?"

She laughed

"Really, what happens? Have you ever tried?"

Now she sat up and hugged her arms about her bare body. "I'm really cold. I should get dressed."

Mark held her tunic out of reach. "First tell me what happens."

She snatched, missed, and fell across him, and for a moment they lay close together. He pulled a cover over her and stroked her back. "What happens?"

She sighed and drew away from him. "I tried it once," she said. "I wanted to go home, to my sisters. I cried and cried, and that didn't help. I could see the lights, and knew they were just a few hundred feet away. I ran at first, then I began to feel strange, faint, I guess. I had to stop. I was determined to get to the dorm. I walked then, not very fast, ready to grab something if I started to faint. When I got closer to the off-limits line—it's a hedge, you know, just a rose hedge, open at both ends so it's no trouble at all to go around. When I got close to it, the feeling came over me again and everything began to spin. I waited a long time and it didn't stop, but I thought, if I kept my eyes on my feet and didn't pay any attention to anything else, I could walk anyway. I began to walk again." She was lying rigidly beside him now, and her voice was almost inaudible when she went on. "And I started to vomit. I kept vomiting, until I didn't have anything left in me, and then I threw up blood. And I suppose I really did faint. I woke up back in the breeders' room."

Gently Mark touched her cheek and drew her close to him. She was trembling violently. "Shh, shh," Mark soothed her. "It's all right. You're all right now."

No walls held them in, he thought, stroking her hair. No fence restrained them, yet they could not approach the river; they could not get nearer the mill than she was now; they could not pass the rose hedge, or go into the

189

woods. But Molly did it, he thought grimly. And they would too.

"I have to go back," she said presently. The haunted look had come over her face. The emptiness, she had called it. "You wouldn't know what it means," she said, trying to explain. "We aren't separate, you see. My sisters and I were like one thing, one creature, and now I'm a fragment of that creature. Sometimes I can forget it for a short time, when I'm with you I can forget for a while, but it always comes back, and the emptiness comes again. If you turned me inside out, there wouldn't be anything at all there."

"Brenda, I have to talk to you first," Mark said. "You've been here four years, haven't you? And you've had two pregnancies. It's almost time again, isn't it?"

She nodded and pulled on her tunic.

"Listen, Brenda. This time it won't be like before. They plan to use the breeders to clone themselves through implantations of cloned cells. Do you understand what I'm saying?"

She shook her head, but she was listening, watching.

"All right. They've changed something in the chemicals they use for the clones in the tanks. Now they can keep on cloning the same person over and over, but he's a neuter. The new clones can't think for themselves; they can't conceive, can't impregnate, they'll never have children of their own. And the council members are afraid they'll lose the scientific skills, the craftsmanship, Miriam's skill at drawing, her eidetic visual memory—all that might be lost if they don't ensure it in the next generation through cloning. Since they can't use the tanks, they'll use the fertile women as hosts. They'll implant you with clones, triplets. And in nine months you'll have three new Andrews, or three new Miriams, or Lawrences, or whatever. They'll use the strongest, healthiest young women for this. And they'll continue to use artificial insemination for the others. When they produce another new talent they can use, they'll clone him several times, implant the clones in your bodies and produce more of him."

She was staring at him now, openly puzzled by his intensity. "What difference does it make?" she asked. "If that's how we can best serve the community, that's what we have to do."

"The new babies from the tanks won't even have names," Mark said. "They'll be the Bennies, or the

190

Bonnies, or the Annes, all of them, and their clones will be called that, and theirs."

She laced her sandal without speaking.

"And you, how many sets of triplets do you think your body can produce? Three? Four?"

She was no longer listening.

Mark climbed the hill over the valley and sat on a limestone rock, looking at the people below, at the sprawling farm that had grown year by year until it filled the whole valley all the way to the bend in the river. Only the old house was an oasis of trees in the autumn fields, which looked like a desert now. Livestock were moving slowly toward the large barns. A group of small boys swept into view, playing something that involved a lot of running, falling down, and running again. Twenty or more of them played together. He was too far away to hear them, but he knew they were laughing.

"What's wrong with it?" he said aloud, and was surprised by the sound of his voice. The wind stirred the trees, but there were no words, no answer.

They were content, happy even, and he, the outsider, in his discontent would destroy that to satisfy what had to be selfish desires. In his loneliness he would disrupt an entire community that was thriving and satisfied.

Below him the Ella sisters came into view, ten of them, each a physical carbon copy of his mother. For a moment the vision of Molly peeking out from behind a bush, laughing with him, came to mind. It vanished, and he watched the girls walk toward the dormitory. Three of the Miriam sisters came out, and the two groups stopped and talked.

Mark remembered how Molly had made people come to life on paper, a touch here, another there, an eyebrow raised too much, a dimple drawn too deep, always something not just right, but which made the sketch take on life. They couldn't do that, he knew. Not Miriam, not her little Ella sisters, none of them. That was gone, lost forever maybe. Each generation lost something; sometimes it couldn't be regained, sometimes it couldn't be identified immediately. Everett's little brothers couldn't cope with a new emergency with the computer terminal; they couldn't improvise long enough to save the growing fetuses in the tanks if the electricity failed for several days. As long as the elders could foresee the probable troubles that might arise and train the young clones in how to handle them, they were safe enough, but accidents had a way of not being foreseen, catastrophes had a way of not being predictable, and a major accident might destroy everything in the valley simply because none of them had been trained to deal with that specific situation.

He remembered a conversation he had had with Barry. "We're living on the top of a pyramid," he had said, "supported by the massive base, rising above it, above everything that has made it possible. We're responsible for nothing, not the structure itself, not anything above us. We owe nothing to the pyramid, and are totally dependent on it. If the pyramid crumbles and returns to dust, there is nothing we can do to prevent it, or even to save ourselves. When the base goes, the top goes with it, no matter how elaborate the life is that has developed there. The top will return to dust along with the base when the collapse comes. If a new structure is to rise, it must start at the ground, not on top of what has been built during the centuries past."

"You'd drag everyone back into savagery!"

"I would help them down from the point of the pyramid. It's rotting away. The snow and ice from one direction, weather and age from the others. It will collapse, and when it does, the only ones who can survive will be those who are free from it, in no way dependent on it."

The cities are dead, Molly had told him, and it was true. Ironically, the technology that made life in the valley possible might be able to sustain that life only long enough to doom any chance of recovery after the pyramid started to tilt. The top would slide down one of the sides and sink into the debris at the bottom, along with all the other technologies that had seemed perfect and infinite.

No one understood the computer, Mark thought, just as no one but the Lawrence brothers understood the paddle-wheel boat and the steam engine that drove it. The younger brothers could repair it, restore it to its original condition, as long as the materials were at hand, but they didn't know how either one worked, the computer or the boat, and if a screw was missing, none of them would be able to fashion a substitute. In that fact lay the inevitable destruction of the valley and everyone in it.

But they were happy, he reminded himself, as lights began to come on in the valley. Even the breeders were content; they were well cared for, pampered compared to the women who foraged each summer and those who worked long hours in the fields and gardens. And if they became too lonely, there was the comfort of drugs.

They were happy because they didn't have enough imagination to look ahead, he thought, and anyone who tried to tell them there were dangers was by definition an enemy of the community. In disrupting their perfect existence, he had become an enemy.

His restless gaze moved over the valley, and finally stopped on the mill, and like his ancestor before him he understood that was the weak spot, the place where the valley was vulnerable.

Wait until you're a man, Molly had said. But she hadn't realized that each day he was in more danger, that each time Andrew and his brothers discussed his future they were less inclined to grant him a future. He studied the mill broodingly. It was weathered almost silver, surrounded by russets and browns and golds, and the permanent green of the pines and spruces. He would like to paint it; the thought came suddenly, and he laughed and stood up. No time for that. Time had become the goal; he had to have more time, and they might decide any day that allowing him time was endangering them all. Abruptly he sat down once more, and now when he studied the mill and the surrounding area his eyes were narrowed in thought, and there was no smile on his face.

The council meeting had gone on most of the day, and when it ended Miriam asked Barry to walk with her. He looked at her questioningly, but she shook her head. They walked by the river, and when they were out of sight of the others she said, "I would like you to do me a favor, if you will. I would like to visit the old farmhouse. Can you get inside?"

Barry stopped in surprise. "Why?"

"I don't know why. I keep thinking I want to see Molly's paintings. I never did see them, you know."

"But why?"

"Can you get in?"

He nodded, and they started to walk again. "When do you want to go?"

"Is it too late now?"

193

The rear door of the farmhouse was loosely boarded. They didn't even need a crowbar to open it. Barry led the way up the stairs, carrying the oil lamp high, casting strange shadows on the wall beside him. The house felt very empty, as if Mark had not been there for a long time.

Miriam looked at the paintings quietly, not touching them, holding her hands tightly clasped before her as she went from one to another. "They should be moved," she said finally. "They will rot away to nothing in here."

When she came to the carving of Molly that Mark had made, she touched it, almost reverently. "It is she," she said softly. "He has her gift, doesn't he?"

"He has the gift," Barry said.

Miriam rested her hand on the head. "Andrew plans to kill him."

"I know."

"He has served his purpose, and now he is a threat and must go." She ran her finger down the cheek of walnut. "Look, it's too high and sharp, but that makes it more like her instead of less. I don't understand why that is, do you?"

Barry shook his head.

"Will he try to save himself?" Miriam asked, not looking at him, her voice tightly controlled.

"I don't know. How can he? He can't survive alone in the woods. Andrew won't allow him to remain in the community many more months."

Miriam sighed and withdrew her hand from the carved head. "I'm sorry," she whispered, and it was not clear whether she spoke to him or to Molly.

Barry went to the window overlooking the valley and looked through the peephole Mark had made in the boards. How pretty it was, he thought, the gathering dusk, with pale lights glowing in the distance and the black hills encircling it all. "Miriam," he asked, "if you knew a way to help him, would you?"

For a long time she was silent, and he thought she would not answer. Then she said, "No. Andrew is right. He is not a physical threat now, but his presence is painful. It is as if he is a reminder of something that is too elusive to grasp, something that is hurtful, even deadly, and in his presence we try to regain it and fail over and over. We will stop feeling this pain when he is gone, not before then." She joined him at the window. "In a year or two he will threaten us in other ways. That is what is

194

important," she said, nodding toward the valley. "Not any individual, even if his death kills us both."

Barry put his arm about her shoulder then, and they stood looking out together. Suddenly Miriam stiffened and said, "Look, a fire!"

There was a faint line of brightness that grew as they watched, spreading in both directions, becoming two lines, moving downward and upward. Something erupted, blazed brightly, then subsided, and the lines moved onward.

"It will burn down the mill!" Miriam cried, and ran from the window to the stairs. "Come on, Barry! It's just above the mill!"

Barry stood by the window as if transfixed by the moving lines of fire. *He* had done it, Barry thought. Mark was trying to burn down the mill.

Chapter 28

Hundreds of people spread out over the hillside putting out the brush fire. Others patrolled the grounds surrounding the generating plant to make certain no sparks were blown in by the wind. Hoses were put into service to wet down the bushes and trees, to soak the roof of the large wooden building. Only when the water pressure failed did anyone realize they had a second serious problem on their hands.   *

The flow of water in the swift stream that ran the plant had dwindled to a trickle. All over the valley the lights blinked out as the system compensated for the sudden loss and diverted the electricity to the laboratory. The auxiliary system took over and the lab continued to function, but on reduced power. Everything was turned off except the circuits directly tied into the tanks containing the clones.

Throughout the night the scientists, doctors, and technicians worked to meet the crisis. They had drilled often enough to know exactly what to do in this emergency, and no clones were lost, but the system had been damaged by the uncontrolled stoppage.

Other men began to wade upstream to find the cause of the diminished flow of water. In the first light of morning they stumbled upon a landslide that had almost dammed the small river, and work was started immediately to clear it.

"Did you try to burn down the mill?" Barry demanded.

"No. If I wanted to burn it down, I would have lighted a fire at the mill, not in the woods. If I wanted to burn it down, I would burn it down." Mark stood before Barry's desk, not defiant, not frightened. He waited.

"Where were you all night?"

"In the old house. I was reading about Norfolk, studying maps . . ."

"Never mind about that." Barry drummed his fingers on his desk, pushed back the charts he had been studying, and stood up. "Listen to me, Mark. Some of them think you're responsible for the fire, the dam, everything. I made the point you just made: if you had tried to burn down the mill, you could have done it easily enough without going through all that. The question is still open. The mill is off limits to you. So is the laboratory, and the boat works. Do you understand?"

Mark nodded. Explosives for river clearing were kept in the boat-works building.

"I was at the old house when the fire started," Barry said suddenly, and his voice was very cold and hard. "I saw a curious thing. It looked like an eruption of some sort. I've thought a lot about it. It could have been an explosion, enough to start the landslide. Of course, no one could have seen it from the valley, and whatever noise it made would have been masked if it were underground even a little bit, and by the noise everyone was making fighting the fire."

"Barry," Mark said, interrupting him. "A few years ago you said something to me that was very important, and I believed you then and still believe you. You said you wouldn't hurt me. Do you remember?" Barry nodded, still cold and watchful. "I say that to you now, Barry. These people are my people too, you know. I promise you I won't ever try to hurt them. I have never done anything purposely to harm any of them, and I never will. I promise that."

196

Barry watched him distrustfully, and Mark smiled softly. "I've never lied to you, you know. No matter what I had done, I admitted it if you asked. I'm not lying now."

Abruptly Barry sat down again. "Why were you looking up Norfolk? What is Norfolk?"

"There was a naval base there, one of the biggest on the East Coast. When the end was coming, they must have put hundreds of ships into dry dock. The ocean levels have been dropping. Chesapeake Bay, Delaware Bay, it will be low there too, and those ships are high and dry—they called it mothballing them. I began to think of the metal in the ships. Stainless steel, copper, brass . . . Some of those ships held crews of a thousand men, with supplies for that many, medicines, test tubes, everything."

Barry felt the doubts fading, and the nagging feeling of something not cleared up vanished as they talked of the possibilities of manning an expedition to Norfolk early in the spring. Only much later did he realize he had not asked the crucial questions: Had Mark started the fire, for whatever reason, and had he blasted loose the rocks that had slid down into the stream, for whatever reason?

And if he had, why had he? They had lost time; it would take several months to clean up the mess completely, but they had planned to discontinue the cloning anyway until they were ready to start the mass production later in the spring. Nothing had been changed in their plans, except that now they would work on the stream, make it failproof, set up a new auxiliary system of generating power and improve everything generally.

Only the human implantations would be delayed beyond the target date already set for them. The preliminary work of cloning the cells, all done in the laboratory, would have to wait until spring when the lab was cleaned, the computer programmed anew . . . Why, then, had Mark been so self-satisfied? Barry couldn't answer that question, nor could his brothers when they discussed it.

Throughout the winter Mark made his plans for the expedition to the coast. He would not be allowed to take any of the experienced foragers, who were needed to finish clearing out the warehouses in Philadelphia. He began training his group of thirty fourteen-year-olds while snow was still on the ground, and by March he said they would be ready to start as soon as the snow melted. He presented his provisions list to Barry for his approval;

197

Barry didn't even glance at it. The children would carry oversized packs, so that if they found salvageable items they could bring back as much as they could carry. Meanwhile, the other, more important forces who were going to Philadelphia were also being readied, and more attention was being paid to their needs than to Mark.

The laboratory was ready to operate again, the computer reprogrammed, when it was discovered the water flowing through the cave was contaminated. Somehow coliform bacteria had infiltrated the pure cave water, and its source had to be found before they could start operations.

It had been one thing after another, Barry and Bruce agreed. The fire, the landslide, missing supplies, misplaced drugs, now the contaminated water.

"They aren't accidents," Andrew said furiously. "Do you know what people are saying? It's the work of the forest spirits! Spirits! It's Mark! I don't know how or why, but it's all his doing. You'll see, as soon as he leaves with his group, it will all stop. And this time when he comes back, if he does, we terminate him!"

Barry didn't object; he knew it would be useless. They had determined that Mark, now a man of twenty, could not be allowed to exert his influence any longer. If he hadn't come up with his plan to scout the shipyards at Norfolk, it would have been done sooner. He was a disturbing element. The young clones followed him blindly, took his orders without question, and looked on him with reverential awe. Worse, no one could anticipate what he might do, or what might stir him into action of some sort. He was as alien to them as a being of another species; his intelligence was not like theirs, his emotions were not like theirs. He was the only one who had wept over the deaths of the radiation victims, Barry remembered.

Andrew was right, and there was nothing he could do to change that. At least, if Mark was responsible for the series of accidents, they would stop and there would be peace for a while in the valley. But the day Mark led his group out on foot, it was found that the corral had broken down at the far end and the livestock had wandered out and scattered. They were all rounded up except two cows and their calves and a few sheep. And then the accidents did stop, exactly as Andrew had predicted.

The forest became thicker each day, the trees more

massive. This had been a park, protected from cutting, Mark knew, but even he was awed by the size of the trees, some of them so large that a dozen youngsters grasping hands could hardly reach around them. He named those he knew: white oak, silverbell, maple, a grove of birches . . . The days were warm as they headed south. On the fifth day they turned west by southwest, and no one questioned his directions. They did what they were told to do cheerfully and quickly and asked nothing. They were all strong, but their packs were heavy, and they were very young, and it seemed to Mark they were going at a crawl when he wanted to run, but he didn't push them too fast. They had to be in good shape when they arrived at their destination. In the middle of the afternoon of the tenth day, he told them to stop, and they looked at him, waiting.

Mark surveyed the wide valley. He had known from studying the maps that it was here, but he hadn't realized how beautiful it would be. There was a stream, and on either side of it the land rose enough not to be in danger of flooding, but not so steeply that it would be difficult to get water. This was the fringe of the national forest; some of the trees were the giants they had been seeing for days now, others were younger, and would make the logs they would need for their buildings. There was level ground for their crops, grazing ground for the livestock. He sighed, and when he faced his followers he was smiling broadly.

That afternoon and the following day he started them building lean-tos for temporary shelter; he laid out the corners of the buildings he ordered them to erect, tagged the trees they were to cut and use for the buildings and their campfires, paced off the fields they were to clear, and then, content they had enough to keep them busy until he returned, he told them he was leaving and would return in a few days.

"But where are you going?" one of them asked, glancing about now as if questioning for the first time what they were doing.

"It's a test, isn't it?" another asked, smiling.

"Yes," Mark said soberly. "You could call it a test. In survival. Are there any questions about any of my instructions?" There were none. "I'll return with a surprise for you," he said, and they were content.

He trotted effortlessly through the forest toward the river, and then he followed the river north until he reached the canoe he had hidden in the undergrowth weeks before. In all, it took him four days to return to the valley. He had been gone over two weeks, and he was afraid it might have been too long.

He approached from the hillside above the valley and lay down in some bushes to watch and wait for darkness. Late in the afternoon the paddle wheel came into view, and when it docked people swarmed out and lined up shoulder to shoulder to unload the boat, passing the salvage from one to the next, onto the shore, and into the boathouse. When lights came on, Mark moved. He started down to the old house, where he had hidden the drugs. Two-thirds of the way down he paused and dropped to his knees. To his right, a hundred yards away, was the cave entrance; the ground had been trampled, the limestone slabs had been covered with dirt. They had found his entrance and sealed it off.

He waited until he was certain no one was below him watching the house, and then he cautiously made his way down the rest of the way, bellied under the bushes that grew thick about the house, and slid down the coal chute to the basement. He didn't need a light to find the package, cached behind bricks he had pried loose months earlier. There too was the bottle of wine he had hidden. Working quickly, he added the stolen sleeping pills to the wine and shook it vigorously.

It was dark when he climbed the hillside once more and hurried toward the breeders' quarters. He had to get there after they were in their rooms, but before they were asleep. He crept to the building and watched outside the windows until the night nurse made her rounds with the tray. When she had left the dorm room where Brenda and five other women slept, he tapped lightly on the window.

Brenda grinned when she saw him. She opened the window quickly, and he climbed in and whispered, "Turn off the light. I have wine. We'll have a party."

"They'll have your skin if they catch you," one of the women said. They were pleased at the prospect of a party, and already they were dragging out the mat, and one of them was winding her hair up out of the way.

"Where's Wanda and Dorothy?" Mark asked. "They should be here, and maybe a couple of others. It's a big bottle of wine."

"I'll tell them," Loretta whispered, stifling her laughter.

"Wait until Nurse is out of sight." She peeked out, shut the door, and pressed her finger to her lips. After waiting a moment, she looked again, then slipped out.

"After the party, maybe you and I can get out for a little while?" Brenda said, rubbing her cheek against his.

Mark nodded. "Any glasses in here?"

Someone produced glasses, and he began to pour the wine. Others joined them, and now there were eleven of the younger women on the mat drinking the golden wine, muffling giggles and laughter. When they began to yawn, they wandered off to their beds, and those who had come from the other room stretched out on the mat. Mark waited until they were all sleeping soundly, then left quietly. He went to the dock, made certain no one had remained aboard the paddle wheel, and then returned and began to carry the women out, one by one, wrapped like cocoons in their blankets. On his last trip he gathered as many clothes as he could find, closed the window of the dorm, and, panting with fatigue, made his way back to the boat.

He untied the mooring ropes and let the boat glide with the current, using a paddle to keep it close to the shore. Downriver, nearly opposite the old house, he snagged a rock and drew the boat into shore and tied it securely. One more thing, he thought, very tired now. One more thing.

He ran to the old house and slid down the chute, then hurried upstairs. He didn't use a light, but went straight to the paintings and started to pick up the first one. Behind him a match flared, and he froze.

"Why did you come back?" Barry asked roughly. "Why didn't you stay out there in the woods where you belong?"

"I came back for my things," Mark said, and turned. Barry was alone. He was lighting the oil lamp. Mark made a motion toward the window, and Barry shook his head.

"It won't do any good. They wired the stairs. If anyone comes up here, it rings an alarm in Andrew's room. They'll be on their way in a minute or two."

Mark scooped up the painting, then another and another. "Why are you here?"

"To warn you."

"Why? Why did you suspect I'd come back?"

"I don't know why. I don't want to know why. I've been

sleeping downstairs, in the library. You won't have time to get them all," he said urgently as Mark picked up more paintings. "They'll be here fast. They think you tried to burn down the mill, dam the stream, poison the clones in the tanks. They won't stop to ask any questions this time."

"I didn't try to kill the clones," Mark said, not looking at Barry. "I knew the computer would sound an alarm before the contaminated water was used. How did they find out?"

"They sent some of the boys down into the water, and a couple of them actually managed to swim out the other side, and after that, it wasn't hard. Four were killed in the attempt," he said without inflection.

"I'm sorry," Mark said. "I didn't want that."

Barry shrugged. "You have to go."

"I'm ready."

"You'll die out there," Barry said, in the same dead voice. "You and those children you took with you. They won't be able to breed, you know. Maybe one girl, maybe two, but then what?"

"I've taken some of the women from the breeders' compound," Mark said.

Now Barry registered shock and disbelief. "How?"

"It doesn't matter how. I have them. And we'll make it. I planned it very carefully. We'll make it."

"That's what it was all for?" Barry said. "The fire, the dam, the contaminated water, the seed grains you took? That's what it was all for?" he said again, this time not looking at Mark, but searching the remaining paintings as if they held the answer. "You even have livestock," he said.

Mark nodded. "They're safe. I'll get them in a week or two."

"They'll track you down," Barry said slowly. "They think you're a menace, they won't rest until they find you."

"They can't find us," Mark said. "The ones who could are in Philadelphia. By the time they get back there won't be any signs of us anywhere."

"Have you thought what it will be like?" Barry cried, suddenly losing the rigid control he had achieved. "They'll fear you and hate you! It isn't fair to make them all suffer. And they'll come to hate you for it. They'll die out there! One by one, and each one will make the survivors hate more. In the end you'll all die mean and miserable deaths.

Mark shook his head. "If we don't make it," he said, "there won't be anyone at all left on earth. The pyramid is tilting. The pressure from the great white wall is bearing down on it, and it cannot stand."

"And if you make it, you'll sink back into savagery. It will be a thousand years, five thousand, before a man can climb out of the pit you're digging him. They'll be animals!"

"And you'll be dead." Mark glanced swiftly about the room, then hurried to the door. He paused there and looked at Barry steadily. "You won't understand this. No one's alive but me who could understand it. I love you, Barry. You're strange to me, alien, not human. All of you are. But I didn't destroy them when I could have and wanted to because I loved you. Good-bye, Barry."

For a moment they continued to look at each other, and then Mark turned and ran lightly down the stairs. Behind him he heard the sound of something breaking, but he didn't stop. He left by the back door, and was through the trees and into the field when Andrew and his companions drew near. Mark stopped and listened.

"He's still up there," someone said. "I can see him."

Barry had broken the boards on the window so he could be seen. He was buying time for him, Mark realized, and keeping low, he began to run toward the river.

"That's what it was all for," Barry whispered again, and now he addressed himself to the walnut head that was Molly. He held the head between his hands and sat down at the exposed window with the lamp behind him. "That's what it was all for," he said one more time, and he wondered if Molly had always been smiling. He didn't look up when flames started to crackle through the house, but he held the carved head tighter against his chest as if to protect it.

Far down the river Mark stood in the paddle wheel watching the flames, and he wept. When the boat bumped a rock, he began to fire the engine and then, under power, continued downriver. When he reached the Shenandoah he turned south and followed it until the big boat could go no farther. It was almost dawn. He sorted the clothes he had gathered together in the women's quarters and made up packs of the boat's provisions; they would need everything they could carry.

When the women began to stir, he would give them tea and cornbread, and get them ashore. He would take the boat out to the middle of the river and let it float downstream again. They would need it back in the valley. Then he and the women would start through the forests toward home.

Epilogue

Mark kept behind trees as he approached the ridge over the valley once more. Twenty years, he thought. Twenty years since he had seen it. It was possible they had set up an elaborate alarm system, but he thought not. Not up here anyway. From all appearances, the woods up here had not been entered for many years. He ran the last few feet to the ridge, concealed himself behind a tangle of wild grapes, and looked below. For a long time he didn't move, hardly breathed, and then he slowly began to walk down the slope.

There was no sign of life. Aspens grew in the fields, willows crowded the riverbanks; around the buildings the junipers and pines that had once been kept trimmed now grew high and almost hid the buildings. The rose hedge had become a thicket. He started and whirled around at a sudden shriek that sounded almost human. A dozen large birds launched themselves into the air and flew awkwardly toward the nearest copse. The chickens had gone wild, he thought in wonder. And the livestock? He could see no sign of cattle, but they would be in the woods, along the riverbanks, spreading throughout the region.

He walked on. Again he stopped. One of the dormitories was gone, no trace of it anywhere. A tornado, he thought, and he saw it now, a line of destruction that time had smoothed over, erased; a path where there were no buildings, no large trees, only the new growth of alders and aspens and grasses that would hold the ground until the spruces made it down the hillside, until the maple and oak seeds could be blown in to land on a hospitable site and take root. He followed the swath cut by the tornado, more certain as he moved that that was what had happened. But it couldn't account for the death of the entire community. Not that alone. Then he saw the ruins of the mill and stopped.

The mill had been destroyed, and only the foundation and rusting machinery indicated that it had once stood there, the mechanical queen ant of the community, giving all the will to live, the energy, the means to sustain life.

The end would have come quickly without the mill, without the power. He didn't go any closer to it. He bowed his head and stumbled down toward the river, not wanting to see anything else.

He traveled homeward more slowly than he had come, stopping often to look at the trees, the brilliant green carpet of mosses, and now and again he watched a glittering locust beat heavily through the sunlight, its iridescent wings appearing in flashes of color, then disappearing when it changed direction and didn't catch the light exactly right. The locusts had come back; there were wasps again, and worms in the ground. He stopped at a mammoth white oak that overlooked a valley and thought about the changes the tree had witnessed silently. The leaves rustled over him, and he put his cheek against the tree for a moment, then went on.

Sometimes the loneliness had been almost too much, he thought, and always at those times he had found comfort in the woods, where he sought nothing human. He wondered if the others were still lonely; no one spoke of it any longer. He smiled as he thought of how the women had wept and screamed and straggled behind him, only to run to catch up once more.

At the top of the hill overlooking his valley he paused, then leaned against a silver maple to watch the activities below. Men and women worked in the fields—weeding the sugar cane, hoeing corn, picking beans. Others had torn down one wall of the bathhouse and were busy expanding the facilities; more of the fired-clay tiles were being put in, fitted closely around the great fireplace in order to have a constant supply of hot water. Some of the older children were doing something to the water wheel—he couldn't tell what.

A dozen or more children were picking blackberries along the edges of the fields. They wore long-sleeved shirts and long pants, so they wouldn't become too scratched. They finished, put down their baskets, and began to pull off the confining clothes. Then, naked, nut-brown, laughing, they started toward the settlement. No two of them were alike.

Five thousand years of savagery, Barry had believed,

but that was time measured on the steps of the pyramid, not by those who lived any part of it. Mark had led his people into a timeless period, where the recurring seasons and the cycles of the heavens and of life, birth, and death marked their days. Now the joys of men and women, and their agonies, were private affairs that would come and go without a trace. In the timeless period life became the goal, not the re-creation of the past or the elaborate structuring of the future. The fan of possibilities had almost closed, but was opening once more, and each new child widened its spread. More than that couldn't be asked.

Four canoes came into view on the river; the boys and girls had been out netting fish. Now they raced one another home. Soon, Mark knew, some of them would ask the community's permission to take the canoes on a trip of exploration, not searching for anything in particular, but out of curiosity about their world. The older adults would be fearful, unwilling for them to leave, but Mark would grant permission, and even if he didn't, they would go. They had to.

Mark pushed himself away from the tree and started down the hill, impatient suddenly to be home again. He was greeted by Linda, who held out her hand to him. She was nineteen, large with child, his child.

"I'm glad you're home," Linda said softly. "It has been lonesome."

"And you're not lonely now?" he asked, putting his arm about her shoulders.

"No."

The naked children saw him then and raced toward him, laughing, talking excitedly. Their hands and lips were stained with blackberries. He tightened his grip on Linda's shoulder. She looked at him questioningly, and he loosened his grasp, afraid he had hurt her.

"Why are you smiling like that?" she asked.

"Because I'm happy to be home. I was lonely too," he said, and it was part of the truth, and the other part he knew he could not explain to her. Because all the children were different.

Fantasy Novels from Pocket Books

I had set out with a feeling of foreboding, but now that we were fairly to sea, with Key West at last below the horizon astern, and steering a compass course for the Tortugas, much of my gloom left me. I began to think that I had been too long alone in that overpowering house; had been doing too much reading on piracy, and this had overburdened my imagination.

... The fresh air had made me more tired than I realized, and in a few minutes I drifted off into a heavy sleep.

... I awoke suddenly in the dark, aware that there was something the matter with the cutter. Her motion through the water was no longer smooth, but uncertain....

The cockpit was empty. The untended tiller swung from side to side. My uncle had disappeared. But dead ahead, dark against the starlit waters, lay an old-fashioned brig with high-pitched bowsprit and her two masts raked well back in the style of the 1700s.

"The yarn is meatier and more skillful than most storytelling and bound to intrigue. ..."

—*ALA Booklist*

"By ingeniously combining such disparate elements as piracy, a search for King Solomon's Mines, reincarnation, and time fantasy, the author has produced a briskly moving adventure story."

—*Horn Book*

Also available from VAGABOND BOOKS

Blackbriar
   by William Sleator

Doris Fein: Quartz Boyar
   by T. Ernesto Bethancourt

Doris Fein: Superspy
   by T. Ernesto Bethancourt

The Forever Formula
   by Frank Bonham

Fours Crossing
   by Nancy Garden

Give Dad My Best
   by James Lincoln Collier

Kidnapping Mr. Tubbs
   by Don Schellie

Leroy and the Old Man
   by W. E. Butterworth

Sarah Bishop
   by Scott O'Dell

The Crime of
Martin Coverly

by

Leonard Wibberley

Vagabond Books

SCHOLASTIC BOOK SERVICES·
New York Toronto London Auckland Sydney Tokyo

ISBN 0-590-32307-5

12 11 10 9 8 7 6 5 4 3 2 1   12   2 3 4 5 6/8

Printed in the U. S. A.   06

For Christopher

The Crime of
Martin Coverly

I can give no explanation for the story that follows beyond one, gaining a little acceptance these days, that all life, all existence, is like a highway, and the fact that each of us walks on a particular part of that highway does not mean that what is behind us and what lies far ahead of us does not exist, and at the same time.

That explanation I did not arrive at entirely by myself. It was suggested to me by Dr. John Wilton, who is both a psychologist and a historian, and who taught history at our local high school.

It took several evenings of conversation for me to tell him all that happened to me — a rambling wild story as you shall see. But Dr. Wilton, clad as always in the evenings in a light sports shirt, jeans, and sneakers and smoking a pipe to which he was so addicted that it seemed part of his anatomy, interrupted me only occasionally and then always over what seemed to me a trifling detail.

He wished to know, for example, of what kind of stone the columns in the treasure house of King Solomon were made, and whether the spearheads of the warrior tribe I had met in Africa were made of bronze or of iron, and whether prisoners in the old Newgate jail in London had to pay for extra water in which to wash.

But let me start with my story, having warned you that it is a wild and rambling one.

My name is Nick Ormsby, I was sixteen years of age when all this happened, living in Key West, Florida, and a junior at the Key West High School. My great love has always been sailing, and I can hardly remember a time when I was not interested in boats. My father loved sailing, too, but was lost at sea in his sloop *Sayonara* when I was fifteen. My mother had died some years before — I have only the smallest memories of her, and I think most of them come from the many photographs of her we had about the house.

When my father died I went to live with my uncle, Hillary Ormsby, in an old and isolated house on the outskirts of Key West. He was a bachelor and a somewhat silent man, not at all like my father, who had been very talkative and lively.

I found my uncle kind and very shy.

He tried to make conversation with me, but it was always stilted and formal, and broke down after a few sentences. His only interest was in books (he owned a bookshop specializing in rare books), and as for sailing, he warned me against it seriously.

"Not only was your father lost at sea but your great-grandfather as well," he said. "There is a family history of death at sea. The ocean is a dangerous place for the Ormsbys."

2

A strange man, my Uncle Hillary, and I put his strangeness down at first to his bookishness, for his study was lined with books in which he read constantly. The contents of his books were, I think, far more real to him than the world around. He would not have a television set and so in the evening I took to reading some of his books myself.

I found several on the sea and the old days of sailing and many on piracy. Among them was one by Alexander Exquemelin, a Frenchman and surgeon who had gone to sea and accompanied Sir Henry Morgan, the notorious West Indian pirate, on his raid on the city of Panama, the golden treasure house of Spain in those days, so rich that it was said that the very statues in the churches, and the altars themselves, were made of solid gold. There was another, written by Basil Ringrose and published in 1685, *The Dangerous Voyages and Bold Attempts of Bartholomew Sharp in the South Seas,* and another, *A General History of the Robberies and Murders of the Most Notorious Pyrates*, published in 1724 and written by a Captain Charles Johnson.

These all became favorite reading of mine, so that my mind dwelt constantly on pirates and piracy. Though I knew little about books, I discovered from my uncle that those I have mentioned were all first editions, and assumed that this was the reason he had collected them. He admitted that they were worth a good sum but added that he had reasons for being interested in piracy (a strange phrase I thought it at the time) and would not part with them.

He was a good figure of a man — broad-shouldered, tall, though a little stooped by age, for he was fifteen years older than my father. The house in

3

which he lived had been the family home for many generations.

He ate sparingly and often in silence, and I soon found that he did not mind at all if I brought a book to the table to read at dinner. He had a nervous habit of passing his fingers between his collar and his neck, as if to loosen his clothing, and he often walked about his house at nighttime as if seeking something.

Mrs. Marsden, the housekeeper, a fat, old, withered woman with, however, a thin, weathered face and a wart at the corner of her right eye, explained that this had been his habit since first she came to "do" for him some twenty years before.

"Pay no attention to him," she said. "It's them books that disturb his mind. Too much reading has made him a little queer, and watch out it doesn't do the same thing for you. He eats too much fish, too."

"Fish?" I cried.

"Bad for the brain," she said. "Any doctor will tell you so."

It is true that my uncle was a great lover of fish, and particularly liked a dish of salted cod called "bacalhau" which had to be soaked in water for several hours before it was edible and, before being soaked, had a most offensive odor.

When I first came to live with him, this nighttime prowling of his disturbed me. But after a while I grew used to it. The house, made entirely of wood, was one of three stories, with an attic above, which was reached by a ladder leading to a trapdoor. It was, in part, over two centuries old, and like all wooden houses it creaked, more often by night than by day. At times the stairs would creak in succession, as if someone were coming up them.

4

Often enough, someone was coming up them — my Uncle Hillary. But several times when the creaking stopped outside my bedroom on the third floor and I, awake and uneasy, opened the door, there was no one there.

Once or twice when this happened, when there was no one to be seen on the landing outside or on the staircase, there was the strangest smell around the stairs — a smell of rotting seaweed. The first time this occurred I mentioned it to my uncle only to be met by an unexpected look of fear and that nervous gesture of his, loosening the clothing around his neck with his fingers.

That look of fear prompted me to ask whether the house was haunted, to which my uncle replied, a little shortly, that there were no such things as ghosts. "It was just your imagination," he said.

"But can you imagine a smell?" I asked. "It was like rotten seaweed — on the staircase."

"The kitchen odors rise up the staircase during the night," he said stiffly. "That is all there is to it. I think you have heard Mrs. Marsden complain, often enough, that bacalhau, before it is thoroughly steeped in fresh water, smells like rotten seaweed."

That explanation reassured me for the moment, and after a while I became entirely used to the creaking stairs and my uncle prowling around the place by night, and the occasional disagreeable smell on the staircase.

By tacit agreement, I never made any mention of his night prowlings to him. They seemed to be something private, something he would not want to discuss, and since I was still a guest in his house, I thought it would be indelicate to bring the matter up, which is why I mentioned it only to Mrs. Marsden.

5

When I had been with him for a few weeks, I began to feel sorry for my uncle. Some great problem seemed to weigh constantly upon his mind — something he could discuss with no one else. Yet he had days when he was almost cheerful, and he once even consented, after much pleading, to go down to the harbor with me and take a little sail in my gaff-rigged cutter *Sea Rover*. To my surprise, in view of his fear of the sea, he proved an excellent sailor and once we were clear of the slip he took the tiller and with the lightest touch filled her sails as smooth as a gull's wing.

He sat loose and easy in the cockpit, and had me lower the peak of the gaff a trifle, when the mainsail set better immediately. When we were out of the harbor and met the waves of the ocean, he took *Sea Rover* over the crests light as a bird.

"Why," I exclaimed, "you're a better sailor than I. I think you must be the best helmsman in this harbor."

He looked at me, his light blue eyes twinkling, and said, "Once I could sail a bumboat against any yacht built." It was a delightful afternoon, the best I had ever spent sailing since my father died. He talked about the Florida coast, on which many a galleon had been wrecked in the days of the Florida Keys, and of the flat coffinlike island among them called Deadman's Chest, which perhaps inspired Stevenson's pirate song in *Treasure Island*.

"Avery is said to have buried three chests of gold *moidores* on Key Largo," he said. "Roberts filled his casks with turtle meat off the Dry Tortugas before leaving for India in the *Royal Fortune*. It had all turned bad when they were a month at sea, but they boiled it into soup and ate it anyway. Rum's the cure for rotten meat. They carried plenty of that."

I wasn't surprised that he should say that Avery had buried treasure on Key Largo. All through the Florida Keys people will tell you of treasure buried here and there by Blackbeard or Tew or the Lafittes and so on. The stories are part of the tourist trade.

But there was an intimacy in that detail about rum being the cure for rotten turtle meat that surprised me. It was the sort of thing that only someone who had been with Roberts would know. And Roberts — Captain Bartholomew Roberts — had been killed in a sea fight in 1721 with a grapeshot through his throat.

2

Several weeks went by after that little sea voyage with my uncle during which nothing out of the ordinary occurred. I say nothing out of the ordinary, but he still walked about the house at night, rather more than usual, and there were still at times the sounds of steps mounting the stairs outside my room, though no one was to be seen.

Then he went away on a business trip to Boston and Philadelphia, buying books, and one evening, poring among the volumes in his library, I came upon a mass of papers hidden in the back of a bookcase and held together between two board covers tied with lacing.

The boards, filthy with dirt, were worn away at the four corners, and had at one time been covered with leather. I discovered this only when I wiped them with a damp cloth. Little patches of leather lay stuck here and there to the wood, and on one of the boards were tooled the letters: "M . . t . n . . v . rly." That was all I could make of them.

The pages within, brittle with age and with long confinement between the boards, were covered with writing, in an old-fashioned, cursive script. The ink had gone rusty with age.

The first several pages were full of botanical notes, and seemed to be the findings of some early-day naturalist on a journey seeking specimens.

Whoever the author was, he was meticulous about his entries, dating them all with care, as if the time of his discovery of a particular plant was in itself of some importance.

Thus, on May 11, 1720, was the entry: "I have found, growing in sandy soil such as lies at the tops of sundry small hills where there is ample exposure to the rays of the sun, a species of legume with a small red flower which I take to be a bean of sorts. Around are the dried pods from the seedings of previous years, tough and black. To judge by the flower and the leaves I would pronounce this plant a relative of the bean commonly known as the scarlet runner, and its seeds seem to be edible."

Another entry was as follows: "June 1, 1720. Although it is an acknowledged feature of the tropick seas that there is little sea wrack to be found, but only coral, and that always most abundant on the windward side of ye islands, yet today strolling the sandy beach in this place I found several strands of sea weed, brown and green and of a delicate texture such as I have never seen before in these regions. It is possible that they are torn up from the depths and that in the colder waters below, sea weed is as abundant as upon more temperate coasts."

Beside this description there was an excellent sketch of whatever kind of seaweed he had found —

a wavy ribbon of vegetable matter, with the notation below "of the color of young leaves in spring time."

The first part of his journal — the greater part of it in fact, covering several years — was nothing but descriptions of plants and snails and insects and fish and other things a naturalist on a voyage of exploration might find of interest.

The handwriting was always neat, each letter carefully formed, and the sketches, which were abundant through the manuscript, were excellent. The man's personality was plainly that of a careful scholar, but he was not without philosophy touched with humor.

On one page, for instance, he noted: "Man holds that all things on Earth are there for his use and so he is told on the authority of Holy Writ. This is surely of small comfort to he who is devoured by a lion or bitten by a poisonous serpent." And again: "Since Man carries no natural armour as does the turtle, the crocodile and the oyster, it would seem unnatural in him to engage in combat. Yet he loveth combat more than any of these creatures."

I spent a long time going over these notes, and with great pleasure. The pages had to be carefully handled, being so brittle, particularly at the edges, where the light had got at them. Then I turned to the back part of the journal and met with a great surprise. Although the writing was in the same hand, the contents were entirely different.

The first entry I turned to read:

Latitude 14.50 N. Longitude by dead reckoning 83 W. At two bells of the forenoon watch sail sighted northward off the starboard bow. Gave chase and overtook her after four hours.

She proved to be the brig *Experiment* of Boston mounting six long twelves and two swivels. Called on her to strike. Captain elected to fight and went briskly to work. Boarded her with pistol and cutlass and all cut down or driven below and the brig taken.

Of her crew, five dead, four heavily wounded, and lost myself three dead and four hurt — one blinded by pistol shot. The following from the brig embraced the piratical life and look good seamen:

William Neville, Welsh, of Cardiff.
Thos. Asby, English, of Salem.
Jos. Thakery, Negro, escaped New York slave.
Phineas O'Brien, Irish, of Boston.
Jeremiah Todson, English, Boston. Mate.

The remainder were put below in irons and under close watch. By this day's work eight dead, eight hurt, profit estimated from sale of brig and cargo, twenty-three thousand pounds sterling.

The terse description of the sea battle, the businesslike brain that counted the profit from the sale of the ship and her cargo against the men killed, shocked me. At the side of the page was a clean, detailed drawing of the mounting of one of the ship's swivels. There was something about the mounting that had struck the writer as being of possible worth to him, and he had made a careful drawing of it.

Fascinated, I turned more of the pages toward the end of what I had at first taken to be a botanist's

11

journal. That first account of piracy was followed by another entry which was a list of payments made following the sale of the Boston brig and her cargo. It read:

Item. To Peter Ramilly, for the loss of an eye, four hundred and twenty pounds sterling, paid before division of spoil.

Item. To James Rackton, for the loss of his left arm, two hundred and twenty pounds sterling, paid before division of spoil.

Item. To Thos. Crawshaw, for the loss of his left hand and two fingers of the other, five hundred and twenty pounds, this price being agreed by the crew, and paid before division of spoil. Crawshaw to remain with the ship if he so desires but not excused from such duties as he may within reason perform.

Item. To Henry Worthsell, for the loss of an ear, ten pounds sterling. He had demanded an hundred but was voted ten only since the loss in no way impaired his ability to earn a living.

Total compensation paid to crew in ye late taking of ye brig, eleven hundred and ninety pounds sterling.

There were no more entries of the taking of prizes, but I realized that the careful botanical descriptions of plants and animals were the work of the same man who set down in businesslike detail the profits and losses of an act of piracy.

The style of the drawings and the delicacy of the detail were identical. The handwriting was the same. Then there were the touches of a philosophical humor, slightly mocking, evident in the botanical notes and the descriptions of the life of piracy.

"Fenistone, lying about the deck two days drunk in the tropick heat, died of a stroke," ran one entry. "The sun being blamed, all are agreed to drink their rum after dark."

All the entries were given under a date, together with latitude and longitude, the latter always by dead reckoning, for there was no method, in those days, of accurately finding longitude at sea.

The last entry in the journal was dated February 22, 1721. It read: "Weighed anchor bound for the Bight of Benin, there to seek the Mines of Solomon, of which I have had a secret chart these many years. Or do I seek my own true self? What doth it profit a man to gain the Mines of Solomon and lose his own soul? My nephew Nicholas wants nothing of the venture, his soul being safe, yet . . ." The rest of the journal was missing.

My uncle was away on business, as I have said, when I came across this journal. I was anxious for him to get back to talk to him about it. Plainly, from its condition, he had not read it in a long time, if at all. But I wondered how he had come by it and why it had been hidden at the back of the bookcase when all the other material he had amassed on piracy was in plain view. It was as if he could not bear to part with it nor yet bear to have it in his sight.

Though I went through all the pages very carefully, there was no clue to the identity of the writer other than the faded letters on the front cover: "M . . t . n . . v . rly." There were no initials, no mention of his name, no mention of a hometown or a home country nor even of the ship he commanded.

I tried to be as logical as I could in sorting out the puzzle posed by this journal. Plainly, the writer, whoever he was, had been far more than a common pirate. He had two personalities, that of an educated man deeply interested in natural things and that of a cold-blooded and efficient sea robber. He was a man divided and at times deeply troubled, a man of sufficient depth to weigh the Mines of Solomon against the salvation of his own soul.

All this was plain. The mystery lay in why the journal should have been hidden. I began to wonder whether those footsteps I heard about the house at night, accompanied at times by the smell of rotting seaweed, were not connected with the strange diary. To try to put an end to the mystery, I decided one night not to go to bed at all but to remain awake in my uncle's study on the second floor, below my bedroom, where I frequently heard the mysterious footsteps.

The first night I tried this, I failed miserably. I stayed awake until a little after eleven and then fell asleep, and woke shivering in a chair in the gray of the dawn. There had been no visitation that night, or if there had, I slept through it.

The second night, I asked Mrs. Marsden to make me a thermos of hot and strong coffee, pleading I had some studying to do for some tests at school.

"I'll be up late in my uncle's study," I said.

"You'd better study in your own room," she replied. "Your uncle doesn't like people to use his study."

"Well, I'm not people," I said. "I'm his nephew, and anyway, my room gets too cold, and I have to have room to spread my books about."

14

She wasn't at all pleased with the idea. Old people, of course, do not like the rule of a house to be broken, and I knew quite well that my uncle disliked others using his study.

After dinner, she brought me a thermos of coffee and once more asked me to do my studying in my own room. But I was determined to use the study.

Eventually she retired to bed, very upset, and I put the coffee in the study and took a stroll around the house to be sure that there was no one hanging around the grounds. There was only one way in which the grounds could be entered and that was through a gate at the end of a long driveway leading to the front door. The gate was new and I locked it and turned on the switch in the house which operated the burglar alarm, installed largely to protect my uncle's book collection. I did all this, I suppose, just to comfort myself — to make myself feel a little more secure.

When I had carried out my inspection, I entered the study, drew the heavy drapes over the windows, and closed and locked the door. I had the curious feeling, in doing this, that I was locking myself away from the modern world and all its comforts. Then, to the solemn ticking of a grandfather clock in the corner of the study, I settled down to my vigil.

3

I had locked myself in my uncle's study at nine in the evening but it was hopeless to try to read anything. I went over paragraph after paragraph in my books, time and again, but could not concentrate enough to get any sense out of my reading. The deliberate ticking of the clock made me uneasy, to the point where I was tempted to stop the swinging of the pendulum. Whenever the mechanism started to whir before striking the quarter hours, I jumped in my chair, and I kept watching the hands remorselessly marking off the minutes.

I had the feeling that whatever was going to occur would take place at midnight, and as that time slowly approached, my anxiety became greater and greater, until the temptation to rush out of the study to the safety of my own room was all but overwhelming.

Still I remained, strengthening my nerves a little

by walking about and occasionally taking a sip of the coffee, for comfort rather than wakefulness. Outside, the tree frogs chirped, each seeming to protest the other. But occasionally they joined in chorus, as if protesting some other presence. Then I would go to the window, pull the drapes aside, and peer out, but see nothing.

When the hands of the clock were close to midnight and my nerves wire-taut, I heard another sound — the distant crunch of gravel underfoot as of someone walking stealthily up the path toward the house.

The study was situated in the front of the house, and so gave a view of the path. I parted the heavy drapes to look outside. A veil of silver mist lay over the ground, so the pathway could not be seen, nor the surrounding lawns, though the tops of bushes and shrubs erupted from the mist here and there, frosted with moonlight and strangely menacing.

Other than that, I could see nothing. But the footsteps came on steadily, making my skin crawl as they approached, until at last they reached the house. I heard the sound of boots climbing the stone steps leading to the front door, heard the door itself groan open, and then I knew whoever it was was inside, standing in the corridor two stories below. I listened in the dead silence which followed the opening of the door. Then the footsteps moved along the corridor and approached the stairs. They mounted the stairs slowly and deliberately until they reached the first landing. There was a little pause then, and on they came again up the second flight, leading to the very study in which I had locked myself.

I looked for a place to hide, completely panicked. The drapes over the windows provided an obvious

17

hiding place — too obvious. There was an old-fashioned round table, with a cloth on it that reached almost to the floor, but it would not hide me for long. Finally, there was a closet in which my uncle stored, all higgledy-piggledy, papers, magazines, and miscellaneous books. That was the best that offered and I was about to shut myself in there when the clock struck twelve. The doorknob turned, and the door, despite the fact that it was locked, opened slowly.

A man dressed in the fashion of two hundred years previously entered. He wore a frock coat, deep red in color, which came down to his knees, was handsomely waisted, and elaborately decorated with silver frogging. He had on white knee breeches and white stockings and blunt-toed shoes with large silver buckles.

He had a strong handsome face, weathered by sun and sea, and his light blue eyes were deep-set. With a shock I realized he had a marked resemblance to my Uncle Hillary. He looked about the room leisurely, gave me a nod of acknowledgment and a glance of mild amusement, walked over to the desk on which I had been working, and looked at my books. He picked up one volume dealing with America in the nineteenth century, read a little in it, and tossed it aside.

Then he said, "I see you have become a scholar since last we met, Nicholas."

His voice was a touch mocking and I sensed that he meant me no harm. I stared at him in silence.

"You don't know me?" he asked. "Why, you and I have stood together in many a hazard. Fair wind and foul, ebb tide and flow. We've seen them all and smelled gravecloths strong enough to make the pious sweat."

"No," I whispered. "I don't know you. Who are you?"

"That's hardly civil," he replied lightly. "Particularly since you have discovered my journal and seen your own name put down in it. But you'll find out in time who I am. Memories, they say, are not lost, but only mislaid."

"Memories?" I echoed.

"Aye, memories, Nicholas. Memories. We have unfinished business together, you and I."

"Unfinished business?" I exclaimed. "What business?"

"A matter of life and death. At a certain place."

"What place?"

"Shark Island in the Dry Tortugas. To start with."

"Whose life and death are you talking about?" I asked fearfully.

"You will find the answer yourself later," he replied. "Matters will begin to be clearer when we meet, as we must, at Shark Island."

"Does this meeting concern my uncle?"

"Yes. You might say it concerns him principally."

"He has seen you?"

"He is aware of my existence."

"You have spoken to him of Shark Island and this unfinished business, as you call it?"

"He knows of it all. But he is afraid of the meeting."

"What is he afraid of?"

For answer my visitor smiled, almost apologetically. "He is afraid of being hung," he said. "Faith," he added with wry humor, "it is enough to dampen

19

the spirits of any man."

I remembered with horror my uncle's mannerism of giving a frightened look and at the same time loosening his collar with his hand.

"Will you tell me plainly who you are?" I asked.

He studied me closely for a while and again the resemblance to my uncle came through strongly for a moment. "Does the name Martin mean aught to you?" he asked.

"Nothing," I replied.

"Martin Coverly?"

"No. Are you Martin Coverly?"

He nodded and I recalled the few initials on the journal, "M . . t . n . . v . rly," and realized that it was he who had written it.

He reached in the pocket of his frock coat and took out a cylinder of ivory, which he placed on the desk. It was inscribed with a curious design of which I could make nothing.

"Does this not stir some memories, Nicholas?" he asked.

I picked it up and examined it and shook my head. "No," I said.

He was silent for a while and then said, "Shark Island. The Dry Tortugas. Do not fail to be there."

"When?" I asked.

"February 20, 1721," he replied, and was gone.

4

My uncle did not return until some days later, and during that time there were no further visitations, nor a sound on the stairs nor a whiff of that seaweed smell on the landing outside my bedroom.

I needed to talk to someone about the whole thing and in the end I told everything that had occurred to Dr. Wilton at the high school.

He was, as I have said, a master both of philosophy and of history, though at school he taught history only. He was a friendly man and a wise one. I flunked a test on American history dealing with the term in office of President Polk, and when he had given me an F he asked me to drop by and talk to him in his study about the result.

"There's something on your mind, Nick," he said, vigorously lighting that pipe to which he was so attached. "I know your uncle is away and that you are living alone. You usually do well at history. You are one of my best pupils. Do you want to tell me anything of what is troubling you?"

Disturbed as I was, I broke down and told him everything. When I had done (and he listened to me without interruption), he said, "I am not going to make the obvious suggestion that this whole thing was a dream. First, a man knows perfectly well when he has dreamed something, for he awakens and recognizes the dream. Then again, dreams, however vivid, are rarely remembered in detail, and what you have told me is full of detail.

"That leaves the possibility of hallucination. You said that you have been reading a lot of pirate lore in your uncle's library, and particularly that mysterious journal.

"This in itself may have conditioned your mind for a deep and vivid hallucination. Don't laugh at the idea. There are such things. People suffering from hallucination actually see others who are not there, hear voices, talk with individuals, smell odors, and so on. I would venture to suggest that every ghost story that has ever been told is the product of a hallucination. That seems to me to be the most logical explanation."

I shook my head. "I just can't believe it was a hallucination," I said. "It was much too real."

"Hallucinations are just as real as reality to those who experience them," he replied. He was silent for a minute and then said, "There is one thing you can do if you wish, which may rid your mind of the whole affair. Go with your uncle to Shark Island.

"There is some danger in doing that, and I should warn you of it. The hallucination may intensify. You may find yourself caught up in matters of the mind — imaginings — beyond your conscious control.

22

"From what you say of your uncle, I think he himself is also suffering from hallucination, and of the same sort. But you are both basically healthy people and I think you will come out of it. I find it significant that you see some resemblance between this Martin Coverly and your uncle, who is so interested in pirate lore and with whom you spend so much time alone. You may be transferring his image into your hallucination."

I still could not believe that this was the correct explanation and said so. He asked me what I could offer of my own.

"Look," I said. "Is it possible that this Martin Coverly is living in the eighteenth century and we are living in the twentieth century but that these two centuries coexist or can be made to coexist for some special purpose?"

Dr. Wilton looked at me soberly and I realized that I was talking wildly, but I was desperate for some kind of explanation, other than talk of ghosts, that I could accept myself for what had happened to me, and plowed on.

"Take memory," I said, catching at any straw or reasoning that offered. "When you remember something, you go back in time — or your mind does, though your body stays in the present. Martin Coverly kept saying that I should remember who he was. He referred to memory as something that is never lost, but only mislaid.

"All right. Supposing I actually did live with this man in the 1700s. Supposing I have some mislaid memories of him that are vitally important to him — a matter of life and death, as he said . . ." I stopped. "Oh, gosh, I'm really not making any sense, am I?" I concluded.

"You may be making more sense than you realize," said Dr. Wilton. "There is a thing called genetic memory — memory handed on through the genes from generation to generation. It isn't, as far as is known, a memory of specific things, but a memory of how to do things — how to breathe, for instance, and how to arrange all the muscular mechanism needed to talk and to grow and so on. It isn't a conscious memory but a subconscious one — a memory of which we are not aware. It seems to be contained in the cells of the body rather than in the brain alone.

"But it is just possible — and for goodness' sake please remember that I said 'just possible' — that a few people have a genetic memory that recalls specific things — other lives, other times — a memory passed along by genetic material from generation to generation. Material which is in a sense immortal. You know," he concluded, "this might be a wonderful opportunity to test that outrageous theory."

"Dr. Wilton," I said. "Are you talking about having lived before?"

He gave me a slow smile and took a meditative puff on his pipe. "I have painted myself into a corner," he said. "And I must now try to find a way out. What I am talking about, I think, is that we contain the same genetic material, by and large, as our ancestors. That's why we resemble our ancestors. The famous Bourbon nose, as you know, existed through several generations.

"All right. If we have a physical resemblance to our ancestors, we may have a mental resemblance as well. And we may — stress the word 'may' — have in that mental resemblance thoughts and memories experienced by our forebears. It's not quite the same thing as having lived before. It is rather that they continue to live in us — physically and mentally.

"Something of the sort," he said. "But let us again stress the word 'may.' You may have genetic memories of that kind. And such genetic memories may account for what are called hallucinations by some and ghostly visitations by others. In which case it may account for Martin Coverly himself. It's preposterous, but then so also was a great deal of what is now regarded as scientific fact. We have an exciting opportunity to test all this now, and I'd be very glad, when your uncle returns, for a chance to talk to him about it."

A few days after this talk, my Uncle Hillary returned from his book-buying trip. In the interim (since most of the end-of-the-quarter tests were over), I spent a lot of time down at the yacht harbor, readying *Sea Rover* for a voyage of a hundred miles or so to Shark Island. I felt my uncle and I just had to make that voyage, and as soon as possible.

There wasn't really much to do, but it is surprising the amount of time you can spend just puttering around on a sailboat. I aired out the life jackets, which were getting a little moldy under the cockpit seats, and put twenty gallons of water in my tanks; put enough food aboard for a week (more than we actually needed), put new batteries in the radio direction finder, and went over sheets and halyards for signs of wear. I put twenty feet of chain on the anchor up forward, for we would likely be anchoring in coral, and, in short, did all the things needed to prepare for a short voyage.

My uncle returned in the mid-afternoon. He asked

me, not quite able to hide his concern, whether anything had happened during his absence. I told him of the journal I had found and of the visit of Martin Coverly and his insistence that we meet him at Shark Island.

He trembled when I had finished, buried his face in his hands, and said, "I have lived with these things for years, but I hoped that neither you nor anyone else in the family would have to endure them. I wish you had not found that journal. I shudder at the very name of Martin Coverly."

"Why?" I asked.

"Your father, I suppose, told you little about our family?"

"Nothing at all," I replied.

"Well, it's time you knew something of it," he said. "Or, rather, something of the history of one notorious member of our family, who disgraced every honest man among them — Martin Coverly."

"Martin Coverly," I cried. "So he was indeed an ancestor of ours?"

"He was. And it was because of Coverly that the family name was changed to Ormsby," said my uncle. "He came of a decent, seafaring family in the west of England, and he was himself until the last few years of his life an honest and highly respected man. Then he turned pirate."

"What happened? For what reason?" I asked.

"I do not know," replied my uncle. "The change was sudden and profound. He became an entirely different person — still interested in natural philosophy, as it was called in his day, but capable at the same time of deeds of outrage and infamy, all done without the slightest trace of pity or remorse."

26

"What was the end of him — how did he die?" I asked.

"I do not know," said my uncle. "I can say nothing of him for sure. There is a story, for which I find no proof, that he was captured, taken to England, and sentenced at the Old Bailey in London to be hung at Execution Dock and his body displayed in chains from a gibbet at Gravesend on the Thames."

"Surely there would be some record in England of his being tried and hung," I said.

"There should be, but there isn't. The records are not complete for the period. There is another story, equally without proof, that by some ruse he escaped capture, though his companions were all taken. It is said that another was hung in his place."

And here my uncle gave me again that frightened look, and inserted his fingers between his neck and his collar as if to loosen a noose.

5

The following evening Dr. Wilton came around to dinner — a meal during which there was nothing but small talk, for we did not want to discuss Coverly in the presence of Mrs. Marsden.

But afterward, when we had retired to his study, my uncle came straight to the point, exclaiming even before the door was shut that nothing could persuade him to go to Shark Island.

"I am deathly afraid of that island," he said. "My feelings are unreasonable, I know, and yet there they are. I have a deep fear that in going there to see Martin Coverly I will lose myself completely — I will become possessed, if that is the right expression. Yes. Possessed. Robbed of my identity, of my mind, my character, and my principles, and turned into another person. Seized by some dominant force from which I cannot escape."

"All the more reason why you should go," said Dr. Wilton quietly. "I think the only way you are going to be able to rid yourself of this fear is to face up to it. Otherwise, it will be with you for the rest of your days. Life lived in fear is not life at all but a kind of hell, and I fancy, Mr. Ormsby, that you have had enough of that sort of existence."

My uncle sighed deeply and shook his head. "We are all talking some kind of madness," he said. "Nicholas has been talking to me and to you of genetic memory and the concept of two centuries existing side by side; of time being not a line, as it were, but a tabletop. All these ideas are, in the plain daylight of reason, nonsense. They have no reality. They are pure fancies."

"Your fear is real enough and it is something which has to be dealt with," said Dr. Wilton firmly.

"You asked me whether my father had ever spoken to me about our family," I said. "Did he know about Martin Coverly?"

"Your father was sailing down the Florida Keys when he was lost at sea," said my uncle. "Nothing was found of him or of his boat, though there was an intensive search by the Coast Guard. Although I had never mentioned the presence of Coverly to him, for I did not want to burden him with the thought that his brother was — well, deranged, I suspect now that Coverly visited your father. I suspect that he made an appointment with him on one of the islands. And I suspect that that was what destroyed him."

"There I draw the line," said Dr. Wilton. "Many boats have been lost off the Florida Keys. They are dangerous cruising grounds even for good sailors. There is no need for something supernatural in the death of your brother."

For answer, my uncle went to a bookcase and took from it a small black notebook. He opened it

29

and riffled through a few pages. "Here is a list of the Ormsby men lost at sea," he said. "There was Tobias Ormsby, lost overboard from the bark *Emerald* in 1764; George Sawyer Ormsby, drowned on returning from a voyage to England two days out of Boston Harbor in 1810 — the record says that he was missed and presumed to have fallen overboard; Peter Maxwell Ormsby, lost at sea, 1865. That was in the Civil War and he was an officer in the Union navy. Once again, the report merely stated that he was missed and presumed to have fallen overboard. That was off the coast of Carolina. And there was James Sawyer Ormsby — grandfather to Nicholas — missing in a small sloop in which he had gone sailing — down the Florida Keys.

"That makes five of the Ormsbys missing at sea and presumed drowned in two hundred years. When you consider that the sea was not their business once they had settled in America and changed the family name, that is a very high number indeed. It is a matter not of accident but of fate, or rather of plan. I believe Coverly was responsible for all those deaths, and I think he seeks mine and this boy's now."

But Dr. Wilton would not be persuaded of that. "The record seems high," he said, "yet it could perhaps be matched in many other families over the same period. You say the Ormsbys were no longer seafaring people, but they were, in that as merchants and importers they plainly had to go to sea frequently. Two were lost overboard, which may be high, but not unique, in a family history. I hope you will not object to my saying that you seem to be becoming a little paranoid on the subject.

"You first said you were afraid of visiting Shark Island lest you become possessed. Now you say that you are afraid of going there lest you be killed. Whatever the cause, you are full of fear. I sincerely believe that it would be the best thing in the world for you and Nicholas to make the voyage. As I said before, I think you have to face this fear and free yourself of it. I am willing to come with you, if you wish, and share whatever hazards may lie ahead."

It was a tempting offer — to have one person with us, wise, sane, balanced, who was an observer, outside of all the events which had previously occurred. But my uncle turned the offer down. Nor could he be persuaded for some time to undertake the venture himself. Indeed, he only agreed in the end when I told him firmly that if he did not make the voyage with me I would go alone. This broke his resolve, and with great reluctance he said he would go.

To give him no chance to change his mind, the boat being ready, we set out the next day, leaving the yacht harbor at Key West early in the morning to get as much sailing done by daylight as possible.

The Dry Tortugas lie to the west of Key West, a scattering of coral islets, once a hiding place for pirates but now a federal bird sanctuary. There are many of them in all, East Key being the first of any size to be met on a voyage from Florida. Then there is Bird Key and Loggerhead and Shark Island a little farther on — the latter nothing more really than a hill of sand and coral, with a few coconut palms, and no water supply of its own.

It was on Shark Island that Dr. Harvey Mudd, who had treated the actor Booth after he shot President Lincoln, was imprisoned for several years.

The wind was out of the east and we tacked and tacked again into it, clawing our way forward. My uncle, his spirits raised a little once we were at sea,

31

rigged a vang on the cutter's gaff so that she would lie closer to the wind. Even so, we made but miserable progress, and after four hours of this kind of sailing, Key West was still plainly in sight behind us.

Toward noon, however, the wind turned a little more northerly and we were able to loose the sheets and make better progress.

Despite the circumstances, it turned out to be a delightful sail. A school of flying fish picked us up, darting about our bows and gliding over the water with twinkling fins for several yards before plopping back into the sea. The water was so blue that I had the feeling that my hand would be stained if I put it into the ocean, and once we were through with the business of tacking, we trailed a line with a spoon over the stern and caught a medium barracuda, which would be welcome for supper.

My uncle proved once again an excellent sailor. He was truly transformed whenever he got to sea. He became less gloomy and was soon speaking again on that subject which had always interested him — piracy and pirates.

"Kidd had a bad name, but he was a poor hand at piracy," he said. "What was brought against him at his trial could have been brought against a hundred men worse than he, all of whom died in their beds.

"He was commissioned captain of the *Adventure* galley by the King himself, to put down piracy, and sailed as far as Madagascar in his efforts to do so. But he met with no pirates and his crew almost mutinied because he refused to attack a Dutch vessel. He got into an argument with his gunner, Moore, over the matter, and losing his temper, struck Moore over the head with a wooden bucket, killing him. A great deal was made of that at his trial, and the upshot of it was that he was hung. The only great ship he took was the Moorish merchantman *Queda,* which was, incidentally, commanded by an Englishman. He made ten thousand pounds out of the sale of her cargo, of which he kept eight thousand for himself.

"But that was the extent of his fortune from piracy. Those who are looking for Kidd's treasure, in my view, are looking for something he never had in his life. Unless it was a snuff box of which he was fond, made of ivory with a silver clasp on it."

There it was again, a little detail which I had never come upon in any account of the life of Kidd.

He had taken the tiller for the greater part of the morning, so I suggested that I take it during the afternoon while he got some rest. Accordingly, he went below, out of the sun, to snooze while I was left to myself in the cockpit, enjoying the slap and surge of the waves against the little cutter's bow, the full curve of the mainsail in the wind, and her easy motion through the water, which made her a delight to handle.

I had set out with a feeling of foreboding, but now that we were fairly at sea, with Key West at last below the horizon astern, and steering a compass course for the Tortugas, much of my gloom left me. I began to think that I had been too long alone in that overpowering house; had been doing too much reading on piracy, and this had overburdened my imagination.

It is surprising how much our moods and thoughts are ruled by our surroundings, and in the bright sun and sparkling sea I recovered my spirits and, almost

33

forgetting Martin Coverly, looked on our little voyage as a pleasant vacation.

It was not until sunset that I left the tiller for a moment to wake my uncle. Ahead, very low on the horizon, I could see the smear of East Key in the sunset, and proposed that we anchor there to spend the night.

"No," said my uncle. "We will go on to Shark Island."

I fixed some hot soup on the alcohol stove and served this with the barracuda for supper. Then I went below myself, intending only to lie down and rest for a while in the cool of the cabin. The cabin was snug and on the bookshelf opposite my bunk lay my Nautical Almanacs for several years and a copy of Bowditch — old and comforting companions. The fresh air had made me more tired than I realized, and in a few minutes I drifted off into a heavy sleep.

I awoke suddenly in the dark, aware that there was something the matter with the cutter. Her motion through the water was no longer smooth, but uncertain. She would fall off the wind, rolling wildly, then sail briskly for a moment or two, heeled over, and then round up into the wind, her sails flapping and her rigging trembling.

I thought that my uncle had fallen asleep at the tiller and called out to him. Getting no reply, I climbed out of my bunk, my heart pounding, and scrambled into the cockpit.

The cockpit was empty. The untended tiller swung from side to side. My uncle had disappeared. But dead ahead, dark against the starlit waters, lay an old-fashioned brig with high-pitched bowsprit and her two masts raked well back in the style of the 1700s.

6

I stared in disbelief at the brig and called wildly for my uncle. There was no reply. Then, as I looked about, completely panicked, for I thought he had fallen overboard, I heard from ahead the thump and splash of heavy oars, and a voice called out: "Ahoy the boat! Heave to, or you're a dead man."

I looked forward and saw a heavily built rowboat propelled by two pairs of oars coming down on me, with a man standing in the stern with the tiller in his hand. The next moment there was an orange flash, something hummed by my ear like a big beetle, and a hole was ripped in my mainsail.

"Heave to," came the order again. I put the tiller over, brought the cutter up into the wind's eye, and backed her jib and staysail — all these actions done automatically and as if in a dream. A moment later the boat was alongside me, heralded by a smell of sweat, unwashed clothes, and liquor strong enough to overwhelm the tang of the sea air. There were seven aboard, dressed in full breeches hanging ragged and wet below their knees, full shirts, too, and around their waists gaudy scarves. Their hair was long and matted and their cheeks unshaven for many days. Two wore drooping mustaches, long as dogs' tails, and one, as soon as the boat was alongside, spat a stream of tobacco juice into the cutter's cockpit and then grinned at me, exposing not his teeth but his tobacco-blackened gums.

"Who are you?" I asked. "What do you want?"

"Why, gentlemen o' fortune, come to pay our respects and request you to kindly step aboard the brig *Swan* — Captain Martin Coverly."

"Martin Coverly?" I cried, and then, full of fear, "Where is my uncle? Have you taken him?"

They made a comedy act of it, each turning to the other with the questions.

"Where's 'is uncle?" asked one.

" 'oo pinched 'is uncle?"

"Anybody seen this 'ere younker's uncle?"

"What swab lost this poor boy's uncle?" And so on.

The man at the tiller said, "Wot's 'is name?"

"Ormsby," I said. "Hillary Ormsby."

"Never 'eard of 'im," was the reply.

The others had meanwhile been eyeing me and the boat.

"Not Salem-built," said one. "No topmast."

"Lateen rig, I'd say," said another.

"Knock 'im over the 'ead, take the cutter, and mum's the word," said a third. He picked up a heavy club and made as if to step aboard.

"Belay that," said the man at the tiller. "You was always too slow to ask and too quick to kill, Jack.

'e's expected aboard. Leave the boy be. You," he said, turning to me, "what's your name?"

"Nicholas Ormsby," I replied.

"Where do you hail from?"

"Key West."

" 'op on board, then. Tinney, take the sail off that cutter and we'll take her in tow."

Tinney stepped aboard, groped for the jib and staysail halyards, and lowered these two sails. I, in the meantime, let go the peak and throat halyards on the mainsail, and in a few moments *Sea Rover* was under bare poles and fastened by a line to the stern of the longboat (such I took her to be). I stepped into the boat to find her bilges full of turtle all alive, though some had been clubbed and were bleeding. Several were of great size and might easily have climbed out of the boat but that a fishnet had been spread over them all, in which they entangled their necks and fins in an effort to escape.

We were soon alongside the brig and I climbed over her gunwale onto the deck and looked around. There were two or three men lying about, half in shadow and half in moonlight, fast asleep and dead drunk, to judge from the bottles that lay nearby.

The brig had several cannon in tackles on each side along the waist. They were long twelves, as I discovered later, and her main armament. From her cabin, aft, below the poop deck, there was the glimmer of candlelight, and up forward by the fo'c'sle, a group of men were sitting around a smoky lantern, playing dice. The light from the lantern lit their faces in patches. Someone shouted, "Hands to the longboat," and the men playing dice left their game reluctantly and, ignoring me, shuffled over to get the longboat with its turtle aboard. Someone seized my shoulder, saying, "Cap'n's waiting for you in the cabin," and thrust me forward to the poop. He flung open a low door and I went down a short flight of steps to find myself in the brig's cabin, illuminated by a large lantern hung from one of the deck beams overhead.

The place was blue with tobacco smoke.

There was a bunk against one bulkhead, and two chairs at a table. Seated astraddle one of these, and smoking a long clay pipe, was Martin Coverly. He blew a stream of smoke in my direction when I entered, and said, "Welcome aboard, Nick. Glad you kept your rendezvous. Will you have a glass of wine with me?"

Without waiting for an answer, he filled a glass from a bottle on the table, filled one for himself, and then proposed a toast. "Fair or foul, Nick. We'll hold together." He smiled at me, savoring my surprise.

"You're taken aback by a change in the wind, eh, lad," he said. His voice was kindly and humorous. "Well, there are strange winds blow in men's lives, many of them unexpected, and a good seaman will keep an eye to weather every now and then, without neglecting the luff of his topsails.

"You've made a far voyage, Nick — twenty leagues and a trifle more from Key West, but the passage took two hundred and fifty years, or thereabout — and them run backward. Didn't you expect such a voyage, Nick, when I saw you last in your uncle's house?"

"I didn't know what to expect," I said. "It's beyond reason . . ."

"Many things are beyond reason," he replied,

smiling. "Reason's but a cockboat, too small to hold the cargo of life. Why, reason would founder if but half a year of living were put into it.

"No, Nicholas. Don't put your trust in reason. You need a bigger vessel.

"And as for Time, why, it is but a tool for measuring change. It was made for man's service, but it has become a prison for his mind. Use it in its proper way — to get up in the morning and go to bed at night, and to mark the watches aboard ship. But don't let Time tell you what can and what cannot be, for it was man himself that invented it, and he should be the master of his tool, and not its slave."

"What year is this?" I asked, ignoring his philosophy.

"Seventeen twenty-one," he replied, "the twentieth of February, and nine in the evening, if you want to be nice about it. But stop quibbling, Nick. Your reason's too small, as I said, to handle the cargo. So just accept matters and let your mind run free of dates and clocks."

"My uncle," I said, "is he aboard? What have you done with him?"

"He is and he isn't," said Coverly, smiling at some secret joke. "And the same might be said of you. Drink your wine, Nicholas. We'll come to your uncle later."

I had never drunk wine in my life, and reached only hesitantly for my glass. It was red wine, darker than blood in the light of the lantern. I sipped it. The taste belied the richness of the color, for it was sour and acidic. I put the glass down.

"You must drain it to the last," said Martin Coverly. His voice was not so gentle. "Down with it."

"I don't like it," I said.

"Why, damn your wormy eyes, who asked if you liked it?" he snapped, suddenly angry. "You're in my cabin and by thunder you'll drink it down if it were bilge water foul with bloated rats."

I drank it down at one gulp, for I sensed that Martin Coverly was no man to cross when angry. I put the glass on the table and gasped for air. The wine burned in my stomach and my head reeled so that the cabin swam around me and the light of the candle lantern turned dim and then slowly glowed brighter again. I shut my eyes to steady myself and felt strange pullings and tinglings all through my body. My hands felt fat and numb and my head seemed to swell and throbbed horribly. I could hear the blood pounding in my ears and, unable to stand any more, sat heavily on the bunk a little way from the table.

Then my head cleared, the throbbing and aching stopped, and I opened my eyes and I knew I was Nicholas Coverly, sixteen years of age, apprentice seaman on the brig *Swan*.

My uncle, Martin Coverly, was sitting opposite me, astraddle his chair, smoking his pipe and shaking his head.

"You're a good enough seaman, Nicholas," he said, "but a poor hand with a glass of wine. Wine's like a pretty woman — better looked at than touched. How many turtle did they bring aboard?"

"Seventeen," I replied. "There's some of them weigh a hundredweight, and others ashore bigger. But no sense taking them, for four men could not have got them into the longboat."

"Was it good sport?" he asked.

"There was no sport to it at all," I said. "Just turning them over on their backs with the oars and

40

dragging them down to the water. Jack Starkhurst fell to clubbing them, helpless as they were. There's four or five will die before we are a week at sea."

"Starkhurst is a swab that would starve ashore and go hungry at sea if there wasn't a ship's captain to take care of him," said my uncle. "There are barnacles growing on the bottom of this brig that have more brains than he."

He paused and looked at me curiously. "Did you see anything of a little cutter out there?" he said.

"Cutter," I repeated and something stirred in me, though for what reason I couldn't say.

"Hailed from Key West — two aboard."

Again something stirred, something like a memory that I could not place and then was gone.

"No," I replied. "Nothing." I stared reflectively at my hands. The nails were broken from heavy work aboard the brig, and the palms thick with calluses. My feet were bare and my long full breeches made of sailcloth, wet and heavy with sand from boarding the longboat in the surf after the turtle hunt.

"You said something a moment ago about your uncle," he said.

"My uncle?" I echoed. "But you are my uncle."

"Why, so I am," he said. "So I am."

7

My uncle had not always been a pirate. He had followed the sea since he was twelve, and through his own industry, intelligence, and honesty had risen to command in his early twenties.

Even as a boy he was fond of learning, though he had little opportunity for scholarship and was, in everything but reading and writing, self-taught. He had early taken a deep interest first in the various ports and places to which he sailed, the people, their habits, and their commerce, and then in the plants and animals to be found in varying parts of the world.

Thus, his sea journals contained but short descriptions of the passages he made, the weather met, the cargoes taken on and discharged, and lengthy accounts of the trees and flowers and fish and birds and other living things which he had noted and studied.

I will give you a short extract from such accounts to illustrate what I say, viz.: "The Rock Fish is called by Seamen a Grouper; the Spaniards call it Bacalhau, which is the Name for Cod because it is much like it. It is rounder than the Snapper of a dark brown Colour; and hath small Scales no bigger than a Silver-penny. This Fish is good, sweet Meat, and is found in great plenty on all the Coast of Peru and Chile. It can be heavily Salted in Brine, in which condition it Stinketh, but on soaking in Fresh Water, becometh sweet Meat again, and a savory Dish fit for any Gentleman."

Indeed, my uncle was very fond of fish, salt or fresh, as I discovered when I was apprenticed to him two years previously as a seaman. But his favorite of all was this bacalhau, or salted cod, and belowdecks every ship he commanded had about it the odor of rotten seaweed, because of his fondness for this food.

His first commands were in the coasting trade, carrying stone from the Welsh quarries, sea coals from Newcastle to London, and so on. But later, his record being excellent and his knowledge of navigation unsurpassed, he was given command of vessels plying to the Levant, and then in the triangular trade from Bristol to the West Indies and thence to Boston in the American colonies (though sometimes also to Philadelphia and New York) and back to Bristol.

It was when he entered this trade in January of 1719 that I was apprenticed to him. He was given command of the snow *Venture*. Though he was strict in his discipline in all matters concerning the ship, he treated me with great kindness, and often took me ashore on his naturalist's rambles around the countryside.

He was most of the time humorous, patient, and much of a philosopher, but there were occasions when he was overcome by gloom, and complained bitterly that after a quarter of a century at sea he had been able to save very little. He showed me, on sev-

43

eral occasions, a cylinder of ivory, curiously inscribed, of which he was very fond, saying it was all he had to show for his many years of honest seagoing. Yet he hinted darkly that it might yet be fortune enough for him. At such times he was morose and sometimes drank heavily and would remark, in or out of his cups, "Honesty is the best policy — to keep a man poor."

He might indeed have prospered had he followed the custom of other captains of keeping some of the profits from the sale of cargoes for himself, receiving "aids," that is to say, bribes, for carrying merchandise without cost and without the knowledge of the owners, and so forth. But he would not do these things. Ships' captains were permitted to carry a little cargo on their own account, and my uncle, without the slightest dishonesty, might have made some money here. But he was the poorest of businessmen, and often, whatever he carried, he sold at a loss or could not sell at all.

So, for all his years at sea, he remained poor, and indeed I think the study of natural things provided him with some consolation for his lack of wealth. One particular incident in his life had turned him from an honest seaman into a sea rover, to my horror.

In our second year of voyaging in the triangular trade together, we were off the island of Barbados (so named, my uncle said, because the moss growing on the trees reminded the Spanish discoverers of beards) when a brig was sighted one morning overhauling us from the stern. Nothing had been seen of her during the night, for she had been sailing without lights, whereas we carried always a light at our masthead.

44

The snow, built to carry as much cargo in her hold as possible, was no match for the brig, which was soon within hailing distance, though showing no colors. She came up to windward of us, so close that you could have thrown a marlin spike from one deck to the other.

"Back your yards and heave to," shouted someone in her main shrouds through a speaking trumpet.

"What ship are you?" demanded Martin Coverly.

For answer a flag was run to the peak of her main and broken smartly out in the wind. The sight of that flag turned my blood cold. On a black background was a human skeleton with arms outstretched. Under each hand was a human skull — the Jolly Roger, then, the flag of piracy.

The ship was none other than the *Royal Fortune*, commanded by the notorious pirate Bartholomew Roberts. There was no question now either of running away or of fighting. The yards were backed, the snow heaved to, and my uncle went aboard to see what was required of him. I contrived to get into the boat with him and so witnessed the whole scene.

Roberts, of middle size but very dark in his face, as if he were a gypsy, greeted my uncle on deck. He was dressed as gaudily as a parrot — a huge hat on his head with the plume of an ostrich stuck in it, a coat of royal blue with silver lacings, a waistcoat of crimson silk, and white knee breeches, which gleamed like snow in the sunlight.

His manners matched his dress. "I'm honored to have you aboard, captain," he said. "Perhaps you will do me the favor of having a glass of wine with me, while we discuss whatever addition you are about to make to my treasury."

"Why, sir," said my uncle, "I'm but a merchantman out of Bristol, carrying manufactured cloths, glassware, chinaware, lumber, flour, tools, and such to Bridgetown, there to take on molasses and sugar for Boston."

"There'll be the ship's money, too," said Roberts, smiling. "And some rolls of velvet and satin for the planters and their wives, and likely a few geegaws such as brooches and necklaces and rings and trifles to please the ladies. Rugs, too, I'll venture, and a few hogsheads of Madeira."

"You're welcome to it all," said my uncle. "Indeed, there is nothing I can do to prevent you taking it. But I would ask you to spare my crew and this boy here, my nephew."

"Have no fear for them at all," said Roberts. "You will find that their lives are in their own keeping."

His crew, meanwhile, ragged but gaudily dressed, lolled about, shouting to the men on the *Venture*, asking where they hailed from and what were their names and bragging of the money they had made as "gentlemen of fortune." There were not many of them, but they were as rough a crowd as you'd find in the worst tavern in any seaport town, and some of our own crew would say little to them. But others grinned at the pirates, who were drinking freely about the deck and who threw a bottle or two to their "brethren," as they called the hands of my uncle's ship.

They gave the impression that life as a pirate was but one long carouse, with plenty of prizes taken and all apportioned on the principle of "share and share alike."

To make short work of the tale, Roberts, having drunk his wine and toasted my uncle's health, ordered his crew aboard the *Venture* and transferred to his own hold all her cargo of value.

What they did not want they tumbled delightedly into the sea, and soon the water around was bobbing with the jettisoned cargo of the snow — bales of paper, chairs, tables, bundles of cheap calico, and the like. Then, to our dismay, the *Venture* was set afire, and from the *Royal Fortune*, having sailed a little distance off, we watched the flames roar up the masts and rigging and sails of our vessel, and expected that in a little while we would be put to death.

The crew was assembled, under my uncle, in the waist of Roberts's ship. Roberts told us that we had no reason to fear for our lives.

"You may either join me as gentlemen rovers," he said, "or swim ashore. As I told your captain, your lives are in your own hands. There's prizes to be taken in plenty and an equal share to every man that signs articles. Look you, you could spend your lives at sea as honest seamen, as they're called, and earn less in all that time than you could make in one cruise with me as your captain.

"What do you have now when you step ashore after a long voyage?" he continued. "A few shillings in your pocket, soon gone, and then a search for another ship. Is that the way for men to live out their lives, all for the sake of honesty?

"Sign articles with me and you'll live like gentlemen, merry and free, with a full vote as to what port you'll sail to or what prizes you'll seek."

"And a rope around your neck at the end of it," called out one of our crew — an old white-haired seaman named Peters.

"Why, there's a chance of it," said Roberts coolly. "But look you, them that dance in the air at Execu-

47

tion Dock for five minutes lived merry for ten or twenty years before that, and they chose to be taken or they'd have fought it out to the end. And look you again, every man must die and what's five minutes choking to death on the end of a rope against starving in your old age or drowning in a shipwreck, which is the lot of most honest seamen, as every one of you knows."

This summing up of the situation, true enough in all reality, had its effect on many of the crew. But old Peters argued that those who did not want to join Roberts should be given a boat and a few provisions to make their way to Barbados, thirty leagues to the westward, as best they could. Roberts replied that he had not a boat to spare and all must either swim or join, for he had lost many of his hands, as I discovered later, and was short of crew.

"Rig a plank," he ordered, and in a few moments a plank of pine was thrust over the side, the inboard end lashed to a gun carriage.

"Well," said Roberts, his fierce eyes fixed on Peters, "would you like to lead the shore party?"

I think he would have gone had not Martin Coverly stopped him. Peters was a stubborn old man, very fixed in his principles. He had been wild enough in his youth, but hearing by chance a preacher talking of hell's fires and eternal damnation for those who were lost, had repented and turned seaman to earn a living. He bore every kind of hardship without complaint, saying he had caused God more pain than he himself now endured, and expressing the hope that he would live long enough to wipe out the sins of his youth by honest living and hard work.

Peters, then, moved toward the plank, calling out to his shipmates that we must obey the will of God and not that of a common pirate. But Martin Coverly stopped him.

"It was never the will of God that a man should kill himself," he said gently.

"Am I to stay among thieves and murderers, the spawn of Satan?" asked Peters.

"You are to preserve the life that God gave you," replied my uncle.

Peters hesitated and then said, in a simple, wondering kind of voice, looking straight into the eyes of Martin Coverly, "You are my captain and I took oath to obey you. Order me to stay aboard and that I'll do."

"Stay aboard. It's your captain's order," was the reply, and Peters moved quietly back among the rest of the hands.

So it was that we who that morning had been peaceful merchant seamen were by sunset pirates by force. Yet force was but a pretext for many of the hands. The taking of the *Venture* was celebrated by a regular carouse on the *Royal Fortune*. Spirits were circulated freely, and many of our crew were drunk by nightfall. Roberts himself drank only sparingly, however, and delegated enough hands to stay sober to handle his ship. It was a tribute to his personality and discipline that these orders were obeyed.

I got no sleep that night. Those of our old crew who were not carousing (there were but half a dozen of them, led by Peters) gathered under the bulkhead forward, keeping to themselves and watching their own shipmates and Roberts's crew reeling about the deck in the moonlight, playing dice and cards or singing songs, which became, as the night went on, more and more unintelligible.

One or two nightmare pictures remain of my first

49

night aboard a pirate vessel — two men grappling with each other at the foot of the foremast in a drunken quarrel. Then the gleam of a knife, a cry of rage or pain, and one of them staggering across the deck, grasping his arm, with the dark blood flowing in rivulets between his fingers.

That was one scene.

Another was ludicrous by contrast — a fellow with a completely bald head and great drooping mustaches, and a bottle of wine in one hand, singing as sweetly as a girl "The Ballad of Barbara Allen," while another cutthroat sat by, maudlin drunk, with tears flowing down his dirty cheeks.

There was yet a third picture, of greater significance — Martin Coverly walking in deep talk with Roberts on the poop deck, after which they went down to the cabin together.

Later, when he emerged from Roberts's cabin, I asked him what they had been talking about and what was to become of us.

"There's a change in the wind, Nicholas, and we must trim our yards and sail with it," he replied.

"Surely it would be possible to escape," I said. "We could wait our chance and take one of the boats. Half a dozen of the hands are still loyal."

"Why, Nicholas," he replied, "Roberts is no fool. And consider the name of his ship — the *Royal Fortune*. 'Tis a good-luck omen, Nicholas, and you will find perhaps that there is more to that name than you think. The key lies here." And he produced from his pocket that cylinder of ivory which was never out of his possession and which he had told me before might prove fortune enough for him.

8

In the months that followed I lived the life of a pirate, constantly thinking of escape, but could hit on no trustworthy plan for doing so. Martin Coverly accepted the life — indeed, observed and studied it as he studied the heights and kinds of palm trees in different places, the times of tides in varying parts of the world, and the strange clawless crabs with armored tails to be found throughout the tropics.

He was reduced to the rank of a common seaman. But he remained, for the most part, a philosopher, and a humorous one. He was on excellent terms with Roberts, with whom he often discussed the philosophy of "free trading," as Roberts called it. But he received no special favors aboard the *Royal Fortune*, and some of his own crew, finding their former captain now at their own level, tried hazing and threatening him. They soon discovered that "captain" is not merely a title but resides in the quality of a man. Martin Coverly was a captain still and ready to prove it.

We had one big fellow in our crew by the name of Thad Waxman, who had been a bosun on the *Venture*. He harbored a grudge against Coverly, who had found him neglectful of his work in the old days.

Finding Coverly one day scrubbing the decks (for Roberts, despite all the carousing, liked to keep things shipshape), he picked up his bucket and emptied the contents over my uncle.

Those around jeered at the former captain, drenched with water. But my uncle got slowly to his feet and said in a level voice, "You should think before you do things like that, Thad Waxman. But to ask you to think is to ask a pig to discuss mathematics." Then he picked up the bucket and struck Waxman such a blow with it on the head as to stretch him senseless on the deck. That done, Martin Coverly restored the man by drenching him with water. When Waxman had recovered his senses, my uncle threw him the bucket and said to him calmly, "Your turn, I fancy, Mr. Waxman."

But Waxman had no stomach for revenge and went off, grumbling. That little scene, followed by one or two others not quite so dramatic, restored my uncle's prestige not only among the men who had been his own hands but among Roberts's crew as well.

There were other things they admired about him.

Whatever he had to do, be the work ever so lowly, he did excellently. He was put, to shame him I suppose, to cleaning the cooks' utensils, and he cleaned them to the point of shining. He was always ahead of the others when it came time to tack or take in sail. To my dismay, he was always first with cutlass and pistol ready when we came to take a prize. He never once spoke of escaping. He had, as I found later, other plans.

We took many prizes.

In the two months after we ourselves were taken,

we stopped a Dutch schooner, a Portuguese merchantman, two French vessels, and a New England brig, plundered their cargoes, and burned the vessels or set them free, according to what might be Roberts's whim at the time.

Some of the crews were pressed into piracy — others were not. It depended on Roberts's need of hands, for in these engagements, of course, he lost men. Three of the vessels decided to fight — the Portuguese, one of the Frenchmen, and the Dutch schooner. The Portuguese was a brigantine, bigger than the *Royal Fortune* and armed as we were with long twelves. We chased her for sixteen hours, for she was a fast sailer, before she was overtaken. When we were within hailing distance, we called on her to heave to and she replied with a broadside that cut down two of our hands, smashed the longboat to splinters, and upended one of our own guns, under which two of the crew were trapped, one with a broken arm and the other with a pulverized leg.

The swiftness and appalling effect of that broadside left me shaken. I had been forced to arm myself with pistol and cutlass but had not expected to have to use them. Now here, lying dead at my feet, was the baldheaded pirate with the long mustaches whom I had seen singing "The Ballad of Barbara Allen" on my first night on board. His torso was one bloody, spongy mass, and the end of one of his mustaches was as drenched with blood as a brush with paint.

Over by the bulwarks, the men with the broken arm and the trapped leg writhed and screamed in the scuppers. The smoke of the broadside from the Portuguese had scarcely cleared away before we replied with a broadside of our own. Over the boom of the explosion I could hear the ringing of the metal cannon, like the continuing chime of a bell. I heard our shot thud home, saw above the curtain of smoke a balk of flaming timber hurled into the air, and heard Roberts roar to our helmsman (none other than old Peters), "Wear ship, damn you. Wear her round and bring our other guns to bear."

He was dressed for battle — plumed hat, snow-white breeches, scarlet waistcoat, and all, and had two beautifully polished pistols hanging on silken ribbands about his neck.

The battle noises stopped as the ship turned before the wind, and the human noises could be heard — orders shouted by Roberts and the curses and screams of the wounded men, and also cheers and laughter — for on some the slaughter and danger had an exhilarating effect.

We turned, then, but the Portuguese had turned before us, and in a shorter arc, so that when we were clear of the smoke we found her up to weather of us, giving her the advantage.

"Fall off. Fall off," cried Roberts, and Peters put the wheel over. But we could not escape the broadside which swept us from the port quarter, raking us almost from stem to stern. Surprisingly, the damage was small — splintered bulwarks and taffrail, and two shot straight through the cabin, one of which buried itself in the mainmast a foot or so above the deck. Peters now, without any order, put our helm up, bringing our own guns to bear, and the foremast of the Portuguese came tumbling down.

It was easy then to come alongside and board her, grappling irons being thrown to clench the two vessels together. Roberts was first aboard the Portuguese, followed by Martin Coverly — not Martin Coverly, honest seaman and naturalist, but Martin

Coverly, pirate. I heard the clap of pistol shot and the high, tinny clattering of cutlasses clashing against each other. I saw my uncle engaged with two men, forced back to the bulwark, and leaped aboard the Portuguese to his aid. A man leveled a pistol straight in my face and fired, and I suffered all the terror of dying, but remained alive, for there was but a flash of the pan and the weapon misfired. I struck his hand down with my cutlass and then I was beside Martin Coverly, who turned, glanced at me a moment, and gave me that little mocking smile of his. Out of the corner of my eye I saw one of his opponents swing at me — a blow which would have cleaved my skull in two had it landed. I ducked and, ducking, thrust upward with my own cutlass, which was immediately forced from my hand by tremendous pressure. Then, in a moment, as if on some signal, all was over. The Portuguese merchantman had been taken, and lying at my feet was a young seaman of my own age, red-haired and blue-eyed. The eyes were full of fear and he was trying with dying strength to pull out of his breast my cutlass, which was thrust through him. I staggered to the side, sick in body and mind.

Martin Coverly pulled me around to face him.

"I killed him!" I shouted. "I killed him!"

"There's worse has happened in the world than this day's work," said my uncle grimly. "You've been a boy long enough. Learn to take the wrack of life naked. Others have endured it and made good ends."

From that day forward, I grew more grave and lost many joys. I became despondent, sick of myself and my life, and sick, too, of my strange uncle, Martin Coverly, and his secret thoughts.

9

Some few months after the taking of the *Venture* and our being forced into piracy, the *Royal Fortune* put in at Charleston in the province of South Carolina, to sell some of her stolen goods and reprovision.

Here I thought would be an opportunity to escape. The royal governor would certainly give me shelter, or if he could not be reached, some of the honest merchants of the town. But when I talked of my plans to Martin Coverly he laughed at me.

"The royal governor is as big a rogue as Roberts," he said. "The two of them will probably dine together the first night ashore. As for honest merchants, the greater number of them wink at piracy and receive stolen goods, paying cash in return.

"Nicholas, my lad, for every pirate afloat there are five to help him ashore, with whom he deals. Not one of them would befriend you, for if you turned witness against Roberts, you would be equally a witness against them. They work hand in glove. Also, it is one of Roberts's rules that anyone who leaves the ship without his permission must, on being recaptured, be tried and put to death. It is a rule he never breaks.

"If we ever put in at any big port — Boston or New York or Philadelphia — there might be a chance to get away. But outside of the big towns, the whole of the American main is but a receiving house for pirates. In short, my lad, attempt to escape here and you'll be back aboard in twenty-four hours, tried and shot. There will be nothing I can do to save you."

Peters and some of the other honest hands also proposed that we try to escape, but my uncle warned them against making the attempt, assuring them that they would be caught. Peters accepted this as coming from his captain. But one of the hands, Thad Waxman, did try to escape, and that surprised me, for he seemed to have accepted a life of piracy completely.

He was brought back two days later, terribly beaten, and trussed up like a fowl ready for the spit. He was put in irons in the hold, chained to a ring, and left there until the *Royal Fortune* had cleared for sea again and was well out of sight of land.

In that time no arrangements were made to bring him food. When I discovered this I got a pannikin of water, some ship's bread, and a little fruit and took these down to him.

He was barely conscious and drank the water avidly. His eyes were swollen almost shut and full of pus, and one side of his face, where he had been hit with a club, was a massive blue bruise.

"Nick," he said, "I'm a dead man. Nothing can be done to save me."

I could offer him no comfort on that score.

"If I could get ride of these irons." he said, "I'd take my chances over the side."

"You could not even get on deck," I replied. "You are too badly hurt."

"Martin Coverly was right," he mumbled. "I have no brains." Then he added grimly, "And he has too many."

I spent as much time as I could with Waxman to comfort him. My uncle also pleaded that he should be set free of his irons, which chafed him terribly, and Roberts finally permitted this. He was free only for a day, however, before he was brought up on deck, shortly after dawn of our second day at sea, and his trial held.

It was law among Roberts's men that two others besides the captain be elected from among the crew to act as judges in cases of desertion. One of those elected was a fellow to whom I had taken a dislike, though I had scarcely said a word to him in all my time on board. He went by the name of Salvation Sims, and was an old man with white hair coming down to his shoulders and a simpering, overly pious way of speaking. There was something exceedingly cruel in his nature — cruel and deceitful, and all glossed over with an air of sanctity which, as Martin Coverly put it, "smelled sweet as corruption."

Sims smirked at the crew when elected, thanked them for reposing in his hands the fate of one of their brethren, whose immortal soul, he said, was a treasure beyond any taken by any ship — and would shortly be seized by the devil himself. He put his hands before his sunburned, withered face in a mockery of prayer and, rolling his deep-sunk eyes up to heaven, prayed for divine guidance in the deliberations which were shortly to begin, which would be greatly eased if a pannikin of rum was issued to one and all.

This horror of a man, then, was one of the judges, and the second was a good seaman and altogether honest fellow — though somewhat slow in his thinking, called Sam Lord. He opposed Sims in the matter of rum, saying that if a man was to be tried for his life, he had a right to be tried by sober judges. But he was hooted down and the rum passed freely around, though Roberts did not touch it.

Sims said a little mock grace over his, some mumbo-jumbo ending with the phrase, very loud, "In nomino domino homino," which, being reckoned part of a Papist prayer, brought shouts of laughter.

There was no prosecutor, nor anyone appointed to defend poor Waxman. Roberts read the charge, saying that in violation of the ship's articles which he had signed he had sought to desert the vessel, knowing that to do so and be recaptured meant death. He asked Waxman whether he had anything to say in his defense, but all poor Waxman could mumble, blinded as he was by the sunlight, with the water streaming from his puffed eyelids, was a request that they get it over with.

He was a pitiful figure, but he aroused no pity among his shipmates, for he had broken that one law which threatened them all, and had he succeeded, would certainly have given evidence against them. His head was still swollen and blue from the blows he had endured, his eyes puffed to blindness, and his clothing filthy from his confinement in the hold.

He stood trembling before his judges, more from pain and wretchedness than fear. So, finding he had nothing to say for himself, Roberts turned to his fellow judges and said that according to regulations he should be executed, a verdict with which Sims immediately agreed. He added, in that lisping voice of his, that he himself favored hanging as likely to provide a little needed diversion for those of the crew who were staunch, and a salutary lesson for others who might be thinking of following Waxman's example. Then the wretch turned full on me and gave me a toothless grin, baring his blackened gums.

The other judge, Sam Lord, was not so quick with his verdict. He admitted in his slow way that the facts were as stated and could not be denied. "But I hear tell the man was drunk and not in his right senses, and that should be put into the reckoning," he said.

Poor Waxman perked up a little, hearing someone speak for him.

"Why, so he might have been," lisped Sims. "There's a thought there, and a good one. But it says in the Good Book that there's truth in wine. And if it doesn't say it in the Good Book, it says the same thing somewhere among notable and ancient writing. So what he did drunk was but what he wanted to do sober and dared not. Being drunk, then, if you follow my tack, but makes him all the guiltier, and he should then hang twice — once for the thought while sober, and once for the action, while drunk."

"Is there anyone to speak a word for this man?" asked Roberts, cutting off the guffaws that followed Sims's remark.

He looked about at the hands, some smirking, some whispering to each other, and some strangely silent. One had tied a piece of marlin around a rope's end and was jiggling it up and down in a travesty of a hanging.

Then Martin Coverly stepped forward, and walking to the table where the judges were seated, stood, hands on hips, looking straight at Sims. "There are apes in Africa could teach you humanity," he said. "But I have a fancy I'll teach that lesson to you myself one day. It'll take time, but you'll learn."

He next turned to Roberts. "Is it your opinion," he asked, "that a man should take the full responsibility for all his actions?"

"It is," said Roberts.

"Under the ship's articles, at first look, this man should be sentenced to death," said Coverly.

"I still hold if he was drunk it should be put into the reckoning," said Sam Lord.

"Whether a man is drunk or sober is his own choosing," replied Coverly. "But being aboard this ship was not of his choosing but mine. It was I as captain who surrendered the *Venture*, not he, who was but a bosun. So you must hang me in his place, for you said yourself that a man should be responsible for his own actions, and it was not Waxman's action but mine that put him in the place he is today."

"By thunder, you're a bold man," said Roberts.

"I am," said Coverly. "Few bolder."

"You'll find me as bold," said Roberts, defiantly.

"Why, then," said Coverly, "you would not stand by and see one of your own hands killed for something that was properly to be laid to your account."

That took them all aback — all but Sims. He took a swig of his rum and simpered, "There's a nice argument there. We should, in all truth, hang the two of them."

But Martin Coverly had not done.

"Come," he said to Roberts, "you're captain, as I was, and must show an example to your crew. They'll have small respect for you if you let them think that they must be put in jeopardy for a decision that was yours."

"You're mistook there," said Sam Lord. "No man's life is put in jeopardy on this ship without his having a vote. It's the crew that votes whether we chase a prize or leave it; storm a city or not. The captain's vote counts but one."

"True enough, no doubt," said Coverly. "But there was no vote taken on my ship whether to surrender or not. I made the decision without consulting my crew. If you decide on death for Waxman — and under your law you can make no other decision — it is I who should die in his stead."

"You're too good a man to hang," said Roberts, scowling.

"And too clever a man to have aboard this ship," said Sims.

Roberts stood up impatiently. "Look you, we've had enough of this lawyer's talk," he said. "It's the rules of this ship — not any other — that we're judging by. I say death."

Sims took another drink of his rum, rolled it around in in his mouth, swallowed it, and said, "Death."

"On the matter of drunkenness . . ." said Lord.

"Vote," said Roberts. "Damn drunkenness."

"Death, then," said Lord.

It was all over in a few minutes. Waxman was taken to the portside, where the boarding gate was pulled away. He was told to kneel and did so, with the open sea behind him. The crew voted (out of pity, perhaps) that he be shot rather than hung, and Sims, at his own request, was appointed executioner and given a musket.

Waxman asked for a few moments in which to

make his peace with God, and old Peters knelt with him and the two prayed together. Sims, meanwhile, fiddled with the musket, winking copiously at the crew, and watched quietly by Martin Coverly, who, I noted, had now thrust a brace of pistols into his waistband.

Then Sims raised the musket, took careful aim — and the weapon misfired, for he had purposely neglected to prime it. He hoped in this way to raise a further laugh from the crew, but he reckoned without Coverly. My uncle knocked the musket from his hands and presented him with one of the pistols.

"Do your work cleanly, Master Sims, for the first time in your filthy life," he said. Then he put the other pistol to the head of the wicked old pirate.

There was a report and Waxman toppled backward through the open port and into the sea. I saw his body hit the water and stared in horror at the place. There was a splash and a swatch of foam on the surface of the ocean and then Waxman floated to the surface, a little farther off, trailing blood and trying feebly to swim.

Despite my uncle's threat, Salvation Sims had not done his work cleanly.

Later I asked Martin Coverly whether he would indeed have given his life for Waxman, leaving me alone on Roberts's ship.

"No," he said. "I was bluffing Roberts, hoping to save Waxman's life. In any case, that was not the trial I have yet to face."

"What do you mean by the trial you have yet to face?" I asked.

He looked at me gravely and said, "The test lies ahead, Nicholas — the test which I failed before and have a chance not to fail again."

10

The attachment between Roberts and Martin Coverly was greatly strengthened by this incident. Roberts, a brave man himself, admired courage in others. My uncle's defense of Waxman, his coolly offering his own life in place of that of the bosun, greatly impressed him. Coverly was often consulted on problems of navigation and ship handling and had far more time for Roberts than he did for me. Indeed, it became difficult to get a word alone with him, and he similarly avoided Peters and the other hands who, like myself, had been forced into piracy. In short, he came more and more under the influence of Roberts, and on the few occasions when I managed to talk to him privately he was either aloof or treated my concern with casual humor.

"You say I am too much influenced by Roberts, against my better nature, as you call it," he said.

"Well, it is but policy to be in the good books of a ship's captain, even though he be a pirate."

"You admire him and his way of life," I said. "Admit it."

"Indeed, I do," replied my uncle. "When you consider it calmly, it is no small thing for a man to set the governments of the world at defiance, and, thus free of them, establish his own government, even if it be only captain of a pirate vessel."

"He is a robber and a murderer," I said hotly.

"Why, that is only because he does these things under his own flag," replied Martin Coverly. "The same deeds done under the flag of any nations of what we call the civilized world would be hailed as acts of the highest patriotism.

"Think on that, Nicholas. Sheep make good citizens, while lions are hunted. But the sheep are fleeced throughout their lives and eventually slaughtered, and the lion leads a free life and may in the end evade the hunters."

"You are mad to talk like this," I said.

"No, Nicholas. I was mad when I talked the other way." That was Martin Coverly in one humor, which now grew more and more upon him.

There were times, however — usually after we had taken some prize which had decided to fight rather than surrender — when his mood changed utterly and he came to me quiet and reflective and very much his old self.

Then he would talk of the rambles we had had together in different ports, of my father (his brother), and my mother, both now dead, and of all the Coverlys back home in Somerset.

He spoke of his boyhood, before he went to sea,

fishing for trout in the upland pools of the Avon, and of the glitter of slate roofs after a storm of rain, and of the shoaling of mackerel in the early spring along the English coast.

After the slaughter of battle his mind turned to such things, and he once confessed he would give all the prize money to which he was entitled for the sight of a hawthorn hedge buried in white blossoms in the spring.

"Bear with me, Nicholas," he would say. "We will get out of this yet."

But such moods were rare, and most of the time he avoided me, as I have said, and kept company with Roberts.

We took the *Swan* off Hispaniola and she proved a special prize, for she had been sent out from England as a privateer and mounted eight long twelves — four to a broadside — besides several swivels and smaller guns.

As with many privateers, she had herself turned at least half pirate. Privateers were privately commissioned vessels of war, licensed to attack enemy merchantmen. But that license was often extended to attacking all merchantmen, which was but plain piracy. When Roberts came up on the *Swan* and raised the Jolly Roger, the captain, thinking him a kind of brother, did not fight but accepted his invitation to come aboard the *Royal Fortune* for the usual glass of wine.

He discovered his mistake when he was informed that he had lost his ship, and quickly agreed to sign articles with Roberts. I half suspect that he hoped to be given command of his own vessel again, but Roberts was not as simple as that.

He summoned Martin Coverly to a conference in his cabin which lasted the better part of an hour. When it was over, he announced that he had put Coverly in command of the *Swan*, for he had found him a staunch man and true, a good seaman, and one who he was sure would prove loyal to him.

I was overjoyed at this news, seeing in it at last a chance to escape and win my uncle away from the influence of Roberts. Volunteers were called for to man the *Swan* and I stepped forward eagerly. Her own crew was excluded from serving aboard her, and not enough of Roberts's men wanted to leave the *Royal Fortune* to serve under a new captain. The decision did not sit well with them. They grumbled about it, saying that by rights he ought to appoint one of his own hands to command the *Swan*. But Roberts was not a man to be crossed, and in the end they accepted the appointment.

Hands were then selected to make up a crew, and among them was the man I detested — Salvation Sims, with his wrinkled mouth, long white hair, and pious lisp.

He gave a knowing nod to Roberts when he was picked. I made a note to watch Sims and the others whom Roberts selected, and concluded that he had given command of the *Swan* to my uncle lest he prove a rival aboard the *Royal Fortune*, but did not expect him to hold that command for long.

Among the new crew was Jack Winthrop, a huge man who was quartermaster of the *Royal Fortune*, Jedediah Truxton, first mate, and Clem Matthews, bosun. All had served a number of years with Roberts. Matthews had some condition of the skin whereby he was never tanned by the sun, but only turned red. As a result of this he was nicknamed Redbird. Although he was only in his thirties, his hair was pure white, including his eyebrows and eyelashes, and his eyes had a pinkish cast to them. He was, in fact, an albino. His eyesight, for all that, was of the keenest and he could throw a knife with great accuracy. This was a great sport for him, and many times, when I was scrubbing down the decks, he would pitch a knife from some distance off so that it fell close to my hand. Then he would laugh, baring his teeth but making no great noise in laughing. The effect was peculiarly menacing.

Others who came with us were more wholesome — Sam Lord, the slow-thinking yet curiously honest pirate who had been one of Waxman's judges, old Peters, and those whom I have called the "honest hands" of the crew of the *Venture*. There were four of these — plain seamen without any ambition but to do their work and stay out of trouble. They were James Phipps, Edward Hyde, Charles Fanshaw, and John Atkins. To these I must add Munro Mcdougal — a Scot who spoke little, but of whom it was known that he dared not set foot in England or indeed in any British territory, his life being forfeit as a traitor.

He was, in fact, a Jacobite — that is, one loyal to the cause of the Stuart kings who had been displaced. He had taken part in some minor riot in Edinburgh in favor of the Stuarts, been arrested, and condemned to the gallows, but made his escape.

Piracy was nothing to him.

He was as contemptuous of pirates as he was of the king's officers who were supposed to hunt them down. There was for him but one rightful king of

68

Scotland and England, James Stewart, son of James II, whom he called James III, and he regarded George I as a villain greater than Roberts.

When the crew had been selected and sent aboard, the *Swan* and the *Royal Fortune* started their cruise together.

My uncle, now installed in the captain's cabin, seemed for a while his old self. His discipline was strict and he would show no favorites, which had always been his way. Yet he now spoke to me more often and in his old kindly way, and I thought that at last a reformation had set in.

On the third day of his command, when I had finished the first trick of the night at the wheel, I decided, instead of going below to sleep in my bunk, to spend some time on deck, for I was not tired and the tropical air was as soft as satin.

We were bowling along nicely under plain sail through seas full of phosphorescence. Each time the bow of the *Swan* crashed into a wave, a sheet of light was thrown upward from the dark ocean to reflect on the bellying sails — a sight so beautiful that, though I had seen it many times, I never tired of it.

The crunch of the brig into the seas, her easy motion, the display of light, and the softness of the air so soothed me that I fell asleep in the shadow of one of the gun carriages. I awoke sometime later, stiff and bemused about where I was, and then heard, from close by, the lisping voice of Salvation Sims, speaking in a whisper, which made his simper the more pronounced.

"Planning to give Roberts the slip, he is," he said. "I'm sure of it as Satan is of Sin."

"Well, he won't be the first that took a ship and went off on his own account," said another. "Smaller crew means bigger shares."

"What makes you think he's going on his own account?" asked Sims. "You're as simple as a milkmaid, Jack Winthrop. Give Roberts the slip and turn us all in — that's his plan. And a free pardon for him, and that nice upstanding nephew of his. Such a sweet boy. He'd have made a fine parson if he hadn't taken to the sea."

"Aye, and you'd have made a fine bishop but for the same reason," said a voice which I recognized as that of Jedediah Truxton. "But then I heard, too, that you couldn't keep your hands off widows and young boys."

"We all have our weaknesses, Jedediah," said Sims smoothly. "But this is just gossip. Coverly intends to give Roberts the slip. Of that I'm sure. Roberts put us aboard — you, me, Redbird, and Jack here, old trusted hands — to prevent that. Do you see the course plain now? It won't be to go on his own account that he'll leave Roberts but to turn us in and get a pardon for himself."

"You say so, but we don't know that it's true," said Winthrop doggedly. "I never saw him hold back when we was in action. He's as good a man as any of us. And I never knew anything but trouble to come out of hands that had suspicions of their captains.

"That happened under Tew on the old *Arrow*. Mutterings and whisperings and suchlike, and then a mutiny and fifteen dead and the ship lost with quarreling afterward, and them that survived hung and sun-dried at Cape Corso Castle.

"Same thing with Tolliver on the *Salem Joy*.

70

Fleming stirred up the hands with whispering and they marooned Tolliver on a freezing island south of Africa, where he had only seals and penguins for company. Then what happens but the hands fall out among themselves and between drinking and fighting they run the ship onto Teachers Reef and only three come away from that alive."

"He was a lovely man, Tolliver," said Truxton. "Keelhauling was his delight; that and the barrel of beef."

"Nailing a man up in a keg and leaving him there until he died," said Redbird. "Well, he'll be sitting on hot coals for the rest of eternity."

"Why, so will we all," said Sims calmly. "So we must take our delight now."

"I won't go for any move against Coverly until it's plain what he intends to do," said Jack Winthrop. "There's been some talk, and most of the crew, I'd say, is of the same opinion. The day he's given Roberts the slip is the day to come to a reckoning. Not before."

"That may be too late," said Sims.

"No. We can take the ship then, deal with Coverly and that nevvy of his, and go on the account on our own. And what's wrong with that? I was ready to split with Roberts six months ago. Let Coverly take the ship and then let us take it from him. That's the true course to follow."

"And who would be captain?" asked Redbird.

"That's for the hands to elect," said Winthrop. "But it won't be you, Redbird. You're too quick with that knife."

"We must elect someone who can keep peace aboard," said Sims unctuously. "Someone who has

the fortune and health of the hands close to his heart
— and is wise as a serpent." Plainly he meant himself.

The talk drifted off then to other ships and captains under whom they'd served. They all agreed that the richest cruising grounds were off the African coast, where there were Moslem ships to be taken laden not with bales of wool and cotton and barrels of molasses but with silks and precious woods and gold from the African mines.

"They know where the gold mines are, them Arabs," said Truxton. "Caves, they say, in the mountains, with veins of pure gold running along the walls, thick as a man's hand. They glitters like sunlight in the light of a candle lantern.

"That's where we should be cruising instead of here picking up merchantmen loaded down with pickaxes and chamber pots."

"Black ivory, too," said Sims. "It is a long time since I had my hands on black ivory." And he gave a little chuckle of delight. By black ivory I knew he meant slaves, and I shuddered to think of the fate of slaves in the hands of such a man as he.

They talked for some time longer, while I lay straining to hear what was said and fearful of being found hiding in the shadow of the gun carriage. Winthrop produced a bottle of spirits, which was handed around. Sims had one weakness, which lay in the fact that he could not resist hard liquor, and soon they were all somewhat befuddled. I then decided to make my escape, and crawling along the gunwale, keeping in the shadow, the deck being frosted with starlight, got back to the break of the poop, where it was an easy matter to gain Martin Coverly's cabin.

He was sprawled on his bunk, fast asleep, when I entered, but awoke in a moment. I told him all I had heard, and when I was done he said, "Why, Nicholas, I thank you for the news, which, however, only confirms what I had already suspected."

"What are you going to do?" I asked. "If we part company with the *Royal Fortune* to make our escape, it will be but to sign your own death warrant, and mine, too."

"As to that, we must wait and see," he said. He was silent for a while, in deep thought, and then said, "They spoke of an African cruise, eh, Nicholas, and of the gold of the African mines? Well, when it comes to play, they may find that though they hold the king I have the ace."

11

Three days later, still keeping company with the
Royal Fortune, we met some heavy squalls during the night, particularly fierce in the hours before
dawn. All hands were called to take down our topsails, for the *Swan* heeled dangerously with the
freshening of the wind.

The squalls were preceded by heavy rains, completely obscuring the masthead light on the *Royal
Fortune*, which was sailing two miles ahead of us.
We had, of course, taken a compass bearing on the
light in case this should happen. But when dawn
came at last, the *Royal Fortune* was nowhere to be
seen, though Coverly himself went to the masthead
with a glass to look for her.

"We've lost her," he announced when he regained
the deck. "She's nowhere in sight, and Roberts appointed no place for a meeting should we become
separated. But the Florida Keys would be the most
likely, in my opinion."

This was Sims's chance to make a move, and he did so immediately. "Mates," he said to the hands gathered around, "I've been expecting something of this sort to happen. Coverly isn't one of us and never was. I say he plans to turn us over to the king's men in Florida and win a pardon for himself. And I say we should take the ship here and now and be rid of him."

"Well, now, Master Sims," said Martin Coverly, "would you say it was part of my plan to arrange a night of squalls so that we lost the light on the *Royal Fortune*?"

"No," said Sims. "But I'd be a fool not to know that you'd take advantage of the first squally night to give Roberts the slip. So we took down our topsails to lose speed, and I found this here clasp knife next to the steering compass, to give a false reading. And what do you say to that, Martin Coverly?" He produced a heavy clasp knife from his pocket.

"Why, I say what everybody knows — that you're a liar," replied Coverly. "Would it be reasonable if I put the clasp knife there that I should leave it for you to find?"

" 'Tis your knife, ain't it?" demanded Sims. "Look at it close, mates," he said, passing it around among the crew. "We all know that it belongs to Martin Coverly, so it's plain as print that he's the one that put it there to sneak away from Roberts by steering a wrong course."

There was no denying that it was my uncle's knife, and I looked at him in dismay, surprised that he should have been so foolish. "Under the articles, the crew is entitled to vote to depose a captain, and I say that we should take that vote now," Sims said.

There was some argument, but in the end a vote

was taken on a show of hands and Coverly ousted from his post. He took it in surprisingly good humor, however, and inquired whether he was still a member of the crew and therefore entitled to vote on who the new captain should be.

"Only Roberts's hands get to vote on that head," said Sims, "the rest being suspect as having signed articles not of their free will." But huge Jack Winthrop would have none of that and insisted that all should vote. The business of voting for a new captain, again by a show of hands, was then begun. But from the start there was no agreement. Some voted for Sims when his name was called out as a candidate — mostly Roberts's men — but some wanted Sam Lord, and some even voted for Coverly. While the arguing and voting was going on, a white squall came roaring out of the west and had the *Swan* on her beam ends, her leeward guns half buried in the water, before the helmsman, with the assistance of two others, could run her off before the wind and bring her upright.

"Why, Master Sims," said Coverly, "here's the first lesson for you in running a ship without a captain. But you were ever more of an old woman than a seaman, and if this ship were put in your hands, I'd say the crew would be dead faster than if I turned them over to the king's men, as you say I was plotting to do.

"But take your pick, men," he continued. "There's Sims here with a mind that would frighten a bilge rat. Or there's Sam Lord. Sam's an honest and able man, but he'll admit himself that he knows no more of navigation than a fish does of periwigs. There's Redbird that would put a knife in you for sport. There's Jack Winthrop. He's one of Roberts's men, and a good choice all round, I'd say. For myself, I wash my hands of you. You're not a crew worth having. The first setback — the first misadventure — and you're all set to elect a new captain. I could have taken you to the Gold Coast of Africa and the Mines of Solomon. Yes. I have a chart, and that is in my power. But there's hardly a man among you has the heart of a sick weevil in a moldy biscuit.

"So pick yourselves a captain and sail where you want. But you'll get no help from me. None at all."

When he had said that, he turned on his heel and strode away.

Sims's face was a study. It was normally a dirty brown, but now it was gray, and his pursed lips trembled. Redbird, with an oath, pulled out a knife and would have buried it in Coverly's back but that I charged him, hitting him full in the stomach with my head, and sending him sprawling across the deck. He was as quick as a cat, however, recovered, and in a moment had me pinned on the deck, his hand groping for my throat.

I thought that was going to be the last of me. Then there was a loud report and Redbird fell off of me, clasping his hand to the side of his face. I looked about and was astonished to find Salvation Sims with a smoking pistol in his hand. Martin Coverly was leaning against the weather rail, smiling at the whole performance.

"Mates," cried Sims, "we've made a mistake. I was the first to make it and I hope you'll bear in mind that I'm the first to repent it. Coverly for captain, I says, loud and clear, and let bygones be bygones."

Such a turnabout was hardly to be believed. But so changeable in its mood was that disorganized crew that half of them roared, "Coverly for captain," a moment after Sims, and in a minute more the lot of them were gathered around my uncle, begging him once again to take command of the *Swan*. He protested that he would have nothing more to do with them, but they continued to plead, and Sims made a speech on their behalf.

"These poor souls," he said, "simple seamen misled by myself — to that I plead guilty like a repentant sinner — are once more asking that you take command of their lives and fortunes. Since I was the cause of their being led astray, it falls on me to lead them back in the right path like a good shepherd. I don't say you didn't leave that knife by the compass to give Roberts the slip, but I was wrong in thinking you meant to turn us all over, you having mentioned the African Gold Coast and a chart of the Mines of Solomon, and I hear the ring of truth come through clear in that remark.

"In regard to my own mistake," he continued, "it arose for concern for the lives of my messmates. Mistake it was, but made out of love and pity for them that has served with me, side by side, good days and bad, through many long years.

"So let us voyage on again, under your command, share and share alike, and come back from Africa with enough gold to make every man a king.

"As for what trust you can place in me now who led this crew in deposing you," he added, "why, didn't I save the life of that beloved boy there, shooting the top of the ear off one of my messmates to do so? There's warrant enough for how much I love you now and that boy whom God has placed in your charge."

It was a lesson in hypocrisy to hear that evil old

man talk so earnestly of the purity of his motives. There were moments when I halfway believed him myself.

In the end, Coverly agreed to accept command again and announced that we would still head for the Florida Keys and the Dry Tortugas, lest it be possible to find Roberts there.

Reflecting on the whole sequence of events, I believe Martin Coverly had planned it all. It could not have turned out better for him. He had forced the crew to beg him to be their captain and had thoroughly discredited Salvation Sims, who could never again challenge his authority.

12

We did not find Roberts at the Florida Keys, nor the Dry Tortugas, where we took aboard enough turtle to provide us with meat for the Africa voyage. I went ashore with some of the hands to get the turtle, and when I came back aboard, Martin Coverly gave me a glass of wine in his cabin and asked me whether I had seen anything of a little cutter with two aboard. Perhaps he was expecting to meet some of Roberts's hands. I had not, and it was then, on my questioning him directly, that he openly confessed his determination to turn pirate on his own. Up to that point I had hoped he would return to an honest life. Now all my hopes were dashed.

He had become, in effect, two men — the one an excellent and honest seaman, kindly and deeply interested in life and nature, and the other daring, adventurous, ambitious, and without the slightest regard for the law. He could switch from one person to another in a matter of a few minutes.

We had no need to water or take on other provisions. All these we had aboard in plenty. Yet we did not immediately clear for Africa, for a few days earlier we had fallen in with the American brig *Experiment*, which Coverly engaged and took as his first prize. We'd lost three dead and four badly wounded in the engagement. I will not dwell on the horrors of that sea fight. Laying over only long enough to replenish our supplies, we took the brig to New Orleans. There five of her crew elected to join the *Swan*, and the rest were set ashore, for Coverly would force no one into piracy. The prize money from the brig — twenty-three thousand pounds — was divided among the crew.

There was no question of my deserting the ship in New Orleans. We anchored far out, and the city itself lay many miles from the mouth of the river in a swampland of saw grass laced with bayous and teeming with alligators.

A watch was kept on all boats leaving and approaching the *Swan*, and I was not allowed ashore. Peters, however deeply he may have been disturbed by the attack on the *Experiment*, voiced no objection nor complaint. For him, captain's orders were captain's orders. He had in effect handed his conscience over to his captain. With me, the position was precisely the opposite. I many times thought myself the true conscience of Martin Coverly. Time and again, when I mulled over plans for leaving the ship, I realized deep down that I could not desert him. To do so, I felt, would be to destroy his last hope of recovering his true self. I loved him despite the change that had come over him. I could not leave him.

81

As for the ship being seized by the authorities in New Orleans for the taking of the *Experiment*, there was no hope of that. All were hand in glove with the pirates of the Spanish main, as were the planters also. They and New Orleans lived by whatever profit came to hand, and they could not afford to be nice about the source of that profit.

Coverly was ashore for several days, arranging for the sale of the *Experiment* and her cargo. When the spoils had been divided among the crew, all demanded a further week for a carouse in which to spend their gains. In less than the week granted, they had squandered it all in drinking, gambling, and carousing.

When their money was gone, they came back aboard, many of them scarcely able to climb up the ship's side. The decks were soon muddy with their footsteps. Empty bottles lay in clutches along the gunwales, and the forecastle was a squalid slum of tobacco smoke and the fumes of liquor.

All this changed when Coverly returned aboard. Truxton had been left in command, being first mate. He was given a dressing down in front of the crew and demoted there and then to seaman. Sam Lord was appointed first officer in his place, the decks hosed off until they gleamed in the sun, the bottles thrown overboard, the forecastle cleaned up, and some now needed stores put aboard—salt cod, salt beef and pork, dried beans, flour, and ship's biscuit. When these stores had been laid in, the aroma of tobacco smoke and liquor between decks was replaced by that of rotting seaweed from the casks of salt cod, or bacalhau, a favorite dish of Martin Coverly's.

A day was spent overhauling the rigging and tallowing the masts so that the yards could be raised and lowered without difficulty. The gun tackles were renewed where needed, and a dozen kegs of gunpowder added to those already in the powder hold.

This place, deep in the bowels of the ship, was lit by a lantern behind a pane of glass, and all the bulkheads were padded. It was death to enter the powder hold smoking a pipe, and it says much about the carelessness of the crew that such a penalty had to be demanded. Without it they would, careless of danger, have fetched powder to the guns with pipes in their mouths.

When all this was done, we cleared the sultry roadstead in which we had lain at anchor for almost three weeks, eastward bound for the Gold Coast of Africa, with all aboard talking about the riches to be had with such glee you would have thought they were already in possession of a shipload of gold.

They never stopped to think that King Solomon's Mines, if they existed at all, must have been sought through the centuries by others, and if found, despoiled of all they contained.

For myself, I thought it all a ruse of Martin Coverly to recover command of the *Swan* and get the ship to Africa, there to pick up ivory and slaves and prey upon whatever shipping he met.

There was more and more talk as the long voyage progressed — for we were ten weeks making the African coast — of the map or chart Coverly had mentioned. In the end I asked my uncle if it were really true that he had such a map, as he claimed.

"Yes, indeed," he replied. "And you and others have seen me with it many times." He reached in his pocket and produced that curiously inscribed cylinder of ivory which he had often shown me, and which he had obtained, he said, during one of his voyages to the Levant.

"That is a map?" I asked, incredulous.

"Yes. An old map," he replied. "And the mapmaker was cunning enough to know that the best way to hide something is to expose it openly. Watch."

He dipped a finger into an inkhorn and smeared the cylinder lightly with ink. Then he took a sheet of cartridge paper and rolled the inked cylinder over it.

A map, about four inches square, was immediately printed on the cartridge paper.

The draftsmanship was exquisite. The map showed a portion of a coastline, with a river winding its way from the interior. There were several mountain peaks, with tributaries of the river flowing between them, one more strongly marked than the others. There were forests and swampland and savannas. That so much could be shown in so small a space is an indication of how carefully the map was drawn.

But there was nowhere any indication of the purpose of the map. It was just a map, without any of its features identified by a single word. My uncle noticed that I was puzzled, and smiled.

"He was a very cunning mapmaker, as I remarked," he said, and pushed against the center of the cylinder with his finger, when another emerged. This also was inscribed with small interrupted lines.

"Here is the key," he said, and covering this slim-mer cylinder also with ink, he rolled it on the paper, and the following was printed on the sheet:

KING SULEIMANS MINE

Volta thirty leagues. White lion rock. Guardian and skeletons. Tributary east bank. Through gorge. First lake and waterfall. Overland N. to second lake and village. NNE 10 leagues. Mines.

That was all. But a dozen questions were raised immediately in my mind.

"You had this cylinder — this map — for years, yet spoke of it to no one," I said. "Were you planning all that time to make a voyage to Africa to discover these mines?"

"At times I believed the mines existed," said my uncle. "At times I did not. But I had no real plan to search for them until I got command of this ship."

"Do you believe that they exist, now?"

"For three hundred years, gold has been traded in quantity off that coast," said Martin Coverly. "Then the supply dropped sharply, until now slaves are more profitable. The sudden drop in the supply suggests that the site of one of the principal mines is lost."

"How could it be lost?" I asked.

"Warfare. Famine. Sickness. There are more plagues on the Gold Coast than in the whole of Europe. Warfare is common, tribe against tribe, and hand in hand with warfare goes famine. It would be no miracle for the site of the mines to be lost."

"Would finding these mines repay you for all your

years at sea?" I asked. "Would you take the gold, and live honestly thereafter?"

He stood silent a moment.

"The treasure each man seeks lies within him," he said. "Yet it is plaguily hard to find, and we are often misled by the glitter of false gold. When I was in New Orleans I saw a swamp bird I had not seen before, and delighted in it as much as if I had found a new island in the world. Is that where my treasure lies? Or is it in the Mines of Solomon? Or in the zest of battle and the taking of prizes at sea? I sail a dark course, Nicholas, with a few lights ahead, but do not know which leads to safe harbor."

Then he said softly, "Do not leave me, for if you do, I am lost."

"What if I become as lost as you?" I asked.

He shook his head. "That can never be," he said. "There are some in the world who never question their course from birth to death, but sail it true. And you are one of those. So do not leave me."

For some days he remained kind and considerate — captain of a ship and yet a genial friend to all aboard, even including Salvation Sims and Redbird, for whom he had a pleasant word whenever they met. For Sam Lord he developed a particular regard and counseled him to give up the life of a sea rover whenever he had the opportunity. "You have more of the husband and father in you than the pirate," he said. "Make your stake, perhaps on this one voyage, and then settle down ashore."

"I never liked the life," said Lord. "Yet I have no friends nor family and would starve ashore." So it was with many of the hands. They were outside the law because they could not live within the law.

Clawing our way down the coast of South America to the bulge of Brazil, we sighted several vessels, but though the hands wanted to give chase, Coverly refused to do so. We were Africa bound, he said, and he would not stop, and though they grumbled about this, such was the force of his personality, they dared do no more than grumble.

When we were in midpassage across the South Atlantic, old Peters was found dead in his bunk when his watch was called. He had complained for a while of pains in his arms and back, which he took to be rheumatism, but would not on account of them shirk his work. He was sewed up in an old sail, with a cannon shot at his feet, and put over the side. His death spread a gloom about the whole ship, for callous as the hands were, they respected Peters for his loyalty to his captain and his constant talk of his desire to make up in his old age for the excesses of his youth. Even Sims had refrained from mocking him when he spoke of this, and there were moments when I thought that Sims himself had a conscience; that somewhere deep inside that gleaming mound of hypocrisy there was still something of worth, something perhaps of the innocence of his childhood. He read the funeral service without his usual jibing, and when the body was dropped into the ocean, he stared at the spot where it went down as if reflecting that it would not be long before he himself went to meet his Maker. Yet it was only a few moments later that he was passing around a pannikin of rum and taunting those who refused to drink from it.

Peters's personal effects, kept in an ancient sea chest, which he had repaired carefully many times, were divided among the crew. There were pitifully few of them — some clothing, a clasp knife on whose bone handle he had inscribed the words "Serve God," a much used Book of Common Prayer, and an equally used Bible. These latter I asked for and was given without question. On the flyleaf of the Bible was the entry: "December 5, 1688. Mary died this day." I assumed that Mary was the wife whom he had deserted, and this date marked the beginning of his conversion.

Other than this, there were no incidents to the voyage, and at the beginning of the tenth week of our passage, we made, following a night of heavy rains and squalls, the African coast. A mountain loomed ahead, next morning, sighted momentarily between heavy downpours of rain, and by evening we were upon the coastline. So good was the navigation of Martin Coverly that we came in within a few miles of the Volta River, and anchored that afternoon at its mouth. The shoreline was low-lying, and covered with vegetation of a poisonous green, and a rank smell of mud and rot settled on the ship. From that moment I developed a fear of the place which never left me.

13

We started out the next afternoon up the Volta
River — two boatloads of us equipped with
powder, shot, muskets, cutlasses, ship's bread, beans,
that dried fish to which my uncle was so devoted, a
little of what was left of the turtle meat, and two
kegs of rum and one of Madeira wine, so sour that
it could hardly be drunk, though it was drunk anyway. Martin Coverly took the first boat and I went
with him; though Salvation Sims wanted me in the
second boat, of which he was in command.

"Leave that precious boy with us," said Sims.
"He'll be a needed influence upon the hands. There's
a full load of sense in that boy's head that's ballast
we could do with."

"He'll come with me," said Coverly shortly. "And
as for sense, just bear ever before you, like a steering
compass, that we're off to get the gold of Solomon's
Mines. That, I fancy, will keep your hands orderly
enough."

"A cloud by day and a pillar of fire by night, it will be for us," said Sims.

The *Swan* was left in the charge of Sam Lord with twenty hands, while twenty went up river in the boats, including Coverly and me. The steadier men remained with Lord, men who could be relied upon, to a degree, not to take the ship and leave us marooned on the African coast. There were, however, several of Roberts's hands among them — the sort of men who would prefer to chance a short cruise than swing on an anchor waiting for the return of the boats. Still, Coverly believed that Sam Lord, whom they all respected, would be able to keep them under control, though not without difficulty.

We were a wild-looking lot as we set up that oily river, which debouched a yellow plume of mud into the clear waters of the bay. Some wore slouched felt hats to guard their faces and necks from the sun. Others relied on colored scarves tied about their heads, turban-fashion. Some wore tattered frock coats, and others loose shirts and jerseys, and one had dressed himself in all the finery he could find — a hat with an ostrich plume, a velvet coat of blue, and soiled red breeches, saying in jest that he wished to cut a good figure should they run upon King Solomon himself. This man's name was Clem Peachurst, but he was called Peachy, and he had all the eccentricity of a hover fly — constantly darting here and there, chatting volubly on every subject. He was overdaring in action, but remarkably good at cutlass play.

Salvation Sims was dressed as always in black, his long white hair hanging loose about his shoulders. From a distance he looked like an elderly, respectable churchman. It was only from close at hand that the slyness and evil in his face could be seen. Before the boats set off, he pronounced a mocking blessing on them, calling on the Almighty to pour forth his riches on all aboard and give them now that golden reward which all hands had sought throughout their lives.

The river flowed but sluggishly into the bay, meandering through low palmetto- and scrub-covered sandhills for several miles. The banks on either hand were thick with reeds, growing out of a matting of water lilies so dense that the boats could not get through it.

It was necessary, then, to stay in midstream, and we rowed all day, sweating up the muddy river, mile upon mile, until the sight of the ocean was utterly lost, and the river, like a great serpent, had swallowed us. It was with a feeling of deep foreboding that I took my last glimpse of the sea and the *Swan*. I had the feeling of being doomed — of starting on a venture which must end in disaster for all. Coverly himself seemed grave, as if sharing these feelings, but determined to go ahead with some fatal part he had to play.

The boats' crews, however, were merry as school-boys, shouting to each other from boat to boat, and singing. They thought themselves already in possession of the riches they sought, and worked willingly. I was glad, pulling at the forward oar, of the calluses on my hands, for they would have been skinned and raw in a short while without them. Each boat pulled four oars, and having ten men aboard, it was possible to relieve the oarsmen every hour. That was the routine Martin Coverly set up, but on Sims's boat no routine was established. On the third day upriver, when the merriment had worn off, there was a lot of growling and quarreling over the work. And in mid-afternoon all refused to work the oars, and Sims's boat fell far behind. When eventually it came up to us, Coverly gave them a tongue-lashing and bade Sims come into his boat, ordering me to take his place. The boat was then put in charge of Jedediah Truxton, who had more command over the men, and there was no further trouble aboard.

White Lion Rock was the first mark to be reached, according to Martin Coverly's chart. We were ten weary days getting there. Before reaching it, we rounded a broad bend of the river, and the current was so swift in midstream that we had to pull over to the bank to make any progress.

The banks were high at this point, of yellow clay, with a tangle of black roots like serpents writhing down their sides.

Above grew tall trees, with dark green leaves and small purple flowers. Several of these had fallen into the river, and we threaded our way among the trunks through these, sometimes rowing, sometimes poling ourselves. Then we reached the bend and rowed around it inshore through a tangled matting of water lilies. When we were through, there, in midstream, was a small island and on it a rock as big as a man-of-war.

Carved on the side was the figure of a lion, curiously stiff in its shape, but crouched to spring. Although vines and shrubs of every kind covered the whole face of the rock, the figure of the lion had been cleared of these, and the white pigmentation renewed. Coverly steered his boat into the shallows by the island, and said, "The Lion of Judah. The guardian of Solomon's Mines."

Salvation Sims, old as he was, had keen eyesight,

and examining the top of the rock pointed with a cry to someone standing almost hidden in the shade of a tree which was rooted on the summit.

"There's Solomon himself," he said. "Peachy, go pay him a visit." Scarcely visible in the shadow of the tree was a giant warrior, clad in flowing yellow robes and armed with a lozenge-shaped shield.

All that was visible of his features was his hair — a round bush of it dyed a bright orange. Redbird whipped up a musket and fired, the explosion ringing loud above the brooding silence of the river.

"Damn you," cried Coverly. "Put that down. With one shot you can raise the whole country against us." Redbird only grinned at him, and when the smoke of the discharge had cleared away, the figure remained there, unmoved, still staring at us.

"Naught but a figurehead," said Peachy with contempt. "A statue to frighten boys with." At that, half a dozen of the hands tumbled out of the boats, myself among them, and started up the rock toward the strange figure. The rock was backed by a hill, and through the tangle of grasses and vines there was a path leading to the summit.

I could see that the path had been recently used, for in the soft mud were the prints of naked human feet. The pirates took no notice of these, but plunged on, and at last all reached the tree under which the warrior was standing.

It was indeed an effigy, a figure composed of woven reeds, clothed in flowing yellow robes, and twelve feet high at the least. But there was something else there, too.

All around the figure was a pile of human bones: skulls, ribcages, spines, leg and arm bones, heaped together in confusion. To some there still clung tat-

tered rags of clothing. They must have been the re-
mains of a hundred men there, and the sight of this
mound of death struck me with fear. Here, then,
were the guardian and skeletons mentioned in the
key to Coverly's chart, proving its authenticity.

The others were taken aback, too, but only for a
moment. Redbird was the first to break the spell.
"Looks like Tew were here," he said. "That was
always his visiting card — a pile of bones put where
they was sure to be found."

"This ain't Tew's work," said Big Jack Winthrop
with a laugh. "There was always rum bottles left
around like on the beach at Campeachy. Threescore
he piled up there — some of them women."

"This weren't done all at one time," said another.
"Some of them's old. Some kind of sacrifice, I
reckon, to that thing." And he pointed to the effigy
of the warrior. He kicked one of the skulls aside, and
added, "Tew were a hard case, but it were done in
slaughter. This here killing's for religion — that I
can't stomach."

"Well, no profit to be made here," said Redbird.
"Back to the boats, I say." And turning, he led the
way down the hill. I took one last look at that pile of
bones with the huge effigy standing over them, shuddered, and followed.

Coverly and the rest of the hands received the
news without a tremor, and pushing off from the
island, we rowed perhaps half a mile up the river and
then found that tributary of the Volta, marked on
the map, which we must follow.

Here the scenery changed dramatically. The scrub-
lands strewn with thorny palmettos through which
we had been traveling gave way to forest trees, thin
at first, but by the end of the day so thick that we

94

traveled even before sundown in a heavy clammy gloom. The trees became huge, and in the forks of the branches whole gardens of orchids and other flowers grew.

Vines and mosses covered the branches, life feeding upon life, and it seemed to me that this was an unhealthy growth. This tributary flowed more rapidly than the Volta, and the water, though dark, was clear.

Overhead, we could hear the devilish scream of flocks of parrots, and at one place, passing under the outstretched branch of a massive tree, we saw, twined about it, the glistening mottled body of a huge serpent. My flesh crawled as we rowed rapidly beneath it. Redbird flung a knife at the reptile, and laughed his soundless laugh as it writhed around the wound he made where the knife plunged into the thick, gleaming body.

A little farther on, we came to a place where there were no trees near the banks and the sunlight struck down strong on the water. It was infinitely comforting to feel the clear warmth of the sun, and this would have been a good place to stop. But Coverly insisted we go on, and once again we entered that forbidding tunnel of trees, with around us the moist damp smell of rotting vegetation.

The banks on either side rose higher and higher, until we were in a veritable gorge — the same gorge mentioned in the key to the map. There we anchored for the first night on the tributary, and all the next day we rowed through this fearsome place in a kind of cold dusk, with steep cliffs towering on either side, and above them trees, small as toys, and far, far away, glimpsed only now and then, a little jewel of blue sky.

We were two days in the gorge, during which time hardly anybody spoke, so depressing was the darkness. In the evenings, when we settled down for the night to sleep in the boats, each man was given a pannikin of rum, which did a little to raise their spirits.

We were low on food, for the hands ate their fill, without any attempt at rationing, and though we tried to fish in the river, we caught nothing. During the latter half of the last day's travel in the gorge, we began to hear a thundering sound from far ahead — first like a muffled drumroll and then, as we went farther and farther upriver, with the current now much swifter, a continuous, though still distant, roar.

"The waterfall," said Martin Coverly. "We will be there tomorrow, with the Mines of Solomon but a day or so away."

This cheered everybody up, and the laughing and shouting started again. On the following day, about the middle of the morning, we were suddenly out of the gorge to find ourselves in a vast lake with, at the farther end — two miles away, I would judge — a waterfall cascading from a height of a hundred feet.

We camped in good humor on the borders of the lake that night, with the rumble of the falls in our ears. But I could detect above the noise another sound — a persistent drumming — and twice I saw the flickering of torches on the far side of the lake. At first I thought them fireflies, but then I realized that, at that distance, fireflies would not be visible.

I pointed them out to Coverly. He looked across the lake steadily for a long time and then instructed the men to look to the priming of their muskets.

14

Our shortage of food, a great deal of which had been wasted, now made it necessary to send out a hunting party in search of game.

The best shots in the two boats were Munro Mcdougal and Jeremiah Todson, who had been mate of the brig *Experiment*, Phineas O'Brien, an Irishman from Boston, and Edward Hyde, a small birdlike man who had lived some years among gypsies and, when drunk, sometimes talked in their language.

Hyde was riddled with superstition, a great reader of signs and palms and cards. When it was decided that he would be one of the hunting party, he took out a deck of playing cards, greasy with use, shuffled them, and put the top six in a circle, face up.

The hands were just as superstitious as he, and peered at the cards. Hyde studied them, very grave, picked them up, shuffled the pack once more, and did the same thing. He went through this performance three times and then announced that he would not go.

"There's death in those cards," he said. "I won't leave the boats."

Coverly cocked a pistol and aimed it at his head. "Perhaps you are not reading the cards right, Mr. Hyde," he said. "There's death in them, to be sure, but the death is right here unless you pick up your musket and go hunting with the others."

"No," said Hyde. "There's the jack of spades and that's death, and there's the three of hearts and that's trees. Those have turned up three times, so the death is in the forest."

Redbird was reckoned the next best shot, but Redbird shook his head when Coverly glanced at him.

"I'll go," I said. "I'm not afraid of playing cards and I'd be glad of a chance to stretch my legs after days in the boat."

Coverly uncocked his pistol and nodded his agreement.

We took muskets, powder, shot, and cutlasses — the latter to cut our way through the undergrowth — and set off through the gloom of the forest. The air was cool to the point of being cold, and we followed, for half an hour or so, a game trail through tremendous columns of trees wreathed with thick vines. Eventually, climbing all the while, we came to a ridge and here Mcdougal called a halt.

"We'll get nothing for our trouble but a long walk unless we divide up — each man going his own way," he said. "Let one stay here, hidden, and watch the game trail. Let the rest of us go off through the trees and see what we come upon."

I said it would be dangerous to split up in hostile country and I reminded them of the torches and drumming the night before. Todson said he didn't like what Hyde had said after consulting the cards, and Mcdougal exclaimed in a rage, "Be damned to Hyde and his cards! The man hasn't the heart of a sick chicken. Are you going to let your life be run by Hyde and his gypsy mumbo-jumbo? Stay if you like, but I'm off. I could do with a barbecued deer for my supper."

After some more discussion, it was decided that we would split up, but not go very far. I was elected to stay behind and watch the game trail. There was a clump of giant ferns growing at the base of a gigantic tree, and when they had gone I hid myself there, able to peer through the fronds and stalks. With a sinking heart I saw the others disappear into the gloom of the forest, leaving me alone — but with the sense all the time of being watched.

For a while there was nothing to be seen or heard — nothing, that is, but the distant rustle of the wind in the treetops overhead, and a curious patter, like raindrops, which I found to be the noise of small twigs, leaves, and pieces of bark falling to the ground.

Then I heard a slight rustle from over the ridge, and my skin crawling, I picked up my musket and cocked the hammer.

The rustling grew louder, stopped several times, and then over the ridge appeared a little deer, not much bigger than a large hound. I had my musket at my shoulder. The deer looked about and then turned its head toward the clump of ferns in which I was hidden. In that moment I fired, the report of the musket shattering the forest silence. The deer tumbled to the ground, and with a shout of triumph I broke out of the ferns and ran toward it.

But I had hardly reached the deer before, somewhere to my left, I heard the report of another musket, followed by a shout and then a scream. The scream was one of pure terror, and then silence settled over the gloomy forest. The silence did not last long. There was another shout, this time almost directly in front of me, but some distance off. Then I heard footsteps running, bodies crashing through the underbrush, and again a scream, and again silence.

Ignoring the deer, I rushed up the ridge and down the other side in the direction of the last scream. Beyond was a rocky slope, and I had scrambled halfway up this when Mcdougal came pelting down it.

"Back to the boats!" he shouted. "Run for your life."

"What happened?" I cried.

"Run for your life," was all he would say, and so I turned and ran behind him. We pelted down the game path, Mcdougal turning every now and then to stare fearfully over his back, and at last we burst out of the forest and reached the boats at the bank of the river.

"Push off," cried Mcdougal.

The hands were lolling about the bank, but tumbled into the boats and we launched into the lake.

We were not an instant too soon, for down the game trail came a score or more of warriors armed with shields, spears, and bows and arrows. In a moment a cloud of arrows and spears was hurled at us, but no one was hit. We pulled hard to the center of the lake and then gave them a volley from our muskets. The shots, from the rocking boats surging through the water, went wild, and a dozen of the warriors plunged boldly into the lake and swam after us. They were prodigious swimmers.

Three reached the boats, and one, brave as a lion, had almost climbed over the gunwale when he was clubbed. Thereupon the others swam back to the shore. They consulted among themselves and then dragged forward the bodies of O'Brien and Todson.

Todson was dead, but O'Brien was still alive. He raised his head to look at us, and his face was a mask of blood. Then he was thrown on the ground and clubbed.

"Pull for that little island there," cried Coverly, unmoved by this sight. "We'll be safer there for a while."

We reached the island minutes later. It was nothing more than a rock with a bank of sandy gravel, covered with shrubs, and of the extent of an acre around it. Two crocodiles lumbered off into the lake as the boats approached, and Coverly remarked that that was a good sign, for it meant that no one was hidden in the thick shrubs.

Then a council of war was held, and some of the hands were for going back down the river to the *Swan*, though Martin Coverly repeated that we were but two days from the fabulous mines.

"Two days off the mines may be," said Redbird. "There's eighteen left of us, and a thousand of those savages primed for slaughter. We'd never get to the mines. And if we did, we'd never get back."

"It's madness to think of going on," said another. "Back to the *Swan*, say I, and let's vote on it now."

Coverly calmly lit a pipe of tobacco and, with his

back to the rock, blew a thin stream of smoke into the air.

"Vote if you wish," he said. "But to vote without any consideration is play for children. There's eighteen heads here, and not one of them being used but mine. Have you thought, any of you, why those two hands were killed and why the warriors attacked us?"

Peter Ramilly, a quarrelsome man, one of the hands who had lost an eye in the taking of the *Experiment*, blurted out angrily, "Why, by thunder. Because they're savages, and that's all the reason that's needed."

"Savages?" said Coverly. "Faith, I think they would give the same name to us — with the exception perhaps of Master Sims here. But they had a reason for attacking us, and it wasn't savagery. Did you notice aught of the man that got to the boat and was clubbed?"

"He was a painted savage," said Truxton. "With his back all covered with scars."

"Yes, and scars — deep scars on his wrists, too. Do you know what those scars signify, mates? They signify that he was a slave. The scars on his wrists were made by manacles and the scars on his back by the whip. They took us for slavers, coming up the river for black ivory. That's why they attacked."

That took them all aback, and I was as surprised as the rest.

"Well, then," said Sims, breaking the silence sarcastically, "it seems we are in need of a missionary — a man of peace and of good will — who will be able to explain that we are like them, God's poor children, cast upon the stormy seas of life, buffeted on every side, and striving toward salvation and the golden shore. Two boatloads of the golden shore," he added, "and we'll be away mild as lambs. Give me a drop more of the rum there, Redbird."

"And who'll play missionary?" asked Redbird.

"Why," said Coverly, "I think that would be a proper role for Sims here."

They burst out laughing at that, and someone remarked that the idea had merit, for it was but plain sense to send the devil as missionary among devils.

But when they were quiet again, Coverly said calmly that he would go alone on the errand. Sims, quick to see implications not immediately obvious to others, said slyly, "How long are we to wait here, captain, for you to come back before returning downriver to the *Swan* to see what pickings we can make, the mines being barred and you dead?"

"Three days," said Coverly.

I opposed Coverly's going at all, calling the plan plain madness. "You will be killed from ambush before you can say one word," I said. "You but throw your life away, crazed by the thought of the gold in King Solomon's Mines. Indeed, you have not been in your senses for some time past."

Coverly laughed at me. "Let each man hazard his life as he wishes," he said. "Come, Nicholas, you have more blood in you than that. What, turn my back on a king's treasure for fear of losing my life? That was never my way."

"How are you to speak to these people?" I demanded. "How can you talk to them except with gestures — easily mistook."

"In Arabic," he replied. "If they know slavers, they know Arabs. And English, too. The English have shipped many a cargo of black ivory from this coast."

But the plan still seemed harebrained to me. There was a great deal more talk, but in the end all agreed, myself alone opposing, that Coverly should try to make our peace with the fierce warriors who lived about the lake.

"All right," I said at last. "But instead of striding boldly ashore, Martin Coverly, let us first make them an offering of good will. Let us take some of the rum and some bright clothing and leave them ashore as a gift. If what we offer is taken, then try to talk with them. I will go with you."

"Before God, why?" demanded Coverly.

"Before God, I do not know," I replied. And, indeed, I didn't.

15

The gifts, a small keg of rum and some bright scarves and shirts, were rowed ashore that night and remained untouched all through the following day. But on the morning of the second day they were gone, and Coverly thereupon decided to go over to the shore and into the forest to find the tribesmen. I went with him, and at the last moment Salvation Sims decided he would go, too.

"I'll stand by the captain, mates," he said. "Live and die by him. And maybe I can put in the right word at the proper time." But I think the wily old rascal had decided to come because he did not trust us. His mind was incapable of dwelling on anything but deceit.

We were soon ashore and walking up that same game trail through the cool dusk of the forest we had taken before.

I had again the sense of being watched, and so did

Sims, for he kept glancing nervously about and made sure not to fall a pace behind us. But Coverly was as cool as if he were on a botanizing expedition, and stopped to examine clumps of ferns and a growth of a jade-green plant with stalks as high as a man and spear-shaped leaves of huge size.

"They have a root, Nicholas, that can be eaten," he said. "We would not starve in this forest, even lacking game."

"This is no time for examining plants," I snapped, for I was as nervous as a cat.

"We're watched, Nicholas," replied Coverly. "We're watched. I hear footsteps about us. To show concern would be dangerous — and unbecoming," he added. "In the face of fear, it is the part of a gentleman to remain calm."

"On which side do you hear the footsteps?" asked Sims.

"All about," replied Coverly, peering into a growth of ferns, from which, in triumph, he picked up a red beetle the size of my thumb.

We passed the place where I had shot the deer, climbed the stony ridge beyond, and entered a deep valley through the forest, at the bottom of which there flowed a small stream, brown as rust.

There was a well-worn path beside the stream, and after following it for close to an hour, up a gentle hill, we came to an opening of the valley on a small plateau. Here the river had expanded into a small lake, and on the far side was a village built on stilts. The roofs were thatched with palm leaves, and the walls were of mud and wattles. This was plainly the village mentioned in the key to Coverly's map.

It was only then that those who had been following us emerged silently from the bush — fifteen or so savages, tall, splendidly muscled, armed with bows and arrows, and painted, and naked except for a loincloth.

They said not a word, but fell in behind us and herded us, like sheep, toward the village. There was a walkway of planks, rough-hewn, from the shore to the lake village, and over this we went, to find ourselves, after passing a few of the huts, in a central place where by a pole, hung with skulls like a coconut tree with nuts, sat a wizened, small, emaciated man, utterly naked, who looked to be two hundred years old. He squatted under the shade of an umbrella made of a brown transparent material.

"Skin," whispered Coverly. "Human skin."

"Why do you invade the forest of the Sesi?" said this man, in excellent English. "Why do you come with guns into the home of my people?"

"We were without food. We were hunting game," said Coverly.

The witch doctor, for such he was, looked steadily at us, as if he were Time itself examining our innermost thoughts.

"Game is not what you were looking for," he said. "You were seeking the white man's food — slaves. You eat the slaves. That we know."

"No," said Coverly. "We are not slavers. We are looking for gold — for the Mines of Solomon, hardly a day's journey from here."

"The mines are forbidden," said the witch doctor. "They are closed and can only be entered by one whom I, Ntelka, will know. I guard the mines."

"How will you know him?" I asked.

"He will be of this time and of another time,"

replied Ntelka. "He will not have come here for gold but for some other thing — the freeing of one man into Life, and another into Death."

He looked at Sims. "You are dead," he said. "A corpse that walks." At this, Sims, unperturbed, only smiled.

He looked at Coverly, who returned his look boldly. "You are between life and death," he said.

"So is every man in the world," said Coverly.

He looked at me and said, "You come from far away in Time. Do you know that?"

"No," I replied.

"That is because you will not let yourself know it. You have made Time your master, but man is the master of Time, and Time his servant."

Some faint memory of a similar remark stirred in me. For a moment I caught a glimpse of myself in Martin Coverly's cabin, when we had been hunting turtle on the Florida Keys and he had given me a glass of wine in his cabin. Then it was gone. I glanced at Coverly, and he had that half-mocking smile on his face I knew so well.

"What is your name?" asked Ntelka.

"Nicholas."

"What is your other name?"

"Ormsby," I said, and I do not know where the word came from. But I had a glimpse of a cutter gaff-rigged, and myself coming out of the cabin to find no one at the tiller. My head swirled and I felt as if I was going to faint, but always before my eyes was the wizened, almost fleshless face of Ntelka.

When my head cleared, I found Sims looking at me queerly with his glittering old eyes. He turned to Ntelka and said, "The boy's a little queer in his head. A touch of the sun, I would say, and I've seen it happen before. But he has an honest heart, and speaketh the truth more than most, according to the commandments of the Good Book. But his name's Coverly and this here's his uncle and that's the plain fact. And he comes for gold as have we all, myself not least among them, for gold is food and drink to me and all us honest hands. And since you have no need for it yourself, I would ask you kindly to let us go to the mines, and not a hair touched on either side.

"As for the two that were killed — that's an old score and forgotten at this moment."

"Quiet," said Coverly. "There's more here than you know of, you fool."

Ntelka, taking no notice of any of this, rose and beckoned me to follow him into a large hut which stood solitary from the others.

During the whole of this interview there was not a soul around, for even the warriors who had herded us into the village had gone. When I got inside, I found the place to be a kind of temple or spirit house. There were grotesque masks hung from the walls and from the central pole which supported the roof. The floor was covered with a woven mat of rushes, swept very clean, and there was a heavy smell of flowers in the air, pleasant, but after a while overpowering.

I had no fear or anxiety in this place, but only a sense of peace, and the wizened Ntelka seemed friendly. He seated himself on a stool carved of ebony and told me to sit before him.

"You are in the House of Dreams," he said. "Look about you." I did so and found that the grotesque masks which covered the walls were constantly changing. They dissolved into beautiful birds with exotic plumage, into trees covered with flowers, and flowed together to produce scenes — one of a large wooden house of three stories, in which I found myself, in a room, waiting while footsteps mounted the stairs outside, another of a gallows with several bodies dangling from it, their faces turned from me. I looked at them carefully and was paralyzed with fear when I saw the last one. For the last body dangling from the gallows was me. There was a crowd of people about, and in the crowd I could distinguish one face — that of Martin Coverly.

Then these visions or nightmares were gone, and sitting on the stool before me was Ntelka.

"What did you see?" he asked.

I told him all that I had seen, and he said, "You, then, are the one for whom I have been waiting. The way to the mines is opened to you, for you are of this time and another time, and it is not gold that you seek but something of far greater value. But it will not be you that finds the key, but the living corpse that is with you."

"I don't want to go to the mines," I said. "I would sooner not be here. I am here because of my uncle, and against my will. I want only my freedom."

"That you must earn," said Ntelka, and beckoned me out of the hut.

The other two, who had remained outside, were now surrounded by the tribesmen, whom Coverly looked at with curiosity. Sims, with a glitter of fear in his eyes, was exhorting them to be merciful to their brethren who had come many thousands of miles across the sea to visit them with loving hearts.

Many of the warriors were grinning at him and fingering the points of their spears.

The crowd parted when Ntelka appeared, and he said something to them softly in their own language. They listened in silence and at the end gave a great shout, which I suppose signified their assent.

Then Ntelka said to Coverly, "You are free to go your way. No one will harm you. Yet I would advise you. Whatever treasure you find will not replace the value of that boy there." And he pointed to me.

"Remember that," he said. "And remember it at another time, or you will never know rest. You must weigh treasure against treasure — that is the task that lies before you."

So we went back to the boats and were cheered to the echo by the other hands when told that the way to King Solomon's Mines lay open to us. But Coverly took me aside and asked me what had transpired when I was in the House of Dreams with Ntelka.

"I saw myself hanging on a gallows and you in the crowd watching me," I said.

He was struck silent for a moment, his face pale, and then said seriously, "Ah, Nicholas, we indeed have unfinished business to attend to together."

Again I had a vivid recollection of having heard those words before, and cried out, "Martin Coverly, I do not know who you are — whether real or a dream from which I must awaken. I do not know whether I am in my right senses or under some spell cast by that witch doctor."

To that he made no reply.

16

Now the way was open to the Mines of Solomon, and we reached them on the second day of our journey. The tribesmen gave us some food in return for what gifts of clothing we could spare, and they particularly welcomed three cutlasses, for which they gave us enough of their flour and a kind of bean to last us several days.

We took with us shovels and pickaxes and coils of rope, and two sea chests in which to bring back the gold — one of them the plain but sturdy chest of old Peters, who had died on the voyage over.

Coverly was now seized with gold fever. He became sharp-tongued and quick-tempered, always pressing on, and once, when I hung back, exhausted from the load I was carrying up a steep slope, he snarled that if I did not keep up with the hands he would leave me there to rot.

The same fever for gold had seized the others. They could think of nothing else. Even Sims found enough strength in his ancient body to break into a trot now and then. So, stumbling, sweating, cursing, taking no time to rest except for a few brief hours at night, we pushed on toward the mines, and entering at last a stony valley between two steep-sided mountains, saw at the far end a white cliff face with, in it, a great dark entrance. All gave a shout and dashed toward the portal.

Redbird was the first to go through. He dropped everything that he was carrying and, outstripping the others, flung through the dark doorway. We, hurrying behind him, heard his footsteps echoing against the rocky walls and then were brought to a standstill by a scream, which grew less and less and then stopped abruptly.

We stared at each other in terror, and Jedediah Truxton was the first to break the silence. "He's dead," he said. "Redbird were always a fool."

"No sense hanging back," said another. "Come on, mates."

But now we were made cautious by whatever had befallen Redbird, and we made torches of twisted brush and sticks, and lit them with sparks from the flintlocks, with a pinch of gunpowder to give a quick blaze. Then we went in, cautiously, Coverly leading, through a high dark tunnel, and came almost immediately to a vast pit, clear across the floor. It was into that pit that Redbird had plunged.

"A hundred fathoms of line wouldn't reach the bottom," said Sims, peering down. " 'Tis a strange fancy. The gold is lying in the pit of hell."

"There's a narrow pathway over this side past the pit," I said. "The pit is but a trap."

The pathway was no wider than a plank, with the black hole yawning below. Along this pathway we

113

inched our way, at times forced to crawl, for the rocks bulged outward, giving no room to stand. When we were past that hazard, we went on, the floor of the tunnel ever descending, and the ruddy light of our torches so uncertain that we hardly dared put one foot before the other. Three times we came to rockfalls that almost blocked the tunnel, and at last reached a rock face on which was carved the figure of that same white lion we had seen on the island in the river. Here we stopped, uncertain, for several galleries led off in different directions.

"The lion faces this tunnel," said Coverly, pointing. "That's plainly the one to follow."

In the flicker of the torches, the lion seemed to be moving. The others went off, but I stayed, examining the figure. Something was wrong with it, some interruption of the lines that puzzled me.

I glanced nervously down the shaft into which the others had gone. Their torches made a ball of light reflected off the walls and ceiling of the tunnel. Against the light I could see their figures in silhouette, a head here and an arm upheld there, and now and again the gleam of a cutlass.

On they went, leaving me alone, for Coverly had the gold on his mind, and now had no care for me. They turned a corner and left me solitary, with the darkness settling about me, gazing at the figure of the lion.

I wanted to be gone, too, but something held me there.

The figure was of no great size — much smaller than the one we had seen on the island. I examined it in detail by the light of my torch and then discovered that there was not one lion carved there but two. The second, not outlined in white, so that it could

114

scarcely be distinguished, was in a sitting position, eyeing me.

While I stared at this, I heard a thunderous rumble rolling up the tunnel down which Coverly had gone. There followed shouts and screams and curses, and first one man and then another came tumbling out of the shaft, all covered with rock dust, several limping.

"What happened?" I cried.

"Ramilly and Hyde pushed ahead and leaped upon a stair cut across the tunnel, and the ceiling came down upon them," cried McDougal. " 'Twas a trap, a damned infernal trap, and it hath killed them both."

Coverly was the last back, panting heavily. "No hope for them," he said. "All I could find was Hyde's boot." Then he added lightly, "He'd have done well to have told his fortune in the cards this morning. He might have hung back with you, Nicholas. He could have kept you company in the dark while others ventured their lives."

"Let each man hazard his life as he wishes, Martin Coverly," I said, angered, quoting his own words. "If fools want to follow fools, while wiser men hold back, then that's their affair. There's five hands lost now that can be laid to your account. There's Redbird that you let run into a pit without a shout of warning. There's Todson and O'Brien, butchered by savages. And now there's Ramilly and Hyde, plunging down a tunnel that you, like the fool you have become, thought the guardians of King Solomon's Mines would leave to point the way to the king's treasure. Five hands gone, and not a pinch of gold to show for it."

"Would you cross me, Nicholas?" said Coverly in a whisper, getting slowly to his feet.

"Yes, I'd cross you," I cried, my wrath rising. "And I should have crossed you before. Would you like to kill me also and make it six dead, Captain Coverly, and still not a pinch of gold found? I could count it six now, for there's poor old Peters, faithful as a hound, who died on the voyage out here."

He quietened at that, all the anger gone from him. "I'll not forget Peters to the day I die," he said.

"You forgot him the moment his body was dropped into the ocean," I replied bitterly.

"There's no gain to standing here quarreling," interrupted Mcdougal. "Try another tunnel, say I, and go more canny."

"Spread out," said Truxton. "Ten paces apart. If there's more deadfalls like that last, but one man would be killed, not two."

"Take what tunnels you wish," I said, still angry. "The entrance is not down those tunnels. You'll find nothing but death in them. Those rockfalls we already passed were traps. Why do you think the gold has been untouched all these years? Because it's been sought by fools; by mice that rush into a trap at a sniff of cheese and do not stop to think of what is before their eyes."

"And pray, brother mouse," lisped Salvation Sims, "what should we see before our eyes?"

"The lion there," I replied. "There's none of you looked at it — you least of all, Martin Coverly. You gave it a glance and plunged on."

"What of the lion?" asked Coverly.

"Look at it," I said. "Read what it tells you."

At this they all fell to crowding about the lion,

jostling each other to get closer, until Coverly told them to stand back and hold their torches steady so he could study the figure. At last he turned to me angrily. "I see nothing but a white lion," he said.

"Because a white lion is what you are looking for," I said. "Look for another figure — another lion."

It was some time before he made it out, and even then he did not know its meaning.

"You who know so much about Nature and natural things," I said. "Answer me this question. Do lions point the way to places — this way or that way? Is that their natural function?"

"No," he replied.

"If you saw a lion sitting and staring at you, what would you say of it? That it was taking it easy?"

"No," replied Coverly. "I would say that it was preparing to attack."

"Crouched, it would be preparing to attack," I said. "But sitting facing you — its back to something?"

"By thunder!" cried Coverly. "It would be a sentinel, on guard."

"Yes," said I. "A sentinel guarding something. And that lion, far less distinct than the other, is, unless I miss my guess, guarding not the entrance to the Mines of Solomon, for the shafts lie all about it, but the door of the treasure house in which the gold was stored. Plainly, it wasn't ore that was shipped back to Solomon's court, but gold kept in some secret storage place. Behind the lion."

That took them all by surprise, but the problem was how to get past the lion — through the rock, behind which the treasure must lie.

It seemed plain that there must be some secret spot which should be pushed or pulled on the lion to move it aside. Closely examined by torchlight, it could be seen that the outline went deep into the rock, and so the figure might be a doorway. But though they pushed at the eyes and the ears and the paws and indeed against the whole figure, the lion remained immovable.

Big Jack Winthrop wanted to try blasting with gunpowder; and some of the others started to dig down with picks and shovel, but after making a hole only a foot or so in depth, found themselves up against solid rock.

Salvation Sims alone remained aside, deep in thought, and Winthrop turned on him angrily and demanded that he bear a hand.

"Bear a hand, is it?" asked Sims. "You've enough hands there to dig your way through Africa, but it isn't a hand that is needed, but a little learning. Solomon's men were great builders and they built a temple, and if I remember right, there were twelve lions, and maybe more, guarding the door. Yes, my dear brothers, that sweet lad Nicholas is right when he says that a lion guards the door."

"We know that," said Truxton. "If you've aught more to say, then speak plain."

"The key to the door lies in the Good Book," said Sims. "A dram of rum and I think I could find it for you."

He was given the rum, which he rolled around in his withered cheeks and drank with great pleasure.

"Out of the mouths of lions comes forth sweetness," he said at last.

"Meaning what?" asked Mcdougal.

"Judges, chapter 14, verse 5," said Sims. "There you'll find the story of Samson, who met a lion that came roaring and raging at him. He seized the lion by the jaws and tore the jaws open and so killed it. Maybe three or four days later, and maybe more — the Bible don't specify — he passed the place where the lion lay dead, and he found a swarm of bees had made a hive in the lion's mouth. There was a comb full of honey in that lion's mouth. Golden honey, shipmates. Golden. Prize open the lion's mouth and there we'll find the treasure."

"Well, if that don't beat all," said Truxton. "But which lion? There's two here."

"The white lion," said Coverly. "That's the one shown roaring."

The open jaws were carved deeper in the rock than the rest of the figure. Coverly thrust the butt end of a musket into the cavity and heaved on the barrel to force the jaws wide apart.

"Bear a hand here," he grunted, and I seized the barrel also, to help him. We heaved until we thought the musket would break at the stock. Then, with a slight rumble, the jaws opened, and the figure of the second seated lion moved upward into the rock face.

The entrance to the treasure house of Solomon lay open before us.

17

A tunnel led from the doorway for a short distance, and beyond, we entered a huge hall carved out of the solid rock but with the roof supported by tremendous pillars of stone. The pillars were like giant, silent guardians of the place, equally spaced and carefully aligned. They were twenty feet high at least, but there were so many of them that those far away seemed not much taller than a man.

This vast hall was lit by natural light, coming, we found, from shafts above. We did not need our torches now. There was enough daylight in the huge chamber for plants to have rooted in the cracks of the vast paving stones that formed the floor.

Creepers spread everywhere, and vines of many kinds climbed up the huge pillars. There was one creeper which grew in profusion and had a sulfur-yellow flower and fleshy leaves which were thick with white hairs. We looked about the hall, half jungle, half architecture, and Coverly cried, "Scatter and search, lads. We will be rich as kings by sundown."

So we fell to slashing through the creepers and vines and bushes with our cutlasses, looking for coffers or chests of stone, or any doorways or removable slabs in the walls behind which the treasure might be concealed. An hour of this revealed three stone chests, each big enough to hold a man. But the tops had been smashed in, and whatever they once contained taken.

"The treasure's gone," said Mcdougal. "There's been others here before us. They dug down through those shafts from above. We're too late by maybe a hundred years."

They all turned angrily on Coverly, cursing him for bringing them on a fool's errand across an ocean and deep into Africa to an empty treasure house.

Coverly took it calmly. "Why," said he, when they had done, "go on back if you will. I'd be pleased to see the last of you, for a whining pack of faint-hearted scum. An hour hacking at bushes and you're in the bilboes. Did you expect to find the gold stacked up like cargo ready for loading? And some of you Roberts's hands. Well, I can see why he was glad to be rid of you."

So they started searching again, but without any method, just slashing away wherever the fancy took them.

The three stone chests had been found against the walls of the hall. After an hour or so more of haphazard searching, four others were found — all of them opened and emptied of their contents — and the anger against Martin Coverly mounted. He, however, after a while turned to examine a clump of

121

those same sulfur-yellow flowers with the fleshy leaves, growing near one of the smashed chests.

"Look close around the base, Nicholas," he said. "You'll find instruction there. What do you see?"

"Nothing but a few insect wings," I replied shortly.

"Insect wings they are, Nicholas," he said. "These plants are great eaters of flies."

"I'll tell the hands you've found your treasure," I snapped. "Six men dead and you have a plant that eats flies."

"A plant that eats flies," he said. "And there is a fate like a plant that eats men, or the souls of men, Nicholas. And that fate may yet be avoided. Do you remember nothing of why you and I are together on this venture?"

"For gold," I said.

"No, Nicholas. Do you remember nothing of an old house and someone who came to you by night, talking of unfinished business?"

"What are you talking of, Martin Coverly?" I demanded.

He looked at me earnestly and said, almost in a whisper, " 'Tis but ten minutes, I think, that a man dances in the air while dangling from a gallows." Recalling that vision I had had of myself upon the gallows, with Coverly watching me from the crowd, in the dream house of Ntelka, so great a fear came on me that I shuddered.

"Do you intend to have me hung, Martin Coverly?" I asked.

"Ten minutes, Nicholas," he said. "Ten minutes. 'Tis nothing. A little gift of love. No more."

At that moment Winthrop, digging with a black, Jack Kott, himself an escaped slave from the island of Barbados, cried out, "Here's a chest unbroken," and Coverly ran to it, leaving me staring after him. The chest was, like all the others, up against the wall. But it was larger than they, and only the top had been cleared away of scrub and earth. More of the earth was dug away, to the depth of about a foot down each side. Coverly pointed to a straight line of hairlike roots growing about two inches below the top.

"There's the lid," he said. "Fitted neat as a whaleboat's planking. Get your cutlasses in there and wedge it open enough to slip the end of a crowbar in."

Half an hour's work was needed to get the lid off, and when it was tumbled aside the chest was found to be full of earth and blocks of stone.

"There's your treasure for you," sneered Truxton.

Coverly reached in, pulled out several of the blocks, and flung them aside. And below lay the gold — huge bricks of it. In that one chest alone there were twenty of them, each weighing about sixty pounds. Since there were but forty men in the crew of the *Swan*, this one find would give each one thirty pounds' weight of solid gold for himself — a fortune, then, for every man.

The finding of that first cache had to be celebrated. What was left of the rum was drunk there and then. Enough dried brush was found to light a roaring fire, and the hands made seats for themselves out of the gold blocks and sat around it, drinking and toasting each other and telling of the great homes they'd build and coaches they'd buy, and the servants they'd have, when they got the gold back to the American main.

Coverly was toasted as if he were Solomon himself, and that great hall, thousands of years old, rang with their songs and tales of ships taken and cruelties of every kind. They looked like demons sitting around that roaring fire, their hair unkempt and their beards and clothing ragged. But at last they fell into a drunken sleep, one by one, leaving only Martin Coverly and me awake. He was sitting on his little throne of gold blocks, staring into the glow of the fire and holding in his hands some of those yellow flowers which ate flies and which he had compared to fate eating the souls of men.

He glanced over at me and then passed his hand around his neck and shuddered.

"You have the gold, but something troubles you, Martin Coverly," I said.

"Aye, Nicholas," he replied. "Something troubles me. Unfinished business. I wish at this moment that I had never turned to this life. Yet it is done, and I see nothing ahead but peril and foul weather."

When at last I fell asleep, he was still toying with the flowers and staring at the fire.

We stayed two days further, searching in that underground treasure house, which I soon came to hate, among the creepers and bushes, but found nothing more. Some of the hands, foremost among them Salvation Sims, were for continuing the search, but we were running out of food. We'd got enough from the tribesmen for several days. But careless of the future, they had thrown away much of it as deadweight in their mad scramble toward the mines.

So we had to go back. It was a lesson in values to see the same men who had thrown their food away as too heavy to carry clinging even when exhausted each to his burden of gold.

We managed to transport the gold blocks in one

trip, though two would have been more sensible. The two sea chests we had brought could carry no more than six of the gold blocks apiece, making a dead-weight of three hundred and sixty pounds or thereabouts. These were strung on poles and placed on the shoulders of two of the hands, which made them easier to manage.

For the rest, each man picked a block of gold, slung it on his back with a rope sling, and staggered along with it. Salvation Sims carried his block of gold in his arms, however, as if it were a child. He staggered along behind the others, his ancient lungs wheezing, his gray, wrinkled face streaming with sweat, his eyes ever on the gold he cradled in his arms. Those of us who were not burdened with the gold carried our weapons and lengths of rope. Now they were in as much of a hurry to reach the boats as they had been to get to the mines, and Coverly, time and again, had to call a halt to bring up the stragglers. We came first to the lake on which the native village stood, and here Coverly, telling the others to wait on the shore, went off, with me accompanying him, to see Ntelka and ask for more food.

But the witch doctor forbade the tribesmen to give us any. "You have what you came for," he said. "Now depart and live off it."

He was offered muskets, clothing — rags to be sure, but still of some value among his people — and even a block of the gold. He wanted none of these things. Of the gold he said that it was cursed among his people. They might get as much of it as they wanted, but so many wars had been fought over it, so many villages destroyed, so many foreigners had come searching for it, that a taboo had been placed upon it.

125

On parting, he looked at me and said, "It is not from lack of food that you will stand in danger, you who are of this time and of another time." Coverly turned strangely pale and once again put his hand to his throat to loosen his clothing.

Truxton and Winthrop were for attacking the village there and then and taking what food we needed. "We've fifteen hands, sound and tried," he said. "Burn them out, say I, and help ourselves."

Mcdougal agreed, and so did the black, Kott, and Sims.

"They've done us no harm," I protested. "Leave them be."

"They're naught but savages," growled Truxton, and the rest agreed and started priming their muskets to make an assault on the village without any plan being formed.

Coverly tried to hold them back, but they could not be dissuaded. The attack failed even before it was launched. Led by Truxton, the men formed into a body to march on the village, when from the bush stepped fifty or more of the natives, armed with spears and bows and arrows. I think Truxton would have charged, but the others held back, glancing nervously at each other. So we picked up the gold and the rest of our belongings, and escorted by these same silent warriors, went on to the other lake, where our boats were beached.

The tribesmen stood on the shore watching us, and remained watching until we had left the lake and entered the tributary which led to the Volta.

We had aboard a fortune for every man — and somewhat less than ten pounds of moldy flour.

18

We reckoned five days to the sea, where the brig awaited us, for we would have the current to help us. But, though the current was swifter than we had reckoned, the journey took a week, for we were beset with troubles all the way. The boats were heavily laden with the gold and not so easily managed with oars and rudder. We got through the terrible gorge without mishap, but when we were on the Volta, Truxton's boat lost its rudder, drove up on a rock, and the planks were stove.

George Fenn, not the best of the hands, was at the tiller at the time, and seeing the boat bearing down on the rocks, pushed it hard over. It was then that the pintles or bearings broke.

The rudder was useless, and the heavily laden boat drove on the rocks with a splintering crash that could be heard above the rush of the water. It was swamped in a moment and then gone, leaving the men struggling in the river. Three were carried away by the swiftness of the stream. The others we picked up, but the gold had gone to the bottom.

The blame was put on Fenn, who was one of

those who lost his life. "He was always a swab," growled Truxton. "He should have seen them rocks half a mile off."

"We must try for the gold," said Sims. " 'Tis lying right there at the bottom of the river. I know the place where I dropped mine. I marked it well before I let go of it."

"You're a bigger fool than Fenn," said Truxton. "Even if you could swim, you couldn't see half a foot in that dirty water."

Yet try they did. They tried probing with oars and they tried with ropes tied around them, groping blindly in the water until they were half drowned. They spent a day trying, and got nothing for their pains. When we left they swore they would come back with grapnels and try again. We had set out with twenty hands and two boats, and now there was but one boat and twelve men left.

Half our little supply of moldy flour was lost, and half the gold was gone. Thereafter we traveled along the banks of the river, close to the beds of water lilies, going downstream not much faster than we had come up. It was no consolation to them that even the amount of gold that remained was enough to make them all wealthy for life. They could think only of what had been lost, and cursed and grumbled all the way.

We were starvation hungry in two days, and our sufferings were made all the worse from the small cuts and bruises we had suffered in getting to the mines and back. These in a moderate climate would have been nothing, but in the tropical heat and damp they festered and attracted swarms of flies. Some of the men's arms were swollen fat as the sausages of Germany. Their hands were puffed and split down

128

the back, and soon there were but three or four who could handle the oars, making it all the more necessary to stay close to the banks in the quieter water of the river.

I think it was on the fourth day that we passed that place where Redbird, now dead, had thrown his knife at the huge serpent coiled along the overhanging limb of a tree. The serpent was still there, still alive, and to my horror, swarming with ants and flies. It had not been able to crawl away, for its spine, I suspect, had been injured.

"They die slowly," said Coverly. "Another week and I think it will still be living." At that I plucked up a musket and shot the wretched creature through the head. The great coils relaxed slowly, and before we had turned the bend of the river, the serpent fell into the water.

That evening, when we had pulled into the bank, not wanting to risk the boat in the dark, I saw the carcass, like a length of cable, awash and rolling down the stream in the twilight. I looked at it in sorrow, for its death had been needless and wanton.

But Sims sidled up to me and lisped that Redbird had met death through harming the serpent, and perhaps shooting it would mean death for me. Another, gnawing on some roots that Coverly had pronounced edible, said there must be two hundred pounds of meat on the creature and he would be glad of a slice of it. Such was the brutality and degradation of these men.

Downstream we went, then, suffering greatly, until at last we came to that part where the Volta River meandered through the low, sandy hills, covered with palmetto and scrub, to its junction with the sea. Twice we were grounded on sandbanks through the weakness of those who could still handle the oars. On these occasions all had to get out so the boat could be floated again, and we had to fire our muskets over the water to prevent the crocodiles from feasting on the hands struggling at the task.

At last, after a voyage as close, I suppose, to Purgatory as one may come upon the earth, we glimpsed the open sea in the middle of the afternoon. A faint cheer went up at the sight of it, but when we rounded the last bend and got finally into the bay, our joy turned to despair.

Not a ship was to be seen.

The empty bay stretched cruel and glittering before us. We had been so certain that it would be there waiting for us that we could not believe our eyes.

The hands cursed and raged at Sam Lord, who had been left in charge. When their first anger and frustration was spent, some suggested that he had gone cruising on his own along the African coast, where there were many rich Arab merchantmen to be taken. He would be back in a while, they argued. Others held that Lord had just taken the *Swan* and left us marooned.

"Lord was a stout man and loyal," said Coverly. "He would not leave, having promised to wait for us. Some misfortune has overtaken him."

"If I gets my hands on him," said Truxton, "I'll have the liver out of him while he's yet alive."

There was nothing to do but beach the boat on the shore, and make camp. We pulled it into a small inlet full of brackish water and overgrown with clumps of mangrove.

These trees, which do not flourish on land, have

roots that reach deep down in the water, and on these Coverly, knowledgeable in such matters, found great quantities of oysters, small but nutritious, which satisfied our need for food for the time. Exploring along a sandy stretch of beach, he uncovered a clutch of turtle's eggs, round and soft-shelled, and added these to our store. The next day he took a musket and went hunting among the sedges at the mouth of the river and brought back two plump heron, and we began to think better of our situation.

Now hopes were raised that Lord had indeed only taken the brig on a short cruise and would be back at any time. But Coverly remained silent during these discussions and seemed as if some deep problem weighed on his mind.

One morning, when we had been three days in that cove, with the desolate sound of the surf constantly in our ears, Coverly announced that he was going hunting again, but further inland, in the hope of finding game other than heron and waterfowl, whose flesh had a disagreeable taint of fish. Truxton agreed heartily with the idea, and said he would find all safe and sound on his return.

"Safe and sound, in all truth," said Sims, "and I think the hands could spend the time in putting up a shelter, for it seems the *Swan* may be a week or more before she's back. The night air is chill with nothing to ward it off."

This was surprising, since Sims had done the least of anybody to add to our comfort, not even bothering to join the others in the daily search for oysters and other shellfish, for there were clams to be obtained in plenty in the ooze at the river's mouth.

"I'll go with you," I said to Coverly when he got ready to depart.

"Nay, Nicholas," he replied. "It would be better if you stayed behind. Have you not noticed how Truxton and Sims are constantly together and talking quietly with the others since yesterday? They are plotting something, though what it is I cannot say."

"Then, why leave?" I asked.

" 'Tis but a ruse of mine," he replied. "I will not be far away. I but want them to show their hand." And off he went.

To save the planking of the boat, which out of water would have suffered under its weight, the gold had been moved ashore and buried. No sooner was Coverly out of sight than the men launched the boat in the cove and started carrying the gold toward it to load.

Mcdougal, the one man on whose loyalty I could rely, had been posted as a lookout on the top of the highest of the low hills that fringed the shore.

"What's this?" I cried. "Mutiny?"

"Nay, mate," said Truxton, grinning. " 'Tis called marooning. We're leaving Captain Coverly ashore and taking the boat and the treasure."

"You're a good sensible lad," said Sims, "and may come with us with the love and good will of all hands, as always. Or you may stay ashore and grow fat on shellfish and seabirds."

"But the *Swan* may be back in a day or two," I said.

Truxton shook his head. "We ain't waiting for the *Swan*," he said. "Lord's gone off with it, and we've no mind to stay here and rot, but will go along the coast and take whatever vessel we can. As for Martin Coverly, the fewer to share with, the bigger the share, and that's enough on that head."

Just then there was the report of a musket from

the hilltop, this being the signal that a ship had been sighted. All rushed to the high ground at the back of the beach and there, just clearing the horizon, was a brig, coming in under full sail. None of the gold had been loaded yet, some being still buried in the sand, and the men rushed for the boat and tumbled in, myself and Mcdougal with them.

We were out of the cove in a moment and, with the oars double-manned, pulled hard for the brig. It was the work of twenty minutes to get through the surf line, for the big rollers came in from the ocean at intervals of a hundred yards. By that time, the brig was much closer — scarcely half a mile away — and Truxton, handling the tiller and standing in the stern of the boat, shaded his eyes against the glare of the sun to stare at it.

He looked for several moments and then shouted, "That ain't the *Swan*, mates. She's carrying upper and lower topsails, and she sails low by the bow."

The boat was turned immediately, in a panic, to head back to the beach. A puff of smoke bloomed from the side of the strange brig, and then another. Two rounds of shot plumped into the ocean so close that we were drenched by the splash they made.

That was enough for the boat's crew. The gun crew of the brig plainly knew their business and had our range. Someone plucked off his shirt and waved it. The cannonading ceased and a boat full of armed men was lowered and pulled toward us.

I thought of Martin Coverly ashore, with much of the gold still buried, and wondered whether he had witnessed the scene. I wondered, too, whether he had not anticipated it; not my Uncle Martin Coverly, but the man he had become — Martin Coverly, pirate.

133

19

The brig was the sloop-of-war *Swallow*, commanded by Captain Edward Smart and stationed off the African coast for the suppression of piracy. Ten days earlier she had taken the *Swan*, after a brisk engagement in which half the hands, Sam Lord among them, were lost. They were the lucky ones. Those who survived were made prisoners and confessed, in the hope of leniency at their trial, that we were to be expected in a few days, coming down the river with gold from King Solomon's Mines.

We were taken aboard the *Swallow* and put in irons in her hold. A party went ashore and remained there several hours, bringing back the treasure and searching for Coverly. They did not find him nor all of the gold.

We sailed first to Cape Corso Castle, where there was an English garrison to protect traders and where we were imprisoned for three weeks. Our jail was the gloomy, insect-infested cellar of the building in which the soldiers were quartered. Here it was almost as dark by day as by night, and the floor, which was of blocks of coral rock, was covered with rotting palm fronds.

For food we were given each day a dish of paste made of corn, with only two pints of water to slake our thirst. Half starved and tortured by flies, we thought we would be tried in this place, but instead were shipped to England in a homeward-bound merchantman.

I will not detail the sufferings of that voyage, which lasted seven weeks. The food was moldy ship's bread, full of weevils and boiled up in a sort of thick, gray soup, of which we received two bowls a day. We were allowed a brief time on deck each day in good weather, but wore leg irons and manacles. These bit into the flesh, and the wounds were further aggravated by the salt water, by our wet clothing, which never dried, and the unending rocking of the ship. When we landed at Tilbury, on the River Thames, to be transported in carts to the Newgate Prison to await trial, we looked more like scarecrows than men.

Newgate jail was worse by far than either the cellar in which we had been held at Cape Corso Castle or the hold of the ship. Not far away was the Fleet ditch, a slow-moving stream into which the offal of the city was thrown — the carcasses of cats and dogs along with rotting vegetables, bones, and other garbage. The stench from this place, when the wind was off the river, provided the basic odor for Newgate, over which was laid the smell of the prison itself.

It assaulted me like a wall when I was dragged out

of the cart and thrust through the terrible door, studded with iron bolts, which was the main entrance.

Inside, all was dark and hot and the air so foul that I hardly dared draw a breath. We were thrust into a room so crowded with others there was scarcely room to sit on the floor.

I now gave myself up to despair. Though I had been a pirate against my will, I had no hope of proving this in court. There was no one to give evidence on my behalf. Mcdougal might have spoken up and offered to do so. But Mcdougal, who was a Jacobite rather than a pirate, was taken away two days later, tried, and hung on a charge, not of piracy, but of being a rebel against the King.

" 'e made a fine figure at Tyburn," the turnkey told us. "There's something to be said for those Scotchmen. I've seen 'alf a dozen of 'em 'ung, and all done it well."

This turnkey, whose name was Thaikes, was a monstrous man with the girth of a barrel. He was never entirely sober, and his face was inflamed with wine. He could procure for the prisoners any favor required — other than liberty — for money. The wealthier prisoners — mostly highwaymen with friends on the outside — were given special rooms, with good beds, and served three- and four-course dinners whenever they wished. Others got such favors as bottles of wine or rum, or candles, playing cards — whatever they could afford. Some paid a shilling a week to be freed of their manacles and leg irons.

We, without a penny among us, could procure nothing. There was, however, a grating, giving out on the street, at which we could beg alms from passersby. The stronger among us were able to struggle to this grating and thrust through it a stick with a spoon on the end, in the hope of receiving a penny or two. When a coin was put in this begging spoon, the others jostled and fought for it, and few received the penny given by a kindly passerby.

Salvation Sims now underwent a remarkable conversion. We were permitted to attend divine services in the prison on Sundays, and he was always there. His Amens were the loudest in the congregation. He spoke earnestly with the divines who conducted the services, and went about through the cell, talking to this one and that one, quoting passages from Scripture to comfort them and assure them that death was but the doorway to eternal bliss if they confessed their sins.

He even arranged a public confession of sins among those of our cellmates who would join in it, first making sure that one of the clergymen who held Sunday services was present. This man, the Reverend Thomas Sweeting, hardened as he was by years of ministering among felons and the like, was completely taken in by Sims. He provided him with a Bible and a Book of Common Prayer, which Sims was sure to be found studying every day by the meager light that came through a double grating high up in the wall of the cell.

With tears in his eyes, the Reverend Sweeting one day assured us that Sims had at last been brought back into the fold. "I have never seen such a true repentance in all my years of service to the Lord," he said earnestly.

"He'd choke you to death with the same Bible if it

137

would get him out of here," said Jack Winthrop, grinning. "Why, I've seen Salvation preaching brotherly love while men were thrown to the sharks."

"Through God's grace, he is a different man now," said Mr. Sweeting.

"Amen," said Sims. "The grace of God reaches the most miserable creatures on earth, of whom I am one. For he remembers, whatever our transgressions, that we are his children, and he loves us all. There is joy in my heart that his grace did not reach me too late."

Soon, Salvation Sims became a figure of importance, not merely in the prison, but among the people of London also. There was always great interest in the inmates of the Newgate. Many of the highwaymen were public heroes. Pirates, too, were very popular. A notorious pirate who had sailed with Roberts, who had witnessed and taken part in every kind of cruelty at sea, who had even entered the treasure house of King Solomon in Africa, and who now renounced his evil ways and preached repentance to his fellows became a popular figure.

Many, of course, scoffed at his conversion. But such was his eloquence that others believed him, and he was one day visited by a bishop, who examined him privately and then announced that Sims had become one of the most truly Christian men in London, if not in England.

Because of this reputation, Sims was given many privileges in the prison. His ancient legs were terribly chafed by the irons he was compelled to wear, and his wrists also. When Reverend Sweeting proposed that the irons be removed, Sims fell on his knees and begged to be allowed to continue to suffer.

"Let me offer this atonement for the evil of my

138

days," he said. "Do not, dear sir, deprive me of this opportunity to suffer for the offenses I have committed against our Sweet Saviour." But the irons were removed and Sims allowed to circulate through the prison, from cell to cell, reading from the Bible, saying prayers, comforting this one and that one, and rejoicing when he was met, as was often the case, with oaths and even blows.

Thaikes was now able to make money out of Sims by accepting bribes from those who wished to see him — most out of curiosity, but some, though this is hard to believe, to receive spiritual consolation.

A special small room, on an upper floor of the Newgate, was set aside for these interviews. When he heard of this, Truxton said, "He'll be out and away in a week — mark my words."

An elderly noblewoman, Lady Margaret Astonberry, arranged for a private interview on some spiritual matter that weighed heavily on her conscience. She arrived at the prison in the evening, her face hidden in a heavy cloak, for she did not wish to be recognized by anyone. She came in a covered coach, and was admitted to Sims, with whom she spent an hour in complete privacy. Then she left and, still covered by the heavy cloak, got into her carriage and was driven away. But when the turnkey went to get Sims, he found Lady Margaret Astonberry strangled on the floor and stripped of all her clothing. It was Salvation Sims who had left and been driven away in the carriage. When the carriage got to its destination, Sims was gone. He had slipped out at some stop in the dark London streets, and though a hue and cry was raised after him and a reward of a thousand pounds offered for his recapture, he was never seen again.

"Why," said Truxton when he heard the news, "there's some good to be gotten out of Bible study after all."

Mcdougal had been hung, then, and Sims had made his escape. The weeks dragged on, and then at last came the day when we were taken to the Old Bailey for trial. The courthouse was connected to the prison by a dark underground passageway called Deadmen's Walk. Under the worn, uneven flagstones of the floor of this corridor were buried the bodies of many who had been hanged.

The evening before our trial, we were visited by a lawyer appointed to represent us, but who had so little interest in our case and so little hope of anything but a guilty verdict that I do not even recall his name.

He was a short, swarthy man, with very thin legs and a very big belly, and during the course of our brief interview he held a sprig of rosemary to his nose as a preventive against jail fever. Jail fever, a product of the filthy air of Newgate, caused the death of many who were confined there, particularly children imprisoned and awaiting trial for some trifling theft.

I told him I had been forced into piracy, and all he did was enter against my name on the list before him the words, "Claims to have been forced to turn pirate." When this was done, he said in a dry, supercilious tone, "That is the common claim. It is no defense unless it can be proved. You have no witnesses, I suppose?"

"There is but one man who can testify to the truth of my statement. Martin Coverly."

"And where, may I inquire, is Martin Coverly?" asked the lawyer.

"He is in Africa," I said. This the lawyer noted down, and that was the whole preparation for my defense.

The foul air of Newgate Prison flowed along the corridor into the courtroom of the Old Bailey where we were to be tried. The judge sat at a high bench against one wall, with two huge windows behind him. On the bench before him, besides a sea of papers among which his clerk shuffled constantly, was a small hedge of herbs, to prevent his being infected by the jail fever from which many of the prisoners suffered.

Before and below the judge's bench was a vast table at which many lawyers sprawled or sat, some of them scribbling notes, others conversing, and one with his head on the table, fast asleep, following a night of carousing. The swarthy lawyer with the fat belly sat at this table, and to one side, in a room separated from the actual court by several pillars, sat the spectators.

The spectators' gallery was crowded that day, for the trial of several "notorious pirates and sea robbers" was the sort of entertainment that Londoners were not going to miss.

My own head was swimming that morning, and the whole scene was as unreal to me as a dream. Several of the others, including Truxton, were tried before me and condemned to be hanged, and when I was at last led to the dock, in irons, trembling in every limb, to be sworn and the indictment read, I had no clear realization of what was going on.

I was asked to plead, and pleaded "Not guilty" in a voice so low that I had to repeat my plea. The evidence against me was presented — that I had engaged in piracy in the company of many others, that

141

I had been a member of the crew of Roberts's vessel, the *Royal Fortune*, had served willingly under him in the taking of several other vessels, and had again served on the *Swan* under Captain Martin Coverly, who was my uncle, and again, under him, voluntarily engaged in many piratical acts.

The whole of the charge was presented in detail. I discovered that others of the crew had testified against me, in the hope of leniency for themselves. When asked whether I had any evidence to produce to prove these charges false, I could only reply that my sole witness was my uncle, Martin Coverly, who had been left on the African shore and was not, then, available to testify.

At this, the judge took out a huge handkerchief, blew his nose with a loud noise, and gave the jury, seated to his left, a significant nod. Some of the lawyers before him chuckled, and my own lawyer rose and asked the court for a delay in my case until a sufficient search could be made to find the said Martin Coverly.

The judge gave a short laugh and asked the lawyer whether he proposed that justice should be delayed so that the whole of Africa could be searched to produce my one witness. The lawyer replied that, with all due respect to the court, he was obliged to do what he could for his client. The judge nodded at him, blew his nose again, and said to the jury, "It is the common defense of pirates that all were forced into this cruel and evil practice by others, more cruel and evil than themselves. Indeed, gentlemen, were these pleas to be credited, not a pirate would have been hanged in the whole of England for several centuries past.

"The Crown has submitted sworn and well-substantiated evidence that the accused" — he glanced over his papers for a moment — "Nicholas Coverly, is guilty. Not one of those who were his shipmates has testified that he was forced into this life. Indeed, several have sworn that, were it not for Martin Coverly and this boy, they themselves would have continued to live the life of honest seamen. The jury will know how much credit to give this kind of evidence.

"There being nothing further to be added in this case, the jury may withdraw if they so desire and consider their verdict."

The jury did not withdraw. There was a little exchange among them and the foreman said that all were agreed on the matter.

"And what is your verdict?" asked the judge.

"Guilty," said the foreman of the jury.

The judge then held out his hand and was given a little black cloth, which he put, somewhat carelessly, over the heavily powdered wig he wore.

"Stand up," he said to me, though that was unnecessary, for I was already standing. He peered at me for several moments, and then pronounced sentence. I was to be taken to the place where condemned felons were held and from thence to be transported to a place of public execution, there to be hanged by my neck until I died.

"And may God have mercy on your soul," he concluded. Then he blew his nose again, and I was led, trembling, my head in a whirl, back to Newgate.

20

We were now removed to that part of Newgate Prison where those awaiting execution were held. Here the cells were not so crowded and we were treated with more humanity. We wore irons by day, but they were removed at night so we might sleep the better. We had also a small courtyard in which to exercise. In this courtyard there was a spectators' area to one side, behind high heavy iron railings, where for a fee those who were interested could come and watch us, and indeed converse with us.

Once condemned to death, we became even greater heroes. We were sneered at if we showed any gloom or depression before these spectators, and were expected to walk about with bravado, boasting of our deeds.

Truxton played the part excellently. He was, in any case, a brave man, though of no great intelligence. He told tales of his life which made him a great favorite. He proclaimed that much of the gold taken from Solomon's Mines was hidden in the sands near that cove where we had been taken, and undertook, for a fee, to provide one of his admirers with a chart showing the exact location of this buried hoard.

With the money, he bought an excellent suit of clothes — a coat of blue velvet, with silver froggings, a fine ruffled shirt of Irish linen, breeches of white satin, and stockings of the finest Holland manufacture.

"Share and share alike," he said. "That was always the rule among the Brethren of the Coast."

He divided the remainder of his money with the rest of us, and when it was gone, he sold another chart to another credulous admirer, for the man had a real talent for piracy of any sort. Indeed, he did not fear the gallows, and little of life being left to him, determined to spend it with the greatest possible enjoyment.

He paid a fee to one fellow to prepare a gallows speech for him, for it was very important that each man, going to his death, be able to make a fine address before the rope was put about his neck. One phrase of that speech especially delighted him. It went: "I have lived freer and richer than any of you standing about here, and will die better than any of you, too." Though I had disliked the man, yet in those last days I came to admire him.

But there were times when we were alone in our cell when he became gloomy and fearful. Once he took me aside and asked me whether there might be any truth in the belief of life after death.

I assured him, for so I believed myself, that only the body died, but the spirit lived on.

"Why, then," he said, "since I have been friend to the devil all my life, perhaps he'll make me bosun

145

when we meet at last." He would have nothing to do with repentance, of which I spoke to him.

"I repent only being caught," he said. "Anything more is for sniveling scum."

We had no notion of when we were to be hanged, or "turned off," as it was called. Hangings at Tyburn took place at regular intervals — on the first Tuesday of every month. They were so popular a diversion that hanging day was a legal holiday for all the apprentices of London, with the idea that the spectacle of many being executed for their crimes would be a stern warning to them to live within the law and attend closely to their work. But there was no regular schedule for the hanging of pirates at Execution Dock, that being, so I was told, at the discretion of the Lords of the Admiralty.

One by one my companions were taken away, for the authorities had decided not to hold a mass execution but to spread the punishments over several weeks.

Those who were executed were taken from the cell at night and removed to a prison hulk, close to Execution Dock, on the Thames. Then the public was advised who was to be hanged and on what day, so that a large crowd of seamen and longshoremen could be present. Jack Kott, the Barbados black, formerly a slave, went first. Then big Jack Winthrop, and so on. Truxton followed Winthrop, and at the end of a month I was the only one left. During those terrible days I did not know whether the following dawn would see me on my way to the prison hulk and to my death. Eventually I reached so hopeless a state of mind that I did not really care. It was as if the greater part of me had died already and the part that remained was but a mechanism that walked and ate and breathed, incapable of sensation.

Then one night, when I had fallen into a fitful sleep in which I found myself again in that spirit house of Ntelka's on the African lake where I had had the vision of myself hanging from the gallows, with Martin Coverly watching me from the crowd, the turnkey Thaikes awakened me. He held a lantern close to me and there was a smile on his wine-flushed face.

"Is it time?" I asked, trembling, thinking I was on my way to the gallows.

"You have a visitor," he said. "Mum's the word."

He led me to a small room, close to the main prison gate, where private interviews were permitted (on payment of a fee) with prisoners. There was a table and two chairs in the room, and a lantern on the table with a bottle and two glasses. Someone was seated in one of the chairs, but out of the circle of light shed by the lantern, so I could not see him distinctly.

"You have twenty minutes," said Thaikes, and left.

"Well, Nicholas," said my visitor, "here's a new turn of the wind for you."

It was Martin Coverly.

For a while I could not believe it. "How did you get here?" I asked. "Surely I am dreaming."

"Much of life's a dream — a phantasy," said Coverly. "We have been through this once before, Nicholas, at another time. But now I am permitted to change the end."

All of this made no sense to me. "How did you get here?" I repeated. "Why have you come to me now,

147

Martin Coverly? To mock me? Had you been a witness at my trial, my life might have been saved."

"I was present at your trial among the spectators," he replied calmly. "I could not have saved you then. Had I come forward to testify on your behalf, I would not have been believed. I would have been condemned myself, and not then had the opportunity to save you now."

"Save me now?" I cried. "How can you possibly save me?"

"By doing what I should have done before — die in your place. Have a glass of wine with me, Nicholas."

He poured out two glasses from the bottle, raised his, and said, "Drink deep."

I would not touch the wine, however, and he put his glass down. "Nicholas," he said, "I have not much time to end our business — the unfinished business we have together. Here. Take off those rags and put on these clothes of mine. Come, we must hurry."

"Why?" I asked, my mind in a whirl.

"Because I am going to take your place, Nicholas." He took off his own coat and shirt and threw them to me. "Give me your rags," he said. At that moment the door opened and Thaikes entered.

"I'm not through yet, Mr. Thaikes," said Coverly.

"Make it fast, then," said Thaikes. " 'Tis almost dawn." Then he left.

"He knows of this," I asked.

"He knows," said Coverly. "We have a slight resemblance, you and I, and in any case, all who would recognize us are dead. Master Thaikes is in no danger and has been well paid. Quickly! Your clothes!"

148

Not fully realizing what I was doing, thinking in fact that I was still dreaming, I took off my rags and put on the clothing Martin Coverly had given me. He, in turn, put on my filthy apparel. When it was done, he picked up his glass of wine.

"Come, nephew," he said, "you will surely have a parting drink with me. I go to where I belong, and you to your proper place in time. Drink deep."

He drained his glass and I drained mine.

"When you leave here," said Coverly, "you will find a coach waiting outside the prison. Get into it. You will be driven to the Blackfriars Stairs on the river. There you will find a boat tied up — a little cutter — with sails set. Get into her, Nicholas, and cast off. All is arranged."

At that point Thaikes returned. He looked at the two of us by the light of the lantern he carried, holding it high for his inspection, grunted, and said to me, "Time's up. Come on."

"Good-bye, Nicholas," said Martin Coverly. "Our business is ended, and well ended, I fancy."

"But how did you get here?" I cried, for he still had not answered that question.

"Think on it at your leisure, Nicholas," he replied. "Remember, I was left ashore with some of the gold buried in the sand."

Then I was led out of the room and let through a small door by the main prison gate through which visitors entered. Outside, as Martin Coverly had said, there was a coach waiting, into which I climbed. We rattled and plunged over the cobbles until we came to the Blackfriars Stairs by the river. Here I got out and found a small cutter tied to the landing stage, her sails set. I scrambled aboard and cast off, and the little cutter moved slowly away, downstream, her mainsail filling in a gentle wind. The effect of the wine, delayed in the excitement of my escape, now began to make itself felt. My head was in a whirl. A great weariness came over me, so that I had to fight to remain awake. Time and again I found myself dozing off, and at length, careless of what happened to myself and the cutter, surrendered myself to sleep.

It was broad daylight when I awoke, and the cutter lay quietly in the water, at anchor. I was lying on one of the small bunks in her cabin, and looked around, unsure of where I was. Slowly I recognized the small stove on which I had heated some soup the evening before, and the bookshelf with its Nautical Almanacs and a battered edition of Bowditch.

I rolled out of the bunk and climbed into the cockpit, and there was my uncle, Hillary Ormsby, carefully coiling up a length of line.

"That's Shark Island," he said, nodding toward the land off which we were anchored. "We've lain here most of the night and it's close to midday now. Not a sign of Martin Coverly," he added cheerfully.

"We'll never see him again," I said slowly. "He was hanged over two hundred years ago at Execution Dock, for piracy. So was Jedediah Truxton, and many others. Martin Coverly was hanged in place of his nephew, Nicholas Coverly, who, although sentenced to death, was innocent."

I paused, and added, "I am, or was, Nicholas Coverly. You are, or were, Martin Coverly."

My uncle continued coiling the line in silence. Then he looked at me and nodded. "I know," he said soberly. "I have known, I think, for a long time."

About the author

Leonard Wibberley was born in Dublin, Ireland — the last of seven children. At the age of eight, he and his family moved to England where he attended a school run by nuns and first learned the pleasures of the written word. In fact, when one of the nuns read *Treasure Island* to the class, young Leonard decided that he would be a writer.

At age sixteen when his father died, he took his first job as a copy boy for the London Sunday *Dispatch*. But upon learning that there were nearly 8,000,000 unemployed in Great Britain he grew fearful of being fired, and he quit, taking to the streets of London as a violin and flute player. From there, he filled such diverse jobs as the editor of a weekly newspaper in Trinidad, a "gandy-dancer" laying railroad track in Nevada, a dishwasher, a fry cook, a bait fisherman, and finally a writer.

He has now published over one hundred titles, fiction, nonfiction, who-dun-its, and children's books. One of his best-selling books, *The Mouse That Roared,* was made into a movie starring Peter Sellers.

Mr. Wibberley is married, has six children, and lives in California.